SWEET WILL BE
THE FLOWER

ISOBEL NEILL

Sweet Will Be the Flower

HarperCollins*Publishers*

HarperCollins*Publishers*
77–85 Fulham Palace Road,
Hammersmith, London W6 8JB

Published by HarperCollins*Publishers* 1996
1 3 5 7 9 8 6 4 2

A catalogue record for this book
is available from the British Library

ISBN 0 00 225488 3

Set in Postscript Linotype Palatino by
Rowland Phototypesetting Ltd,
Bury St Edmunds, Suffolk

Printed and bound by
Caledonian International Book Manufacturing Ltd, Glasgow

The bud may have a bitter taste,
But sweet will be the flower

WILLIAM COWPER

Acknowledgements

The author would like to thank the staff of the following: Paisley Library, Edinburgh Central Library, the National Library of Scotland, Vancouver Library, the Mitchell Library, the Salvation Army Heritage Centre and the Royal Botanic Garden, Edinburgh.

Chapter 1

If she stamped a little bit harder as she passed each entry, her boots made a reassuring din in the dark. Just a few yards further and she would be round the corner, then a short run along and she would be into Canal Street. Grannie's house wasn't far then. 'Ten steps to the corner, Dandy Baxter,' she told herself. Of course she had been to Grannie's hundreds of times on her own . . . well, maybe not hundreds . . . but never in the middle of a cold, dark night. It helped keep the terror at bay if you counted. It didn't pay to think about all the hidden things and wonder what those strange bumps were when Mammie needed you to fetch Grannie. She knew what Grannie would say: 'It's your drunken faither that should be out in the dark, no' a wee lassie like you.'

She turned the corner and gasped. The strange bumps were louder and flaming torches moved in the foggy dark. Two Clydesdales snorted and stamped, seeming enormous and threatening in the shifting light. Then she was lit up and a raucous voice accosted her, 'Here, wee lassie, whit are you daein' oot at this time?'

'I'm . . . I'm . . . to fetch my grannie. Mammie's not feelin' well.'

'Whit age are you?'

'I'm ten.'

'Could your faither no' . . . ?'

'He's got his work to go to in the morning, Mammie says, and I'm the biggest. I've got six wee brothers and sisters.'

'My Goad! So that's the way o' it. Here! Johnnie! You light this wee lass along Canal Street. She's in a hurry. I'll tak' your turn at the heaving. There you are, lass. There'll be lights on the main road.'

The face under the torch was a younger one and Johnnie certainly knew how to run. 'It's awfully kind of you,' she gasped.

'Don't mention it,' he said. 'It's a treat to get away from the bloody stink.'

'Aah . . . I didn't know . . . you're the cludgie men.'

'Aye.' There was bitterness in the clipped syllable.

'It canna be nice . . .'

'Naw. It's hell. I don't know how these auld yins can stick it. I'll be out o' it as soon as I can get something better.'

'Could you not get something better before?'

'I had a fight with my boss. He was drunk, you see.'

'It's a terrible thing the drink, my grannie says.'

'Aye. You listen to your grannie and steer clear. There you are, hen. There's lights on Neilston Road. I'd better get back. You'll be all right with your grannie.'

'Aye. There's not a soul in Paisley can frighten my grannie. Thanks, mister.'

It was true, Dandy reflected, as she slowed a little to get her breath back. Grannie was scared of nobody. She didn't have to shout or anything, but she said things in such a cutting way that even Faither was forced to shut his face at times. She grinned with satisfaction at the thought. 'When I'm big . . . even before I'm very big . . . maybe when I'm fourteen, in 1908 . . . or 1909, I'll be like Grannie and nobody will dare take advantage of me. Just wait. Faither will never dare slap me again.' Her hand came up to caress her cheek which had burned for a long time after . . .

*   *   *

2

Last night. It had all happened so simply. There they were, crammed round the kitchen table as usual – Faither getting one end all to himself; Mammie at the other with wee Jack on her knee and May stuck in beside her; the big boys, George and Billy on one side; and herself with the twins, Jinty and Peggy, on the other. It had been the usual muddle with Faither glaring at the boys, who never behaved themselves, Mammie expostulating gently as she spooned food into the toddler on her knee; Dandy herself getting little peace to eat for the demands of the twins to have bread buttered, jammed and cut up, and in the middle of it all she had to remember gentle little May, who made few demands.

It was when Faither asked Mammie for another cup of tea. 'You've *had* a cup of tea, Faither,' Billy had said.

'Aye, and I'm having another, my lad. What's it got to do with you?'

'Dan Stewart in my class at school said that his mother said that if you didna drink so much, Mammie wouldna have so many bairns.' George's foot had met Dandy's under the table then, forcing her to lose control. It was her stifled snort that had sent Faither into a blazing temper. His chair bounced on the linoleum as he jumped up with a roar. 'You can tell your Mrs Bloody Stewart to mind her ain bloody business,' he said to the astonished Billy, 'and I'll make you laugh on the other side of your face, Dandy Baxter.' The vicious slap had knocked her sideways. May started to cry then and the twins joined her in fright. Tears were running down her mother's face, but she didn't dare say anything. They all jumped as the door slammed.

'That's him off to the pub,' muttered George. He punched Billy. 'You are stupid.'

Then Billy was crying. 'I just said . . .'

'Aye, you just said. That was enough for that . . .' He broke off then. Dandy knew why. If he said what he

3

really thought and one of the younger ones repeated it – well! It didn't bear thinking about. As she went on hugging her aching jaw she reflected that George, newly nine, must have learned the same thing that she had heard from that big girl in the playground. At the time she had found it all so difficult to believe, but Faither's reaction and that sly kick from George forced her to think the big girl had not been taking a rise out of her after all. Fancy her wee brother George knowing! It wasn't nice. Her grannie certainly wouldn't approve. She liked everything in order. There was never any mess in Grannie's house. Her three daughters had learned to put their things away tidily. But there! She was at Grannie's close now. It would be easy to wake Grannie up. Faither said once that she slept with one eye open, but Dandy wasn't sure if that was true and didn't like to ask.

After the first knock she heard a distant bump. She opened the letter box and called, 'It's me, Grannie.' A candle flickered at the end of the hall and then the gas mantle flared. Grannie looked a wee bit funny in her big hairy dressing gown and floppy slippers, but her crisp questions helped to restore Dandy's confidence. 'Go into the kitchen, lass, while I get dressed. Take a biscuit from the barrel on the dresser. I'll not be long.'

Grannie Jordan's biscuit barrel was a thing of beauty. The silver bands which girdled it shone with constant polishing. Grannie took care that none of the polish ever got on to the shining oak of the rest of the barrel. The biscuits inside were of a different quality from any that ever appeared in the Baxter household. George and Billy would make short work of any biscuits and her mother never had a penny to spare, Dandy knew. Grannie had said, 'Take *a* biscuit.' That was a pity because the ones she liked best happened to be the smallest ones. If only she had said, 'Help yourself to the biscuits.'

4

But Grannie wasn't given to saying things like that. Dandy settled for her second choice. If she swithered much longer, Grannie could well be dressed and ready to leave and her chance would be gone.

The door had been closed quietly and locked behind them, but still Grannie held a finger to her lips. 'We'll talk when we're out in the street,' she whispered. Even in the street it was some time before Grannie said, 'Right! Tell me again . . . your mother fell off the table, that was in the afternoon, you say.'

'Aye – I mean, yes. I heard a bang and when I ran through to the kitchen, Mammie was lying on the floor and the table had capsized on top of her. I asked her what she was doing on the table and she said she was trying to knock down a cobweb. I asked her what she had been trying to knock it down with and she said a feather duster. I said where was it and I would knock it down for her and she said she had forgotten it and was going back for it and that was when the table had capsized and would I help her up and straighten the kitchen and I wasn't to tell anyone. I can't see any cobweb anyway. She was being far too fussy.'

'Aye,' Grannie sighed loudly. 'Poor Nettie. It's a pity she hadn't been more fussy years ago. When I think what a good-looking lass she was, so superior . . . and she had to take a drunken dyer who'll never be anything in this life. And what was she doing when you left to come for me?'

'She was sitting on the parlour floor with her skirts kind of spread round her. Our May and the twins were fast asleep there and she said she would get a wee bit of peace. She didn't want to disturb the boys in the kitchen bed.'

Mrs Jordan's step quickened. 'It's like a model lodging house – seven bairns already . . . sleeping in two rooms. She'll never get a chance with that drunken devil. It's a good thing her father's not here. It would have broken his heart to see what she's come to. If she has any more ... Oh, God, I hope not. We'd better hurry. I canna speak ... I need my breath.'

There was nothing but the sound of their hurrying feet till they neared the closemouth. 'Would any of the neighbours hear you, pet?'

'Maybe Aunt Violet, downstairs. She doesn't sleep very well.'

'Aye, and I expect they get plenty to keep them awake,' said Lily Jordan ominously.

Though they tiptoed carefully up the stairs, the door on the landing beneath the Baxter house opened gently as they passed. Miss Violet McLaren looked funny too, thought Dandy, with her fine greying hair screwed up in paper twists. But Miss Violet was properly dressed and was opening the door wider. 'If we could be of any help ... take the children in here ... or give Dandy a rest?' The look she was giving Mrs Jordan puzzled Dandy. There was something in it she did not understand. 'They get plenty there to keep them awake,' Grannie had said. It couldn't be the children; they usually fell asleep quite early. The boys' wild games had them exhausted by bedtime and though they always made a token resistance when Mammie urged them towards bed, once there they were soon sprawled out, dead to the world.

Grannie took her time in replying, even though she had been in such a hurry to get to Mammie. 'Perhaps if you could have Dandy for a little while,' she said. 'She needs her sleep if she's to go to school in the morning. Yes, I'd be grateful.'

Dandy experienced her usual feeling of relief when she stepped into the haven of the flat which was home to the Misses McLaren. The sense of peace and order always struck her so forcibly. And yet people said that

6

Miss Alice and Miss Violet had come down in the world. They had been brought up in a house with servants, but something had happened to their father's business – nobody knew quite what, so the stories were varied – and soon after, both parents had died; their brother, newly married, had moved with his bride to a small cottage in Espedair Street while his sisters had been forced to move to a small flat with a shared WC on the landing. The general opinion was that they were ladies all right, but they weren't stuck-up.

Dandy, unaware of the niceties of the situation, only knew that Aunt Alice and Aunt Violet seemed to be able to give her life a different colour. Their voices were gentle and not tired like Mammie's. Meals were simple but always nicely served and in an atmosphere of peace. Whenever her mother could spare her, Dandy found her way to the spinsters' house, knowing that she would always be sure of a welcome.

The kitchen fire was blazing cheerily and Aunt Alice was lifting the singing kettle to fill the teapot. 'Maybe you'd like to make yourself a bit of toast, Dandy,' she was suggesting. The McLarens' toasting fork had always intrigued her. It was quite heavy and had a little brass handle ornamented with the figure of a monkey. With no struggling weans to knock the thing out of her hand, Dandy could give herself up to guiding the fork to the hottest area of the fire then watch the golden glow deepen on the surface of the bread till a tempting smell confirmed that it was ready. Sometimes she had been so mesmerized by the dancing flames that the fork had had to be rescued by Aunt Alice and the burnt surface of the bread scraped into the fire. But that was when she was younger. It was a matter of pride now to produce a perfect golden slice, ready to melt the generous pat of butter that Aunt Alice would plop on to it. A dainty tray was set down on the tall stool beside her; steam drifted from the cup of sweet tea; nobody would jog her elbow when she drank it. Dandy spoke her gratitude. 'When I'm big, I'm going to have a house like this with no weans, just nice things and quietness and flowers in a dish and books and things . . .'

'But children are lovely,' said Aunt Violet. 'Surely you love your little brothers and sisters?'

'Not much,' said Dandy truthfully. Violet McLaren looked vexed.

'You can get an overdose of the nicest things, isn't that right?' asked Alice.

'Aye,' said Dandy, 'and they're not always that nice anyway. If George hadna kicked me last night –' She stopped suddenly, remembering what had sparked off that little fracas.

'Your brother kicked you?' The sisters spoke almost in unison.

Dandy paused to consider. These aunties were 'ladies'. Would 'ladies' know about the thing that big girl in the playground had said? But if it was true, all the grown-ups would know about it, surely. She could test if it was true now. These two would show by their faces. She would watch them. And if it *was* true. Then . . . they would know what that creaking was that she could hear through the wall from Mammie's bed . . . that is, if it *was* true what the girl said. And she was pretty sure now that it was. George's kick had helped confirm it. Could that be what Grannie was thinking of when she said that the McLarens would get plenty to keep them awake? They were watching her now, puzzled and a little anxious.

'Well, I wouldn't have laughed and made Faither angry.' She paused. Her listeners said nothing.

'You see, we were at the table having tea and Faither . . . my father asked for another cup. Our Billy tried to stop him and Faither couldn't understand why and then

Billy said that Dan Stewart in his class at school's mother had said that if Faither didn't drink so much, Mammie wouldn't have so many weans. It would have been all right if George hadn't kicked me under the table, but that made me laugh and Faither was that angry. He swore at Billy and slapped me hard on the face and then he banged the door shut and went to the pub.'

During her recital Dandy had been keeping a careful eye on the two women. Alice who was plump was always pretty rosy, especially in the firelight, but Violet was easier to spot. The pink line had gradually risen and broadened in her neck. Now she was clutching it anxiously. 'George kicked you?' she gasped out.

'Aye, or I wouldn't have laughed,' repeated Dandy.

Alice spoke firmly. 'Oh, well, there's no need to worry here. Just enjoy your wee supper – or is it breakfast?' She gave a forced laugh as her hand rested on Violet's shoulder. Dandy noticed the warning pressure. So the big girl was right. If the truth had been otherwise they would have wanted to know why she had wanted to laugh and why George had kicked her.

Unlike Grannie, the Misses McLaren never criticized anyone. They simply slipped off into a siding, you might say. And yet, somehow you knew what their real attitude was. Though Dandy agreed most of the time with her grandmother's sentiments, it didn't really help to be told the same old thing; her mother had been a gentle, well brought-up girl – Grannie had seen to that; Grannie supposed you could say that Faither was handsome then: tall, with fair hair and bold blue eyes that seemed to knock the girls silly – and not only her Nettie. Grannie wished to heaven that one of the others had got him and not her fine girl. None of Nettie's sisters lived in a dump like theirs; none of them had bairns making a mess all over the place; none of them got

9

every decent piece of china you gave them broken by a couple of wild devils their father should be keeping an eye on; instead of that he was off to the pub to spend the money her daughter should be having to feed her bairns; she couldn't see what the end of it would be.

It was this last remark which irked Dandy most, because she couldn't see the end of it either. One thing she was determined on was that it would never happen to Dandy Baxter. Never! But though her mother irritated her with her dumb acceptance of her fate, she couldn't help feeling protective towards her – and to May, the gentle little sister who smiled shyly and never seemed to lose her temper, even when her wild big brothers managed to damage the doll her Sunday School teacher had given her. May had asked Dandy then to help her bandage the bedraggled creature and called out in protest when Dandy had turned on the culprits with her ready fists.

'They said they didn't mean it, Dandy,' she had pleaded.

'They should be looking after their wee sister instead o' breaking the wee doll for her. That bairn's too good to live,' Lily Jordan had remarked. It was a common phrase but suddenly its full import had struck Dandy. She looked then at May in a sort of daze; the delicate little wrists were busy with the bandage; everything about May seemed to be gentle. If only I could buy our May nice clothes, she could look like an angel, she thought. But, really, she didn't want an angel. She wanted her wee sister to be strong and healthy. A sudden fear struck her and she resolved to make sure that May got her share of whatever food was available and was not thrust aside by the Gannets, as she thought of them. She turned a baleful glare on her brothers.

But it was better to forget all that and just enjoy the peace. 'Make yourself another bit of toast, if you like,'

Aunt Alice was urging. 'Here, Violet, take a cup of tea to keep our Dandy company.'

Was the cup of tea meant to restore Miss Violet's shattered nerves? Dandy watched Miss Alice with the teapot. They were fond of each other. No wonder Miss Violet thought bairns were lovely things. If Dandy only had May to consider . . . Oh, it would be lovely! They could go for nice walks into the country and pick wild flowers and put them in a vase with no fighting boys to knock them over. Mammie wouldn't need to buy so much food and maybe would be able to buy herself a new coat now and again. It was a shame that she couldn't. Everything Mammie wore was passed on from her sisters. She said she was grateful to get the things, but Dandy saw how her mother sighed at some of the shop windows.

Her own clothes were mostly passed on from her cousin Betty, a lumpish stupid girl who thought she was 'something' simply because her father worked in a lawyer's office. 'Him! He's just a glorified pen-pusher,' she had heard her father say in derision. 'A day's work would kill him.'

Of course, it didn't pay to listen to Faither's opinions. He was drunk most of the time. Grannie said that was what gave him his courage and a lot of men who drank were just weaklings who had to hide from themselves. It sounded like something that someone else had said to Grannie. But there was maybe a lot of truth in it. When the noise in the house got too much or one of the weans was hurt or sick or something, Faither would slam out to the pub. She knew from the girls at school that all fathers were not like that. Some girls sat on their father's knees and told them things, and some fathers made jokes and said when they liked a hair ribbon and asked the girls what they had learned at school that day and could they say the new poem to them. Dandy sometimes had to pretend that her father did things like that too. She didn't want them all feeling sorry for her. It was bad enough being off school so often. Most of the girls had to help at home sometimes, but she was missing as often as she was there.

She hated missing school. She wanted to know things. Every time it was Mammie's turn for the washhouse, it went without saying that Dandy would have to stay at home and keep an eye on the wee ones. Not only that; while Mammie toiled away in clouds of steam down there in the tiny building beyond the backyard and the cellars, Dandy had to see to the housework and the cooking and the frequent attentions that the twins and Jack demanded. Then, if the rain came on, she had to rush down with the twins at her skirts to help Mammie take in the washing and lug it all up the stairs where it steamed round the fire, leaving the room without its only cheerful spot.

The McLarens' house was exactly the same as theirs in shape, but the way they lived was so different. Upstairs, her father and mother slept in one of the kitchen beds while the two boys had the other and Jack, the toddler, still slept in the cradle. She slept in the recess bed in the parlour with May beside her and the twins at the foot of the bed. No wonder Grannie was hoping that her mother wouldn't have any more! At Sunday School on the first Sunday of the year they had been asked to make a little prayer of the things they hoped for in 1905. Dandy's fervent wish had been that there would be no more weans in the house, for 1904 had been a big enough squash. A new bairn in 1905 would mean that wee Jack would have to give up the cradle and sleep at the foot of the boys' bed, and they were that restless!

Her mother always tried to keep the parlour decent in case anyone dropped in, but sometimes when the boys were wild and noisy she was glad to send them through there to play, just to get a minute's peace. They had managed to break the two lovely little chairs that had belonged to her mother's grandmother who was called Janet too. Mammie had cried sorely when that happened and Dandy had stood helplessly by, listening to her sobbing complaint, 'Rosewood with mother-of-pearl inlay . . . I'll never get anything like that again . . . I never have anything nice and your grannie will be so angry . . . they were her mother's treasured chairs.'

And then, as the family grew, more and more things had to be stored in the parlour. Hooks had to be screwed in to the lovely varnished doors to give them hanging space for coats and things when the lobby cupboard overflowed. More and more boxes were jammed under the set-in bed because the two chests of drawers were in the same state. Grannie said that this was most unhygienic – you couldn't keep the dust down – but Grannie was awfully fussy about cleaning. And what was Mammie to do? She couldn't afford a bigger rent. Of course, if she said that, Grannie would say they could afford a lot of things if her father would only give up his drinking. 'I hate him,' Dandy muttered to herself.

'What was that?' Miss Violet asked.

'Sorry, I was sort of dreaming,' said Dandy. Another nice thing about the McLarens was that they didn't pester you for awkward explanations.

'Maybe you'd like to slip into my bed,' Miss Violet said. 'I tidied it and put in a fresh hot bottle in case any of you needed it.'

Now, there was another thing about the McLarens! They had a bed each. When she had remarked on this to her mother once, Nettie Baxter had assured her that Alice and Violet would have had a room each in the old days and a maid to fold away their clothes and

13

mend them and all that. 'But you never hear them grumble,' her mother had added; 'they're real ladies.'

It would be nice to sample a bed all to herself. The McLarens moved about so quietly. 'I think I *would* like to go to bed for a little while,' said Dandy. 'I expect Mammie will need me when the wee ones wake up, for she hasn't had much sleep.'

She was half-awake. May didn't seem to be beside her. Her toes were free – not tangled up in somebody else's feet. Then she remembered. She was in Miss Violet's bed. It was lovely! She couldn't be bothered opening her eyes. Then she heard the murmuring voices; her own name.

'It's a shame that a child should know of these things,' Aunt Violet was saying, 'and not only Dandy but little George – barely nine years old. They're losing their childhood. Dandy never gets any girlish pleasures. Just think of the games we were playing at that age! And the trips to the seaside!'

'Yes, it's a great pity.' That was Alice's voice. 'If only we had a little money. There are so many things we could do for her, but we must do the best we can within our limitations. She is a fine girl; strong character; a quick intelligence. We can certainly give her the things that don't cost anything: quietness to recuperate from that turmoil upstairs, sensible conversation and a different outlook, perhaps, on human nature. Yes! We must be positive, Violet my dear. Remember, that was what Mama was always telling us. Her advice has stood us in good stead since we came down in the world – as the world has it.'

'She loves flowers – told me once that she wished *her* name was Violet. She never gets a chance to look at them properly, for every time she goes to the park she is burdened by her younger siblings. It's a shame.'

'You're right, Violet. I've just thought of something.

14

We'll have to be a little devious in a good cause. She asked me one day if our brother had a garden. Could we try to borrow Dandy to "help" us carry things next time we go to see James? Certainly the weather's still cold, but he has a few things in the garden and, though to us a cottage garden is nothing too wonderful, I have a feeling that Dandy might see it differently. She has a longing for "territory", I think; there's no space in that menagerie for her to keep anything that is "hers".'

'But James could be difficult. He never talks to children.'

'Well, he doesn't really have much opportunity, does he, Violet? We're rather cut off from the people we used to associate with; losing Rachel *and* the baby is bound to have affected him, and maybe he has got out of the habit . . . but Dandy is so refreshing. I think it would be worth a try. It's a pity we can't do anything about those boys. I fear for them when they are older – no guidance. But, our resources are limited. We shall have to channel them towards our Dandy.'

'I wonder what's happening upstairs. Mrs Jordan is very capable, of course, and has no fear of her son-in-law. It's a pity her daughter hadn't inherited a bit of that grit.'

'That crash we heard must have been the table going down. It's dreadful to think what she's been driven to. She could have a damaged baby, if she's not careful.'

'From what I overheard one day, Alice, I gather that that little trick has worked once or twice before. It may seem dreadful, but I hope it has worked again. Dandy has enough on her hands with six of them.'

Dandy puzzled sleepily over the idea of a trick. How could a table stop her having a bairn? Or could it be, maybe, that Mammie knew there was another one growing inside her and if she went up on the table and jumped down . . .

It was a puzzle all right. Would the baby fall out? But there was no sign of a baby. Was Mammie sitting on the parlour floor with her skirts spread out like that to hide something? Aunt Violet hoped the trick had worked. They were on her side. It was lovely. The bed smelled so nice and clean and the room felt . . . peaceful . . . yes, that was it. She drew a deep breath and went back to sleep.

Chapter 2

'Just you get ready for school, Dandy,' Lily Jordan said. 'Your Mammie's staying in bed this morning. That fall has upset her. But I've got to be home in the afternoon – the factor's man is coming to look at a tap I've been complaining about.'

'Will I tell the teacher . . . ?'

'No. We'll keep our business to ourselves. Just you come back for your dinner as usual. Tomorrow you can tell her your Mammie was a little sick and you had to look after the wee ones, but not a word about your Mammie falling off the table, mind.' She turned to Nettie, 'God knows they get enough to gossip about with that man of yours!'

Well, half a day was better than nothing, Dandy reflected, as she hurried to school. But it was such a pity to be off on a Friday afternoon again. That was the day Miss Martin always read them a story unless one of the wilder boys in class had upset her. That didn't happen often now. She grinned to herself. She had seen to that. You had to be tough with boys. It was no good complaining as Jeannie White did or crying as Louise McGowan did. No! You surprised them with a good thumping and tripped them up before they hit back. She had learned a few things dealing with George and Billy. If they put a hand up and you grabbed their thumb and jerked it, you could land them on their backs. The shock usually left them too scared to fight back and they pretended that they were badly wounded so that you would leave them alone. Grannie Jordan was right when she said that Mammie should stand up to Faither. 'I'd put something in his tea,' she had said, 'give him something else to think about. A bit of peace is what our Nettie needs, but is she likely to get it from that drunken devil!' Grannie hadn't said what the stuff was that she would put in Faither's tea. That was a pity. It probably cost a lot anyway. Still, it would be worth knowing.

The school bell stopped as she reached the gate. Dandy ran the last few yards to join the end of her line. 'Late again, Dandy,' Miss Martin remarked.

'I couldn't help it,' gasped Dandy, 'my wee sister ...' but Miss Martin had moved to the front of the queue and was reminding the boys to remove their caps as they entered the school premises.

Dandy sniffed the familiar smell of chalk and varnish as she entered the classroom, but felt the usual humiliation as she took her place in the front row among the dunces. It was unfair, she knew. She wasn't a dunce. These others were painful to listen to when they got up to read, stumbling over words and pronouncing them wrongly. But she missed so much and Miss Martin didn't seem to understand. They finished the Lord's Prayer and sat down. The register was intoned and at last Miss Martin was ready to begin. Dandy looked up hopefully. 'Last Friday morning we did some parsing. Let's find out how much you remember. Write down the following sentence, *This morning I went to school.*

The pencils squeaked on the slates. Some people said that the sound made their blood run cold, but Dandy liked it. There was a funny kind of excitement about it. The words you wrote on a slate could take you far away; you could do anything with words.

'Finished?'

'Yes, Miss.' The answer came in drawling chorus.

'Right. I'll start at the front. Dandy, what part of speech is *Morning*?'

'I don't know, Miss.'

Miss Martin gave a sigh. 'Louise, can you enlighten Dandy?'

'Yes, Miss. It's a noun.'

'Noun, Dandy, noun. Have you got that into your head?'

'Yes, Miss.'

'Right! Now, perhaps, you can tell the class what a noun is.'

Dandy felt the hot blood rise into her face. 'I don't know, Miss.'

'Really, Dandy, for a girl who reads so well, you amaze me. Don't you want to know what kind of words you are using when you read?'

There was a pause as Dandy seethed inside. If she had been at school last Friday she would have known what a noun was. She wasn't stupid. The self-pity which she usually had under control welled up inside her. She felt the shaming tears spring to her eyes.

'Well, Dandy?' Miss Martin urged.

The answer came out in a fierce whisper. 'Of course I want to learn. I wasn't here.'

Elizabeth Martin was startled. Dandy Baxter, that ragamuffin who was more than a match for the wild boys in the class, almost in tears. There was a pause while she drew herself together.

'No, if you weren't here, you wouldn't know. Stay in at the interval and I'll see what I can do.' Quickly she moved on to another pupil. Dandy let out her breath carefully. Attention seemed to have been diverted. Nobody would have noticed her lapse. It didn't pay to let people see they could upset you. Look at Mammie. If she had stood up to Faither or, failing that, put something in his tea, she wouldn't have had all these weans and she, Dandy, would have been able to go home without getting a bairn stuck in her arms and a shawl wound round her when other girls were out playing peevers on the pavement or rounders in the park.

The bell rang for the interval. There was the usual scuffle, the thudding of desk lids and the shuffling of many feet. As Louise McGowan passed her she whispered, 'Poor you, I've got a skipping rope today.' Her sympathy was misplaced. Far from feeling punished, Dandy was relieved. At least she would learn something about nouns and things like that.

'Well, Dandy, I'm sorry I forgot you weren't here last Friday – you are off so frequently – but if I write some of these down as I tell you, perhaps you could take them home and read them at your leisure.'

Dandy glanced at Miss Martin. Was she being funny? No, she had spoken automatically. Other girls had leisure. Her big cousin Betty had leisure – only one wee brother, and her mother took care of him. Betty grumbled about having to practise the piano when some of her chums were out playing in the garden. That was another thing. Betty had a garden and never bothered to do a thing in it, except play. Dandy longed to plant seeds and see them grow. Seeds were so tiny, a miracle. How could Betty not want to . . . but Miss Martin was speaking. 'Now these are the ones we covered this morning. I'll write out some sentences for you to parse at home. Ask me for them before you leave this afternoon.'

'Yes, Miss.' Dandy answered automatically and then remembered; Grannie had to go home this afternoon! She would have no list of sentences to work on at the weekend. Miss Martin would think she didn't care. Desperation made her take a risk. 'Please Miss, could I possibly get them before I go home for lunch? Sometimes my dinner isn't ready . . .'

The last part was true at least. Nettie Baxter was usually relieved to be able to hand the youngest over to Dandy while she concocted a sketchy meal.

Elizabeth Martin smiled. She seemed to have stirred some sort of interest here. She congratulated herself. 'I'll see what I can do, Dandy. Ask me. Oh! There's the bell. It's taken longer than I thought.'

She didn't get her cup of tea, Dandy thought. I wish I could tell her . . . What would Aunt Alice do?

She cleared her throat. 'I appreciate it, Miss.' Then, as she blushed, was glad to hear the clatter of feet in the passageway.

Elizabeth Martin automatically hushed the returning mob. 'We walk in the classroom, William. We do not run. There is no need to bang your desk lid, Andrew. Now, sit up straight and fold your arms. That's better.' All the while she was marvelling at her new knowledge. Wait till I tell them in the staff room. They all laugh at the way Dandy can manage the boys in the playground. This is something new; 'I appreciate it, Miss.' Just wait till I tell them that one!

With the precious paper safely folded in her deepest pocket, Dandy resigned herself to a frustrating stint of domesticity. Grannie greeted her. 'I went out for some cheese. Maybe you could toast some, Dandy. Don't put it on too thick, mind! These boys never know when to stop. See that your Mammie gets some. She's needing rest and nourishment. If only I could get her out of here!'

If only someone or something could get us all out of here, Dandy thought, and you and your grumbling, she mentally added, then felt guilty. In spite of all her grumbles, Grannie always responded to her daughter's calls for help. I'd feel the same, I suppose, only I think I *would* put something in Faither's tea if I knew the magic recipe. The thought cheered her up as she

21

stretched to the high shelf where the big breadknife was stored.

She was busy in the scullery when she heard Grannie. She wasn't really speaking loudly, but she had that cutting sort of voice that carries. Then her mother was hushing her, 'Dandy'll hear you, Mother.'

'Not her – she's busy.'

Dandy kept tapping the knife on the board as she edged her body nearer the open scullery door. 'Now I've warned you, my girl. You've been lucky this time but it's no thanks to him. He'll have to think of you for a change. You'll just have to tell him that you have all the bairns you want and if he canna take care of you, he'll just have to go without.'

'He would roar the house down, Mother. The neighbours would hear.'

'Oh, God, I expect they hear enough. If only you had a brother, Nettie. What that man of yours needs is a good hammering to frighten him. It's the drink, of course. If only you could have got him to the Band of Hope before you married him. It's too late now for that.'

Dandy stuffed her fist in her mouth while she went on tapping the chopping board. Faither in the Band of Hope! Grannie could be a laugh too. And yet she was being serious. If Mammie had told him to take the pledge or she wouldn't marry him, would he have done it? No; Grannie had said that there were plenty girls willing to take him. What Faither really needed was someone like Grannie who could lash with her tongue and was scared of nobody. 'I'm going to be like that when I grow up,' Dandy vowed. 'But I won't be a grumbler.'

Miraculously she managed to get the twins and Jack to lie down for a little while after lunch. Nettie Baxter was grateful for the silence. 'I don't know what I'd do without you, pet,' she said.

'You should be tough like Grannie, you know, Mammie, and then folk wouldn't take advantage of you.'

'I take after my father, Dandy. He got quietly on with his work while your grannie did all the arranging. It worked. He appreciated his nice home and meals always ready. Though Jean was always a wee bit bossy and Margaret the pretty one and a wee bit spoiled, we were three well-behaved girls and there was a bathroom . . . how I miss that bathroom!'

'Well, I suppose it's better to have a WC on the landing than a cludgie in the close. The cludgie men were moving that horrid stuff . . .'

'Night soil, Dandy. I'm sure the McLarens wouldn't understand you if you said "the cludgie men".'

'What would *they* say?'

'I think they'd call them "the sanitary men".'

'I wonder what they call themselves – the cludgie men, I mean,' Dandy said. 'Johnnie – the one who lit me along Canal Street when I was fetching Grannie – was going to get something better as soon as he could.'

'I didn't know about that. You were actually speaking to one of them? They're the roughest of the rough. Oh, it isn't fair that I've to send my wee daughter out in the dark.' Nettie was crying.

'It's all right, Mammie, he was a nice fellow; said he'd be out of the stinking job as soon as he could get something better. You see, the boss he had before that drank and Johnnie said there was a bit of a stramash and he left. Don't worry, Mammie. The auld yin was nice to me too and he told Johnnie to light me, you see. He had a big smoking torch – it was kind of exciting – and we got Grannie all right, didn't we?'

Nettie sniffed. 'Mhm . . . and she'll be back at teatime. She'll get your father to take the boys out for a walk so that she can attend to me in peace.'

'Good old Grannie!' said Dandy, and meant it. If

23

Grannie was there and bossing Faither she might manage to slip down to see Aunt Alice and Aunt Violet after the twins were in bed. She could take May with her. She was nice and quiet. They might let her make toast again. 'Good old Grannie,' she repeated in silence.

Monday morning brought school and the inevitable explanations as she handed over the completed work to Miss Martin. 'It's a great pity, Dandy, you miss so much with these frequent absences.'

'I know' said Dandy, 'especially Friday.'

'Why do you say that?'

'You read us a story and I miss so many bits . . .'

'You like books?'

'Oh, yes, I'd love to have lots of books when I'm big.'

'Have you thought what you would like to train for? I mean, what sort of job you would like to do.'

'I don't know. Mammie will need the money, so I expect I'll have to go to the thread mills. They're always looking for workers and things seem to be peaceful now – I mean, no strikes. It's hard work they say, but it makes a difference to have a pay coming in instead of money going out.'

Elizabeth Martin sighed. This was the fate of most of the girls who passed through her hands. For some it was fine – good wages and companionship, then marriage and children. The strike in 1900 had opened her eyes to the sort of lives that so many of these young women led. No wonder the standard joke persisted: that Paisley girls married young to get away from the mills! That particular strike had been sparked off by the introduction of a new patent which had made work heavier and wages smaller. Women complained that the yarn baskets were too heavy to carry and also that there was favouritism being shown by the foremen. Not only the cop winders but the reelers – whatever these

24

words meant – had been affected by the stoppage. It was difficult to find out the various processes which went on in the thread mills. At one time she had thought of studying them for a geography lesson since the children always perked up when she came to that statement in their text book, PAISLEY IS WORLD KNOWN FOR ITS THREAD MILLS, but her efforts to obtain information had been thwarted. It seemed to her that the mill owners who were very progressive were unwilling to let people have the overall picture of the workings, perhaps afraid of possible competition. Maybe she was imposing her own feelings on the matter, but she wished that some of the girls who succumbed to the lure of the thread mills had wider horizons. If only she could kindle a spark! She lifted the desk lid and brought out a morocco-bound copy of *David Copperfield*. 'Would you like to take this home, Dandy? You could read the bits you have missed; but see that you return it before Friday. The rest of the class will want to hear the story too.'

Dandy, speechless, caressed the leather bindings gently for some time. Then she raised shining eyes and breathed, 'Oh, Miss.'

Elizabeth Martin gave herself top marks. Thirty years of teaching had taught her not to expect too much, but now and again there was a flash of light. This was what the job was all about – inspiring people. That book was a treasured memento of her childhood – a school prize which she had read and re-read many times. Now it was 'opening windows on faery lands forlorn' for this most unlikely child.

At lunchtime May was waiting at the school gate as usual. 'What's that you've got, Dandy?'

'Are your hands clean? No, I think you'd better wait till you're home and have washed them. See, it's one of Miss Martin's own school prizes and she's letting me

25

take it home to read because I've missed so much on Fridays. Isn't that kind of her?'

'Oh, yes!' May squeezed her hand, sharing Dandy's pleasure. 'Maybe you'll be able to tell me what the story is about when we're in bed.' Their brothers ran past. George took the opportunity to jostle Dandy, knowing that she could not run fast with May's hand in hers.

'You'll need to take care that the boys don't get it,' May said earnestly.

'I'll murder anyone who touches it,' said Dandy with finality. May looked troubled. Dandy could be fierce when the boys annoyed her.

Dandy hid the book in the parlour till May had the chance to slip through to look at it and then, climbing on a chair, she carefully stowed it on one of the ornamental shelves of the fireplace overmantel. 'It'll be safe there,' she said.

'Your flowers are fine,' May was sniffing the few blooms in the jam jar on the hearth.

'Yes. It was nice of Aunt Alice to spare me some. Their kitchen smells gorgeous with the big bunch. "Daphne", it's called. Their brother has a bush in his garden. I'd love to see it. Grannie says the brother is a recluse. That means he keeps himself to himself, doesn't talk to folk.'

'Why does he not talk to folk, Dandy?'

'Well, lots of reasons, I think. They lost all their money and he had to move from a nice big house to the wee cottage, and then his wife died and their wee baby.'

'Oh!' May's lip was trembling.

'But his sisters look after him, take him food and things and he works in his garden a lot now that he's finished with the office. He audits books at home. I'm not quite sure what that means, but I'll ask Aunt Alice some day. Fancy getting paid for sitting reading books

26

at home! I expect there's some sort of snag. It sounds too good to be true.'

Grannie had relayed a few more items of gossip which were less than flattering to Mr James McLaren, but they maybe weren't true. That he never, never smiled, for example. Well, if he was all alone maybe he didn't have much to smile about. And Grannie said that he had raised a stick to some boys that had climbed into his garden and tramped on some of his precious plants. If I had a garden I'd thump anyone who damaged it, thought Dandy, and I bet Grannie would do the same if it had been hers. If he had sisters like Aunt Violet and Aunt Alice he surely couldn't be as nasty as Grannie made out. Maybe he just didn't like nosey folk prying into his business.

Grannie got them to start tea early so that the boys would be ready to go out with Faither as soon as he had had his meal. As soon as she saw them start to fidget she sent them through to the parlour – 'And mind you play quietly. We don't want to disturb the neighbours,' she added. Dandy had taken the twins into the scullery to wash; and their father, subdued under the eye of Grannie, was quietly eating his meal when there was an almighty crash from the parlour. George's shout and Billy's crying lent wings to Dandy's feet. Miss Martin's book ... they couldn't have ... they couldn't have. She catapulted into the room. George was picking up the book from the puddle and broken glass in the hearth. Dandy slapped him viciously with one hand and grabbed the book with the other. 'Here!' he cried indignantly. 'It wasn't me. I told Billy you would go mad.' Dandy whirled round. Years of frustration and anger rose in her. She punched and punched till her father's roar shook the room and she was pulled back by her grandmother.

'That's enough, Dandy,' she said.

'Mair than enough. What's all the din about?' her father demanded.

Dandy held up the sodden book which had slivers of glass embedded in its once beautiful covers. 'Miss Martin gave me it,' she sobbed.

'Just look at the mess of that fireplace,' scolded Lily Jordan. 'You can't take your eyes off that pair for ten minutes. If you took more control of your sons, Will Baxter, they wouldn't be the pests that they are. Now get them out of here. It's time their mother got some peace to wash.'

He waved the boys out of the room then turned on Dandy who stood, white and shaking. 'All this fuss for a bloody book, you daft bitch. I'd put it in the back of the fire.'

Dandy gave him a look of pure hatred. 'Aye! That's about your level,' she said in her grandmother's voice.

Will Baxter started forward in fury, but found his way blocked by Lily Jordan. 'You've nobody to blame but yourself. Now get those limbs of Satan out of here and we'll all get peace.'

The door banged behind them. Lily Jordan hurried off to attend to her patient, sending May through with the twins to their bed in the parlour. Dandy, sobbing bitterly, walked past them with dragging steps and made her way to the sure refuge of the McLarens.

'Dandy, my dear, what's wrong?' Violet's arm was round her and Alice was hurrying from the scullery. Dandy held up the sodden spiked mess which she had stroked caressingly that morning. 'Miss Martin lent me it,' she sobbed, 'because I had missed so many Fridays. She was so kind and look! It's been a school prize. I don't know what she'll think. She'll hate me. It was Billy. I hate him. I could murder him.'

'No, you don't. Now, don't say things you'll regret later, Dandy, my dear.' Alice was edging her into a big

28

armchair by the fire and easing the book out of her grip. 'Violet, what do you think? Linen towels perhaps? We don't want any fluff on the pages.'

'I'll get some,' said Violet.

'Will it dry at the fire?' Dandy asked through her sobs.

'Oh, no, that would be the worst thing,' Alice said. 'The leaves would go yellow and curl. We'll have to do it slowly on a flat surface. Help me clear the table, dear, and we'll be able to work carefully; first the gentle drying and then we'll take tweezers and get all that glass out. But I'm afraid that the glue has been affected. Tomorrow I'll take it to James. He has some rare old books and will know, perhaps, what to do about it. The dampness is bound to take some time to disappear in this weather. We daren't hurry it in any way. Had it been summer . . . but James will know.'

'Won't he be angry, Aunt Alice – I mean, feel that we are wasting his time?'

'Not at all. James is fortunate in being able to work in his own time. His garden is too small to keep him occupied for many hours at a stretch. But he is a book lover and will feel as upset as you are, my dear, at the destruction; though, I daresay, your brothers did not mean this to happen.'

'That's what May would say. Grannie says she's too good to live. I think the boys are pests. Grannie told Faither – I mean my father – that if he paid more attention to them they wouldn't behave like that.'

'Certainly boys tend to model themselves on their fathers just as we tend to model ourselves on our mothers.'

Dandy was startled. 'I don't model myself on mine. I'd put something in Faither's tea. That's what Grannie says she should do.'

Violet McLaren's handkerchief went up to her face

and there was a little explosion which might have been a cough. Alice kept her equilibrium. 'Your grannie is a great help to your mother, as you are, my dear.' Dandy paused to consider while Alice's patient hands held the book flat and Violet stretched the dish towel gently over each page. Aunt Alice had managed not to utter a word of criticism again. You knew that she didn't approve of Faither; had reservations about Grannie's pronouncements and yet wanted her, Dandy, to see Grannie's good points. It was a kind of strength Aunt Alice had because she was never put out when other people got flustered and worked up. Maybe that was what being 'a lady' meant. It would be worth studying.

'Shall I tell Miss Martin tomorrow?' she asked.

'No! We'll wait to hear what James has to say. Of course when you take it back you will have to explain. It will never be perfect. That would be too much to hope for.'

'That's what I'm dreading,' said Dandy, the tears starting again. 'She was being so nice, staying in at playtime to teach me about verbs and things. She wouldn't get her cup of tea because the bell rang . . .'

'Oh, you've put *me* in the notion of a cup of tea,' said Alice. 'Do you think you could put the kettle on, my dear? The tea caddy is on the shelf above the cooker and there's a biscuit tin in the right-hand cupboard of the sideboard, here.'

It didn't seem like work doing things for these aunties. I'd like to live with them all the time, Dandy thought. I could model myself on them. But I'd still want to thump Billy, she added truthfully.

The following day was a difficult one for Dandy. Grannie arrived in time to allow her to go to school, yet this was the one day she would have been glad of an excuse to stay at home. She shied away from meeting

Miss Martin's eye, even when she said, 'Well done, Dandy' after her turn at reading.

Alice McLaren was having her worst fears confirmed too. James tut-tutted when he saw the damaged book. 'A lovely edition, that one; quite moderately priced at the time; beautiful binding; Rachel had the identical; it's in her own bookcase – a present on her fourteenth birthday. An accident, I assume?'

'Well, yes, you could say that, though Dandy, our little protégée would not allow that. I gather she was dealing very drastically with the boy responsible till her grandmother tore them apart. You see . . .' She went on to explain the circumstances.

'Poor child!' he said. 'I understand her feelings. Well, leave it with me, Alice. I'll see what I can do, but I'm afraid it will never look . . .' He paused in thought.

'Thank you, James,' Alice said. 'Violet is busy baking and we'll be back in the afternoon with a little steak pie and some nice cakes. Just do your best. It's all we *can* do.'

She walked home thoughtfully, a plan forming. 'What did he say?' Violet raised a floury hand to push a lock of hair from her eyes.

'Not very hopeful, I'm afraid but . . . you know, Violet, it stirred him. He deplored the destruction of the book, of course – any book lover would – but he seemed interested in Dandy and genuinely sorry for her. I have a little stratagem planned. If Mrs Jordan is still upstairs when the child gets back from school I think we should try to "borrow" Dandy to help us carry our things to Espedair Street today.'

'But they're not any heavier than usual, Alice, are they?'

'No, but they won't know that and it would be a break for Dandy. She's worrying about the book anyway so she might as well see what James has managed to achieve with it as soon as possible. You know you remarked on her love of flowers and I thought it would be pleasant to take her to see his little garden but didn't feel he would welcome it. This would be a reasonable time to introduce her. I feel it would do James good. We were saying that he never mixes with young people nowadays . . .'

'No, and he certainly won't have met many like our Dandy – "I'd put something in Faither's tea".' Violet's mimicry was not very accurate but it was enough to send two gently-nurtured sisters into gales of laughter.

One surprising thing about Grannie, Dandy reflected, was that she chased her out, even when she was needed. Grannie Jordan worked hard herself but still had some sympathy for her young granddaughter. 'You go and help your aunties, Dandy, the fresh air's good for you. I'll keep these young tykes in order.' To her daughter she added, 'She'll learn nothing but good from these two – real ladies. I wouldn't mind hearing what that cottage of his is like. He never has any visitors, they say.'

A real lady wouldn't be nosey, Dandy thought, and then had to grin when she thought how she had longed to see that garden. This was her chance. It was a pity it had to be spoiled by the nightmare of the book. The heavy load she had to help with wasn't heavy at all – not to a girl who was used to lugging a half stone of potatoes every other day. Grannie said that that should be George's job, but somehow he always managed to slip off before Mammie could catch him. 'I'd see that he got an empty plate for a night or two,' Grannie had said. 'That would stop his nonsense.' But she would forget Grannie and look forward to seeing that garden with the bush that had such a wonderful perfume; fancy a plant choosing to flower in the cold weather! It was strange.

They were at the front door. It had lovely wee yellow flowers like tiny stars growing round it. Alice rapped the brass knocker and they listened to the approaching footsteps – muffled because they were on carpet, not linoleum like the Baxters' house. Dandy hadn't known how to picture this man who was a recluse; who never smiled; who used to be rich and now had to live in a little cottage she thought was wonderful; who had lost his wife and baby.

He was older looking than she had imagined, though he was the aunties' little brother. Grannie, who was nosey about ages as with everything else, had guessed that Violet McLaren would be sixty-three and Alice two or three years older. James was their wee brother and they had enjoyed playing with him. That meant he was probably under sixty. But what did that matter? She was getting as bad as Grannie!

He *did* smile, faintly, but it was a smile. And he *kissed* his sisters on the cheek as they shook hands. Fancy a man kissing his sisters! Of course they were fond of one another. Alice and Violet looked after each other. Well, she looked after the younger ones herself, but that was to help Mammie. Yet there was May. She was like the sort of sister ... but she had to pull herself together; she was being introduced. 'And this is Dandy, our little protégée, James.'

'The girl who likes books.' His voice was gentle and she got a sort of half-smile. 'I expect you are worrying about the Dickens. Come and see what I have done.'

He led her into the sitting room while the sisters continued towards the kitchen with their parcels. She gave a quick glance round. There were bookcases on every wall and each one crammed with books. A cheerful fire was burning in the grate and shabby comfortable leather armchairs dotted around. One was drawn close to the hearth. James McLaren stepped forward and picked up a book from the table beside it. 'Well, my dear, what do you think?' he asked.

Dandy gasped. She had heard about miracles at Sunday School. She knew she should believe in them because they were in the Bible but somehow . . . well, they never happened to anyone she knew. And now this! This was a miracle. She stood, staring.

James broke the silence. 'Well, my dear, what do you think?'

Dandy licked the tears which had begun to run down her face. 'I think,' she gulped, 'I think you're as clever as Jesus. It's a bloody miracle.'

Chapter 3

Nothing in James McLaren's experience had prepared him for such an accolade. He stared helplessly at the child and then beyond to his sisters, who had reached the doorway in time to hear the last remark. It was Alice who recovered first and stepped forward to remove the book gently from Dandy's hand. 'A miracle, indeed!' she said, smiling warmly at her brother. 'Now, Dandy, what about a hug for Uncle James before we sit down and hear how he managed such a clever thing? I think I've guessed.'

If James had been taken aback by Dandy's remark, he was staggered by the fierce hug she gave him before standing back and beginning to blush. Recalling her resolution to behave like these aunties, she said, 'I can't tell you how grateful I am. I'll remember this for ever.'

Having seen his guests disposed, James took his seat thankfully. 'Well, first of all, let me say it is no miracle. A very fortunate coincidence would be a more apt explanation. You see, Dandy, my late wife had a copy which was identical to that of your teacher. It had been a birthday present when she was fourteen years old. I simply used a razor blade to remove the inscribed title page on her book. Then I cut a narrow strip of strong paper and glued it in to the backing. When that was ready, I removed the title page from your teacher's book and glued it carefully on top of the strip. Of course, if you look you can tell, but no one would normally notice anything.'

'Shall I have to tell Miss Martin?' Dandy had turned to the aunts, but James chose to answer.

'I think it would be better if your Aunt Alice wrote to the teacher and explained things for you before you took the book in. You might feel embarrassed and muddle things up a little, don't you think.'

'Aye! I would. But surely she won't mind . . . it looks the same.'

'No. I'm sure she won't mind if your aunt has explained. It's easier for a grown-up – eh, Alice?'

'Yes, of course you're right, James. I'll be happy to do that. Now, shall we have a cup of tea and sample Violet's cakes? Then James could maybe show Dandy his garden while we do a little bit of polishing. I'll take your coat, Dandy, but you'll have to put it on again before you venture outside.'

The cakes were delicious and the room a delight with all those books to make you feel safe. Why did they? Was it because they had been written a long time ago? She couldn't work it out. It just felt cosy. Dandy warmed to it all. But she wasn't sorry when she saw James wipe his lips with the big linen napkin then lay it down. 'Well, young lady,' he said, 'shall we wrap up against winter's chill and venture forth?' Dandy laughed. He was talking like a book, playing with the words as she loved to do. And no one had ever called her 'young lady' before. Maybe she *was* managing to copy these aunties who were 'ladies'.

The garden which they called 'little' seemed anything but little to Dandy. It was narrow certainly, but it stretched and stretched with funny little winding paths and there, quite near, was the daphne bush she had longed to see. She almost ran to it, then, leaning over the fragrant blossoms, she said, 'It's exactly what I imagined when Aunt Violet told me about it. Fancy a plant wanting to bloom in this cold weather!'

36

'Perhaps it knows that we appreciate it more at this time of year. When the air is heavy with the scent of the rose, I doubt if we would notice that of the daphne, strong though it seems now.'

'Mmm, I hadn't thought of that. It makes sense. It's no' daft, then. You think that flowers know things?'

'It's just a manner of speaking,' James said hastily.

'You mean that God makes them that way?'

'Yes. I think that is nearer the mark.'

'And yet, I think that if this was *my* garden I would feel that the plants knew me and were blooming for me.'

'You have the heart of a true gardener, my dear.'

'I'd murder anyone who destroyed a bonnie bush like that.'

'Well,' said James, 'I think I'd stop short of murder. I don't fancy a prison cell.' They laughed together.

James's sisters heard the laughter. 'Would you have believed it?' asked Violet. 'The difference that child has made to our James – in a matter of minutes almost.'

'Violet, I think there has been more than one "bloody miracle" in this house today. We'll have to be careful or we'll be picking up Dandy's rather colourful language.'

'Don't you think we should correct her when she swears?'

'I've thought about that, Violet, but I think we'll have to take things step by step. At the moment she sees us as a refuge from the turmoil and the rowing that goes on upstairs. I hope that gradually she will see that we don't use language like that. She probably knows it is wrong but hears it so often from her father and, when she is vexed, it is the only way she knows to express herself.'

'Mmm. When you think of it, Alice, she has a great deal to feel vexed about.'

'Precisely! I think James's eyebrows were telling me to enlighten Miss Martin as to her background. As a lover of books he will know that, no matter how good the substitution is, she will feel a little deprived at the loss of her original book. The last thing I would want to do is to deny books to Dandy. They are more important to her than to most children, stuck as she is in that maelstrom of domesticity. I expect she'll have to go home quite soon to help when her grannie is leaving.'

'Shall we remind her, Alice?'

'We may have to. It could spoil her chances of coming here again if we don't. I'm not only thinking of Dandy, either. She's the best medicine we could ever have devised for our James. "Clever as Jesus." He'll remember that for a long time!'

James was explaining things in his precise way and Dandy, hands clasped tightly to her chest, was hanging on every word. 'You see what I mean, Violet?' Alice muttered as they made their way down the garden.

'Some seeds respond to heat,' James was saying. 'When I plant parsley, for example, I take a kettle of boiling water down and pour it over the seeds before covering them. On the other hand, the seeds of the alpine plants respond to chill and like to be in a frosty spot before planting.'

'I'm afraid you will have to think about going home, Dandy,' Alice said as they drew near. 'Your grandmother will be anxious to get away.'

'Oh bugger – it's not that time already!' Dandy, oblivious of her slip rushed on, 'Uncle James knows thousands of things about gardens.'

'Well, if you don't annoy your grandmother by being late today, perhaps she will let you come to help us again,' said Violet.

'Aye! She *can* be a twisted auld bi ... besom,' said Dandy.

'We're very grateful for your help, Dandy,' said Alice. 'Here's a penny. Buy yourself some sweets.'

'Oooh!' Dandy suddenly looked like the child she should be, 'I'll get dolly mixtures. That's May's favourites – and the twins.'

'Do your brothers like them?'

'They eat anything – greedy devils,' she assured them.

James cleared his throat. 'Would your mother care for some leeks? That's the only vegetable which is in plentiful supply here at the moment.'

'Oh aye, that would save her a ha'penny,' said Dandy ingenuously.

James cleared his throat again. 'I have some newspaper in the hut; shan't be a moment.' He was soon back with a large fork and easing up the leeks before Dandy's astonished eyes. 'That's twice what we usually buy. Mammie will get two pots of soup.' She watched him shake off the surplus soil and roll the leeks in the large sheets of paper. 'I hope the paper doesn't get too dirty,' she said. 'I'd like to read it.'

'Doesn't your father get a newspaper, my dear?'

'Only the racing paper and it's no use . . . just what's racing at two-thirty and all that sort of thing. Grannie says the lavvie is all it's good for.'

Violet coughed. Alice gave her sister a warning glance as she turned to Dandy. 'Yes, it's time you were getting off, my dear.'

'I think I shall adjourn indoors now, too,' said James. 'The air is definitely chilly.'

'I hope I didn't keep Uncle James standing too long in the cold,' whispered Dandy as she and Alice led the way back to the house.

'No. I'm sure he would have said,' Alice replied in her comforting way.

'Fancy him doing that for me – the book, I mean. And he didn't even know me. Of course, he loves books.

39

Like me. But he must have wanted to keep that one that was his wife's – I mean, he's kept it all these years.'

'Yes. It *was* kind of my brother to do that. It is good for us to be kind. We develop that way, don't you think?'

'I don't understand,' said Dandy hesitantly.

'No, I was forgetting. In some ways you are so grown-up, my dear. But, to take your case, I think that all the kind things you do for your little brothers and sisters and all the sacrifices you have to make because of them will make you a very special person when you grow up; strong, I mean, and unafraid; able to look everyone in the eye.'

'Yes, I've made up my mind to be strong like Grannie, but I'm not going to be a grumbler like her.'

'No, I'm sure your grannie doesn't mean to be a grumbler, but she feels unable to help your mother as much as she would like. Frustration can make us rather grumbly as we get older, I fear.'

'But you're not grumbly. Aunt Violet isn't grumbly.'

'No. We have each other. That is a great blessing. Also when we look at James and what he has lost we see how much more he has had to grumble about – not that James grumbles; he has simply become a little withdrawn. He was such an amusing little boy. Aunt Violet and I had lots of fun playing with him. And he said such comical things; you wouldn't believe! Shhh, I'll tell you at home,' she whispered as Violet and James caught up with them.

Dandy skipped most of the way to the sweet shop, then started to skip the rest of the way home. Grannie would be relieved to see her back; so would Mammie. May would love hearing about the garden. *And the book!* That was the most wonderful thing of all. Aunt Alice would write to Miss Martin and Miss Martin would

40

know that her aunties were 'ladies' by the way she wrote – not that they were her real aunties, but Aunt Alice had said, 'Give Uncle James a hug,' as if she was real family. Would Uncle James kiss her if she went back? That would be a wee bit embarrassing. A hug was easier. Maybe they wouldn't take her back! Yes they would. She was sure of it. Uncle James liked her. He hadn't said much, but he had been a little bit funny too – that bit about a prison cell. He couldn't be a recluse, really, if he didn't like being shut in. He had said she had the heart of a true gardener. Could that be right? The McLarens were clever. They understood things that other people didn't understand. Fancy Uncle James being a comical little boy. She wondered what the things were that he said. But Aunt Alice had whispered that she would tell her. Dandy skipped happily on.

That evening while Violet tackled a pile of ironing, Alice spent some time composing her letter to Miss Martin. 'What do you think of this?' she asked Violet at the end. 'I've started with the bit about the book; purely a factual account of the affair. You know it all, so I shan't bore you with it, but James gave me firm guidance on what the teacher should be told.'

Because Dandy is a brave child, I feel that she probably does not reveal the difficulties she encounters at home and, because of that pride, I hesitate to betray her confidence. However, I trust your discretion in this matter and hope that you may find the information helpful in dealing with the child and her unsought absences from school. Her mother is a timid woman who is unable to cope with her large brood and her hard-drinking husband. The house is hopelessly overcrowded and Dandy has no privacy or peace there. Thanks to the grit of the maternal grandmother, who visits quite often, matters do not get completely out of hand but they are on a knife edge at times. Dandy is kept working non-stop till most of the younger children are in bed. Occasionally she manages to escape to our house for a short time then. Her grandmother does her best to give Dandy a little freedom, but it is nowhere near the amount any normal child should have. On washdays Dandy has to do all the housework in addition to looking after twin sisters and a baby brother. She treasures her time at school and particularly enjoys hearing you read on Friday afternoons. My sister and I feel that she is a very intelligent girl with a great love of reading who could go far, given a chance. We would be very happy to help in any way we could. Perhaps when she has missed some lessons, it would be possible for you to give her a note with the outline of the subject and we should be very happy to fill in.

Finally, I should like to reiterate our regret at the damage to your book. My brother, who has a fine collection, shares this feeling. He also thinks that Dandy is a brave child who deserves support. We wish to thank you for your work with her.

I remain,
Yours truly,
Alice M. McLaren

'Well, what do you think?'
Violet placed the heavy iron on the hob and paused for a moment. 'Very good, Alice, but don't you think . . . perhaps a little flattery . . . she has been teaching for thirty years.'
'No. If she has learned anything in those thirty years

42

it will be how to sniff out insincerity. Anyway, I don't particularly feel like flattering her. It took her quite a while to realize that Dandy loved reading. She is weak enough, from what Dandy has let slip, to prefer the well-dressed little girls who come from safe back-grounds.'

'Well, weren't we – till we met Dandy?'

'Yes. But we have developed, haven't we? Our brother is clever as Jesus, remember?'

'Oh Alice, wouldn't our Mama have been shocked at that!'

'Yes, certainly she would. Her life was even more sheltered than ours. I *would* like to have money again, but I'm not sorry we made the acquaintance of our little Dandy and that certainly wouldn't have happened in the old life. So! Have I permission to seal this and send it to Miss Elizabeth Martin?'

Violet dropped a spoonful of water on the base of the iron and watched the steam rise before tackling the next article on the pile. 'I expect so. You're the eldest after all. But I've had a wonderful idea while you were writing. You know that Dandy asked us to keep the beautiful book here till it is time to take it back. I was thinking that I could clear a drawer in that big chest in the lobby – the bottom one which is difficult anyway – and let Dandy keep her precious things there. What do you think of that?'

'An excellent idea. James gave me the damaged book too. Dandy will be able to have it always. He kept the title page with the inscription. When I tried to sympath-ize with him, he said to me that Dandy had given him a new outlook. He had been too busy thinking about the past. Her lively interest in things had made him realize there was a future too. Maybe he has been hang-ing on to old ideas as well as old books. A good part of his collection, of course, was left to him by Uncle

Cornelius and even when James lost all his money, he felt unable to part with it. Now, I think, he's looking at it with new eyes. These are books which he never reads himself but would be very valuable to a collector simply because of their rarity. I think he is now wondering if he did the right thing all those years ago, taking Rachel to a little cottage with no bathroom when he might have been able to offer something better.'

'But Rachel was happy there. It was obvious. She simply adored James.'

'That's exactly what I said, Violet my dear. Now, what about some supper?'

On Thursday morning Dandy called on her way to school to pick up the substitute book. 'Just in case something happens and I don't get to school tomorrow. Miss Martin will know, won't she? She won't be too angry, will she?'

'She certainly will know by now,' Violet replied. 'Your drawer is very stiff, as you see, but I'm sure it is worth the struggle to be able to keep your treasures safe.'

'Oh, yes!' Dandy breathed. 'Fancy a drawer all to myself. It was so kind of you to give me it – and kind of Aunt Alice to write to Miss Martin. Uncle James was right. I *would* have got muddled and maybe made her angry, but Aunt Alice would know exactly what to say. Shall I take it in its little box?'

'Yes. James wrapped it in tissue paper and found that box for it. He believes in protecting his precious books from the elements.'

'Me too!' said Dandy, who had never thought of the subject in her life.

'Well,' said Alice when Violet regaled her with this reply later, 'Dandy seems to be identifying with the McLaren family. We shall have to behave ourselves, sister dear.'

44

'I am beginning to think, Alice, that people who don't behave quite so well are a little more interesting.'

'Mmmm, me too!' said Alice.

In spite of all the reassurances, Dandy was none too happy about approaching Miss Martin that morning. Several members of her class had been late and a few of the boys had been dilatory about getting in line in the first place. Miss Martin's jaw had been set in a hard line when Dandy stole a glance at her in passing. But now the moment had come and she had to go through with it. What was it that Aunt Alice had said? – something about all the sacrifices that she had had to make for her little brothers and sisters would make her strong and unafraid. It wasn't happening yet, but Aunt Alice was always right. She approached the desk and handed the box to Miss Martin. 'That's . . .' she started hesitantly.

'My book. Thank you, Dandy. Just sit down now and we'll get on with the register.'

Elizabeth Martin raised the lid of her desk and picked up the register, balancing it on the edge. From where Dandy sat she could see the teacher's hands taking the book out of the box, unfolding the tissue, then replacing it hurriedly before lifting the register and closing the desk. As she found her page she gave Dandy a quick half smile, then began.

Dandy let out a long, slow breath she had not realized she was holding. It was going to be all right. She relaxed. The grammar lesson found her adequately prepared this time. In fact, she was disappointed when the bell rang for playtime. Reluctantly she put away her slate and pencil, wiping the dust with the little rag she kept for the purpose. Miss Martin touched her arm. 'If you will wait for a moment, Dandy . . .' Dandy looked up startled, but Miss Martin was smiling reassuringly.

Some of the girls glanced at her and made faces behind Miss Martin's back.

'As you will know, Dandy, I had a letter from your neighbour, Miss . . . er . . . McLaren.'

'Aunt Alice; there's two of them. The other one is Violet,' said Dandy helpfully.

'I see. Their brother is a collector, I understand.'

'Yes, Uncle James I call him. He has books and books all round his sitting room. You can't see the wall. It makes you feel so . . .' she paused. Miss Martin might think she was being silly if she said 'safe'.

'I love a book-lined room, too,' said Miss Martin. 'It makes you feel cosy and yet you know that those books can take you far away to places that may not be cosy at all but can be exciting and very beautiful.'

'You feel that too?' said Dandy in astonishment. 'I thought I was maybe a wee bit daft when I found books magic. Lots of people don't.'

'Lots of people don't know what they are missing then,' said Elizabeth Martin. 'I have replied to Miss McLaren's letter. Perhaps you could convey my thanks to her brother also for an excellent job. Perhaps he would make a good forger, eh, Dandy?'

Dandy laughed in delight. Miss Martin was being funny – a bit like Uncle James. 'He might land in prison,' she retorted, 'and he told me he didn't fancy a prison cell – that was when I said I would murder anyone who damaged his daphne bush.'

'You like flowers, Dandy?'

'Oh, yes!' The little ragamuffin who dealt rough justice in the playground gave a fervent sigh. 'Uncle James is going to teach me all about them . . . if I get time to visit him, that is.'

'I hope you do. Your young brothers should be fit to help at home, surely? I have one of them next year, I believe.'

46

'Oh, yes,' said Dandy slowly. 'I wasn't thinking. Yes, George will be in your class.'

'Perhaps I'll be able to persuade him to take some of your present responsibilities.'

'Oh my God, if you could!' breathed Dandy, then hastily averting the reproof she foresaw, 'I mean, that would be wonderful. I'd be most grateful.'

Dandy wandered slowly into the playground. None of her classmates, busily skipping, noticed her; nor did she wish to join them. Grown-ups could be so surprising. Fancy old Marty-farty being daft about books! Well, maybe if you were a teacher ... but *she* found them magic too. Maybe lots of people found them magic. Of course, Uncle James must find them magic when he kept so many of them. He was going to show her a book which was very valuable and had lovely illustrations of flowers – hundreds of them. He said that it would maybe be a good thing to do if she came on a wet day and they couldn't get out to the garden. That sounded as if he thought she would be going back again to the cottage. If only! It depended on Grannie. What was the best way to handle Grannie? The only thing that interested her was housework and furniture and things. She was nosey about Uncle James's cottage. Maybe if she told her little bits about it – made her want to hear more ... By the time the bell rang Dandy had her strategy worked out.

Grannie had been in a hurry to get away the previous afternoon, but she *had* seen and admired the leeks. 'Uncle James dug them up,' Dandy had informed her proudly.

'Oh, it's "Uncle James" is it?'

Yes. Grannie had been impressed at that. And there was that time she had assured Mammie that Dandy would come to no harm with the McLarens. Properly handled she could be an ally. Certainly Grannie was the only one who could foil any objections that her father might choose to think up. You never knew with Faither. He wasn't interested in her himself, yet he seemed to be jealous of any other interests she had.

She wouldn't say that Uncle James kissed his sisters. Grannie would tell people and somehow that didn't seem right. She *could* tell her about the cosy sitting room, full of books and with big comfy chairs; she *could* tell her how clever Uncle James was; how many books he had read and could talk about; how he knew thousands of things about gardens. She *could* say that he was going to be planting seeds in a few weeks and if she could get back to visit him, he would let her help. Actually he hadn't quite said so, but she knew in her heart that it could be true. Uncle James had said she had the heart of a true gardener. Grannie would be impressed by that. It shouldn't be too difficult.

She walked slowly that afternoon, thoughts and plans churning in her head. She could afford to take her time. Mammie wouldn't be so het up trying to get a meal ready. Faither was always late on a Friday. He spent more time in the pub, spending his pay. Grannie always had plenty to say about that. She walked home the long way so that she could admire the lovely church with all the steps leading up to it. Folk thought she was daft if she said she liked nice buildings. All her mother ever craved was a house with a bathroom like the one she had left to marry Faither. Eventually she turned downhill to the familiar surroundings of home. George suddenly catapulted out of the close and grunted something as he passed her. Next came Billy. 'Hurry up, Dandy,' he cried. 'Faither's drunk and he's gie'in' us a' pennies.'

'Here! Come back,' she called. 'Where's Mammie?'

'She went to see Mrs Stewart when she heard she was no' weel. She took wee Jack with her. Faither's awfie drunk but he's happy ... singing.'

'Give me that penny! I mean it!' she said, gripping his wrist. 'Mammie will likely need it. If she doesna, you'll get it back. Run and catch George. Make him share his sweets with the rest of you.'

'He'll never ...'

'Oh aye, tell him I'll bash him to pulp if he doesna. Nae messin'!

Billy saw when he was beaten and quickly raced after his brother. At that moment May appeared with the twins by the hand. 'Sorry, May,' Dandy said. 'I'll need to take the pennies in case Mammie needs them. If the auld devil's as drunk as that, there's no knowing what's happened to the rest of his pay. I've sent Billy to tell George to share his sweets with the rest of you.' The twins were beginning to whimper. 'Hurry!' said Dandy. 'George has got sweeties for you and tell him I'll bash him if you don't get them.'

They were too wee to understand, of course, but they'd probably repeat her words. She mounted the stairs purposefully with the four pennies jangling in her pocket. She'd see what she could screw out of the drunken old devil herself, before he sobered up.

It wasn't easy. He was in the big chair and the tuneless singing was interspersed with snores. She would have to think quickly. 'Did you hear about the leeks that Uncle James gave me, Faither?'

'Ho! Uncle James! That's a good one,' he grunted.

'Saved Mammie a penny, they did, and they're nicer than the ones in the shops. Maybe I'll get more next time I go. That would save your pennies, wouldn't it. Billy said you were giving them pennies.'

Faither grunted. Then he fumbled in his pocket. 'Here! Will that stop you blethering? Now, wheesht!'

Dandy whispered her thanks as she quickly extracted the penny from his shaking hand. That fivepence weighing down her pocket now might be essential to Mammie. He must have left work early to be as drunk as that at this time of day. Well, she had done her best for Mammie and the vegetables she was going to grow would surely be an even bigger help – that is if the heavy rain kept away and she could get to the cottage.

The weather proved an ally. There were fine windy days when the washing all dried nicely out of doors. Grannie was less grumbly. Mammie seemed back to normal and next time the McLarens asked her to help them on their trip to Espedair Street, Lily Jordan happened to be present and practically chased Dandy off after seeing that she washed her face and brushed her hair.

'It was lucky Grannie was there when you needed me,' said Dandy as they set off.

'Wasn't it,' said Alice, tranquilly winking at Violet behind Dandy's head.

'Will Uncle James be planting seeds, do you think?'

'I'm pretty sure he will. The weather is just right to get some of the early planting done. He has been asking after our little porter, as he calls you. He *will* be pleased to see you!'

'Really?' Dandy gave a little skip of pleasure and went off into a daydream.

The winter jasmine by the door was still blooming, but no longer alone in its glory. Clusters of crocuses brought sighs of delight from Dandy. 'Look at them,' she said, 'kind of cheeky wee things, so bright! They make me want to laugh somehow.'

'The birds laugh too when they see them,' said Violet. 'They love attacking the crocuses.'

'Why's that?' asked Dandy.

'I don't really know . . . do you, Alice?'

'No. I've forgotten, but your Uncle James will be sure to know. Here he is!'

Dandy suddenly found herself afflicted with shyness. Would he kiss her? But James, having greeted his sisters in his usual fashion turned to her with a shy seriousness and shook hands briefly saying, 'I'm so glad you could come back. Perhaps you could help me plant some seeds today. I've prepared a bit of ground.'

Dandy flushed with pleasure. 'Sure, I'll help you.'

'Perhaps we could go out now while you have your coat on,' he suggested. 'Would that be all right, Alice? We could have tea a little later.'

'Yes, it's early,' said Alice. 'You two go ahead.' She watched them move off, Dandy practically skipping. 'That was a good idea of yours, Violet, going to warn him that we hoped to bring Dandy today. He might not have had the ground ready. She has this idea that seeds are magic. She's never had the chance to plant any in her life. It seems to mean such a lot to her.'

'Wait till she finds that James is allocating a bit of the garden to her for her own use. That was his own idea, Alice. I never even thought of it. I'd love to see her face when she finds out . . .'

'No, Violet. That's James's department. We have our own niche at home – and just think! Dandy's language might not be fit for our delicate ears!'

Violet choked. 'What about James's ears?'

'They'll be rosy. But he *has* read a few books in his time, little sister. I don't think the words will be new to him, do you? Of course, with Dandy you never know. Our baby brother could be completing his education.'

Chapter 4

'And, guess what, Grannie – Uncle James is going to let me have a bit of the vegetable garden and another bit for a flower garden all to myself. He asked me what our favourite vegetable was and I said tumshies. He didn't seem to know what a tumshie was; he calls them swedes. He says they are properly Swedish turnips. Sweden is a very cold country in the winter time and they probably feed their cattle on tumshies. You don't plant them till July and he said that maybe he'll dig up a bit of the lawn near the bottom of the garden to give me extra room for the tumshies – they're big and have to be spaced out. They need a lot of water to make them swell, "but that is seldom a problem in Paisley," he said, and he laughed. Do other places get less rain than we do, Grannie?'

'Oh, aye, but we don't get as much as the Greenock folk, Dandy. At least, that's what we think. My uncle always said they had webbed feet, but I had a neighbour who was brought up in Greenock and she used to get angry when folks said that; declared that Greenock was no wetter than anywhere else.'

'Well, anyway,' said Dandy, 'I'm glad we get plenty rain. I'll be able to grow right big tumshies for nothing and that will be a help to Mammie. I'll maybe be able to give you bunches of flowers for the parlour window, Grannie. I planted candytuft to day. You'll like that, won't you?'

'Aye, aye, that'll be fine.' Lily Jordan spoke absently. 'Were you upstairs? Did you see how many rooms there are? I can see two sets of windows from the street, but you can't see round the back.'

Dandy hesitated. She had no idea, but Grannie's noseyness could make her twisted if she didn't get an answer. A white lie could be useful. 'I'm not too sure, Grannie, but I'll look next time. When could you be here to let me go again?'

'Oh, we'll see how things work out,' said Grannie. Dandy swallowed her disappointment. She would have to go carefully. Grannie was not just tough; she was stubborn. If she wanted you to do something there was no way you could get out of it. The promise of largesse from the garden did not seem to weigh much with her. Her interest lay in the house and its contents; and maybe the sisters who were 'ladies' and the brother who allowed Dandy to call him Uncle James and who seemed to have taken to her granddaughter. Yes, Grannie was none too easy to handle. Still, there were so many cheery things to think about now, to help her forget the noisy disorder that surrounded her most of the time at home. That afternoon there had been the never-to-be-forgotten thrill of hearing that she was to have a little garden all to herself. The ground was dug over, riddled and ready for planting. Uncle James had rummaged in the pocket of his baggy old coat and produced jewels, yes, jewels! There they were, glowing pictures of the flowers to come on the outside; and inside, the tiny seeds that were magic. She sniffed the exciting smell of the damp earth as she held the precious gems in her hands and, under Uncle James's instructions, let them slither gently through her fingers as she proceeded along the row. Then there had been the business of marking the row. Dandy knew that that was quite unnecessary. She would never, never forget the place, the exact spot where she had first planted seeds in the brown earth. She knew without a doubt that she would walk to it in her dreams for the rest of her life.

Fancy Uncle James saying that he would dig up a bit of the little lawn at the foot of the garden! On her next visit Dandy had felt bound to demur. 'It's pretty with the little trees – I mean shrubs – all round it; a sort of place for the fairies to dance – not that I believe in fairies,' she assured him.

'No, of course,' he had said, 'but I see what you mean, Dandy. You are a remarkable child, my dear – an inner eye which sees things hidden from lesser mortals.' He mumbled the last bit and Dandy stood in bewildered silence. What had she said – something stupid about fairies – but Uncle James seemed to think she had said something important.

She pondered while he stood silent for a moment, then turned slowly to his vegetable garden. 'I thought you could have this piece – it gives you room for five rows or thereabouts. We'll start with spring turnips. They're fast growing. It's always difficult to plant them thinly enough, but I use the thinnings as a green vegetable; most people simply throw them away, but I find the flavour intriguing, somewhere between spinach and turnip itself.' Dandy was at a loss for an answer. She had never tasted spinach; didn't even know what it looked like. Uncle James was talking almost to himself again. 'It's a mistake to plant a long row of vegetables; having them all ready at once is not good husbandry. I usually plant quarter of a row at a time; however, in your case, probably half a row would be better . . . yes. The next row will be for carrots. Then we will have to plant onions. Do you know why, Dandy?'

'What?' said Dandy, startled.

'Why we plant onions next to the carrots?'

'No. Why?'

'Because it keeps the greenfly away, that's why.'

'Don't they like the smell of the onions, Uncle James?'

54

'That is probably the explanation, but I couldn't swear to it. However, they do seem to be effective. Otherwise you would have to spray the carrots with soapy water as we do the roses in summer.'

'Oh!' said Dandy.

'You'll enjoy spraying the roses, I think,' said James. 'When I was a little boy our gardener used to let me have a go. It seemed great fun. Then one day I got too bold and pretended it was a gun I was handling and started spraying all round. He got some in his eyes and flatly refused to let me help him again.'

'Not even when you were bigger and more sensible?' asked Dandy.

'By that time I was probably playing cricket or going off with my school chums and the garden didn't get too much attention.'

'When did you start enjoying the garden again?'

'Oh, now . . . let me think . . . It was probably when I met my wife. She was very fond of flowers and knew a lot about them. I was pleased to air my knowledge. Somehow I had not forgotten the things our wise old gardener taught me. And, of course, when we came here I became head gardener and had to look to my laurels.' He smiled at Dandy suddenly. He was being funny again, making the best of things. She recognized that now. Aunt Alice said that that was how people developed, and Aunt Alice knew such a lot.

The time seemed to fly past even though she was just planting things and helping pick out weeds. Again it was Alice McLaren who had to remind her that her grandmother would be anxious to get back to her own house. 'Bugger Grannie and her own house,' was Dandy's silent response. Aloud she said, 'The time always passes so quickly here, but you're right, Grannie might not let me come next time if I'm not careful.'

On the way home she had much for reflection. Aunt

Alice had shown her into the downstairs toilet, saying apologetically, 'There's a smarter one upstairs, but I'm afraid your boots will be rather muddy, no matter how well you scrape them.' Fancy having two lavvies in one house! At home they had to share theirs with the other folk on the landing – as if their own crew were not enough. She thought of the times she had suffered listening for the sound of the WC door slamming and the neighbour's footsteps returning upstairs. Mammie always said that you should wait till they were back inside their house before you opened your door: it was immodest to be seen going to the lavvie. But sometimes you were that desperate! Well, when she was big she would see that she had a house with a bathroom – something like Uncle James's cottage. Still that would be something else to tell Grannie – two WCs! She was bound to be impressed.

Grannie's ration of information that day included the fact that there were three bedrooms, a big one, a middle one and a small one which was used as a boxroom.

'Which one does *he* sleep in, then?' asked Lily.

Dandy said truthfully that she had no idea, but she would probably find out next time she was there. 'And I hope that's enough to make you let me go,' she prayed. The thought would not leave her for the next few days. All these seeds were waiting to be planted and she knew that if she did not get back in time Uncle James would be forced to do the job himself. The seeds would not wait for Grannie Jordan to make up her mind. She would have to watch out, be on her best behaviour, say nothing to annoy Grannie. They said at Sunday School that if you prayed hard enough God would listen and give you what you asked. Dandy was never too sure of that. God always seemed to give the cousin Bettys of this world what they asked, not folks like her with fathers who drank and mothers who had more weans

56

than they could manage and never enough money for anything. Surely Mammie had prayed for a coat that wasn't a hand-me-down from her lucky sisters! It was a bit of a puzzle and it took a lot of swallowing. But things were desperate. She *must* get those seeds planted. As she pocketed the penny that was her Sunday School collection, Dandy vowed to pray as hard as she could.

George and Billy had whooped off ahead of her. Dandy took May's hand out of habit though, really, May was past needing any attention that way. In fact, May was becoming a useful ally. All of a sudden, it seemed, the twins had got off nappies. It had taken ages, but there it was. Mammie dealt with Jack most of the time and May had taken to washing the twins while Dandy cleared up after the evening meal. This had meant a little more time for visiting the McLaren sisters and catching up on her missed school lessons.

The boys were nearly out of sight when they suddenly cut off the main street. 'Now where d'you think these two are going?' asked Dandy. 'That's not the way to Sunday School. Let's run and see what they are up to.'

'Grannie says that you shouldn't run on Sundays,' panted May.

'She's just jealous. She couldna run any day o' the week,' said Dandy. 'Look! That's our Billy outside Capaldi's. George must be inside.'

'Maybe he's spending his Saturday penny,' said May.

'Don't be daft. George couldna keep a penny. I'll bet he's spending his Sunday School collection. See! he's out and running on and there's Billy going in. We'll catch him all right.'

'But he'll have nothing to put in the bag when it comes round.'

'Maybe he'll say he's lost it. I wouldna put it past him. No, that wouldna do. They're both at it and the teachers would never believe that. I think I know . . .'

Billy, emerging with a bulging cheek, nearly choked to death when Dandy grabbed him. 'Let me see your collection,' she hissed. Billy fumbled in his trouser pocket. 'Hurry up, I want to see it.'

Candy dribbled down his chin as he held up a ha'penny for her inspection.

'Wait till I tell Mammie about this,' said Dandy, 'and Faither. You'll get walloped. It was George's idea, I expect.'

Billy, a sorry sight by this time, sucked and sobbed an affirmative.

'Why did George go in first?' asked May.

'They wanted two ha'pennies in their change,' said Dandy. 'Mr Capaldi would have guessed what they were up to and maybe refused to serve them. I'll take charge of the rest of those sweets,' she said, turning to Billy, 'and you can tell George that he'll pay for this.'

While Billy ran off, still sobbing, Dandy and May proceeded at a more dignified pace. 'You won't tell on them, will you, Dandy?' asked May.

'Oh aye, I'll tell. Did you see how little money Mammie had in her purse when she was looking for our collections? And she's only at the beginning of the week. They had their Saturday penny yesterday like the rest of us. It's no' fair and I'll see that they don't get up with it.'

'Oh, Dandy, you sounded just like Grannie, there.'

'If Mammie was a wee bit more like Grannie, Faither wouldna get off with so much and we would have nice clothes like cousin Betty and plenty to eat. The money he earns just goes on drink.'

'Aye, but we always get *something* to eat,' said May, 'not like the little black boys and girls in hot countries where the fields all dry up.'

'No. That must be awful,' agreed Dandy. 'I need the

rain for my tumshies. It'll be a help to Mammie when I can grow lots of things.'

Dandy's thoughts were far from the lesson that day. George's perfidy angered her. Though she grew impatient with her mother's timidity, she still resented this sign of disloyalty. He'll grow up like Faither, that one, if I don't stop him; and he'll make Billy as bad as himself. He doesn't deserve to get off with it, in spite of what May says. So busy was she with those thoughts that they were starting the final hymn when she remembered. Oh, God, let Grannie send me back to the cottage soon so that I can plant my seeds myself. And, God, keep sending the rain when the tumshies are in. It would be some time before she was planting the tumshies, but there was no harm in giving God some advance warning, she told herself.

'You're hurting me,' squealed George.

'Aye and there'll be worse to come,' said Dandy, 'when they hear what you were up to.'

'What's a' the stramash?' Will Baxter roared. 'Stop twisting his arm. Let go, I tell you. What's this?'

'These two went to Capaldi's on the way to the Sunday School and spent half of their collection on sweets. They were fly enough to go in separately to get two ha'pennies in their change or Mr Capaldi would have guessed what they were up to. It was George's idea, of course. I warned him I'd tell you.'

Dandy waited but her father was shaking, not with anger but with appreciative laughter. 'The fly wee devils. That yin will go far – two ha'pennies . . . Ha-ha! I never thought o' that one. I just spent mine and didna go . . . and they found out . . . Two ha'pennies, I should have tried that one . . .'

'But it was for the little black boys and girls,' said May in distress.

59

'Well, these two are black enough half of the time,' Faither laughed again. George stuck his tongue out at Dandy and she promptly clipped his ear.

'That's enough from you, Dandy,' Faither snapped. 'You get mair like that grannie o' yours every day.'

'And thank God for that,' said Dandy to herself as she turned away. 'They're not going to learn any sense from Faither, that's for sure. Grannie's the only one that can manage them. Oh, I wish I could be rid of the lot of them – except May. If I could stay with Aunt Alice and Aunt Violet and go to see Uncle James whenever I wanted . . .'

After the next visit to the cottage, Dandy regaled Grannie with more news of the layout. She would rather not have divulged these details, but it was obvious where Lily Jordan's interest lay and it was not with seed packets.

'Uncle James used to sleep in the big bedroom before his wife died, but now he's in the little bedroom and he won't let anyone change the big bedroom round. It's kept the way it was when Rachel was alive – that was his wife's name; I suppose she would have been my Aunt Rachel.'

'What's the furniture like?'

'Where?'

'In the big bedroom.'

'Oh! There's a lovely little bookcase that was Rachel's when she lived with her parents and it's full of books . . .' Dandy made a quick reassessment. Lily Jordan was not interested in books. What *would* interest her? Dandy didn't mind how far she wandered from the truth if she could fix Grannie's interest. 'It's a big, big bed and it isn't in a hole in the wall – it just stands . . . sticks out.'

'Aye. What kind of bedspread is there?'

Dandy closed her eyes pretending to remember. 'It's pink silk with big roses embroidered on it – lovely. Oh, and there's a little chair like the ones that George and Billy broke.'

'Rosewood with mother-of-pearl inlay? Aye. My hand still itches to warm their backsides when I think of these lovely chairs . . .'

Grannie was off on one of her favourite grumbles. Dandy hoped that she had stimulated enough interest to ensure her next visit. 'Oh, God, let it be soon,' she prayed. 'The weather's so good and Uncle James will be digging up the bit for the tumshies next month.'

The long nights of June allowed Dandy a few blissful visits to the cottage after the twins were in bed. Then July was upon them and school was ending. She was surprised to find a lump in her throat when Miss Martin wished them all a happy holiday and urged them to return in September determined to make a success of their next year. Ever since the affair of the book, Dandy had felt a sort of bond with old Marty. *She* loved book-lined rooms and peace too. *She* felt that books were magic; could take you to far-away places. It must be irritating to have to keep dealing with all these noisy folk at school . . . and the slow readers. And if you were one of the Bettys of this world and hadn't been kept off school yourself, it would try your patience to have pupils who kept missing lessons and holding the class up.

The sentimental notions soon left her when she hurried out of the school grounds. Weeks of freedom lay ahead . . . Not that she ever had freedom, really. Mammie would need her, but there would be no school, no absences to worry about and maybe more visits to the cottage in the warm evenings. Uncle James was going to dig up the little lawn and she would be planting her tumshies. She had experienced the thrill of spraying the roses and Uncle James had said it was a bad year for greenfly and they would need to spray them often. There seemed to be no end of jobs to do in a garden, yet it did not seem like work at all. It was a fascinating game with rewards that other people could not understand. If you had put the tiny, tiny seeds in the damp brown earth in spring and they had magically become rows of candytuft, white and purple and dark pink and pale pink as she had experienced it that year . . . well! She stopped to breathe a deep sigh and then hurried off home.

The first few days in the house tried her patience because her grannie did not appear. 'The weather's so good, she'll be washing bedspreads and things,' said Nettie. 'She's the only one in that building that uses the washhouse, so she can get it any time she likes.'

'What do the other folk do?' asked Dandy.

'Well, the man next door is on his own and the woman who cleans for him takes the washing home. The folk on the top floor send their things to the laundry. It's too far to carry washing up all these stairs, you see.'

'That'll be dear.'

'Oh, aye, and your grannie says that the things are never so clean, but your grannie's fussy, you see.'

'Aye. But one thing about Grannie – she doesn't let George up with his nonsense. If I'd set *her* on him he'd never have spent his Sunday School money again. Faither has made him think that it's clever.'

'I'm afraid you're right,' said Nettie with a sigh. 'Oh, I forgot to say, Dandy, that the Miss McLarens would like your help tomorrow afternoon. They said to tell you that their brother has started to dig up the extra ground for you.'

Dandy gave a whoop of delight then quietened. 'But if Grannie doesn't come . . .'

'It's nice and warm outside. I could carry Jack round to the park – he's trying to walk and that would be a good place to get his wee bare feet on the grass. The twins will take May's hand. She's quiet and gentle, but she can get them to do what she wants now that they're a wee bit older.' A wave of relief swept over Dandy. If things went on like this – no more weans for Mammie – and the wee ones getting less bother, she would be nearly as free as Cousin Betty. Of course they would still be overcrowded, but you couldn't have everything. Aunt Alice and Aunt Violet must find their flat very pokey after the big house they had lived in, but they made the best of it. She thought back to a little talk she had had with Uncle James one day in the garden. He had been telling her something about his wife and Dandy, without thinking, had said, 'She would be a lady like Aunt Alice and Aunt Violet.'

He had looked a little surprised. 'No, Rachel didn't really resemble my sisters . . . she was much younger, of course.'

'I mean, a *real* lady.'

Uncle James still seemed puzzled.

'The neighbours all say that Aunt Violet and Aunt Alice are *real* ladies though they have come down in the world.'

'Yes, I see what you mean, my dear. Well, I would say that a *real* lady matches her behaviour to the occasion. Though my wife had been brought up in very comfort-able surroundings, she came with me quite happily to this little cottage and never gave the slightest impres-sion of being sorry for herself. In fact, she used to remind me how lucky we were and would point out that many people were much worse off. That was when I was worrying about not being able to give her the life I had planned.'

Tomorrow she would see Uncle James again and he

63

would let her plant her tumshies. That night she sang gaily as she cleared up in the tiny scullery. 'Listen to Nellie Melba,' said her father.

George and Billy started to yowl. It was gentle little May who reprimanded them this time. 'Keep quiet. Dandy's a lovely singer.' They broke off astonished and soon the door slammed behind them. 'Go on, Dandy,' said May. 'I'm listening.' Dandy, surprised, was silent. Nobody had ever said she was a lovely singer. She didn't really sing much – just when she was washing the dishes; and maybe when she was planting seeds. She hadn't thought about it. It was usually Friday afternoon that they had their singing lesson at school and half the time she missed Fridays. But if May liked to hear her ... well, it was a simple way of pleasing her. Who was Nellie Melba? She wouldn't give Faither the satisfaction of asking him. She would ask Aunt Alice; she would know – if it was worth knowing, that was!

Dandy woke early. The sun was shining. It looked like a grand day ahead. I'll need to water them in if the ground is too dry, she thought. Sometimes Uncle James takes the watering can along the drill before he puts the seeds in. *Drill*. That's another new word. I think I've learned more from Uncle James than I've learned in a whole year at school. I wish I was really his niece ... or better still, his daughter. I could have lived in the cottage and I would have looked after him when Rachel died ... but I'd be quite old now. I'm getting silly. Hurry up, Dandy Baxter. Get as much done as you can and it'll keep Grannie quiet.

'Aye, it's a grand day to get them all out to the park,' Lily Jordan said. 'Brush your hair, Dandy, and let me see you before you leave. I've taken Betty's dress in a bit, but I'm not sure if it's right for you yet. Mind you, gardening will no' do it any good.' Dandy held her breath.

'I think she should wear it, Mother,' said Nettie. 'If she's out with them . . .'

'Aye! She's got a bit o' sense – not like these brothers of hers. I've mended their things again for you, but it never seems to finish. You're far too soft with them . . .'

Here we go again, thought Dandy, making her escape to the parlour with her new hand-me-down dress. It wasn't that she disagreed with the sentiments, of course. How could she when, thanks to their nonsense, there wasn't a mirror left in the house except Faither's little shaving one. She would have liked to check the dress herself. Grannie's ideas were at least twenty years out of date. Aunt Violet said that once she had a bit more time . . . when the twins were ready for school maybe, she could have a shot at dressmaking on their sewing machine. It was just a knack and she would soon pick it up. You could save a lot of money by making things yourself. I wish I could make shoes, thought Dandy, studying the loose sole of her worn-out boots.

The sound of the front door being flung open startled her. Billy hurtled into the room. 'I *said* I would get here before George. We met Dan Stewart – him that's in my class at school – and he said that there was a polisman here this morning and then a cab came along and the two McLarens were standing at the close waiting for it and they were wearing funny veils, but he said you could see they were greetin' and his mither knew the polisman and she asked him what was wrong and he said he really shouldna tell her but their brother had been found dead in the garden. They thought he had been lying there all night.'

'No!' screamed Dandy and whirled round to the door. 'Here! Where d'you think you're going?' asked Lily Jordan, but she was talking to thin air. The clatter of

Dandy's boots echoed round the walls of the common stair and disappeared into the sounds of the street.

Heads turned as she pounded along with tears streaming. A few kind souls, eager to help, tried to stop her, but she dodged them all and ran on like one demented. Alice, opening the cottage door, scarcely recognized Dandy in the unfamiliar dress as she staggered in with bloated face and hair hanging tangled on her shoulders. 'Uncle James?' she gasped.

Alice's arms went round her. 'How did you know, my dear? We came without telling anyone; we were too upset.'

'Billy met somebody ... where's Uncle James?' She started to sob loudly.

Alice's voice broke as her arms tightened round Dandy's shuddering little body. 'We must be brave, Dandy my dear. Uncle James would not have wished to see you so upset.'

'But he was fine ...' Dandy stammered. 'We were going to plant the seeds and the weather was just right ... There was nothing wrong with him.'

'No. He seemed quite normal and very happy. We must always remember that, my dear. He died in the garden he loved.'

'Maybe he shouldn't have been digging up that bit for my tumshies,' croaked Dandy.

'He enjoyed seeing you in his garden, my dear. You made him happier in these last weeks of his life than he has been for some time. Now we must all stick together and strengthen one another. That's what James would have wished. Mr Aird, his lawyer friend, is looking after things for us. He has been exceptionally kind. It was his young assistant who was passing the end of the street when he saw the postman speaking to the policeman and leading him round the back of the cottage. The young man knew Uncle James, of course, and

66

sensed trouble. He was able to tell Mr Aird immediately and he kindly took over and sent word to us. Violet is clearing up in the kitchen. I think we should have a cup of tea there, then tidy ourselves and make for home. Mr Aird will keep in touch with us there.'

'There'll have to be a funeral, won't there?' muttered Dandy.

'Yes, my dear. You might find that too great a strain . . .'

'I want to be there. I've got to be there. He was so kind . . .' Dandy choked into silence.

Alice held her close. 'That must be your decision, my dear.'

Chapter 5

'She canna go to a funeral without a black dress and she would need new boots and a black hat – no, Nettie, you'll just have to say it's not suitable.'

Grannie had her back to her, ignoring her, but Dandy broke in. 'Aunt Alice said it must be my decision. I want to be there. She said I had made him so happy ... and he was digging up the bit for my tumshies ...' she came to a halt, overcome.

'It's fine for them. They don't know what it's like for your mother, trying to bring up all these bairns and the money goin' on drink that should be hers by right. They've no idea. I'm telling you Nettie,' she turned to her daughter again, 'there's no way.' She jumped as the door slammed. 'Where's that girl?'

Nettie Baxter did not answer. She listened as Dandy's boots clattered down the steps and then the sound of the McLarens' letter box echoed round the walls. 'She's gone down to them, Mother. She's awfully fond of them, you see, and she seemed to take a trick with their shy brother. It's hard for her. She can't help it that she never has a new dress. Think of the nice things we all had, Mother, when we were that age.'

'Aye. Your father knew when to take a drink and when to leave it alone. I got my housekeeping money every week ...' Lily Jordan was safely diverted on to one of her favourite recitals.

Alice McLaren's arm was round her, drawing her into the room. 'I know, my love, I know. We are all feeling sad, but we must try ...'

'But Grannie says I can't go to the funeral because I would need a black dress and a black hat and I'm needing new boots.'

For the first time in Dandy's hearing Alice McLaren showed disapproval of the Baxter family. 'Oh, no, your grannie is wrong. James would never have wanted you to wear a black dress or to cover your lovely yellow hair with a black hat. He would not have recognized you in that sort of dress. Oh, no, if you wish to come you should wear the pretty white dress you wear to Sunday school. We have lots of black velvet ribbon here and Violet would make you a band for your hair and a sash for your dress. If you polish your black boots nicely, I'm sure you will be perfect. Tell your grannie that we would love to have you with us and that we promise to look after you. Let's have a little cup of tea first. Fetch the biscuits, Dandy, while I see if the kettle is near boiling.'

Dandy took a few deep breaths as she mounted the steps to her own flat. Grannie had great respect for the McLarens, but she also had fixed ideas of what you wore for a funeral and she would be angry at Dandy's departure. What would be the best way to handle her? Grannie had told Mammie that day not so long ago that no harm would come to Dandy with Alice and Violet. They were 'ladies'. Maybe if she showed Grannie that it was rubbing off on *her* a bit – behaved a wee bit like a 'lady' herself; after all, speaking like Aunt Alice was almost like saying poetry and she was good at that. What would Aunt Alice say?

Dandy knocked on the door and steeled herself. 'I'm sorry Grannie, running off like that. I was feeling so sad.'

'Aye, well . . .' Lily Jordan was at a loss when approached in this fashion. Emboldened, Dandy went on to tell her what Alice had said. She repeated the words in Alice's clear tones.

'Well, if she's sure . . .' Lily said. 'If the ribbon is nice and broad, it would nearly cover the top of your head, I suppose. I was going to buy you new boots for your birthday in September. Maybe I should just get them now – but you'll get nothing on your birthday, mind you,' she warned.

Dandy threw her arms round her in a rare show of affection. 'Oh, Grannie, that would be worth two birthdays. I'll be a credit to you, never fear.'

'Aye, well, see that you are,' Lily mumbled. 'Just you tidy yourself up a bit and we'll see about these boots now. I'll get the money at the bank.'

It was funny how things could change within a matter of minutes – or maybe the best part of an hour was nearer the mark, Dandy thought. She had been in despair, Alice had supported her and given her hope, and now, there was Grannie doing exactly the right thing. It paid to study what you said. If she hadn't sounded like Aunt Alice, Grannie would never have paid any attention to her. Of course, if you were dealing with George and Billy, it was a different matter entirely. Uncle James had said that a lady matches her behaviour to the occasion. She had done just that. Or had she? Was plotting to get your own way what he meant? She doubted it. But the important thing was that she was not going to miss Uncle James's funeral. Alice and Violet wanted her there. They would all be sad, but, in a way, there was a kind of joy in a sadness that made them all need each other.

Half an hour before the cab was due to pick them up, Dandy presented herself at the McLarens' door. Alice's voice was mufffled and she seemed older, stooping a little, but she smiled kindly. 'Come into the parlour, my dear, and you will be able to watch Violet arrange things for you.'

Dandy had assumed that their parlour would look

very much like her own – except that the chairs would not be broken, of course. She stood and looked round. The only thing that looked the same was the fireplace and overmantel. And even that was a wee bit different, for none of the tiles was chipped. The wallpaper was like a picture with roses entwining all round it. The carpet was deep and soft: you could have snuggled down and slept on it. Then, the room looked so spacious! No bed. That was what made the biggest difference. The doors had been removed and in the recess was a beautiful little bookcase, a pretty walnut table with flowers in a crystal vase and two dainty little armchairs – ladies' chairs, obviously. The long silk curtains were the colour of the deepest pink roses on the wallpaper and they were looped up with bands of green velvet. Alice waited patiently while Dandy's eyes took in the scene, then she gently propelled her towards the oval pedestal mirror in the corner just as Violet hurried through with her workbox.

The nearest Dandy had been to seeing herself for some time was her reflection in shop windows. Visits to her grannie's house had dwindled to nothingness as Nettie's unmanageable brood grew. And she had no chance of seeing herself at home. She watched Violet measure and snip and then do the clever little fold and clip at the end which gave the ribbons a finished appearance. A beam of sunlight caught her yellow hair. It reminded her of Uncle James that day when she was being a little too energetic with a spade and the earth had sparked up over her. 'Dear, dear, dear,' he had said, 'you mustn't spoil your lovely yellow hair.'

'It's straight as a poker,' Dandy had said. 'I wish I had curls like my cousin Betty.'

'Your hair is perfect, my dear,' James had replied. 'Curls would only dim that wonderful gleam.'

It was the first time ever that anyone had complimented her on her appearance. The comfort his words brought to her had deepened her love for James almost to the point of adoration.

Remembering now, Dandy felt the tears welling up. Violet's arm went round her. 'I know, my love, but just you remember that you were Uncle James's sunshine girl. He often asked us, "Where's my sunshine girl?"'

Dandy bit her lip. She owed it to Uncle James not to be a burden to his sisters, especially today. She would try. Keeping busy was a good way. She would be as helpful as she could. Violet was awarded with a watery smile.

Dandy was surprised to see how many people – mostly men – were crowded into the little sitting room at the cottage. The coffin was upstairs and lots of the men trudged up to see the body before the undertaker nailed the lid down. Dandy hoped she would not be expected to go up. She could not imagine what a dead body would look like, but she was sure it would not be like Uncle James in his old gardening jacket with a little wisp of hair tickling his forehead while he explained the ins and outs of gardening to her.

'Alice and I said our goodbyes before the others came,' Violet whispered. 'I think you would rather remember Uncle James in the garden.' Dandy nodded, her lip trembling. 'We'll be depending on you now to keep us right about the planting and things since James told you all his plans.' Dandy lifted her head. This was something she had never dreamt of in her wildest imaginings. All had seemed lost – the cottage, Uncle James, the garden, the books and the exciting trips which had given her some relief from the demands of her turbulent homelife. The solemn men around her were forgotten. The cottage would still be there! Of course, it would belong to her aunties now. And they would move. There would be no refuge for her on the landing below. Trips to the cottage would be difficult to engineer. But if Violet and Alice needed her for their garden, and her tumshies came up and all the other vegetables which she would plant, Mammie would be glad of the saving, surely. Handling Grannie would be more important than ever, but she would learn . . . she would learn . . .

The minister had come in. There was a lot of throat clearing. Then he began to read. The words were so beautiful – solemn, strong, reassuring. Then the minister was talking about Uncle James: how he was a quiet man, but those who knew him well treasured his friendship, his integrity (she would ask Aunt Alice about that word) and his loyalty. No one knew this better than his sisters, who would miss him sorely but could take great comfort from the fact that he had been the object of their care. His great love was his garden. Recently he had had the opportunity to share that love with a young devotee; to pass on his enthusiasm and impart some of his knowledge. That's me the minister's talking about, Dandy thought. Wait till I tell Grannie!

Soon the undertaker's men were there and tramping up the stairs. She could hear the carriages at the door, the impatient stamping of the horses and the slight jingling of the harness. She had come with Alice and Violet in a carriage – a strange experience. But now there were so many people! Would they have to share coaches? The men were picking up their black hats and their gloves and some of them had canes. Her aunts were not making any move to fetch their coats. 'Shouldn't we be getting ready too?' she asked Aunt Violet.

'Oh, ladies don't go to the cemetery,' Violet said, 'only the men. We'll stay here and prepare the food. His closest friends will come back, you see. Probably quite a number of people will join the cortège at the cemetery

– his fellow elders from the kirk and people like that. Of course, most have to get back to work, but some of the people who are retired will want to come here and talk about James.'

'Won't that upset you and Aunt Alice?' Dandy ventured.

'In one way, yes. But it is comforting to have our brother appreciated. He was extremely reticent himself . . . yet so loving to Rachel. If only the baby had lived . . .' She was talking almost to herself.

Alice approached. 'Now, Dandy, do you think you could help us lay out the food? Then when the men come back you could go round with the plates for us. You are far smarter at those things than we are.'

It was a relief to have something to do. In a way she was doing it for Uncle James. There were five of them on the job – the aunts, Mrs Brown (the lady who had cleaned for Uncle James) and Miss Bell who worked in the lawyer's office. Jean Bell was the only one who seemed anxious to talk. 'You know, my dear, Mr McLaren enthused so much about you to my boss that we christened you Miss Fine-and-Dandy. How do you like that?'

Dandy was stuck for a reply. To think that people in a lawyer's office had been talking about *her*, Dandy Baxter! That was surprising enough; but to have been given a nickname by all these important people! Miss Bell was waiting for her reply. 'Uncle James knew such a lot about gardens and he was teaching me . . .' she tailed off. That teaching would end now. But she knew enough to carry on with a lot of the vegetables and there were all those lovely gardening books that Uncle James had said she could study on a wet day. If only Mammie didn't have more weans, there would be time for that, for there were always plenty of wet days . . .

Miss Bell was looking at her curiously. She hadn't

74

really finished her answer. It was difficult to know what to say. Then she remembered Aunt Violet's whispered conversation and seized upon it. 'My aunts will be depending on me to keep them right about the garden now. You see, Uncle James told me all his plans for this year's planting.' Miss Bell's lips gave a funny twist. Was she laughing at her? No! It was a sort of tickle in her throat – probably with talking too much. She seemed a bit of a blether anyway. Of course, it could be her idea of politeness. Some people were like that. But at that moment Dandy found it quite annoying. All she wanted was to think of Uncle James and remember all the things he had told her. *He* never talked rubbish and yet he was polite. Probably he thought a gentleman matched his behaviour to the occasion. Yes, she was sure of it! She knew her Uncle James. Violet called her to arrange biscuits on plates. It was a finicky job, but Miss Bell was called away for something else so Dandy was able to speculate on what would happen to the McLarens now. How soon would they move? What would happen to her drawer with the special things in it? Would they allow her to keep it in the cottage? She was pretty sure they would – especially after the nice things the minister had said. It was as if she was a member of the family. Her new boots were still a little stiff and squeaky. She had to be careful not to hurry too much in them because Grannie had bought them on the big side so that they would last her for a while. Still, she was glad that Grannie's fussiness had taken her in a practical direction. It wouldn't have seemed right to come to Uncle James's funeral in boots that had had to face the worst of the garden muck.

Serving the crowd of people who came back to the cottage kept her happily employed for quite a while, but gradually they all drifted away. 'I don't know about you, Dandy, but I feel absolutely done in,' said Aunt

Alice. 'Miss Bell has certainly been very helpful over the dishwashing, but keeping up a conversation is so wearing . . . I was glad to see her go. That's naughty of me, isn't it, Dandy?'

'No. I was glad to see her go too. I just wanted quietness to think about Uncle James and what he would want me to do in the garden . . .'

'What I propose is that we just finish the necessary clearing; leave the rest till tomorrow when we should be in better trim. I really feel I would like to crawl into bed.'

'That's exactly how I feel,' said Violet, 'and I think Dandy has done enough work for one day. Let's get home.'

Grannie had waited as Dandy expected she would. 'Here, lass, a wee cup of tea,' she said with unwonted gentleness. Dandy felt that she had tea coming out of her ears, but it was such a treat to sit in Faither's chair and be handed a cup and saucer. 'Were there lots of folk there? Did you get any of their names?' Grannie prompted.

One thing about Jean Bell's chatter that had been useful was her naming of the various people present who were clients of their firm. Dandy mustered her forces. She was going to have to keep in Grannie's good books and that meant thinking ahead all the time. 'Well, there was a Mr Watson who's a cousin of the provost,' she began. Grannie nodded approvingly as the names were reeled off, stopping her now and again to ask questions about their appearance. Dandy nearly blotted her copybook when she described one as a very old man.

'Mercy on us, lassie, his big sister was in my class at school.'

Dandy thought quickly. 'Well, he looks an awful lot older than you, Grannie. Maybe he's been ill?'

'Aye, that could be it. I havena seen him for years,' Grannie said, mollified.

Dandy was feeling exhausted and running out of ideas when Lily finally said, 'Well, you've had quite a day. I think you should get through to your bed, lass. I've left everything ready for your Faither's tea. Your Mammie will manage fine.'

The McLarens, in spite of their tiredness, did not crawl into bed. 'I know I would only turn and toss,' said Violet, and her sister had to admit that she felt exactly the same.

'So many people said really nice things about James,' Alice said. 'At times I was glad to make for the kitchen and Miss Bell. She was so busy talking that she didn't notice that I was struggling to keep control of myself. I kept wondering what was in James's letter. Mr Aird advised me to keep it till the funeral was over and we could concentrate.

'He was probably right. I still can't really believe it. Somehow you never think of your little brother being away before you. He never showed any signs of being ill ... Dandy was worried that digging up that bit of garden for her swedes had done it.'

'Well, in a way, it probably was, but I'd never let the dear child think that. Now, where did I put it ... yes, here it is!'

'Could you read it out slowly, Alice, right from the beginning and I'll try to concentrate.'

Alice pulled a little table towards her, slit the stiff envelope and spread the neatly-written sheets out.

My dear sisters,
   By the time you read this I shall be gone. Please do not be too vexed. I have known for some time that my heart was impaired. The doctor put the case clearly to me. I could become a semi-invalid

and in that way possibly live a few years longer, but even that was not guaranteed. I chose to carry on as normally as possible, enjoying my garden. That enjoyment has increased so much recently with the arrival of Dandy. That is one of the many, many things I have to thank you for, my dears. I know I have not always made my appreciation clear to you but hoped that you would understand.

Recently, Dandy in her devastatingly direct way has made me take a fresh look at my life. Compared with what that bright child has put up with, my sojourn in this vale of tears has been a picnic. I now see how selfish I have been to bury myself in my grief at the loss of my lovely Rachel and the child we would have treasured. This cottage breathes Rachel to me and I have selfishly kept it to myself when I should have offered you a home that would be more fitting to your needs. I hope that you will move here and make Dandy head gardener. If there is any help needed with the digging, Mrs Brown would be sure to know a young man who could oblige.

I have consulted Mr Aird on the matter of how to leave something to Dandy without her wayward father being able to grab it or for family loyalty to blackmail her into handing it over when her mother's need is desperate. I wish her to have Rachel's bookcase with its contents and also, on her eighteenth birthday, the sum of £200. I reckon that by that time she will know how to deal with her family. Alex Aird is arranging things in such a way that his firm is trustee for the bequests, but you will house the bookcase. It is a pity that we cannot let Dandy know and give her something to look forward to, but we have decided that this method is safer.

I think her joy at using Rachel's books will be considerable and we know that her boisterous brothers will not be able to reach them in your care.

Some time ago I thought of having an extension built so that there could be a proper bathroom upstairs. I consulted my fellow elder, Sandy Forbes. He drew up plans for the building. It entailed extending the kitchen wall and providing a laundry and some useful deep cupboard space downstairs while, above that, there would be the new bathroom and a small bedroom or boxroom. The plans seemed just right to me and I was ready to go ahead when the doctor told me the position. The upheaval then seemed an unnecessary risk.

I would advise you to get in touch with Mr Forbes and get the job done before you move in, as there is bound to be a lot of dirt involved. You will not find a better builder or a finer man, I can assure you.

I find it very difficult to voice my regrets when I realize the neighbourhood you have lived in. It was only through Dandy that I got a picture of a life that was far, far from what I saw as my modest style here. You who had known the privilege and comfort we enjoyed as children must have suffered deeply. I apologize for my blind selfishness. There is only one blessing I can see in it. We would never have known Dandy had you not been sharing, to a certain extent, her deprivations. I bow to the superior spirit of that poor child.

I know that you will always wish to help her, and Mr Aird and I have worked out the financial plan. As you know, I have hung on to Uncle Cornelius's books out of a kind of loyalty. I now realize that that was stupid. I could have eased your financial burden years ago. Many of them are valuable simply because of their rarity. I have not read them for years and I'm quite sure you would find no pleasure in them. I have studied many catalogues and worked out possible selling prices. I suggest that you sell them in lots as I have designated. As they are increasing in value all the time, it pays you to do it this way rather than dispose of the whole collection. Mr Aird will give you any advice you desire as, of course, will the bank manager, whom you both know.

Well, my dears, I hope I have thought of all the practical matters. Again I thank you with all my heart. Give my love to Dandy and see that she does not grieve.

Your loving brother,
James

'To think he knew that his heart was weak and he didn't tell us,' said Violet, who had been sobbing quietly through the reading. 'I would have stopped him ... insisted on getting someone to do the digging ...'

Alice laid down the letter and wiped her eyes. 'It was his own choice, my dear. We have no right to deny him that. Mr Aird had a quiet word with me today; said that he would like us to make an appointment so that he can discuss things fully with us. I gather that we will be quite comfortably off for the rest of our days. James had a life insurance which he put in our favour when Rachel died.'

'It *does* seem odd,' Violet said, 'that James had no idea what life here was like till Dandy came on the scene. He was so absorbed in his grief over Rachel ...'

'Well, they're united now.' She paused. 'Now we have the prospect of a bathroom in the not too distant future. That *is* something to look forward to. It won't be quite so easy for Dandy – to keep in touch with us, I mean. But we shall be living quite near to her grandmother and are bound to bump into that lady sometimes. I think it would pay us to invite her in to the house now and again. Though she does not seem to be all that keen on gardens herself, she is bound to be impressed by Dandy's work.'

'That's a good idea, Alice. Dandy *did* say that things were a little less frantic upstairs. Mrs Baxter has managed to take the younger children round to the park herself recently. The dear child's worried, however, that May will be overburdened. Really, that is the only one of her family she seems to be fond of; it seems so sad.'

'But, Violet, we mustn't try to compare our feelings with Dandy's. Siblings to us meant playmates. To Dandy they have meant grim slavery at times, and always self-denial.'

'Well, you said not so long ago, my dear, that you wished we had even a little money to help Dandy. James has made that possible. Thankfully we have Mr Aird and the others to help us with the business side. Handling Mrs Jordan will be our chief difficulty, I think.'

'Just watch me, Violet.'

Chapter 6

August was pretty good – some heat and a little rain. Dandy had a wee word with God, thanking Him for the nice dry days that got Mammie's washing out of the way quickly and let Jack and the twins play in the park all day. She reminded Him, however, that the tumshies would need a bit more rain than they were getting and if He could send it at night, that would be best. She toiled in her own beloved domain every day. The builders had set up a stand pipe in the garden and this was actually easier than trailing back to the house would have been when watering her young plants or spraying the roses – those loved tasks, entrusted to her, she felt, by James.

As soon as her mother could spare her, she hurried down to the McLarens' flat to tell them she was off. They followed later at a more leisurely pace, bringing delicious home-made lemonade and sandwiches for lunch. These picnic lunches were heaven to Dandy: sitting on Uncle James's seat in the shade of a copper beech with the scent of the roses she had helped prune and had sprayed religiously. The pansies which bordered the rose beds were a blaze of velvety colour, thanks to all the dead-heading she had done. Yes, it was heaven!

Alice and Violet had decided that while they were at it they would have a little conservatory. It had been a tentative suggestion from Mr Forbes, the builder, when he was showing them how far the extension to the kitchen would stretch. They would be able to step out of the kitchen and have meals there even when the weather wasn't very hot and, as Mr Forbes said, it saved a lot of wear and tear on the dining-room carpet. Dandy wasn't quite sure what to expect of a conservatory, but if her aunts thought it was a good idea, it probably was.

God decided to send the bit more rain she had asked for in a sudden thunderstorm in the middle of the month. Mr Forbes forecast it when he visited the site that afternoon. Dandy, who had been working solidly for several hours, suddenly felt headachy and flopped onto the garden seat. A voice hailed her, 'Hello! You must be Dandy. Mr McLaren used to tell me about you. I'm Sandy Forbes. James and I were elders in the kirk together.'

'You're Mr Forbes the builder?'

'That's right. My men tell me you work like a Trojan. I'm glad to see that you've had the sense to stop for a wee while. There's a thunderstorm brewing if I'm not mistaken.'

'Oh! Is that what it is? I'll get plenty rain for my tumshies then. They need it to make them swell.'

'Aye, that's right. Later they need a bit of hard weather. I think they're always sweeter when they've had a touch of frost, don't you?'

'I hadn't noticed. You see, Uncle James had his ready when I came and, before that, we just bought them from the shop. So I never really noticed.'

'If you've anything loose, get it tied up before you leave today. If we get thunder, the rain will be sure to batter everything down. See – that pillar rose over there, the top is dangling. If you get another wee bit of twine and tie it further up . . .'

'There's some in the shed,' said Dandy and was off.

She was struggling with the twine a few minutes later when Sandy, who had been touring the garden, came back. 'Here, bonnie lass! I'm taller. See! it's got to be firm so it won't wiggle and tear the stem, yet we mustn't choke it.' His strong hands were dealing deftly with the twine. 'Now, let the thunder come! We're ready. I've had a look round the rest of the place and everything seems quite safe.' A large drop of rain fell on his nose as he spoke. 'That's it,' he said. 'I wasn't wrong. Are you here on your own?'

'Aye. My aunties always go home soon after lunch.' She nearly added, 'There's no lavvie, you see, while the water's off,' but stopped herself in time. Her aunts would certainly not tell a man that *they* could not last out as long as *she* could. It would not be ladylike.

'Get your things, lass, and I'll run you home in my trap. There'll be no more gardening today.' Dandy's eyes opened wide and she beamed at him. 'I see why James called you his sunshine girl,' said Sandy Forbes, laughing.

The rain pattered on the oilskin cover of the trap and Sandy had to shout to make himself heard, but Dandy wished that the journey would never end.

'Our youngest is your age,' said Sandy. 'She's up north right now on holiday. Her uncle up there is an expert on gardens. People come from all over to see the rare plants he grows.'

'Do you have a garden, Mr Forbes?'

'Oh aye, quite a bit. My wife is the boss gardener. I just dig where I'm told.'

Dandy looked to see whether he was being funny. He was. 'I tell her I'm not taking her up to Ardgrian – that's where the wee one is – again. She just gets big ideas up there and our climate isn't quite so mild. They're nearer the gulf stream, you see.'

'Aunt Alice was telling me about the gulf stream the other day while we were in the garden. I think they've had it at school, but I'm off quite a lot.'

'Oh, well, I'm sure James's sisters will be able to tell

84

you lots of things. They were lucky in the way they were brought up, but I maintain that now we have free libraries, anybody that's keen can improve on his education.'

'Aye, if they've got time to go to the library and can get peace to read the books without wee buggers o' brothers knocking them to smithereens and drunken faithers threatening to throw them on the fire,' said Dandy. Mr Forbes was the sort of man you could say things like that to. Though she had only known him a wee while she could tell . . .

'Aye, there's that, bonnie lass,' he said, as they drew up at the pavement. She saw him give a quick frowning glance over the building. 'Maybe some day when our girl, Madge, is back from Ardgrian your aunts will bring you over to see our garden. Would you like that?'

'Oh God, would ah no'!' she answered. It came to her as she slowly mounted the stairs that she had said the wrong thing. She should have said, 'Thank you, Mr Forbes: I'd love that.' That's what Aunt Alice would have said. And maybe she shouldn't have told him about her drunken faither. Grannie grumbled plenty, but she was always urging Dandy not to let the neighbours know their business. Yet Mr Forbes had given her a wide grin as he drove off. But if he had a girl just her age, would he want *her* to be taking the Lord's name in vain? Would his wife, the boss gardener, want her girl to hear things like that? Maybe *she* wouldn't find it so easy to grin. They said at Sunday school that if you weren't actually praying, you should not use the Lord's name. It was difficult to know sometimes what was praying and what wasn't. Faither wasn't the praying type and he used the Lord's name plenty. Miss Wotherspoon at Sunday School said that if you took the Lord's name in vain you would go to the fires of hell. You wouldn't like that to happen to Faither, even

85

if he was a drunken dyer and all the other things Grannie said. But forget Faither and think of something nice. *He* was nice, Mr Forbes – a wee bit like Uncle James in some ways, though you couldn't call him shy.

The McLarens' door opened as she drew near. Violet said, as Dandy stepped in to the lobby, 'We were worried about you, dear. The storm blew up so quickly.'

'Yes, Mr Forbes saw it coming and he got me to tie up a pillar rose in case the rain battered it down. He's nice! Then the rain came suddenly and he said he would bring me home in his trap. It was fun. The rain was hammering on the oilskin and we had to shout.'

'So you've made friends with Mr Forbes? That's good.'

'Aye, well! He says his youngest girl is my age. She's up north on holiday now and he said that you would maybe bring me round to see his garden when she gets back, but I don't think he *will* invite me now . . .'

'What makes you think that?' asked Alice.

'I think I took the Lord's name in vain. I was so excited that I didn't take time to think it out – my answer, I mean.'

'Well, we'll see, won't we,' said Alice. 'If we don't think too much about it, it will be a lovely surprise when it comes. This rain will help your turnips, won't it?'

'Yes. They're only wee green leaves just now, really, but Uncle James told me that they seem to get a move on quite suddenly and you see them ease up out of the ground as they swell. I'm looking forward to that, but I'd maybe better get upstairs now. May will be getting too much to do.'

As the door closed behind her, Violet started to laugh. 'I wonder what exactly she said to Mr Forbes. I'd love to know. You didn't ask her.'

'No, I wasn't sure that my reaction would be sober enough.'

'Do you think she'll have spoiled her chances of a visit to their garden?'

'I'm not sure.' Alice paused to consider. 'From what I've seen of Mr Forbes, it would take more than the odd swear word to rock him, but if he has a girl of his own and his wife would be worried .... It's difficult to tell. We would never have been allowed to associate with anyone whose language was not *comme il faut*, after all. But Dandy realizes her mistake, so, I think if the invitation *does* materialize we'll have nothing to fear. Look how well she behaved at the funeral.'

'The schools will be starting in just over a fortnight, Alice, so their daughter is bound to be back quite soon. We won't have long to wonder.'

The thunderstorm broke the spell of good weather and was followed by some cool, showery days. This meant that Dandy was more tied to the house. She felt guilty about her discontent, knowing how her burdens had been falling on May to a certain extent, though May herself showed no resentment and was avid for stories about what was happening at the cottage.

I wish I could get May away too, she thought. She would love my garden and the lovely quiet picnics with the aunties. Soon we'll be back at school and May really hasn't had any fun – not like me; though, she hasn't had the sorrow either. She didn't know Uncle James.

And it was May who suggested on the first warm dry day that it would be a fine chance to take the wee ones to the park: they always enjoyed it so much. Nettie hesitated only a moment. Truth to tell, the park was a pleasant rest for her too nowadays with the twins teaching Jack to walk or tossing his soft ball at him, and May keeping an eye on them, ready to run if necessary.

Dandy had been idly playing with the soap bubbles while she thought of her beloved garden. It only took Nettie's, 'Right, then,' for her to clear the sinkful of dishes in record time, dry them vigorously and wipe round, leaving the scullery spick-and-span. Grannie had her own key, and keeping Grannie in a good mood was her constant worry. One glimpse of a messy scullery and she would be in Grannie's bad books for Dear knows how long.

It was only a few days later that Aunt Alice just happened to be leaving her flat as Lily Jordan came up the stairs. 'Oh, Mrs Jordan, I wonder if you could step in for a moment,' she whispered. 'I don't want Dandy to hear.'

Lily Jordan was only too pleased to be shown into the McLarens' parlour. 'My,' she said, 'what a difference from upstairs. It's not my daughter's fault, mind you.'

'No, Mrs Jordan, we all know that,' said Alice with a significant look that satisfied Lily. Nothing had been said, but she could tell that they knew what her Nettie had to put up with and didn't blame the poor lass for it. Lily warmed to them.

'It's like this, Mrs Jordan,' Alice went on. 'Mr Forbes, the builder, asked me if we could bring Dandy round to his house next Sunday afternoon. It's the last one before school starts and he thought it would be nice for her to meet his little daughter and see over their garden. I didn't want her to be disappointed if it wouldn't be possible for her to get away. What do you think the position will be on Sunday?'

'The position will be that her father will be snoring in bed half the morning and getting in Nettie's way by the afternoon. See here: I'll come on Sunday. I usually keep out of the way in case I say too much. But I'll see that Will takes these two scamps a guid walk up the Braes to get rid of their energy, or my name's not Lily

Jordan. The rest are fine now – Jack toddling about happily and the twins doing what wee quiet May tells them ... Aye, you leave it to me!'

With a resolute nod of her head, Lily Jordan was off.

'Well, that was worth waiting for, Alice,' said Violet.

'Yes, it was. I thought she was never going to come. She's nearly an hour later than usual. But we might have had the ... er ... "pleasure" of her company for a considerable time if she hadn't been late so, as you say, that was worth waiting for!'

'I expect she will break the news to Dandy. I'd like to have been the one to do it, just to see her face widen into that wonderful smile.'

'We mustn't grudge our pure and spotless Lily her moment of glory. Oh dear, all this plotting and scheming! Dandy is having an effect on us, Violet, and I'm not quite sure whether it is a beneficial one.'

'I like it,' said Violet. 'It's fun. D'you think she'll manage it, Mrs Jordan, I mean?'

'I'll be very surprised if she doesn't. I propose to tell Mr Forbes that the visit is on. I'm not quite sure how much James told him of our Dandy's circumstances, but I shall take the liberty of filling in any gaps. If he and his wife know the background, they'll understand the dear child better and make allowances.'

Aunt Alice had said that if she didn't think too much about it, it would be a lovely surprise when it came, but she couldn't help thinking about it. Uncle James had talked about her to Mr Forbes. That gave her a warm glow of importance. Perhaps Aunt Alice was right when she said that the sacrifices she made for her family would make her a stronger person when she grew up. But, really, May was making more sacrifices. *She* couldn't run off by herself as Dandy could. Maybe May didn't need to be alone, didn't need quietness to think things out, as she did. Still, if you had all that housework to do, you *had* to think of something else, something more interesting, or you would end up like Mammie, always down in the mouth, as she was now because Grannie had said she would come and hadn't arrived. The doorbell rang. 'That'll be Grannie,' said Dandy rushing to the lobby.

Lily Jordan had the door open before Dandy reached it. 'Aye, I had the key in my hand as I came up the stair, pet,' she said.

Dandy noticed the 'pet'. She was in Grannie's good books.

'Shall I make you a cup of tea, Grannie?'

'Aye! That would be a good idea and maybe May could take the weans into the parlour for a wee while. I want to talk to your Mammie.'

Dandy tried to listen from the scullery, but Grannie seemed to be whispering. First the kitchen door and then the parlour door banged shut. 'I don't want the wee ones to hear in case they let slip in front of their faither,' she was saying, 'but I've been in the McLarens. Alice – that's the plump one, isn't it? – called me in for a wee while to ask me my opinion. You see, she didn't want Dandy to get a disappointment . . .'

Dandy's hand shook and the heavy kettle splashed a few drops on her hand. She ignored the pain as her brain began to race. What disappointment was she in for now? Something to do with the cottage? Had they decided to sell it or something? Or were they going to get a 'proper' gardener? Yet Aunt Violet had said they would be depending on her because she knew Uncle James's plans. If it wasn't the cottage, what was it? There was nothing else so important to her as her garden . . . Quickly she carried the heavy tray into the room and deposited it on the sideboard.

'Here, I'll pour that, lass,' said Grannie kindly. 'I've

got some good news for you, but I didn't want the wee ones to hear. You see, I was just coming up your stairs ... I should have been earlier but I'd met one of my neighbours and she said there was a slate sliding on our roof ...'

I wish to God she'd get on with it, thought Dandy, and then felt guilty. She was taking the Lord's name in vain again and that was what had maybe lost her the chance of seeing Mr Forbes's garden. Aunt Alice had said she must be patient about that. Aunt Alice would probably say she should be patient with Grannie, too, but who cared about silly old slates anyhow!

'Well, Miss McLaren wanted to know what the position would be on Sunday afternoon and I said that I would be here and make sure that your father took these two devils up the Braes and you would get peace to go with the ladies. They want to take you to see Mr Forbes's garden. That'll be nice for you, won't it?'

Dandy felt the breath go out of her body for a moment. Nice! Nice! 'Oh, Grannie, that'll be heaven! It's awfully good of you ...' She was almost in tears.

'Here, lass, watch your tea, your cup's tilted. I was just thinking it's a good thing you've got decent boots.'

'Oh, yes, and Aunt Violet said that there are some lovely ribbons in Aunt Rachel's workbox that will be just right for me. Set off my pretty hair, she says. Uncle James thought I had pretty hair too. I didn't know it could be nice if it was straight. I always wanted curls like cousin Betty.'

'Your cousin Betty's got frizz, no' curls, Dandy. It's the only nice thing your faither's done for you, lass, as far as I can see.'

She was off again on her catalogue of complaints, but Dandy had new food for thought. It was Faither's bonnie yellow hair and his blue eyes that had captivated all the girls, according to Grannie. She, Dandy Baxter, had blue eyes too. But she couldn't imagine any boys being captivated by her. They were all too scared of her. She grinned at the thought. It paid to keep the boys scared of you. Then she started thinking about Sunday. She had only the one decent dress and it had to be a warm day for that one. What if it rained? It would be quite a long way to walk in the rain and her aunts couldn't walk very fast. At least, it didn't seem fast to Dandy. 'Few people walk so fast as you do, my dear,' Aunt Alice had said one day when she was asking Dandy to slow down a little.

When she voiced her fears about the weather and her dress to Violet, there was quick reassurance. 'We are going to have a cab, my dear. Your white dress is so pretty and if it's cold you could wear a little silk shawl that was Rachel's. I'll fetch it over here, just in case. All her elegant clothes are still in the trunk we put them in when she died. James couldn't bear to talk about them so years have drifted by ... The material is absolutely beautiful, such pretty colours – she was young, you see. Perhaps in the winter when you won't be gardening, I could teach you how to use the sewing machine. Then you could have some lovely things at no cost at all. Perhaps we could make some things for May, too?'

'Oh, yes!' Dandy was overjoyed. 'I'd love to see May in pretty clothes.'

Violet looked at her sister and saw Alice's lip trembling. It wasn't all that long ago that they had been wishing they had some money to help Dandy. Now, they had lost a precious brother, but his books were going to make that desire a reality.

For ever afterwards, Dandy remembered that visit to the Forbes family as a turning point in her life. She seemed to go through it in a dream, absorbing impression after impression. The house itself had seemed huge to her, though it probably wasn't so big as the one her aunties had lived in, for the Forbes's didn't have a gardener – only a little maid and a lady who came to do the washing, Madge had told her. Madge! At first she had been as shy and awkward as Dandy herself. Then Mr Forbes had said, 'What about taking Dandy for a quick tour of the house while we wait for tea in the garden? Then we'll get down to the real stuff – showing you the rare plants that my lady wife has acquired.'

Dandy glanced at his lady wife. She was smiling fondly at him while her arm went round Madge's shoulder. 'That's a good idea. Off you go, pet, and show Dandy where you all sleep, but don't start playing with toys or Dandy will never see the garden. Tea in ten minutes and no surrender!'

They walked together in silence into the hall, then Madge said, 'Will we run up to the top, then work our way down?' Dandy nodded, without saying a word. 'They're not watching, race you!'

Dandy, surprised, was left standing, but only for a second. Soon the pair of them were pounding up the stairs, panting and giggling. After that it was easy. Madge reeled off the names of her grown-up brothers who were in the big bedrooms in the attic, beside the boxroom and her mother's little sewing room. The first floor had lots and lots of doors. 'Beth, my oldest sister, has that one to herself,' said Madge. 'This one is for Jeannette and Margaret. They're grown-up too. Then the next one is for the Wizzies. That's what we call my wild schoolboy brothers. They're really Walter and William. This is my room.'

'All to yourself?' asked Dandy in amazement.

'Yes. I'm the youngest, you see. The big girls wouldn't like to share with me. I think they talk about boyfriends

93

and things,' she whispered, though there was no one near to hear. Dandy stood and stared at this wonderful room that was Madge's alone – the neat single bed, the tiny wardrobe and chests of drawers and the shelves – oh, the shelves! Books and books and books! And another shelf with teddy bears and dolls, masses of them.

'D'you play with dolls?' she asked in amazement.

'Oh, no, I *did*, of course when I was young. All our teddies and dolls are there. Sometimes my big brother, Alex – he's twenty-three – comes in and plays with his teddy just for fun. He's a comic. I giggle so much at him that I get sick sometimes. But we'd better hurry. When Mother says "no surrender" she means it. The next door is the bathroom, then Mother and Father's room and the spare room. On the half-landing there's another bathroom and an extra WC. Let's get down.' She waved a hand as they hurried through the hall. 'That's the drawing room, that's the snug where Father keeps his papers and books and things, that's the dining room and that's the kitchen. We'll cut through the conservatory to get to the garden. We all helped get the chairs ready. The rest of them are all away out. Father thought we would have more fun on our own.'

As Alice had forecast, Dandy behaved perfectly over tea. She had had plenty of opportunities at the McLarens' house to see how they handled things. Madge, no longer shy, said, 'Be sure to try the German biscuits, Dandy. I iced them and stuck the cherries on.'

'Aye, you should see her, Dandy,' said Mr Forbes. 'She's got a big bowl of cherries and it's "one to me and one to the cakes".'

'I don't,' said Madge. 'I only eat the ones that get squashed.'

'Aye, there's a lot of them get squashed!' her father teased.

If only I had a faither like that, thought Dandy.

And that was the pattern of the visit. When the scrumptious tea was finished, they all went round the garden while Mrs Forbes told them about some of the rarer plants and Mr Forbes did a bit of teasing. For a long time Dandy had been determined that she would never, never have the homelife her mother endured. The Forbes family formed for her the positive side of that thought, the goal she would aim for and reach.

'Some day I'll have a house like this,' she vowed.

Chapter 7

Dandy's feelings were mixed as she made her way to school on the first morning of term. There was always the thrill of smelling the chalk and the varnish, but Miss Bryce was an unknown quantity. Of course, she had dreaded Miss Martin, who had a reputation for being a martinet, and look how she had turned out. But that might have had something to do with Aunt Alice's letter. Soon the aunts would be moving to the cottage and would not be on hand to help her with her homework problems, though they had promised to be available whenever she could get away. There was one ray of hope. One of the older girls had said of Miss Bryce, 'She's always wanting to teach you silly old botany. If it's not sepals, it's petals. Daft, I call it.'

Botany wasn't daft. Botany was what some of Uncle James's huge books were about. Aunt Violet had assured her that they would never sell those and any time she was free, she could study them. 'They'll still be there when you are grown-up, Dandy,' she had said, 'and I think they will still be of interest to you.' It had crossed Dandy's mind then that these aunts were quite old ladies. What if they died before she was grown-up . . . or even when she was newly grown-up? The twins and Jack were still wee and Mammie was going to need help for a long time. But Aunt Alice had said that she would be a strong person when she grew up. That meant she would do what she wanted, and spending time in the library would certainly be one of the things she wanted. Aunt Alice was fond of saying that if we were patient, things would work out – and look how patient these two had had to be. It was sad that it was losing their precious brother that had given them a nice home and money to buy things.

'Sit anywhere you like this morning, boys and girls,' Miss Bryce said. 'I'll soon sort you out.'

It's Mammie's washday that will sort me out, thought Dandy. I expect May will take her turn now, but I hate to see her miss school too. She's so quiet that the teacher will never guess.

They finished the prayer and the register. Miss Bryce clapped her hands. 'I want your attention, please.' Dandy watched the chalk dust dancing in the rays of September sun. That sun would be shining on her tumshies. It was difficult to keep her mind on school when her garden needed her. Miss Bryce had a wide mouth and rather big teeth, but she seemed to be used to smiling. That was a good sign. She was busy telling them that these last two years in the junior school were so important, could determine their futures; many new subjects would be introduced in the coming year – botany, for example. Who could tell her what botany was?

Fancy anyone not knowing that, Dandy thought scornfully.

'Can no one . . . ?'

She was really waiting for an answer. Dandy's hand shot up. 'The study of plants, Miss.'

'Yes, of course. Thank you, Dandy.'

Dandy relaxed. This term wasn't going to be too bad – apart from her aunts moving away, that was. She hoped that May liked her new teacher. Then she remembered George. 'I hope Miss Martin remembers what she said. If she could only get him in order . . .' Her imagination wouldn't take her any further along that path. Only brute force had ever worked for her

97

with George and that just stopped him pushing her around, it didn't get him to do his share in the house. Even if Miss Martin got control of him at school, Faither would spoil it by his attitude. He had no respect for teachers – or school, come to that. He would have put Miss Martin's lovely book in the back of the fire – at least, that's what he said. Mind you, Miss Martin had a lot of Grannie in her. Maybe she would know what the stuff was that Mammie should put in Faither's tea. Maybe not. She wasn't married.

Inevitably the talk at the tea table that night turned to their new teachers. May's had commended her for her neat writing. Billy's shouted 'Be quiet!' every ten minutes. Dandy enthused about the botany lessons she was about to start, confident that Uncle James's teaching would help her shine. George was noticeably quiet.

'And what about yours, son?' Faither asked.

'Bloody awful,' said George.

Faither threw back his head and guffawed while Mammie tut-tutted.

'And what was she up to, then?'

'Oh, I didn't get my cap off quick enough. My hands were dirty. I forgot the rag for my slate. She said I was shuffling my feet and blamed me for punching that new boy; he was taking up too much of the seat and wouldn't move so I *had* to punch him! It was George Baxter this and George Baxter that. I thought the bell would never go.'

'That's women for you, son. There's nae pleasin' them.'

Dandy kept her eyes down over her plate. If her father saw what she thought of him, she would probably get another slap. It was all he was good for. I hope Miss Martin makes life hell for George, she thought. Else he's going to grow up like Faither.

Of course, she still had to stay off on some washdays,

though Grannie was being real good about coming round, now that she felt the McLarens were her allies. Alice had met her near the cottage one day and invited her to see what the alterations were about. She had said that Mrs Jordan would have to come and see it all when they were settled in. 'They're having new curtains everywhere when the decorating's done,' she told Nettie. 'Their brother had kept the same ones for years and the ones they have here don't fit the windows.'

Good old Aunt Alice, Dandy thought. She's keeping Grannie sweet. I'm sure she's doing it for me.

Soon the day came when all the alterations and the decorations were complete. Aunt Violet had been busy sewing the new curtains. A cab was coming to transport them with their awkward bundles, but Aunt Alice actually managed to recruit George to help the three of them carry the load upstairs to the various rooms. He looked round in amazement as they entered. Dandy realized that George had never been in anything more spacious than his grannie's flat, and that rarely. He seemed to be in awe of Aunt Alice too, but reverted to normal when she handed him a whole sixpence for his pains. 'Perhaps you could share it with Billy,' she said. 'I'm sure he would have helped as well, but he's really not big enough.'

Dandy reflected that they could easily have carried the bundles upstairs one by one. There was no real need for George. Aunt Alice was up to something. She would know that a ride in a cab would tempt him, of course. Was she trying to get him in order her way? It was very different from Miss Martin's. *She* seemed to have started with a reign of terror. Faither was still stupidly backing George up in his complaints. He'd even threatened to go to the school and sort them all out that night when Billy said that George had been sent to the headmaster and had been strapped.

'What were you doing?' asked May, round-eyed.

'I took a short cut across the desks to get to my place.'

'On top of them?' May was horrified.

'You should have heard her, Faither,' George went on. ' "Homework never done, inattention in class and now hooliganism. No, George Baxter, *I will not have it.*" She was screeching. The headmaster was in the corridor and heard her. He's a bugger that one! They say he soaks the tawse in vinegar – gave me four, cross-hands! And if my homework's not done tomorrow, he says he'll do the same again.'

'God! I'm glad I'm done wi' a' that,' Will Baxter said.

Dandy guessed that all his bluster about sorting them out at the school would come to nothing, and she was right. He was soon off to the pub as usual and nothing more was said about his threats. Probably he boasts about George to his drinking cronies, she thought. Miss Martin's doing her best. I wonder what Aunt Alice's plans are.

A few days after the new curtains were up, the Misses McLaren were off to their new home in Espedair Street and the Baxter children were left wondering what the new neighbours would be like. They didn't have long to wonder. On the Saturday afternoon following her aunts' departure, Dandy found the door of the McLarens' flat open. She couldn't help peeping in. A man with tattoos on his arms was up a stepladder tearing off wallpaper. A girl about May's age was scraping away nearer floor level. Suddenly an older boy appeared with a bucket and started scooping discarded paper into it. She hurried on to her own flat. 'There's people in the McLarens' house,' she burst out as she entered the kitchen.

'Aye!' Nettie said. 'They're getting it ready. Want to move in as soon as possible. Mrs Stewart asked the factor. He said that they're coming from the coast. The wife has just died and the man has left the navy – or maybe not the navy, but the boats somewhere. Anyway, he was a ship's carpenter and he's got a job in the carpentry shop at the thread mills so that he can be near his weans. She says we'll need to give him a wee hand. A man doesn't know what's what in a house.'

'He was up the steps tearing off wallpaper,' Dandy said, 'and there was a wee girl about May's age helping him.'

'Aye. He has two boys and a girl, Mrs Stewart says. He couldna think o' them being left without their Mammie, so he gave up the sea.'

'He sounds nice,' said Dandy. 'I mean, if he chose to go to sea, that must have been what he wanted . . .' She was wondering how much Faither would have given up for them. The answer was depressing. In the next few days the contrast became even more acute as the information on the new neighbours began to feed in. She had been right about the girl's age. Cathy Keir was put in May's class at school and they naturally walked home together in the afternoon. The boy she had seen gathering up the paper was only a few months older than herself; Drew, he was called. He was in her own class. Jim, the next brother, was in Billy's class, though he was a little younger.

In the early days, most of the information about the Keirs came from May as she and Cathy soon became bosom pals. At the table her father often shut her up, telling her he was fed up hearing their name, but in bed at night or in the morning May found Dandy a ready listener. 'They all helped their Da – that's what they call him – get the house ready, she says. Cathy gets very sad at bedtimes for she misses her Ma but her Da cuddles and kisses her. She says that when he came home from sea he always brought presents for every one of them – funny things that you don't buy here.

Now they all work together. He says the Keirs are a team and they want to keep the house the way her Ma would have kept it. They've agreed something, a duty something, I can't remember the word, Dandy, it sounded something like a hen . . .'

'A hen?' asked Dandy. 'I can't think what that will be, but go on, May.'

'On Sundays they sit round the table and discuss the duties for the week. Then their Da draws up the lists, one for each day. It tells them what jobs they are to do. And d'you know, Dandy, they have to sign their names when they finish the job and say how long it took them and their Da studies them afterwards. He keeps saying they have to keep the house ship-shape and Bristol fashion. It sounds like a song the way Cathy says it. The boys do lots of the things that you have to do yourself, Dandy. I wish George and Billy could help like that. He says that their homework is very important and making a nuisance of yourself at school is a stupid waste of time. Learn all you can, he says and it will eq-q- . . . something you for life.'

'Equip?' asked Dandy.

'That's right. What does it mean, Dandy?'

The more Dandy heard of Tom Keir, the more she approved. Aunt Alice, too, thought he sounded a wonderful father. 'Your brothers will learn only good from those two boys, I should think,' she said. That remark inevitably reminded Dandy of her grannie's approval of these same aunts. And of course that had turned out to be true. Aunt Alice's answers were always brisk and helpful. Grannie was still being invited round to the cottage when they met accidentally. Dandy had heard her recounting one visit to Nettie. 'I told them how I had always aimed for the best for you and your sisters and she said that she could see the same ideals in Dandy. She always wanted to do her best and was so quick to learn. They haven't missed much, you know, Nettie. She said they knew what a tower of strength I was to you. Mind you, they never said a word against Will but I'll bet they think plenty.'

'I'll bet they do,' muttered Dandy to the soap bubbles in the scullery sink. 'There's not much Aunt Alice doesn't know. I've got a puzzle for her next time I get over to the cottage.'

A few days later she got her chance. 'Aunt Alice, May said that the Keirs drew up something like a hen to tell them what their duties were . . .'

'Like a hen?'

'Yes, to share out the jobs . . . take their turns . . .'

'Ah! A duty roster. Roster! She's been thinking of rooster.' She laughed. 'Isn't that funny. It reminds me of some of the things your Uncle James used to say to us when he was a little boy.'

Dandy treasured her short visits to the cottage even more, now that there were no brief trips down to the flat. It was soon dark in the evenings and there was little chance of any gardening, except when Grannie told her she would be there in the afternoon and Dandy could go straight from school to her aunts. Soon she was coming out of school in the dark and there was no hope of gardening at all. Aunt Violet took the opportunity then to teach Dandy some sewing. It seemed a shame to cut up the beautiful garments that had been Rachel's, but Alice said one had to be sensible about such things. It was easy to get a museum mentality. Did she mean that that was what had happened to Uncle James and he had regretted it? Dandy wasn't sure and didn't like to ask. Violet congratulated her on her lovely straight seaming on the machine. She said that most learners kept pulling the cloth about: Dandy had the sense to guide it gently. This information surprised Dandy. She found the machine quite fascinating and was happy to let it do its work practically unaided. Thanks to the big mirrors in the cottage, she was able to see the fittings and give her opinion about what she wanted. Having a dress that was actually her choice was such a treat after all these years of cousin Betty's hand-me-downs.

Only May knew how important this was to Dandy. In their murmured conversations in bed she had learned over the years the frustrations that Dandy suffered in this field. Nothing could be said – that would vex Mammie, who shared the same privation. Grannie did her best, but that best was very limited. Now at last there was something to be hopeful about.

George was being forced to do some homework, thanks to Miss Martin's stern measures. Billy followed his example. It was funny to have a bit of quietness in the kitchen when Faither had gone off to the pub – May in the parlour, settling the twins down for the night and Mammie rocking Jack in the cradle. Dandy took to shutting the scullery door so that she could sing as she worked. It had never dawned on her that she sang automatically as soon as the water started running. There had always been so much noise in the house. Of course, you had to think of other things when you were doing dreary housework or you would go daft. Not even Faither could stop you thinking. That was a cheering thought. She had always laughed at her grannie's noseyness about the McLarens. Now she found she was just as nosey herself about the Keirs. May's 'Cathy said' held promise every time. On the face of it, the Keirs had a lot of handicaps – no mother to run the home, moving quite a distance from the coast where they would know all the neighbours, and probably not having much money either. Yet everything seemed to run smoothly for them. Certainly Drew often had lines puckering his brow. She had watched him occasionally in class. Cathy cried every night for her mother and, she said, sometimes Jim cried too. Did Drew feel like crying but he was the 'big one' and not allowed? She had suffered from being the 'big one' herself, especially since Faither refused to take a hand in disciplining George and Billy. These two were goggle-eyed when May explained about the duty roster. When Faither roared with laughter at the idea, they joined in.

Faither was stupid, damned stupid, Dandy thought, encouraging them to laugh at a decent family like the Keirs. George played up to Faither and enjoyed boasting about the silly things he did. May worried about George and Billy too. Her friendship with Cathy made the Keir boys seem almost like brothers to her. It hurt her to hear George and Billy sneer at the fine things that Mr Keir was teaching his sons. Cathy had some lovely toys that her father had made her himself. Whereas May was lucky if there was an old piece of frayed clothes rope for her skipping games, Cathy had smoothly polished wooden handles and nice new rope for hers. She was showing May a new skipping game, singing the while, when George came catapulting down the stairs one day. Cathy tried to stop to let him by, but his foot caught on the rope and he bumped his arm heavily against the wall. 'You stupid bitch,' he shouted. 'Take your bloody ropes somewhere else.' He tore the ropes roughly from Cathy's hands. She cried out with the pain while May gasped in sympathy.

'What's this?' Drew Keir jumped down the last few steps.

'He tripped on my ropes,' wailed Cathy.

'That's his stupid fault and no excuse for swearing at my sister,' said Drew. He grabbed George's hair forcing his head back. 'Now you will apologize to Cathy and you will never try that foul language on her again.'

'Who says? You and your bloody stupid rosters. Faither would sort you lot out.'

'I'm waiting.' Drew's voice was grim. George wriggled suddenly and aimed a vicious kick at his captor. Drew Keir grunted with pain. 'Right! If that's the way you want it. Take that – and that – and that –' The blows were deft and seemingly effortless. 'Had enough, George? There's plenty more. No? Just remember that if ever I hear you use that language to my sister again I'll wipe your mouth out with soap – carbolic! And then I'll paste you!' Come on, Cathy. We'll find something to cool your hands.'

That night, Dandy waited grimly for George to report. He kept quiet right through the meal and waited till Faither was on his third cup of tea and the twins had scampered off to the parlour to play with a new toy Cathy had passed on to them before starting to rub his arm ostentatiously.

'What's up wi' you, son?'

'Bloody Keirs.'

Nettie tut-tutted but Will ignored her as usual. 'What have they been up to this time?'

'I was in a hurry and Cathy caught my foot in her bloody skipping rope and I got banged against the wall so I told her what I thought of her. Then that big sumph, Drew, grabbed me by the hair and punched and punched me . . .'

'But you swore at Cathy,' said May, for once made bold.

'Bloody hell! That doesna mean he can wallop somebody younger than himself,' said Will. 'I'll just go and tell that wee shrimp, Tom Keir, a thing or two.'

As he pushed back his chair Nettie pleaded, 'They're our neighbours, Will. Please, please don't fight. George shouldna swear . . .'

'I'll show him,' said Will, ignoring her. Nettie started

106

to cry and Jack joined her. She picked him up in her arms. It was difficult to tell which of them was doing the comforting, Dandy thought. Will threw the outside door open with a bang and she heard him stamp down the stairs, closely followed by George and Billy. Then he was thundering on the Keirs' door. 'The neighbours will all hear him,' Nettie moaned. There was the sound of the Keirs' door opening. Dandy felt May's hand creep into hers and they moved on to the landing to listen.

'I've a bone to pick with you,' Will bawled.

'Since I'm neither deaf nor drunk, there's no need to shout,' said Tom Keir. 'Say what you have to say.'

'Naw! I expect a pint would land you on your back, but I'm no' going to let your big bully o' a son take a swipe at a fellow younger than himself. And if you don't smash him, I'll dae it. Where is he? I'll teach him to fight someone his ain size . . .'

'You for example? Look, if you've got time to waste, I haven't.'

'Naw. I expect you've to get back to your embroidery.' This brought guffaws from George and Billy.

'Right! The story: from what I've heard, your George tripped on Cathy's skipping rope and swore at her. Drew rightly objected to anyone swearing at his sister and demanded an apology. George refused, so Drew chastized him . . . gently, I understand. He has a pretty powerful punch when necessary. Let me make this clear. Neither I nor her brothers will have Cathy sworn at. Drew has done all that is necessary this time and as far as we are concerned the matter is closed. We shall carry on as before, trying to be decent neighbours.'

'I'll see about chastizing, you miserable wee shrimp,' roared Will, but his voice had lost a bit of its assurance.

'Any time you like, Baxter, on the back green in daylight. That's all I've got to say.' Tom Keir stepped back and shut the door firmly.

'Aye, creep back in to your wee funk hole,' shouted Will for the benefit of the neighbours who had gathered at the foot of the stairs. Still mumbling abuse he lurched back to his own door. May was safely in the parlour and Dandy in the scullery by the time he reached the kitchen swearing under his breath.

Dandy guessed that her father would slam off to the pub and was not wrong. As soon as the door banged behind him she gave a loud sigh, threw down the dish towel and made for the big chair by the fire.

Chapter 8

For a few days George tried to get his father's approval by keeping up the talk about his confrontation with Tom Keir. 'I told the boys at school that you could paste wee Keir with your hand tied behind your back.' At first Will would assure him, 'Aye, you're right,' but gradually his voice seemed to lose a bit of its conviction. Dandy relied on Cathy's reports, relayed by May to get the picture of the Keir family's reaction. George and Billy were both within hearing when May said, 'Mr Keir says it is not the boys' fault. They just don't get any guidance from Faither. He's sorry for Mammie, but he won't have his daughter sworn at. The boys will have to learn to keep clean tongues in their heads. He says that neighbours should treat each other with respect. That way makes life easier for all concerned. Cathy has still to say "Hello" to the boys when she meets them. He's sure that Billy will still be friends with Jim and he says Drew and Dandy have too much sense to be anything else. He thinks Dandy is a fine girl and has too much to do, but it's not his place to interfere with that.'

'It's not his place to interfere with anything, cheeky bugger,' said George. To Dandy, watching, Billy's face was a study. He had been used to echo George's sentiments on such things, but May's report had impressed him.

'We'll show him,' said George. 'Faither will sort him out.'

From habit Billy grinned in agreement.

It was different when they learned about Drew and

Jim going with their father to the sports club where he exercised. Billy forgot to be discreet at the tea table that night. 'I wish we could go to that,' Billy said. 'Jim says the young boys only pay one and sixpence. That's for a whole winter. They're going to learn to box when they are older.' He paused hopefully, but Faither pretended he hadn't heard.

George and Billy were gradually drawn more and more into the lives of the Keirs, though they had the sense to keep quiet about it. The jobs which Faither regarded as the province of stupid womenfolk were tackled in good heart by Drew and Jim, who reckoned that the workouts they performed at the gymnasium were building up good muscles. Cathy's pride in her brothers was relayed by May. 'She goes to the gym with them though she doesn't do the exercises – it's only for boys. She sits in a corner and does her crochet – her Ma taught her, you see – but she can watch the boys at the same time. She says it's fun, although sometimes she worries when they are sweating and it looks too hard for them. Cathy's going to teach me to crochet and then she says I can make wee dresses for the twins. She wishes she had twin sisters.'

This affection Cathy showed for Peggy and Jinty was a plus as far as Dandy was concerned. Because Cathy sought every opportunity to play with them, Dandy felt less guilty about leaving May to cope. In fact, there were quite a few compensations for the removal of her aunts, if she chose to think of it. One important advantage was the lessening of Faither's influence on George since the Keirs' arrival. They heard less abuse of 'Old Marty' at the supper table now. But it was an innocent remark by Cathy that really put George on his mettle.

Dandy had struggled back from the cottage one Saturday afternoon in late October. It was one of those beautiful days in autumn when the Gleniffer Braes were bathed in a golden light. The low sun made you blink but there was a chill feel in the shade – a grand day for gardening. She had dug out two magnificent tumshies and carried them home. It was on the last lap that she suddenly felt tired. As she slowly mounted the stairs with her burden, George shot past her. Cathy, who was on the Keirs' landing with May, said, 'Is your brother not very strong?' May was too surprised to answer. Cathy went on, 'Da says that girls mustn't carry heavy things because it can harm them when they grow up. My brothers have great muscles. You should see what *they* can carry.' Just then Drew came up behind her. 'Here, Dandy, I'll take that.' He relieved her of the bag, ran up the flight of stairs and deposited it on her doorstep before running back down. 'Thanks Drew, I'm grateful,' she said.

As Dandy passed George in the kitchen, he gave her a quick glance. He had heard all right! She summoned up Aunt Alice. What would she say? Nothing. A dignified silence. The bit about the muscles would get through to George.

She had proof of that a few nights later when May said, 'Billy saw you with a bar of chocolate in the playground. Where did you get the money, George?'

'I didn't need any money. Old Marty gave me it. See!'

'You're a liar,' said Dandy.

'Ask Jim Keir, then, Dandy Baxter. He was passing in the corridor and saw us. You'll believe *him*.'

'Were you good at your lessons, then?' asked May doubtfully.

George hesitated, but he was too pleased with himself to keep silent for long. 'Old Marty asked if three strong boys would help her to rearrange some desks at the interval. Alec Stewart and the new boy put their hands up right away. I thought I would show them. And I did! We worked in twos, you see, and Old Marty chose me and we were finished before the other two. She gave us all bars of chocolate. They were only wee bars . . .' he tailed off.

'Aye,' said Dandy meaningfully.

'You could have given me a bite,' said Billy.

'Oh you! Go and shift some desks yourself. Give us a hand to get this table cleared. I want to get my bloody homework done or it'll be nag, nag, nag tomorrow.'

Dandy smothered a grin as she made for the scullery. George had never lifted a hand to clear the table in his life. The Keirs and Miss Martin between them might make a decent job of him yet.

Will Baxter's resentment festered on. It took the form of sarcastic remarks when he saw Tom Keir engaged in any domestic task. Sometimes the remarks were muttered, but when he was drunk they gradually got bolder as Tom Keir offered no response. 'A grand day for the white things, Missus,' greeted the sight of Tom lugging a basket of washing upstairs. Late one night when Tom was polishing the brass doorknocker and handle, Will staggered past, roaring with laughter. 'Bloody cissie,' he called over his shoulder.

Tom broke his silence. 'Repeat that when you're sober, Will Baxter, and we'll see who's a bloody cissie.'

Will laughed all the louder as he struggled to find the keyhole and stumble into the flat. The next morning, in a fiendish temper, he was stamping down the stairs when he found Tom on his knees, preparing to scrub the stairs. Will stepped on the bar of soap and skidded. Enraged, he took a kick at the bucket of hot water, sending it rattling and splashing down the next flight. 'I tellt ye ye were a bloody cissie and I meant it,' he roared.

Doors opened on every landing. Dandy heard Tom Keir's firm voice. 'Right, that's it! Down on the green and we'll settle this.'

'Bloody shrimp,' said Will. 'I'll make mincemeat o' ye.'

Tom Keir saved his breath. Dandy made for the scullery where she would have a view of the back green. Her mother was hurriedly dressing. Tom Keir hung his jacket on a clothes prop, but Will Baxter with a flourish threw his on the ground, muttering imprecations. From her angle, Tom Keir *did* look slight compared with her father's six foot two inches. But as Will launched himself forward with a roar she could see the paunch which his drinking had brought about. The fierce blow he aimed at Tom's face went over his head. One quick bob, a left jab to that paunch which doubled Will up, and Tom Keir ended the argument with a sharp crack on Will's jaw which sent him reeling and sprawling. With blood trickling from his mouth he started to rise, bawling, 'I'll get you for that, you little runt,' but Tom Keir unhooked his jacket from the pole, ignoring Will completely, and re-entered the building. Nettie by now was hurrying down the stairs. Tom spoke tiredly as he passed her. 'I'm sorry, Mrs Baxter, but there's a limit to what blood can stand.'

'Aye,' thought Dandy, listening at the open door. 'If Mammie had only recognized that limit and put something in his tea a long time ago, we would all have had peace.'

Tom Keir set off to work at his usual time and it was Drew who went on to wash the stairs, Dandy saw. She wondered how he felt, doing a job that none of the other boys in class would be faced with. But they were proud of their Da, the Keirs, and probably all the more so now that he had shut Faither up. Grannie had always said that what Will Baxter needed was a hammering.

When she heard the footsteps dragging on the stairs, Dandy hurried through to the parlour and busied herself with dressing the twins. She knew that the sight of

113

her always made Faither worse. She was too like Grannie, in spite of her bonnie yellow hair which was the only good thing he had ever done for her. May made a quiet foray to the scullery and came back with a plate of bread and jam which would be all the breakfast they would see that morning. 'Mammie's holding cold cloths to Faither's face,' she said.

Dandy could not help feeling a pang of sympathy for her mother, married to a drunken dyer who would never give her a chance, as Grannie put it. If only she had more guts! But it was no use worrying about that now. It was time for May and her to set off for school. Quickly she gathered a few tired old dolls in a circle, made them do a dance while she sang a daft little song and then set the twins to doing it themselves. It would keep them quiet till Mammie could get away from Faither.

She had known that the defeat of Faither at the hands of Tom Keir would not improve the atmosphere at home, but it was worse than she had anticipated. Faither took to visiting the pub on the way home, in his messy workclothes. He would come home in a foul temper, criticize the food offered and often just roll into bed with his clothes on. Mammie, brought up in Grannie's clean house where the sheets were always snowy, was appalled to see the smelly dyeworks clothes defiling the washing she had slaved over. Dandy had told her aunts about the fight on her next visit. Their reaction had not been like hers. When she said, 'That should keep him in his place and we'll all get peace,' they had obviously had misgivings.

'I hope you're right, Dandy, dear, but a man who drinks heavily is not rational in his resentments. The innocent are apt to suffer.'

A funny kind of loyalty had kept Dandy from mentioning this business of Faither coming home and going into bed in his dyeworks clothes. When she looked round the shining cottage and relaxed in the calm atmosphere, it was difficult to believe that Faither could create a world that was so different. It wasn't just money, either. Tom Keir was probably earning less than Faither, but his children had adequate food and the sort of orderly homelife she craved.

She sighed. If Faither was like Tom Keir, George and Billy would be getting rid of their wildness in the gymnasium and building up some useful muscle – something to be proud of. When you came to think of it, they hadn't much to be proud of. She wouldn't have been any better off, either, if these aunts hadn't chosen to take her under their wings. She beamed at them in sudden gratitude.

'That's better, Dandy,' said Alice. 'Things will work out. What's George up to these days?'

'Well, not as much as he would like.'

'What do you mean?'

'Mr Keir takes Drew and Jim to the gymnasium. They are members of the junior club and love it. They're building up good muscles and when they are older they'll learn boxing there too. Our boys are jealous. They told Faither about it early on, but he pretended he didn't hear them. It would only cost one shilling and sixpence for the whole winter, but there's no way they can get the money. Faither's drinking has just got worse.'

'That's a shame,' said Violet.

Alice was quiet. Dandy looked at her. Something was brewing. 'You said that your brother was doing his homework now,' she began, 'and he actually carried home the potatoes one night?'

'He's done it three times,' said Dandy.

'Good!'

'I was just thinking, Violet, the garden hut is in need

115

of cleaning out. It's a messy job. Mrs Brown's chest has been bothering her recently so I didn't let her do the outside of the windows. Supposing I drew up a roster – they're used to that word now – and Dandy offered it to George and Billy: a Saturday's work; wages, one shilling and sixpence each with morning snack, lunch and afternoon tea thrown in. Do you think they'd be interested, Dandy?'

'They'd be bloody daft . . . I mean, it sounds a great idea,' said Dandy hastily.

'And if you don't work hard, I'll bloody well paste you,' George threatened.

Billy was indignant. 'I work as hard as you. Just because you're older . . .'

'If that's the way the two of you are going to carry on at the cottage,' said Dandy, 'you can forget it. The aunts are used to civilized speech. I thought you would be dancing at the chance. I'll just tell them . . .'

'No! We're going to do it. We'll get to that gym. Tell the wifies we'll be there.'

'They're not wifies, George Baxter. They're ladies. Remember that. And if I were you, I'd say nothing to Faither or he'll bugger it up 'cause he's jealous of Tom Keir. Just get up quietly on Saturday morning and have your breakfast as if you weren't going anywhere special. Take your big scarves. It's cold out in the garden but the kitchen fire will be blazing when you go in for your tea and things. I wish I could go in the morning, but Mammie will need me, I expect. I'll try to get over in the afternoon.'

'We'll be fine without you,' said George.

'I'm no' worried about you. It's the garden. I've to watch that bits don't get waterlogged at this time of year. And Aunt Violet was going to find some nice material to cut up for a dress for May. I'll be sewing it

116

myself. Now, I'm warning you, behave yourselves or you'll never get another chance. They may be ladies, but that doesna mean they'll put up wi' nonsense from the likes of you.'

She remembered those words as she hurried to the cottage on the Saturday afternoon. It was too much to hope that her brothers would ever behave like the Keirs, but if they had given her aunts any trouble, she'd . . . well . . . she'd better be patient and see exactly what they *had* been up to.

It was Alice who opened the door. 'Come and see this, Dandy, your Aunt Violet has two assistant chefs.'

'What! I wouldn't trust these two . . .' Dandy said as she hurried towards the kitchen. Billy, who was in the act of flipping over a pancake, turned as she came in. The pancake caught on the edge of the pan and fell on to the hob of the cooker. 'That's your fault, Dandy Baxter. I'd been getting them all right till you came in.'

'I didn't do anything, you silly wee . . .'

'Here now,' said Aunt Alice, 'that reminds me of an English cook we used to have. She insisted on calling our Scotch pancakes drop scones. Now I know why. What Billy said is true, Dandy: the two boys have been turning out perfect pancakes and it was Billy who beat up the batter while George was out in the cold washing the windows. They managed to get the hut finished before lunch. It looks perfect now. You'll find everything clearly labelled and that will make your work easier.'

'I beat up the egg-white for the meringues before that,' Billy volunteered. 'Aunt Violet put in the sugar and they're in the oven now. They'll be there a long time.'

Dandy frowned. A surge of resentment swept over her when Billy said 'Aunt Violet'. They were *her* aunts. She knew she was being unreasonable but wished

117

suddenly that she had kept quiet about the boys and their gymnasium. Aunt Violet had been spreading the cloth and setting the kitchen table while they spoke and George had gone on systematically making more pancakes while his brother was otherwise engaged. Billy shouted in indignation when he found that the batter was finished. Alice put her hand on his shoulder. 'George didn't get the chance of beating up the meringues, remember.' George, for once, had the sense to keep quiet.

'You could write out the recipe and make them at home some afternoons,' she urged.

'No, we couldn't,' muttered Billy. 'They need an egg and Faither always gets the eggs.'

Violet stared. Alice spoke quickly. 'Since your hands are nice and clean, Billy, you could arrange the pancakes on this big plate – any design you like ... two circles or two rows ... as you like. They won't stay long like that anyway. I can remember once our little brother was stretching out for another one when our nurse, who had been dreaming, I think, suddenly asked how many he had had. "This is my ninth," he said. Of course he had a sore tummy later.'

As she watched her brothers laughing heartily, Dandy again chalked up a mark for Aunt Alice. She had eased them all out of an embarrassing situation and given the boys something happy to remember. 'I'd love to have that gift,' she thought. It stayed in her head while she spiked the damp patch near the foot of the garden with a fork and then dug up two large swedes. Then it was reinforced when Aunt Alice, wrapping them in many sheets of newspaper, said, 'These are beauties, Dandy. It's a good thing your brothers are here to carry them home. It takes a lot of muscle.' For a moment Dandy wondered if Aunt Alice had maybe overdone it and the boys would realize they were being

118

manoeuvred, but George and Billy, each with a shilling and a sixpence jangling in his pocket, laughed as they pretended to drop the monster turnips on their toes. Dandy walked (like a lady, she thought) with only a neat little parcel of pancakes to encumber her. 'I'll see that Mammie and the wee ones get these before Faither comes in,' she determined.

When the door closed behind the three Baxters, Alice and Violet with one accord made for their sitting room and collapsed into the fireside chairs. 'You too!' said Violet. 'I thought I was the one who was wilting.'

'Oh, no, I was exhausted,' said Alice, 'simply trying to keep one thought ahead of them.'

'Just fancy, all the eggs are reserved for that no-use father of theirs!'

'Yes, I saw your face, Violet. But, on the other hand, these children all seem perfectly healthy. They eat everything that's put in front of them. They get porridge every morning. Their main meal seems to consist of soup and bread most days, from what I have gathered. Probably there's not much in the way of meat in the stock, but the barley and lentils will be giving them a little nourishment. We'll have to see that Dandy gets the chance to grow plenty of vegetables, that's all.'

'But, Alice, did you hear little Billy say that the mince was so different from the kind they get at home?'

'Yes. I gathered that it's well watered when it *does* appear on the menu. These boys certainly stuffed themselves well, but I don't think we should get too involved there. We'll leave them to Tom Keir now that they have the money for their exercise gym. I think we should concentrate on Dandy. She is the one who has carried the biggest burden.'

Dandy's fears about being usurped soon died. Her brothers had no interest in anything else once they had found their way to the gym. It became a game to them, trying to talk about it without their father picking up the subject – not that this was too difficult. Ever since his fight with Tom Keir, Will Baxter had been morose in the house, coming home late after visiting the pub and often refusing food. He had lost a lot of weight and was gambling seriously. Nettie was finding the struggle to make ends meet worse than ever. The vegetables that Dandy grew had become a necessity.

'If that man o' yours gets any worse,' Lily Jordan said to her daughter one day in Dandy's hearing, 'he'll get the sack, that's what!'

'But he's good at his job. He was foreman before he was thirty.'

'Aye, but a lot o' drink has crossed his thrapple since then – drink that's cost money you should be getting for all these weans.'

Nettie was sobbing, no longer able to make her usual defence of Will's little ways. 'It's getting worse, Mither, I don't know what's going to happen to us. It's the gambling, you see. The drink was bad enough. He's in bad company . . .'

'Him – in bad company! He *is* bad company, lass; nane worse!'

'If I could only get him away from here, I'm sure he would change, but then, it's so far away.'

'What's so far away?'

'Canada. That's where Will's talking about. He heard about one of the dyers that went there to be with his married sister and he's doing great and he wasn't the foreman like Will.'

'You're never thinking of going to Canada?' Lily was aghast. 'I'd never see you or the bairns again. He could do what he likes to you if I'm no' there to settle his hash. He's managed to keep his job here so far – I don't know how – but they'd never put up wi' his damned nonsense over there. They're all pioneers that go there, hard workers – no' drunken shirkers.'

'He kens they have to work hard, Mither. I think he just canna help himself here. It's his nature, you see . . . he didna want all these bairns . . . he canna help himsel', but it's no' much fun coming home to a wee crowded place. He canna grumble about it because it's nobody's fault but his own. I'm sorry for him, Mither. He says there's that much room in Canada: we wouldna be squashed in a wee place like this: the bairns could run about and there would be good jobs for the boys when they're a wee bit older. They're offering free land grants to folk from this side. It's a country that's just starting up, even though it's so big that you could tuck Scotland in a wee corner of it.'

'It's the other side o' the world, lass. And what does your Will know about farming?'

Nettie started sobbing again. 'We'll never get out of the bit if we stay here, though.'

Dandy looked at her hands which had stayed still on top of the suds in the basin. Leave Paisley! Leave her garden! Leave her aunties! Never! She would hide if it came to the point. They wouldn't get her on to that boat. Mammie was daft. Faither better if he got to Canada – fat chance! He'd be a drunken devil wherever he went. Why could Mammie not see that? But May would go too if the rest of them went. She would have no right to stop her wee sister, for she wasn't in a position to look after her. 'Oh, God! If only I were older and could get a job,' she thought.

Grannie was leaving. She had forgotten to say 'Cheerio'. That meant she was upset: that the move to Canada was a distinct possibility and not one of Faither's blusters. But Grannie could be getting it wrong just because it would mean so much to her to lose her daughter. She constantly moaned about Dandy's Aunt

Jean, whose husband had stupidly taken a job in Coventry and robbed her of her eldest daughter.

For once, Dandy hoped that her able Grannie might be wrong, but a little warning bell in her head started her thinking out possible escape routes. 'Folks are always saying I look older. Maybe it won't be long till I can pretend that I'm old enough . . .' But there were the school authorities to consider. Her aunts would never assist her in any act of deception. But they were 'ladies' and 'ladies' didn't land in this sort of predicament. She would have to think things out on her own. Grannie was on her side, but this time Grannie's interference could easily backfire and then she, Dandy Baxter, could be swept along and on to that ship, leaving everything she held most dear . . . except May, of course. 'I am *not* going to Canada,' she whispered fiercely. 'It's the other side of the world. There's nothing to stop Faither from mending his ways here. Mammie is only making excuses. She should have put something in his tea. I wonder what the stuff is? I could ask Grannie now that I'm bigger. No! She would do it herself if it was that easy. Maybe it's just pretend stuff and it keeps her happy to think about it. Tom Keir might know. He'd be shocked if I asked him. I could try Drew – but he might be shocked too, even if he *is* my age.'

One big compensation in these worrying times was that she was doing well at school, thanks to having fewer absences. Miss Bryce was a real enthusiast about botany. Dandy had not only Uncle James's expertise to draw on, but had safely 'borrowed' one of the botany books from the cottage, now that her brothers had less time to create havoc in the home. There was no doubt about who was going to walk out for the botany prize in July 1906. 'It'll be me. I'll see to that,' Dandy vowed.

When she did, it was in the comforting knowledge

that her success was not just on paper. In fact, many days their main meal at home consisted of a variety of her vegetables, carefully cooked and then covered in a thin grating of cheese. Her mother would say, 'I don't know what I would do without you, Dandy.' Dandy gulped with pain, for she didn't know either but one thing she was sure of – they would never get her on that boat to Canada. The seeds she had carefully sown in the prepared ground in spring had all come up dutifully. Some colourful rags fluttering from sticks had kept the pigeons off her peas. The parsley round the rose beds had kept the greenfly at bay. Nothing Uncle James had taught her had been forgotten and now her aunties were adding snippets of remembered lore to her store of knowledge. Miss Bryce smiled her wide smile whenever Dandy amplified the textbook answer. George and Billy were far from being reformed characters, but they had begun to appreciate an audience for their shows of strength and Dandy, modelling herself on Aunt Alice, awarded those displays with the right degree of surprise and praise. Then it was easy to call, 'Two strong men wanted,' when she needed to have a heavy basket of washing humped up from the drying green.

Aunt Violet's sewing lessons were a joy too, because she didn't stick to plain useful stuff. No! She showed a lot of imagination. The styles of Aunt Rachel's youth had demanded a great deal of material and Violet revelled in thinking out ways of using it to Dandy's advantage. Even the serviceable dresses she needed for school were made to fit neatly and comfortably. 'Your height is in your legs, you see,' Aunt Violet pointed out. 'That's why it is important to have these properly fitted; then you see your lovely trim waist.'

'I thought I was just a skinnymalink,' said Dandy.

'Not at all. You have a good bone structure. I should

think your father was a very handsome, tall young man. Once you fill out a little, as you *will* do, you will be a very elegant young lady.'

Dandy looked sharply at this spinster who was a real 'lady'. Could she be making fun of her? No, Aunt Violet was holding up a length of fabric to the light, then holding it against Dandy and studying the effect in the tall mirror. Could it be true? Dandy Baxter, an elegant young lady? She pulled herself up a little, straightening her neck.

'Oh, yes,' said Violet. 'Posture is so important. Too many tall people stoop. It is a big mistake. You look like a lily, my dear. Always remember that and never stoop.'

'I love lilies,' said Dandy. 'Uncle James said that there are countless varieties and we don't exploit them enough.'

'Well, many of them need to be under glass – the exotic ones, I mean. I don't think we have room for another glasshouse in our limited space here.'

'It's my vegetables that take up most of the room,' said Dandy. 'Maybe that's what is stopping you . . . ?'

'Oh, no, glasshouses are very expensive.' Violet was briskly dismissive.

The contrast between the Baxter flat and the cottage seemed greater than ever to Dandy. The space which Violet regarded as limited was her idea of heaven. The aunts had decided that they had grown used to sharing a room. 'You see, as you get older, Dandy, sleep does not come so easily. We can lie and talk to each other. It's quite comforting,' Aunt Violet had said on another occasion – just before New Year. That was the day they had given her the most wonderful thrill of all.

'Come and see what we've done with Uncle James's room,' Alice had said, as they climbed the stairs. 'We call it "Dandy's room" and we hope that as your duties at home get lighter, you'll be able to stay with us overnight sometimes. Now, shut your eyes!'

Dandy heard the squeak of the door. 'You can open your eyes now. See how you like it.' She was pushed forward gently into ... paradise! There was no other word for it. Cream paintwork gleamed against pale apricot walls. Flowers rioted over the cream curtains and the same fabric was used for the frilled bedspread and the cushions on the delicate little chairs. But, perhaps most thrilling of all, there, in a corner, stood Rachel's bookcase with all those beautifully bound books to be read, fondled and mooned over.

'Well?' said Aunt Violet, eagerly. 'Does it suit you?'

Dandy was beyond words. Tears ran down her cheeks as she drifted round gently, stroking the bed, the brushes on the dressing table, the little floral handles on the clothes cupboard. Then her shoulders began to shake and the sisters saw something that few people had ever seen – Dandy Baxter completely broken: Dandy Baxter who never had time for the self-indulgence of tears, whose griefs had always found their outlet in anger and action. She turned, sobbing, to be enfolded in their arms.

Later, when they sat by the sitting room fire, Alice said, 'We both had the same idea all along about that room but, of course, it was Violet who did all the lovely needlework. Some day, when you have a home of your own, you will be able to make lovely things too because Violet says you are very adept with the machine already. It takes so much out of the labour of making curtains.'

'Did people sew curtains by hand in the old days, then?' asked Dandy. 'It's funny, I never thought of that. You know, our May loves the parlour curtains you passed on to Mother when you left.'

'Oh, yes. Everything was sewn by hand not so long

ago and at a time when fashions were very elaborate too.'

Dandy was quiet, then the tears began to trickle down her face. 'What's wrong?' asked Violet, but Dandy couldn't answer her.

'I think Dandy likes her New Year present,' said Alice.

Chapter 9

The glorious room remained something to dream over for a long time. There was always some reason why Dandy could not be spared. Though Faither had never been told of it, Dandy knew that he would put a spoke in her wheel if possible. Maybe it was safer to keep it as a dream – unspoiled. If he dragged Mammie all the way to Canada, she would stay behind. Of course, she would be expected to stay at Grannie's flat and she still would not enter that beautiful domain and call it her own. But Grannie's flat was not too far from the cottage and Grannie had a bathroom. Dandy always had a little sniff at the scented bathsalts in the cottage. A scented bath would be heavenly, even if it had to be at Grannie's and not near 'Dandy's bedroom'. Always as she drifted into sleep these nights, she thought of that lovely room and then it would become entwined with Madge's bedroom at the Forbes' house. Madge didn't say 'Mammie'. She said 'Mother'. It sounded more grown-up. If she was going to pretend to be older, it might be better to practise saying it now. It would be better to do it gradually, start with her aunties . . .

Faither came home black as thunder – but sober – the following Friday night. There was dead silence at the table as everyone sensed his mood, until Billy dropped his knife on his plate. 'Watch what you're doing, you silly bugger,' Will barked. Then, as Jack began to whimper, 'Can you not keep that wean quiet?' Dandy noticed how her mother's hand shook as she tempted Jack with a spoonful of jam. Rage choked her,

127

but she knew that anything she did or said would make matters worse. They all waited, tense, for their father's expected exodus to the pub but, instead, he made for his armchair and drew the racing paper out of his pocket.

'He's ready to explode about something,' thought Dandy. 'Mammie's scared. I'll have to work something out the way Aunt Alice would – avoid trouble.' She started to pick up some dishes, gave George a kick under the table and a look which said, 'Follow me'. He balanced a few things on his forearm – good for the muscles she supposed – but a damn silly risk with Faither in that mood. In the scullery she grabbed his ear and, clattering dishes with one hand, whispered, 'Get down to the lavvie, the two of you, before May takes the twins. Then get your books and disappear to the gym club. You'll just have to do your homework there.'

'Right!' said George without a moment's hesitation.

'Thank goodness Miss Martin's knocked a bit of sense into that one,' she thought. Then she began to wonder. Without Aunt Alice's initiative in getting the boys to earn money for the gym club, *that* escape route would not have been open. Tom Keir's attitude to school work would help too. Aye, there were quite a few things to be thankful for.

There was no singing in the scullery that night. Dandy worked quietly, listening as hard as she could, but the only sound seemed to be Mammie shushing Jack as she got him ready for bed. He couldn't still be reading that daft paper – there was next to nothing in it. He never read anything else. She had finished clearing up but was reluctant to draw attention to herself in case it brought on another display of bad temper.

Then she heard the rustle of the paper, the creak of the chair and Faither's voice. 'Where are the boys?'

Panic seized her and she quickly opened the scullery door. Nettie was saying, 'I'm not quite sure...'

'They're out playing. One of the boys has got a football and they all meet up,' said Dandy.

'It's getting dark,' said Will.

'Aye, but there's probably lights near where they play,' Dandy improvised.

Her father turned away. 'I was going to take them for a walk up the Braes, smarten them up...' He walked out of the kitchen and a few minutes later the outside door banged.

'It gets dark up the Braes too,' said Dandy.

'Aye!' Nettie was out of her depth. 'He seems different tonight, don't you think? Maybe he's no' well.'

Dandy reflected. Her father had seemed almost sober though bad-tempered as ever. Before Uncle James died, normally on Faither's exit she would have checked up on May and the twins and then made her escape to the McLarens' flat. Somehow tonight she felt that it would not be safe to leave her mother, even if there *was* somewhere to go. She might open her mouth and tell Faither about the gym club, for one thing. And for another, this was a funny mood he was in. There was no saying what might happen. She stared into the fire while her mother went on clearing away Jack's toys and clothes and rinsing things in the scullery. The sound of the doorbell startled her and brought May into the lobby.

The man on the doorstep was unknown to Dandy, though the mixed smell of beer and whisky was a familiar one. 'Is Will in?' he asked.

'No. I think he went for a walk,' she said warily. 'Did you want him?'

'Aye, well, aye, well, you see, he's usually at the pub ... I'm Sam Murdoch ...'

'Come in, Mr Murdoch,' said Dandy. Nettie stared as Dandy led the stranger into the kitchen. 'Mr Murdoch expected to see Faither in the pub tonight,' she explained.

Nettie indicated a seat but could not find a word to say.

'Had you something to tell my father?' asked Dandy.

'Aye, well, just solidarity, y'ken. He was upset wi' the boss threatening like that.' He hiccupped. 'Will's a fine fellow, kens his job, nane better. Of course, the boss has been on at him before, many a time. But this time . . . well. Ah'm sorry for Will: threatening to put him out without a reference, like that. Will was that angry: tellt us he was going to Canada – faur frae this damned place. Then, Jim Spence – him that's cousin went to Canada – said that you've got to have references . . . simply got to. They're that keen on references in Canada. Mind you, reference or no reference, I'll bet Will could show them. He's a fine fellow; sink a pint wi' the best of them.'

'I don't doubt it,' said Dandy. 'Well, we've no idea when Faither will be back . . .' she added meaningfully.

Nettie said, 'Would you like a cup of tea, Mr Murdoch?'

'No, no . . . dinna bother. I'm no' that fond o' tea.' He lumbered to his feet. 'I'll see Will . . . probably . . .'

'I'm no' that fond of tea,' mimicked Dandy after closing the door behind him. 'I'll bet he isn't. Did *you* smell it, May?'

'Aye. He's had a lot,' said May. 'I wonder why men like that stuff so much. It smells like horrid medicine.'

'Aye, medicine to make men horrid!' said Dandy.

George and Billy rattled the letterbox softly. Dandy opened the door. 'He's out,' she said.

'Oh, good!' said George. 'I didn't get my homework done, we got a chance of the punchball, y'see . . .'

'Get into your bed,' Dandy interrupted. 'You can do

your homework there. But the minute you hear him, start snoring. No, don't! You daft galoots!' – this when the two of them started an exaggerated impression of deep sleep. 'I'm telling you, there'll be no fun tonight. He's in a bad mood and likely to be worse.'

'How d'you know that, Miss Martin?'

'Just you take my word for it, George Baxter. *Now*, the two of you – I mean it! Mammie's got enough worries. I'll help you with your homework in case he comes back soon.'

George sobered instantly. Such an offer had never come from Dandy before. His clothes were torn off instantly and rolled in a bundle on the chair by his bed.

'I've got homework too,' bleated Billy.

'Aye. Stop girning. We haven't time for that nonsense. You read your questions, George, while I run through Billy's with him.'

She gave a sigh of relief when the hated homework was completed and the boys pulled the bedclothes over their heads. Dandy automatically straightened chairs and folded clothes, wondering all the while if her mother needed her backing or if her presence would only be an excuse for Faither's wrath.

'Would you like me to stay with you, Mother?' she asked. 'Or do you think it would be better if I did my homework in the parlour?'

'I don't know, pet. I'm that worried. What if he loses his job? Things are bad enough now. What will your grannie say?'

Dandy knew only too well what Grannie would say – every last word of it. *What did I tell you? I kent fine they wouldna put up wi' his nonsense. Why you had to pick a drunken dyer, I'll never know* ... Oh yes, Dandy could go on and on as Grannie certainly would do. But that didn't help anyone, did it?

131

'Sometimes seeing me seems to make him worse,' she ventured.

'Aye, you remind him of your grannie in spite of your bonnie yellow hair. Maybe it would be better if you went through. I'm just wondering what he's doing. Maybe if he's depressed . . .'

'He'll go to the pub. That's what he always does, Mammie.'

'I think he's determined to get to Canada. If that means giving up his drink, he'll no be happy.'

Aye, and if he's no' happy, the rest of us will have a hell of a time, thought Dandy as she made her way through to the blessed escape of her books.

It was late when she heard the dreaded step on the stair. He was not stumbling. The key went into the lock without all the usual scrabbling, scraping and accompanying curses. She sat up to hear better. He was sober. That was a good thing – or was it? Since his drinking had got worse, she had not heard that regular creaking of the bed. What if he started again? What if Mammie had another bairn? How would he ever get to Canada then? He was speaking – not too loud. She strained her ears. Mammie was speaking now, softly as usual.

Then Faither let out a roar. 'What does Sam Murdoch think he is, coming here spreading gossip?'

Then Mammie was speaking again, pleading. Faither's voice was a little quieter. 'Aye, well, maybe he did, but it's a gey queer way o' being kind.' She heard the bedsprings twang as he climbed into the bed. She listened, not wanting to hear. 'Oh, God! Don't let him do that to Mammie.' The first abrupt snore made her almost laugh with relief.

The next few weeks justified her foreboding about having a hell of a life. It was a good thing that George and Billy seemed to be learning a little sense. Maybe Tom Keir was getting through to them. Certainly that gymnasium had become an obsession. The slightest threat that Faither might manage to put a stop to their visits was enough to ensure their co-operation, albeit reluctant, to any scheme Dandy proposed. They had become a united family, united against the storm of Will Baxter's uncertain temper.

Dandy noticed that the racing paper had been replaced by the *Paisley Daily Express*. While going unobtrusively about her work, she watched to see what it was her father found so interesting. Sometimes he would take a cutting from his pocket and hold it against the paper, comparing the two. 'You can tell he never reads much,' thought Dandy. 'His eyes move across it and he's that slow.' Louise White at school was like that. She read one word at a time. It nearly drove you daft. Though Miss Bryce didn't seem to bother much, Miss Martin had been exasperated with her sometimes and told her she must practise at home. In the play-ground, Louise had confided to Dandy that she *did* practise at home but it was no use and asked how Dandy managed to read like a grown-up. Dandy had been unable to give her an answer.

It was frustrating to find that Faither always folded the paper up and put it back in his pocket before he went out on his mysterious walks. It was never left lying in the morning, either. 'It's always the same page he gets stuck at,' she thought. 'I must find out what's on that page.'

Her aunts would be sure to have a copy every day, but there was no prospect of visiting them till Saturday. Who else? Tom Keir . . . possibly. Drew usually over-took her as she entered the school gate. She would have a word with him.

'Aye, sure, Dandy. Yesterday's, you said? I'll slip it through your letterbox at lunchtime.'

133

'Great. I'll let you have it back when I've found the bit I want.'

Drew was a bit like the Aunties. He didn't pester you with nosey questions about why you wanted it. It had been a good idea to ask Drew Keir.

She wasn't long in the house at lunchtime when she heard the sound she was listening for and darted into the lobby to retrieve the paper. In the parlour she opened her prize. Faither always folded it like so . . . and ran his finger slowly down . . . CANADA! The word leaped out at her. So he *was* in earnest. Carefully she read:

Work plentiful . . . Men and Women . . . unequalled organization . . . advice free . . . conducted parties at frequent intervals from Glasgow . . .

Then she burst out laughing at the final sentence:

Write Colonel Lamb, Salvation Army, Glasgow

That was one advertisement that Faither would not be answering. Maybe there were different ones different days? Where had he got that cutting that he sometimes held up against the paper? She would risk asking Drew if he would mind slipping the paper to her for a few days . . . say the thing she had been looking for was not in that one.

As she had hoped, Drew readily agreed. For a few days there was nothing of interest. Then the Salvation Army one appeared again. Surely Faither wasn't really thinking of joining them. Was he *that* desperate? Then she saw the other one.

Scottish Men and Women can earn more money and find more comfort and prosperity in the great dominion of Canada. *Canada* illustrated weekly

134

paper is giving, this week, free passages to Canada and £25 in cash.

'Well,' thought Dandy, 'that might be the one he is looking for. Maybe somebody gave him the cutting. Maybe he borrows the paper like I do. *Free passages* – I'll bet that doesn't mean with six weans. Maybe he's planning to go on his own . . . No, I'm getting daft. I'll keep borrowing the paper, just in case . . .'

It was early in February she came upon the next advertisement:

75 nurserymen (Scotch preferred) required by large firm. Good wages; steady employment. Conducted parties to sail Mar. 9th and 23rd. British E.T.C. Society.

'Faither knows nothing about gardens. Surely he wouldn't be considering that one? Maybe he thinks it's that easy that anyone can do it. Faither always thinks that everyone else's job is easy.' She watched carefully. The ritual went on. He still had that cutting in his hand and he still folded the paper carefully and put it back in his pocket. That maybe meant that she was right, he was borrowing it from someone. Night after night he came home sober and surly. The muscles on his face looked tight now. After he had read his paper, he was off without saying a word to anyone and it was always late when he came in. Mammie said that he walked till he was exhausted and he was needing new shoes. Dandy wondered what he did with the money he had always spent on drink. Was Mammie getting more? Gradually she realized that their diet was improving. Mince appeared more often and it was the kind of mince that the Aunties made – thick and tasty. And, joy of joys, a baked rice pudding had greeted them at lunch-time one day – rich and creamy and dotted with lovely raisins. Mammie had smiled happily at their oohs and aahs. 'Your grannie made that often for us when we were girls,' she said. Dandy mentally took back some of the things she had thought about Grannie.

Yes! Grannie! Her worried questioning of Nettie produced no results because Will had not bothered to tell his wife anything more about his thoughts on emigration and she was obviously afraid to ask him. Dandy kept quiet about her observations. Grannie might get used to the idea and not insist on backing her up in her determination to stay behind. It was better for Grannie to get a shock. Then she would cling to her granddaughter for want of anything better.

Spring gave way to summer. Her garden was flourishing and Mammie was definitely looking better, thanks to her frequent trips to the park with wee Jack. The twins could dress themselves now, so May also had a little less to do. Faither looked very tall and forbidding these days. With all the walking, his paunch was disappearing. Dandy couldn't believe that he could keep up his sober ways much longer. Daily – or nightly, rather – she expected to find him staggering in drunk. The newspaper came out every night and also, she noticed through the crack in the scullery door, a little book rather like Grannie's bankbook. Was he saving for the fares to Canada? The Salvation Army advertisement had said *Normal fares*. What would normal fares be to the other side of the world? But some people there seemed to be so anxious to get Scotch workers that they were offering money. Maybe it depended on which bit of Canada you were going to. Miss Bryce said in the geography lesson that Canada was a huge country with a small population. 'A few like Faither would soon change that,' she thought.

It was towards the end of July that she saw an advertisement that was much longer than the usual ones:

158 men urgently needed Manitoba and Ontario harvest; high wages. 25 superior Britishers with £20 to earn own first fruit ranch in B.C. Conducted party Aug. 3rd. British E.T.C. Society.

'The third of August!' thought Dandy. 'That's less than two weeks away. How could folk get ready in that time? It must be meant for young men with no family, surely. The folk that are arranging it must have their passages booked, though. Maybe there's always space on these big ships. Somebody said that they were like floating cities.'

That night she positioned herself inside the scullery door in good time. She held her breath as her father's finger moved slowly down and stopped at the magic word: CANADA. She heard him give a little snort and shake his head, then he was reading across again. There was a subdued roar and, 'That's . . .' before he recollected himself, folded the paper quickly and jammed on his cap. As the door slammed behind him, Dandy emerged from the scullery. Her mother was straightening the bedclothes round Jack, who now slept at the foot of the boys' bed. 'Your father's in a hurry tonight,' Nettie said, musingly. Dandy hesitated. What would happen if she told her mother what she knew? It was difficult to know. There were pitfalls in every direction. Maybe it was better to leave her mother in ignorance. Will Baxter probably had little chance of being taken by anyone once they knew the size of his family.

'Would it be all right if I went to the cottage now, Mother?' she asked.

'Aye! Off you go. I expect your flowers are waiting for you.' Nettie smiled kindly, making Dandy feel guilty about keeping her in ignorance. She worried about it all the way to the cottage, but the sight of her 'own' garden soon washed away her worries. 'We've done a bit of dead-heading, but not much else,' said Alice. 'The blackcurrants were ready and another lot of rasps decided they liked these two wet days we had and swelled up suddenly. I've been very busy in the kitchen and Violet is enjoying herself, decorating little bonnets for the twins for when they start Sunday school.'

As Dandy started some energetic weeding it crossed her mind that that Sunday school might well be in Canada. 'I don't care what anyone says, I'm not leaving here. I'll miss May, of course, and the wee ones are quite cuddly now that they're not always wanting something. I don't suppose George and Billy would be all that bad either . . . Maybe if they'd had a father like Tom Keir, they would have been as nice as Drew and Jim. But this is where I belong. This is my garden. It's what Uncle James wanted. He knew I would never let him down. And that lovely wee bedroom upstairs is mine: it's waiting for me.' She clung to that thought as her lodestar.

She needed it in the weeks that followed. Everything happened so quickly. She had been newly in bed that night when she heard her father return, much earlier than usual. 'Is he back to his drinking?' she wondered, but no, he had managed to fit the key in the door first time. She pressed her ear against the dividing wall. It was too risky to go into the lobby. He might decide to go to the lavvie and she could be caught. His voice was muffled and he was speaking quickly. Then she heard her mother's wail, 'Oh, no! Ten days! Oh, no! We could never pack in that time. What will Mother say?'

Will's voice rose. 'We're not taking your bloody mother. This is our chance. I'm fed up being treated like dirt by that young devil . . . sitting there in the office as if he was the emperor of China. I've put up wi' his nonsense these last months because we've got to have references for Canada. Jim Spence's cousins have been helping me. They gave me that cutting a while ago. It came from Canada. Their brother's out there; says it's a land of opportunity. In some of these fruit-growing places the young boys can earn money; do our George and Billy good to put these muscles they're so proud of to some use.'

'But Dandy's determined she'll never leave here.'

'Well, she can stay. She'll get on fine wi' her grannie – they're two of a kind. She'll cut herself on that tongue of hers some day.'

'But how will I manage without my wee lassie? Oh, Will . . .'

'You've three ither wee lassies. This is our chance, Nettie. We'll never get another like it. Nancy Spence says that folks are making for Canada from all over the world. It'll no' be easy in a few years' time. So stop your girnin' and think what's worth taking with you. They say just clothes, bedlinen and tiny precious objects. Accommodation is provided. I'm off to Glasgow first thing tomorrow to see them. I hope my best shirt is ironed. I bought new shoes the other day, in case. Nancy says it is important to give a favourable impression.'

'And what will we do with all our furniture here?' Nettie's voice was rising again.

'Your mother can sell it and send us on the money.'

Nettie's sobs started then. Dandy could not make out her next remark, but it drove her father mad. 'No' take me? You'd like that, you bitch, if they didna take me. Stuck in the mud in Paisley, that's you, you and that auld bitch of a mother of yours. Now, I've got to get peace to sleep or I'll no' be ready for the morning.'

His shoes clonked down on the linoleum. Dandy felt the vibration against her ear as he heaved himself into bed. Long after his snores punctuated the darkness, she could hear her mother's stifled sobs. Dandy felt like paraphrasing one of Grannie's frequent complaints: 'Why could you not have married somebody like Mr Forbes?'

Chapter 10

Her mother's doubts about his being accepted had seemed quite reasonable to Dandy. Of course, nowadays Faither held himself proudly. When dressed for departure the morning of his interview he had looked almost distinguished, in fact. What they were looking for was superior men who were hard workers. If you didn't know better, that was just what Faither looked like. That was what he probably looked like before he started drinking so heavily. But he must have been a drinker when he was young too. Grannie always referred to her daughter's choice as 'a drunken dyer'.

Grannie for once had nothing to say when she dropped in that morning and Nettie, in a storm of tears, broke the news. Lily Jordan sat and gasped. Dandy rushed to put the kettle on for a reviving cup of tea. By the time she carried out the tray, however, Lily was in full spate. There were all the usual complaints and observations which even Billy could mimic now. The colourful additions were more interesting. 'I hear that it's that cold in winter that folk can wake up frozen to the bed. And they've got big grizzly bears that grab a wean if you turn your back. Why do you think they're asking folk to go there? If it was that wonderful they'd be trying to stop them coming. That man of yours doesn't know what to be up to next. I warned you when you took him . . .' and they were back on familiar territory.

Faither returned that night, their fate was already

141

sealed. He had signed all the papers, paid the necessary money and it was to be 'up sticks and away' on 3 August. He'd have to eat dirt for a few days at the dyeworks to make sure of his reference. 'Big Heid' would be glad to be rid of him, Will reckoned. 'He kens damn all about dyeing; just sits there counting up figures and profits. I can tie rings round him when it comes to the real work, but he ignores that. I'd like fine to spit in his eye, but I've got to have that reference for the other side. Now, you two,' he turned to George and Billy, 'you're aye boasting about your muscles. What do you think about earning some money picking apples and what do you think about owning your own ranch, eh?'

His sons looked at him uncertainly. 'Space, boys!' Will waved his arms expansively. 'Space all around you. Rivers to fish in – they say the salmon just jump out at you – plenty of swimming in the hot summer days. Snowfights in the winter; big log fires. You can use these muscles of yours to help cut up the logs. Wild berries all over the place for your mother to make jam. The Spences say that it is a land flowing with milk and honey. No more of being crushed into a pigsty like this.' He waved his arm round their kitchen, provoking a storm of tears from Nettie.

Indignation almost made Dandy forget her resolution to handle her father carefully. Pigsty indeed! What made it a pigsty? The Keirs' house was not a pigsty and it was exactly the same size. Her mother did her best but what chance had she had? There were a few things she could tell Faither but Alice's words came back to her. 'My dear, you must not count on being left in Paisley if your father chooses to go to Canada. You are still a minor and I am sure that by law he could insist on taking you. You will have to be very careful indeed if you cross him.'

142

'But he doesn't really want me.'

'I would not be too sure, my dear. You are his flesh and blood. It may be because you tend to remind him of his inadequacies as your grandmother does, that he seems to shy away from you. It is difficult for you to understand at your age, my dear, but perhaps your father longs for your approval and knows he is unlikely to receive it. That hurts a proud man. None of us is perfect, my dear. Always remember that.'

But Aunt Alice didn't know the half of it, Dandy reflected. There were some things that you did not want other folk to know, no matter how kind and understanding they were: things like Faither falling into bed in his filthy dyeworks clothes, for example. She knew that there were some things that had happened at home that Mammie didn't know she had seen; things she would never tell anyone – ever!

Then she had a flashback to Faither reading that newspaper – slow, oh so slow! Had he had a teacher like Miss Martin who had got exasperated with him? Had the other lads laughed at him behind his back? They wouldn't have dared do it to his face, not if his temper was the same in those days. Maybe that accounted for his loud-mouthed contempt for school and teachers. All his bluster never produced any results. Was he still scared of them after all these years? Maybe throwing her precious book on the fire would have been a sort of revenge when he was stuck for something else to say. He wasn't very good with words. That might explain why he swore so often. It was easier.

Aunt Alice would probably say you should pity him. It was all right for her. She hadn't had to put up with his vicious slaps all these years. Of course, if Grannie got on his nerves and she reminded him of Grannie . . . Well . . . But Alice and Violet didn't know the half of it. That day Mammie fell off the table and brought it down, they had guessed what it was all about. And later, when she was lying in Violet's bed and they thought she was asleep, she had heard them declare that she was too young to know what she knew, but she'd been a lot younger than that the time that Mammie was vomiting and roaring in pain.

It was Aunt Margaret who had happened to drop in with some of her old clothes. Come to think of it, she'd been relieved to see Aunt Margaret that time and had clung to her, begging her to make Mammie better, and Margaret, say what you like, had turned up trumps. 'Do you think you could go to Grannie's house on your own?' she had asked.

'Aye, I ken the road fine, but what about Mammie?'

'I'm looking after your mother. I want you to walk quickly to Grannie's. Don't start running in case you fall. Ask a lady to see you across the main road and then knock on Grannie's door and tell her that Aunt Margaret wants her to come. Clever girl!'

She could remember little of that journey now – except a feeling of self-importance. She knew the way to Grannie's and Aunt Margaret had treated her nearly like a grown-up. Grannie, her face purple with effort, had practically run all the way with her granddaughter, having quite a struggle to keep up while she tried to answer questions. In between times, Lily Jordan had been muttering, 'If Margaret sent for me, it's serious. She's no' the sort to fuss.'

Once in the house, Dandy had been set to keeping the younger ones quiet, but her ears had been flapping just the same. While her mother continued to retch and groan, Margaret had informed Grannie of the situation. 'One of these ignorant women told our Nettie to take a lump of caustic soda – *caustic soda*, Mother – and to encase it in butter and swallow it.'

'And has it worked?'

'Worked! Mother, it might have killed her. Look at her!'

'And we darena send for the doctor, Margaret.'

'Oh, I don't know . . .'

'No, no, no,' muttered Nettie between groans. At that point Dandy had been chased through to the parlour with the young ones. Later, Aunt Margaret had taken the four of them to her house and Grannie had stayed with Mammie. Aunt Margaret had spread blankets on the floor of the wee spare room and they had all fallen asleep there. The next day, Aunt Margaret's charwoman had watched them most of the time. Somebody had come to fetch Aunt Margaret and there was a great deal of toing and froing. They had slept on the floor another night after they had all had a bath in the big bathroom, but then Aunt Margaret had said that a surprise was waiting for them at home and Dandy was a big girl now and would be able to help Mammie with the lovely surprise. That so-called lovely surprise turned out to be two tiny babies who mewed like kittens most of the day. They were in the cradle beside Mammie's bed and Faither slept with the boys in the other bed and Grannie slept in the parlour with May and her till Mammie was strong enough to get up. That seemed to take ages, for Grannie was always saying, 'You're a big girl Dandy, could you . . .' It was fine being a big girl, but you could get too much of a good thing. It was a relief when the spring holidays were over and it was time to go back to school. At least they let you sit down there.

She brought herself back to the present with a jerk. It was as well there was no school to go to right now. Everyone had to lend a hand. The boys had even to take Jack and the twins to the park because May was busy helping Mammie with the mending. They would need all the clothes they had. Faither said that nearly all the money he earned would have to be used to pay

145

up the ranch. But he assured them that things grew easily there and they could catch fish; nobody needed to go hungry. Dandy thought of all her hard work growing the vegetables for the 'pigsty': all the work which Faither had ignored completely. He had no idea how long it took to grow enough food to feed a family their size. Poor Mammie! She had been looking so much better with no bairns to trail at her skirts. Maybe she *would* get a much better life out there, but Dandy doubted it. It had taken Grannie to make life tolerable for her in Paisley. What if Faither started drinking again over there? Mammie would be helpless with not even her eldest daughter to help her. Still, they were all growing up. Mammie had 'three ither daughters' as Faither said. May was soft, but Peggy and Jinty were active and outspoken already. And George had shot up quite a bit. Billy would do what he told him. Maybe they had absorbed enough of Tom Keir's ideas to see them right . . .

The thoughts kept whirling round as she washed bedlinen, scrubbed and polished. Nettie's pride would not let her leave a dirty house. 'Your mother and Dandy could see to that when the house is empty,' Will said. Dandy sighed with relief. Will had accepted the fact that she was staying behind: there was to be no insistence on his flesh and blood accompanying him. He could have done it out of twistedness, she thought.

'Mother will be that upset,' Nettie replied. 'She's not getting any younger. And Dandy has her garden to do.'

'Oh, aye,' said Will. 'We all know about Dandy's garden.' For a moment Dandy felt fear again. What if it crossed Faither's mind that she was the only one in the family that knew anything about gardens? He had eaten his share of the produce without ever offering a word of praise, but he had heard the others say things

146

. . . The moment passed. I'll be glad to wave them off, she reflected.

But, standing at Renfrew ferry, shielding her eyes from the hot August sun, she had an overwhelming rush of feeling for what she was losing. There was something about the majestic big ship, coming slowly, proudly, so close to the bank that you felt you could touch it. She swallowed several times. The emigrants were crowding the rails and the other spectators round about her kept getting in her way. Then she saw the little group. Nettie was crying with Jack hanging on to her, his thumb in his mouth. May was crying too. The twins were watching her and forgot to look for Dandy. George was waving furiously. Billy started to climb the rails still waving. Will hauled him back and cuffed him on the ear. George put his arm around him. The ship moved inexorably on and, funnily enough, it was her father, his long arm waving a white handkerchief, she saw last.

Dandy had expected her grandmother to be upset but it shocked her to see that stalwart figure completely broken. She looks as bad as Mammie, she thought, gulping back her own tears. It had surprised her when her aunts had said that they would accompany her grandmother and herself to see the ship go downriver. Now she blessed them for their thoughtfulness. Alice was supporting Lily Jordan, while Violet had her arm round Dandy's shoulders. She leaned down to whisper and the waft of her perfume was comforting somehow. 'Your Aunt Alice bespoke a cab, my dear. We thought your grandmother would find this an ordeal.'

'Won't that cost a lot of money, all the way to Paisley?'

'This is no day for cheeseparing, my dear.'

Dandy remembered her uncle's words: 'A lady

147

matches her behaviour to the occasion.' How apt they were! Nothing else could have been so helpful as being bundled into the privacy of a cab and clip-clopping along the dusty road all the way to the cottage, that oasis of peace and beauty. They sat in the little conservatory. As always, Dandy found tranquillity in the sight of her flowers. Lily Jordan was much restored by being treated as a lady and noting how comfortably Dandy settled in to this way of life. She congratulated herself. 'I always said she would learn nothing but good from these two and I was right.'

Grannie's bed was big and it stood in the middle of the bedroom. The bathroom was big, too, but Dandy's dreams of hot scented baths were shattered. Grannie had no intention of burning coal for hot water in the summer time. A big kettle, boiled up on the gas ring, was enough to give anyone a good wash down, so Grannie thought. She could take the basin into the bathroom and stand in the bath if she liked but that was little improvement on the parlour at home, Dandy reflected. A wash down had always been possible there once the twins were asleep and May turned her face to the wall. In justice, she had to admit that Grannie was probably hard up and had to be careful with her pennies. Nobody was paying her for looking after her granddaughter. She would have to see that Grannie got plenty vegetables and jam fruit. That was the best she could do for the present.

The big bed was not the luxury she imagined, either. Every night Grannie started crying and bemoaning the fate of her 'Poor Wee Nettie'. As the sobs lessened, she returned to the old refrain that left Dandy near to screaming. Her last murmurs before the snores started were always about a 'drunken dyer'. And those snores! They made the wee lamp on the wall near the bed vibrate. Dandy could hear it. The twins, once asleep, had certainly wriggled a bit, but they never snored. May was so peaceful in sleep that she looked like marble. Dandy had to remind herself many times that if it hadn't been for that selfsame grannie's support, she would have been bundled off to Canada with the rest of them.

One thing she had never known about Grannie was that she had *a stomach*. It surprised her that she had never found this out till she reflected that Grannie had never actually sat down for a meal in their house – a cup of tea, yes. But a meal, no. Having *a stomach* did not stop Grannie eating the things she liked, but it meant having frequent recourse to a big bottle of white stuff she called 'Bishy Magneesha'. Grannie was a good cook too, but the contrast between meals served by the McLarens and those in Grannie's flat was unbelievable. Even when they had lived in the flat and had the simplest of food, her aunts had sat down together; Aunt Alice would say a brief grace and they would calmly lift their cutlery. Grannie, on the other hand, slammed the food on to the plates, stuck Dandy's portion in front of her with an admonition to get started and she would catch up when she had given the pots a doing. 'It's aye better to get the rough off them while they're fresh.'

When she joined Dandy at table she invariably managed to bump her chair against the nearest leg. Sometimes it was the table that suffered: other times it was Dandy. Then came the pepper – in clouds! Dandy soon came to the conclusion that her grandmother could not taste food that wasn't poisoned with pepper. 'Maybe that's what makes her aye short-tempered,' she mused between sneezes.

There had been vague talk about her going to a different school in September – one nearer Grannie's house – but everyone had been so caught up in the rush of preparation that the matter had not been pursued. Nor had Dandy encouraged any discussion. She had a secret plan forming. It was daring and it would be a miracle if it succeeded, but miracles *did* happen. The Bible said so, didn't it? Sometimes there was an explanation for them, like Uncle James switching the books. Maybe there was really an explanation for all the miracles. Or did that stop them being miracles?

Her secret plan ran along these lines. None of the family would be back at school. Though some of the neighbours knew that Dandy was staying with her grannie, they would think she had just changed schools and none of them would be likely to be quizzed by the education authorities, anyway. It would be assumed that the tribe of Baxters had gone to Canada and that would be that. She was tall for her age. Aunt Alice kept saying that she seemed so much older than she really was. If she stuffed her bodice with something, she could pretend she was fourteen and get a job. One of the newspapers that Faither had been studying had told of a new works department being built at the Anchor Thread Mills. That surely meant they would be looking for workers. Of course, she knew nothing about the thread mills. It was a pity there was so little time. Drew Keir might be able to give her some information.

She had asked questions in a casual way, but without much success. Drew seemed to know very little and was obviously not very interested. She couldn't really blame him for that.

'They all have to work hard, Da says. Nowadays it's a five and a half day week, fifty-five hours, but he reckons that's long enough for some of the women.'

'How do they start?' asked Dandy. 'I mean, what sort of job do they learn at the beginning?'

'Oh, nothing very interesting, I think. I know they need lots of young sweepers. There's always so much fluff flying around and I suppose it would gum up the machines. Da says he's sorry for some of the young ones when he sees them choking on the stuff, but they seem to make their own fun; "monkeying about", he calls it. Wouldn't suit me!'

'What would you like to do, Drew?'

'Marine engineering,' he said crisply. Drew Keir knew his own mind. Dandy had no doubt that he would be a marine engineer in due course.

Her plan would not be divulged to Grannie, who would be sure to bugger it up. Hastily, Dandy amended the words of her thought. Grannie would spoil things. Yes! That would be a more acceptable expression for her aunties. She was shaking off the background that had limited her for so long. She would learn all she could from these aunties, now it was so much easier to visit them. It was amazing how often they bumped into Grannie in the shops and invited her round for coffee or tea while Dandy got on with her gardening.

These happy spells almost wiped out the misery of Grannie's snores from which there seemed to be no escape. And Grannie's feet! Dandy supposed that she had always known that Grannie hirpled a bit, but she had assumed it was because she was always in a hurry. She soon learned that Lily Jordan was a martyr to her feet. Every night without fail she sat down in the big chair by the fire and, with many a groan, stuck her feet in a basin of hot water with an aspirin in it. Her feet were horrible; there was no other word for it – all bony lumps and twists and blue veins. Dandy had never thought much about Grannie's age before, but her feet were certainly a lot older than the rest of her. She supposed she should feel pity: those feet had run after Mammie and her wild tribe of weans for many a year but somehow all she could feel was disgust. She wished Grannie would take her basin to the bedroom. Yet that

151

wasn't really fair. It was Grannie's house. She averted her eyes and tried to think of something else.

The letter which came from Coventry suddenly jerked Grannie out of her misery.

Surely now that Nettie's gone you could manage to visit us! The children don't know their Grannie and Hugh will never bother to go up to Paisley. Rents are that high here and we're saving to buy our own house. He spends all his time in the garden or the allotment. You could bring Dandy with you, though that would mean going back in time for school. Maybe she could stay with her cousin Betty – they're not much different in age, after all, and you would know she was all right there. Do think about it, Mother. I've nearly forgotten what you look like. While Nettie was in such a fix I didn't like to say too much. I only hope that awful man of hers pulls his socks up in Canada.

Don't we all? thought Dandy. Her brain was racing. She didn't want to go to bloody Coventry: she wanted to go to her own room at the cottage. This was her chance. She would have to think quickly, say the right thing. Everything depended on it.

'Fancy the wee ones not knowing you, Grannie, and we used to see you umpteen times a week. It doesn't seem fair. You must go. The aunties would love to have me, I'm sure. It's not as if they can't afford to feed me. They depend on me for the garden and I would be near enough to check up on your house while you are away and wash the stairs when it's your turn. It will do you the world of good. Aunt Jean's right. You've spent all your time helping Mammie. She certainly couldn't have done without you, but this is your chance to have a wee holiday and meet your other grandchildren.'

Had she overdone it? Would Grannie realize she was

being manipulated? She watched carefully. Various expressions flitted over Lily Jordan's face. 'Aye . . . Aye, the McLarens would see you right. I'd forgotten about the stairs. That's important. I wouldna like to be beholden to any of them – not but what they're nice neighbours – still, it would be better if you were there, just round the corner. Maybe I'll go. D'you think you could write to your Aunt Jean for me? I'm out o' the habit. Just say I'll come. Oh, we'll need to see about trains, and I'll need to go to the bank first. Oh, there's that many things . . .'

'But I'm here to help you, Grannie. We can go to the station together. I'll write the letter while you get ready and then we can put in the train time after we've been to the station. How would that do?'

'Aye. Aye. But I've my clothes to get ready. That'll take time.'

'I'm sure your things are always ready, Grannie, cleaned and pressed. You won't need to take too many because you can wash things at Aunt Jean's.'

'Aye, there's that!' Grannie suddenly exploded into action. 'Just you get on with that letter. Then we'll away to the bank and the station. There's nae time to waste.'

Everything seems to happen in a hurry nowadays, thought Dandy. For years, nothing but dreary house-work, and then, all of a sudden, meeting Uncle James, getting the garden, Faither giving everybody ten days to get ready for Canada. What next? She had to school her expression. It would not do for Grannie to see how thrilled she was at the thought of going to stay at the cottage in her own room at last. Life was funny. Wasn't it especially funny that the remark that had made up Grannie's mind for her was the one about washing the stairs. Her aunties would laugh at that one. There were lots of things her aunties would laugh at. They would have time to talk, really talk, when she didn't have to hurry home. There was one very important piece of information which she hadn't passed on to the aunties, mainly because she wasn't sure how to frame it. And she didn't want Grannie putting her foot in it either. Definitely not!

That particular piece of information had been one of the most cheering in her life and yet it was surrounded with embarrassment. The others who knew were safely away to Canada, but if Grannie opened her mouth . . . It was better not to think of it while Grannie was around. She had the uncanny knack of sensing what was in your mind – or maybe it was because you were trying to hide something . . . Anyway, Grannie would soon be gone. She could lie in her bonnie wee room at the cottage and think it out.

It took all the tact and ingenuity she could muster to get Grannie organized and safely on her journey. Once or twice there had been little hiccups, threats of a change of mind when Grannie had said, 'I hate leaving you. Nettie put you in my charge and you're all I've got to remind me of her . . .' Things like that had to be circumvented by cheerful remarks like, 'But I'll be here when you come back, Grannie, and you can tell me all about my cousins in Coventry. They probably speak funny. We'll get many a laugh together in bed at night.'

And that would be a big change, she silently added.

Aunt Alice came to the station with her to see Grannie off. 'My sister would have come too, Mrs Jordan, but she has a big cake in the oven and wanted to keep an eye on it.'

'Aye! Eggs are dear. You don't want to waste them,' said Lily in her practical way. 'It's kind of you to come. I wouldn't have liked leaving the wee one on her own.'

'Not such a wee one now, Mrs Jordan,' laughed Alice. 'We think she's quite a young lady.' She couldn't have said anything more comforting – or more likely to be quoted – to Lily Jordan.

Later, as they left the station, Dandy remarked, 'I do appreciate it, you know, you coming, I mean. I was scared Grannie might change her mind at the last minute.'

'Yes,' agreed Alice, 'there was always that possibility, but it didn't happen. Let's hope she enjoys her holiday and seeing her other grandchildren. We shall certainly enjoy having you with us. Now, remember, I can't walk so fast as you can! Can you manage to pick up your belongings from Grannie's flat or would you like help?'

'Oh, no, I packed my case when Grannie was blethering to a neighbour. I haven't really got all that much . . .'

'No, and if you've forgotten anything it's only a step or two round the corner. When we get there, I'll walk on and there will be a cup of tea for you as soon as you arrive.'

Dandy's step was jaunty as she swung her light suit-case. 'A cup of tea waiting for me when I arrive. Fancy me . . . getting looked after as if I was important. I think I really *am* important to them. I wonder why they picked me and not May. She always behaved better. Of course, she was too wee. I was the oldest. And I like books, just as they do. I feel so happy. Maybe I shouldn't, with Mammie and them all away . . . but I suppose this is what people feel when they're going on holiday. We never had holidays.'

The bedroom felt exactly as she had always dreamed it would. It was hers, hers alone and it was fairyland. All these flowers . . . brightness . . . peace . . . and the books! What would a wet day matter if there were all these books? And she had that wonderful piece of infor-mation she would love to impart to the aunties. But Grannie would be back . . . it was better to keep it to herself meantime. She brought back the scene that had made all the difference. Faither had opened the tin box where the rent book and things like that were kept. 'I'll need all their birth certificates, Nettie, for the authorities. There's a thousand things it seems . . .'

'You'll not need Dandy's.'

'No. Here, lass. You take care o' that and keep it safe at your grannie's. You'll need it when you get mairried . . .'

He had barked a laugh when Dandy said, 'I'll never get married.'

'Naw! you'd scare any man.'

The paper was tightly folded. Dandy opened it carefully. 'Lily Jordan,' she read. 'This isn't mine,' she said. 'It's Grannie's – Lily Jordan.'

'Your grannie wasna born in 1894, you daftie. You're called after her, and took her sharp tongue wi' her name,' he added.

'Why do you all call me "Dandy" then?'

'That was a laugh! Remember, Nettie?'

He turned to his wife, his blue eyes twinkling and for the first time in her life Dandy got a glimpse of the attraction that must have been between her parents.

Nettie was smiling fondly back at him. 'Aye, it was like this, pet. Your Grandpa Baxter was at your christening. Your other grannie was dead by that time – she died not long after we were married. He was dandling you on his knee and all of a sudden . . .' She laughed helplessly. Faither with his arm round her was laughing too.

'What happened?' asked Dandy.

'Well, he jumped up, holding you out at arm's length. He was soaking. You had wet him, you see, and he said, "Lily, b'Goad. Dandelion, mair like." '

'Aye and it was the good suit he had bought for our wedding,' added Faither. 'After that, every time he visited us he would ask how Dandelion was and I would say, "Fine and Dandy." I suppose it just got shortened. Wee George picked it up when *he* was learning to speak and you were "Dandy" from then on.'

She had envied Aunt Violet her name. Somehow she had never thought of Grannie's. Of course, no one ever called Grannie by her first name. Aunt Violet had said something once about her looking like a lily. Now she knew she had a right to be called that.

'LILY JORDAN BAXTER,' she whispered it slowly. It sounded a lot better than 'Dandy Baxter' – a hundred times better. But even though the aunties were so loving and kind, somehow she would not like them to know how she got her nickname. It was not ladylike. If it weren't for the danger of Grannie letting the cat out of the bag, she could say that her father had the habit of saying she was fine and Dandy when Grandpa Baxter asked after her. That was quite true. That wouldn't be telling a lie. But if Mammie found it funny to tell what she as a baby had done to Grandpa, so would Grannie. She had better say nothing, yet.

Chapter 11

The housework in the cottage seemed to get done so easily and quickly. Of course, the cleaning lady came to do the floors and windows. There didn't seem to be as much dust as there had been in the flat. She had remarked on that in the garden one day. 'Well, all the trees and plants absorb a lot of it,' Aunt Violet had said.

'So they're useful as well as beautiful,' Dandy had mused.

'Of course. They give off oxygen too. That's why we feel so well after a walk in the country.'

'Aunt Alice and you know so many things. Were you at school for a long time?'

'We weren't at school at all, my dear. We had governesses – I mean, one governess at a time. They taught us at home. And a music teacher came in too.'

'So you wouldn't have silly boys interrupting the class with their nonsense and the teacher would be able to help you all the time.'

'Well, I never thought of it that way, but I suppose you are right. We always felt that her eye was upon us constantly and wished sometimes for the freedom of school as we saw it.'

'That's funny,' said Dandy.

'Yes. Things *do* look different from different angles, I suppose.'

'Aunt Alice and you teach me better than any schoolteacher could.'

'Oh, I wouldn't say that. You are keen on learning

and have a quick intelligence, my dear. It is just that in a classroom of forty pupils your teachers have not had the time to give to individuals.'

'Aye, and I wasn't always there,' said Dandy.

'No. Still, you make up for that with all your reading. Now, I must go in and see about our lunch. Alice is polishing silver – a job I hate. She says she simply thinks of other more interesting things. My sister has a strong mind. Don't tackle too much. Lunch will be ready in ... let me see ... sixteen minutes.'

And Dandy knew that that was a fact. Lunch would be on the table in sixteen minutes. Aunt Violet had said so. No baby would have to be changed; nobody would knock anything over and spill things that had to be swept up; nobody would decide that they wanted to go to the lavvie and couldn't find the key because somebody had forgotten to put it back. Nothing like that would happen. Aunt Violet would have the big oven dishes cooking gently in the range. The plates would be warming on the rack above. The table would be beautifully set with a tiny posy of flowers in the middle. The silver cutlery would be gleaming. Nobody would gobble the food. When the meal was over the aunts would take their coffee cups out into the garden or the conservatory. Dandy would have delicious lemonade and peace to drink it without someone jogging her elbow. This was what life should be like. She hoped that Grannie enjoyed Coventry and stayed there for a long time. Meantime she had less than sixteen minutes to get on with the weeding.

The footstep on the path jolted her. 'Surely it's not that time,' she started to say, then turning, was taken aback to see her cousin Betty approaching. Her face was funny – stiff and important. 'Dandy, you've to come in. Mother has something to tell you.'

Dandy stared. What could Aunt Margaret have to tell

her? Aunt Margaret never said much to her at all. Aunt Margaret was what they called a socialite. Seemingly that meant she went out visiting a lot and didn't have much to say to the family. What information could Aunt Margaret have that Betty couldn't tell her? Then it struck her: the ship! The ship must have gone down. But it couldn't – it was huge!

'What's wrong?' she asked.

'I've not to tell you. You've to come in,' said Betty primly.

For a moment, Dandy was tempted to try one of the tactics she would have used on George in a similar situation, then remembered that she was trying to behave like her aunties. She threw down her gardening gloves, whirled round and ran, leaving Betty lumbering behind.

'I suppose I could take her, but it's an expensive fare,' Aunt Margaret was saying in that drawly voice of hers.

'We should pay her fare happily,' said Aunt Alice, 'if she wishes to go, but I feel the child has already had too many upheavals and needs a little continuity and peace.'

'Exactly,' drawled Aunt Margaret as Dandy hurried in.

Alice came to her quickly, putting a hand on her shoulder. 'My dear, your aunt has had some rather sad news . . .'

Dandy stared at her Aunt Margaret, whose face was puckered in a rather comical expression. There was a pause while neither of them said anything. Then, 'It's your grannie, Dandy. I got a telegram from your Aunt Jean. Grannie took a stroke. I'm afraid . . .' she fished out a handkerchief.

Dandy continued staring. Alice's hand tightened on her shoulder. 'Your grannie is dead, Dandy, my dear.

160

That is what your aunt has come to say. She will be going to the funeral in Coventry. If you wish, you can go too. It is your decision, but I do not think it would be wise.'

'No. A funeral is no place for a child. Betty isn't going,' Margaret hastened to add.

Dandy said nothing, stunned by sudden guilt. She had been wishing that Grannie would stay in Coventry for a long time. Grannie often knew what was going on in your mind. But Grannie was tough. If she thought you wanted her to stay away, she wouldn't. 'She was fine when we saw her off.' Her voice trembled.

'Yes, indeed,' said Aunt Alice. 'But it is the nature of strokes, my dear, that they happen suddenly – often to people who are excitable. Your grandmother had had quite a shock at the departure of your mother.' She turned to Aunt Margaret. 'It is a good thing your sister was with her – her eldest daughter, I believe.'

'Oh, yes, Jean's very capable. The wire said that a letter would be following, so we'll find out all about it then. Well, Dandy? I don't think you should go and Miss McLaren agrees with me.'

Why did her Aunt Margaret get her back up, Dandy wondered. This time, however, it was quite useful. She didn't want to go a long way to a miserable funeral. It had been bad enough going to Uncle James's. Grannie was a busy, busy person – not a strange corpse in a coffin. 'You probably know best, Aunt Margaret,' she responded, as meekly as that lady could have wished. Then a thought struck her. 'Mammie won't know ... won't know for ages.'

'Perhaps that is a good thing,' said Aunt Alice. 'It would not do for her to be grieving when she is unable to go to the funeral. By the time she reaches Canada she will have made new friends, probably going to the same place. There will be countless things to do, new places to see, and your brothers and sisters are becoming more independent all the time, remember. Your mother will not need so much help.'

Mammie was the sort who would always need help. Dandy knew that in her bones. That was why she should never have married 'a drunken dyer'. But maybe he seemed nice and helpful then . . . She shook her head. She was getting to be as bad as Grannie. Oh, that was an awful thing to think, and Grannie just dead! Would Aunt Alice think she was odd, not crying? She didn't really feel like crying. Maybe she would later. There had been enough crying with all the getting ready for Canada. What was it Aunt Alice had said that she needed? 'A little continuity and peace.' Yes, that was it. Aunt Alice understood perfectly.

And having seen Aunt Margaret off the premises it was Alice who thought up the idea that they should go to the station the next day and see that lady off. 'If you pick your choicest rosebuds, Dandy, we could pack them carefully in moss, then wrap the parcel in silk – it breathes, you see. That tiny little basket with the lid would not be difficult for Aunt Margaret to manage; she is being met at the station at the other end. If you write a little loving message, we could wrap it in waxed paper to go on the top of the basket. What do you think of that?'

'It's . . . it's . . . perfect,' said Dandy, bursting into tears.

Alice edged her to the big armchair and held her in her arms, murmuring softly. The sobs grew louder. Dandy didn't know why. Aunt Violet came through from the kitchen.

'It's all right, Violet,' Alice said. 'She's been holding this back for long enough and this is the right time and place to get rid of it.'

*   *   *

It was peaceful in the big armchair with Aunt Alice. Dandy didn't feel like speaking. Her throat was sore for one thing with all that crying. She had been there for ages but the best thing was that she could feel that she wasn't expected to talk, just to have a little peace and continuity, as Aunt Alice put it. Violet was baking again. It was surprising how much time she spent doing that. Cousin Betty would have nothing to sneer about any longer. She had seen all the wonderful things that surrounded 'poor Dandy' now. But she hadn't seen the most wonderful thing of all. Only very special people would see her beautiful bedroom. Who, for example? She cudgelled her brains. There weren't really all that many in her life. Then she recalled the Forbes family. Yes, Madge would like her beautiful room and Mr Forbes' 'lady wife' would appreciate her garden, even though it was not a patch on theirs. Perhaps Miss Bell, if she came on business, and wasn't being too talkative . . .

She stirred herself. 'I left my gardening gloves on the ground, I think, and the weeding wasn't finished . . .'

'Well, perhaps you should get on with it while the weather is fine. It is getting dark earlier in the evenings already. James always said that you had to be diligent in a garden: the weeds were unmerciful and would delight in getting the better of you. Off you go!'

Alice sat on with her chin in her hands. After a few minutes, Violet wandered through. 'Couldn't you have stopped her, Alice? I'm sure she's not fit to be working like that.'

'Stop her! I chased her out. Best thing for her!' She paused. 'I hope I'm right, Violet.'

Dandy seemed to have recovered by the time she set off, accompanied by both aunts, for the station next morning. 'We thought it was time our gardener had a treat,' said Violet. 'We are going to have lunch in a restaurant. What do you think of that, my dear?'

163

Dandy stuttered a little, 'But isn't it silly . . . I mean, you make such nice things . . . lunch in the cottage is wonderful.'

Violet had to swallow hard. 'It's good of you to say so, dear, but don't you think it will be nice to have a menu to choose from instead of simply eating what we put in front of you? I'm looking forward to having a chance to choose and having it brought to me.'

'Of course,' said Dandy quickly, 'you're always cooking, Aunt Violet. It will be lovely for you and I always feel happy anyway when I'm with you. I can't imagine what it is like. I've never been in a restaurant. Won't the other people know and laugh at me?'

'Nonsense! It will be rather like visiting the Forbes family, remember? All the nice things were handed to us without our having to do anything. And it will be very pleasant for Alice and me to have you with us – quite a little party.'

Dandy turned to regard Alice, who had remained silent throughout the exchange. 'Alice is thinking of how she will handle your Aunt Margaret, I think,' said Violet.

Dandy grinned widely. 'I bet you win, Aunt Alice.'

Aunt Margaret was surprised and none too happy to be handed the little basket. 'I've got far too much stuff already,' she muttered.

'You *are* being met at the station, I understand,' said Alice McLaren. 'There are sure to be porters on hand to carry the heavy things. Dandy grew those roses herself. A lot of loving work went into them, I can assure you.'

'Of course,' said Margaret, knowing she was beaten. 'Have you had details . . . ?'

'Oh, yes. Here! I've got the letter with me. Take it and read it to Dandy later.'

164

'You *are* kind,' said Alice, tucking the letter into her old-fashioned handbag.

Dandy found it difficult to look suitably solemn as she waved her aunt off on her sad journey. She was going to a restaurant. There would be a menu. She could eat what she liked. In a dream she walked slowly up the High Street, Aunt Margaret forgotten. A restaurant!

Somehow or other she found that her arm was tucked in Violet's and Aunt Alice was consulting the head waitress. All round her were tables decked in snowy damask. Little silver vases held their quota of carnations. 'A wee bit stiff,' thought Dandy. 'I prefer Aunt Violet's little pansies and rosebuds but I suppose carnations will keep better in the heat.' The waitresses walking smoothly here and there had snowy starched aprons and funny little starched hats on their heads. They'll need a lot of pins to keep these on, she thought. Then they were being shown to their table.

The knives and forks were huge. There were umpteen shining things at each plate. She would never know which she was meant to use. If she just watched which ones her aunts picked up it would be easy. She mustn't panic. She had dreaded her visit to the Forbes family and look how easy that had turned out.

The big menu was very spaced out. The choice made her feel quite dizzy. Alice didn't take too long to make up her mind. 'I think I'll have oxtail soup followed by salmon mayonnaise,' she said. Violet was undecided. 'What do you fancy, Dandy?' Alice asked.

'Ooh, I don't know. They all look marvellous.' Her brain was working furiously. It was the sweet course that dazzled her, but Aunt Alice hadn't chosen anything from there. Perhaps ladies didn't eat puddings in restaurants. She hesitated, then blurted out, 'There's so many nice puddings.'

'Yes, aren't there,' said Alice. 'It's a good thing we

165

don't have to order them till we've had our main course. I don't know what I'll feel ready for by that time. You like most things, Dandy. Why not try the same as I am having?'

'Yes,' said Dandy, relieved. After that it was unalloyed bliss as course succeeded course. Then Alice was turning to her. 'Would you like to have your lemonade here or in the conservatory at home?'

Dandy hesitated only a moment. The aunts always put their feet up comfortably while they were sipping their coffee. They couldn't do that here.

'It would be nice at home,' she said.

Dandy insisted on making the coffee when they got back. It had never occurred to her before how much they would miss being waited on, brought up as they had been. 'This is a treat,' said Alice when the tray arrived. 'Now, as soon as you are settled, you can read us that letter. I've laid it beside your place.'

'Aunt Margaret said *you* were to read it to *me*.'

'I can't think why, can you? Is *her* daughter not very bright?'

Dandy, laughing, did not see the congratulatory wink that passed from Violet to Alice.

Aunt Jean's writing sprawled all over the page, but she was excited, of course. You had to allow for that. Dandy said, 'I'll skip the bits she's written about meeting Aunt Margaret at the station and things like that. Here's the important stuff.

She tucked in heartily to that dinner. I thought she would have been tired after the long journey but, oh, she never stopped talking. In between bites we got all the old stories which I'm sure you've heard before about Nettie throwing herself away on a drunken dyer. Then she has such a funny idea of Canada; thinks that they'll all be eaten by grizzly

166

bears. That's why they have to keep sending for more people, she thinks. They just get eaten up. It took us all our time not to laugh. Our wee Duncan was choking. Then Charlie, who's big enough to know better, excused himself from table and went off and brought a book he has – one of these lurid adventure books that boys seem to revel in. There was a picture of an enormous bear crushing the baddie to death. That convinced her she was right, of course. She went on and on till we were fed up trying to talk her out of it. Mind you, it didn't stop her asking for a second helping of trifle. The boys were groaning because they had been counting on eating up what was left. She certainly hasn't lost her appetite. Oh, what am I saying, Margaret! Poor mother. She always did her best for us and I'm sure she slaved after Nettie. She *did* say that Dandy is a great wee worker. It's not often she admits that about anyone. I thought it was funny that the wee one hadn't gone with the rest, but Mother seemed to approve. She sounds an odd wee thing, Dandy. Where was I? Oh, yes, she went up to bed as soon as her coffee was finished – seemed tired all of a sudden. I'm ashamed to say we were glad to see her go, never thinking, of course. In the morning I took her up an early cup of tea. She always woke at the crack of dawn in the old days. I knocked before going in, but she never answered. When I opened the door . . . oh, Margaret, she was sort of half hanging out of the bed and her eyes were staring at me. I nearly dropped the tray. I really haven't stopped shaking since, but there were so many things to do. I never wear black but mother was so strict about funeral dress I had to start thinking about all the details. Well, we'll be able to talk when this sad business is over. It will be nice for me to have one of you with me. I just wish Nettie could have been there too.

'Am I an odd wee thing?'

'Oh, yes, without a doubt,' said Alice. 'You put up with us for one thing . . .' Dandy grinned uncertainly. It was unbelievable that Grannie, so strong, so positive, should be puffed away like that. Yet she didn't feel like crying again – she had cried all she could. She *must* be an odd wee thing. Or maybe she was just tough, like Grannie. But Alice was going on, 'I think your aunts are cast in your mother's mould. They probably take after their father. You are a much stronger character, more like your grandmother and, perhaps, dare I say it, your father.'

'I'm not like Faither!' Dandy was indignant.

'My dear, you got his lovely yellow hair and his tall slender build. Is it so unlikely that you inherit some of his characteristics?'

'What ones, Aunt Alice? What do you mean?'

'Well, my dear, you have just shown one, I think . . . your quick response to a slight. You almost put your fists up. No, my dear, I am teasing, but think of it this way. We are all shaped by the people who deal most closely with us. From what I have deduced, your father was by far the youngest of his family. The older children would indulge him. His mother, being that little bit older, would have the gentleness of a grandmother . . .'

'My grandmother wasn't gentle.'

'Not with the baby? Little Jack?'

'Well . . . sometimes . . . but she wasn't gentle with the rest of us.'

'That was because she was defending her own child, your mother. If you think of it, Dandy, all her fierceness arose out of a desire to help her daughter.'

'Aye, you're right there, Aunt Alice.'

'To return to your father. I gather that he was an exceptionally handsome boy; wilful, probably. He left his home for Paisley at quite an early age, whereas his brothers stayed on in Govan and seem to have led contented lives. Of course, I am only judging by things your grandmother said when she visited us here now and again. What I am trying to get over to you, Dandy, is the thought that our characters are shaped by others and we must be aware of this. Sometimes we have to guard against an undue influence when it could harm us. Your father would probably have benefited from a firmer mother. There! That's enough lecturing for one day. It was pleasant having a meal out for a change, but isn't it nice to be home!'

Dandy looked out at 'her' garden and breathed a fervent, 'Yes, isn't it.'

'You know, Dandy, we'll have to think of enrolling you at school. Or would you rather keep on at your old one where you have friends?'

'No,' said Dandy, pausing, 'I'd rather not think of it just yet.'

'Dandy has had an upset,' said Violet, as near to admonishing her sister as she could get.

They think it's Grannie I'm worrying about, thought Dandy. I'll let them think that. She had her own ideas and it was time to put them into operation. The Anchor Thread Mills must need workers or they wouldn't have built their new Works Department that the newspaper talked about. It was time she contributed something to these aunts and it would be best to get everything fixed up herself for they would certainly raise objections. How could she manage things without arousing suspicion?

Next morning she was out bright and early working in her garden. It was a good place to think things out. Problems never seemed so insurmountable when the birds were singing round about and the sweet scents catching you unaware as you turned a bend in the path. She could say that she would like to follow the Espedair Burn, even though it was smelly and therefore avoided by her aunts. It would give her an excuse to wander off on her own. She could work her way round to the thread mills by cutting through the East End Park. Yes! That was the answer.

The burn was sluggish and discoloured and it was no sacrifice to leave it behind. She had tidied herself up a bit when she stopped for her mid-morning cup of tea. The worktaker at the mill wouldn't expect her to be dressed too well. In her roomiest blouse with a light shawl draped round her shoulders, her augmented figure was safe from Aunt Alice's sharp dressmaking eyes. She would have to sound confident . . . old enough. On the other hand she mustn't speak like Aunt Alice. She didn't want to draw attention to herself. She reminded herself of some of Alice's remarks. She seemed much older than her age: she was a strong character. Yes, Aunt Alice had said things like that, but what would she say when she went back to the cottage to announce that she was a mill-worker? They were so kind but, really, it wasn't fair to sponge on them, and the only job she had a hope of getting without too much trouble and danger of being found out *was* in the thread mills. So! She would be strong and speak up clearly. The sooner she got it over with, the better.

The red brick building was very new and alien some-how. She marched in erect. The doorman was not impressed. 'Can I see the worktaker?' she asked.

He eyed her up and down in a surly fashion. 'Don't think it'll do you any good. I think he's got all he needs.' Then, seeing that she stood her ground, he pointed along the passageway. 'Try that door there. Ask for Mr Sorbie.'

Mr Sorbie was a fidgety, impatient-looking man. 'I'm just standing in. I don't know what he sent you to me for. What age are you?'

'Fourteen,' said Dandy, confidently.

'What have you done before?'

'I've just left school.' That was true enough. 'But I'm strong and I'm good at counting,' she added.

'Well, this is no' the counting house. I heard them say that they were short of sweepers. I shouldna ... but, here, I'll risk it. The sweepers are always leaving anyway,' he muttered, as if to assure himself.

The note he gave her was not impressive, but it was her passport to independence. Dandy folded it carefully and tucked it in the pocket of her skirt. Now to tell her benefactors that she would be starting work early on Monday morning.

It was worse than she expected. The aunts gaped at her in horror. 'The thread mills?' gasped Violet.

'Whatever possessed you?' said Alice. 'You who love your garden – to work in a dusty unhealthy mill. Dandy, my dear, if it was money you wanted you had only to ask. You seemed quite happy to us – we never thought you might like to have more ...'

'It's not that!' Dandy was shocked. 'It's the opposite. You've given me so much and now that Grannie's dead and I'm living with you all the time ... Don't you see, I want to pay my way.'

'We've never thought you owed us anything, my dear, and your schooling is so important.'

'But you can teach me all the things they teach at school. There's so much time wasted, waiting for the slow readers and things like that ...'

Alice looked at the scarlet face and the hint of tears. She took a deep breath. 'Well, my dear, we are certainly willing to help you all we can in those ways: you are such an apt pupil – but why the thread mills? They work very hard there, I'm told. Some of the older women look really careworn.'

'Where else would I get by with my age and all that? If I go to a shop some of the folk from my school might see me. I could be reported. The Anchor Mills are far enough from the old place . . . I don't think anyone will notice me.'

'Well, my dear, since you have gone to the trouble of an interview I suppose you had better try the job. But do remember that if you do not like the place, we are here and very happy to have you living with us. Goodness me, if we paid you for all the gardening you do we would be in the poorhouse!' This brought the chuckle she had hoped for from Dandy.

In spite of their disapproval, the aunts tried to make Dandy's entrance into the world of work as easy as possible. 'There may be a canteen for the workers,' said Alice. 'I know you didn't think of asking, my dear, but there would be no harm in taking a picnic lunch. Aunt Violet is an expert in that department, you'll agree.'

'Oh, yes,' said Dandy. 'I loved our picnic lunches when the builders were here.'

'It may be, too, that you will long for a little peace and quiet after the noise of the machinery . . . We shall be anxious to hear how you get on in any case and, remember, there is no need for you to do this. If you are at all unhappy about it, let us know and that will be the finish of it.'

Chapter 12

Their words were ringing in Dandy's ears as she stepped out for work in the early morning light. It was difficult to know what to expect – much worse than a new teacher at school! And she would have to be careful what she said to the other girls in case they guessed her age and gave her away. Still, she had learned from Aunt Alice to think carefully before she spoke. It had worked often with Grannie and had ensured her visits to her beloved garden. Her garden! Yes, that was a pity – only to see it at night time . . . well, early evening . . .

Her steps slowed a little when she came in sight of the imposing new building. The paper in her pocket rustled reassuringly when she pressed it. It said she was engaged to present herself for work. Funny that – the surly little man would surely never put it like that normally. It must be something they taught them at the mill. She was going to learn a new language. What would the girls be like? Cousin Betty? No, she wouldn't go out to work in a mill. She would probably get a nice little job in her father's dull office, making the tea for the clerks and things like that. She tried to think of the older girls who had lived in the nearby tenements, but it was difficult. She had always been too embroiled in work for her own family to join the groups chattering in doorways. What would they talk about? Clothes?

Aunt Violet had taught her quite a bit about sewing, but would these girls have time for sewing after a long day at the mill? What *would* interest them? She could tell them about her flowers. But Grannie had not been interested in flowers. Cousin Betty was not interested in flowers. Was she, Dandy Baxter, as the letter had said, 'an odd wee thing'?

Her smile was not answered as she handed over her note. 'Aye, you're on the list. Along that corridor, second door on the left – ask for Miss Meikie. When ah say "ask", ah mean shout or you'll never be heard.' Dandy's spirits were not raised by the last bit of information. Was she to spend all day shouting and being shouted at? Was she mad, leaving her lovely garden with the birds singing . . . ? Aunt Alice had seemed genuinely surprised that she should want to pay her way. Maybe that was an insulting thought to them. Maybe true ladies didn't think like that. But how else could she show her appreciation? They had said that she saved money for them by doing the garden. Well, maybe that was true but they knew that she would have done anybody's garden for nothing. Gardening wasn't work – not *real* work. It was . . . oh, she couldn't think . . . She was at the door. The noise told her that it would be no use knocking.

The heavy door needed all her weight to budge it on its huge hinges. The sudden surge in volume rocked her. No wonder he had told her to shout! A group of women clustered at the far wall, slightly beyond the bank of machines, seemed her most likely target. She edged along behind the busy operatives, who ignored her completely. Their hands, darting swiftly about in incomprehensible movements, made her feel slightly dizzy. She mustn't stagger here. Apart from making a bad impression, it could be dangerous. What if she fell in among all these flailing, clanking steel arms?

As she approached the group, she took a deep breath. In spite of that her voice came out in a shaky croak and she had to try again. 'Miss Meikie?'

'Aye,' came the answering shout. Miss Meikie was a

thickset little figure with a surprisingly thin, sharp face. Dandy handed her the paper.

'Jenny,' shouted Miss Meikie without a glance at Dandy, 'take this lass to the brushes and show her whit to dae. Start here. You'll maybe need to shift to the cop winding later. See that she ties her hair up, mind!'

A girl with wide grey eyes detached herself from the group, grinning encouragingly at Dandy and gesturing to her to follow. As the heavy door swung to behind them, shutting out the din, she mimicked, 'See that she ties her hair up, mind,' and giggled. 'That's auld Meikie. You'll get that every day.' She repeated it again, 'See that she ties her hair up, mind.'

'But my hair *is* tied up,' said Dandy, fingering the securely pinned plaits on top of her head.

'Aye, but it's the regulations, y'see – in case we fall in among the machinery or something goes wrong wi' a machine and it catches our hair. The bosses would get into trouble and have to pay compensation if we were scalped, y'see. That's why we have to tie our hair up and it has to be done right. I'll show you.'

In the small changing room, Jenny was immediately expansive. 'You can hang your shawl up there. What's your name? Dandy? That's funny – nice, though. Watch out for old Meikie. She's aye chasing us up, especially if there's a nice laddie around – not that there's all that many. Have you got a laddie of your ain? What age are you? Only fourteen! My, you're nearly as tall as me and I'll be sixteen in, let me see, four and a half months. Just think of it, I could get married then without my faither's consent. Wait till you see Andy – he's one of the porters. He's that handsome. Mind you, I've got my eye on him, so you keep off,' she said with a warning giggle.

'I'm not interested in boys,' said Dandy.

'What?' Jenny was aghast. 'Why not?'

Dandy drew herself up. She would have to take care. Maybe all the girls here of that age were interested in boys and they would guess she was too young. She tried a careless laugh, remembering a line in a book she had read, 'I'd rather wait for a rich old man.'

Jenny doubled up. 'You're a caution, Dandy. Wait till I tell the lassies that one. Oh here, we'd better get on wi' the sweeping or old Meikie will be on our tails. See, these are the brushes out here. You've always to stack them carefully when you put them back in case one slides and somebody trips over it. That's another thing you can expect old Meikie to be on about,' she added in a whisper, glancing over her shoulder. 'And you've to brush slowly or clouds o' the stuff will come up and the women will gie ye hell ... No! Grip it like this or it'll topple over.'

'They're huge,' said Dandy.

'Aye, they've got to be. It's a non-stop job wi' all the cotton dust and the wee bits o' thread. No' much fun unless the lads come through,' she added again in a whisper. 'Watch me do the first wee bit.'

Dandy watched and echoed Jenny's words in her head. No' much fun! Was this what she would be doing day in, day out?

No wonder her aunts were appalled. At school she would at least have been learning. Maybe the bosses would let her do something better later. But Jenny was nearly sixteen and had probably started when she was fourteen. She seemed quite happy. Fancy anybody looking forward to seeing boys! Maybe she would have to pretend that she liked boys. After all, Madge Forbes had said that her big sisters talked about boys and they wouldn't be silly – not in that house. Well, she had often had to pretend things to get Grannie on her side, so maybe she would have to do the same again. It might be years before they let her work at the machines, even.

None of the women with the fluttering hands looked all that young. Dandy smothered a sigh. This was what she had chosen and she would just have to get on with it. Aunt Alice had said – what was it again? – 'If you are at all unhappy about it, let us know and that will be the finish of it.' Well, if the worst came to the worst, she could fall back on that. But things would have to be gey bad before she lost the chance of a pay packet to take proudly to her aunts.

It didn't take her long to find her fears justified. Jenny and the other girls she met at the tea break seemed to have nothing at all to talk about but the lads who had spoken to them, tickled them when the foreman's back was turned, or, giggle upon giggle, 'caught' them in the broom cupboard. This last piece of information always brought a squeal of delight tinged with envy from the others. Dandy responded as nobly as she could, but found this increasingly difficult, especially when they started asking her to relate her experiences. 'No, I told you I was waiting for a rich old man' soon sounded unfunny in her own ears even if it still brought giggles.

Though she had had no regrets about not going to Canada, she always watched eagerly for the postman. She knew that letters would take ages to reach her, and Aunt Alice had warned her that it would take her family a little time to settle before they were free to write at all. It didn't need anyone to warn her that the cost of postage would be a consideration not to be ignored.

The first one was delivered by her Aunt Margaret. It had been addressed to Grannie's house, but a neighbour had been kind enough to forward it. Somehow Dandy had not considered this eventuality. It had been written by May on the ship.

Mammie has been so sick. I don't think it's just the rough sea – she is missing Grannie and is worrying about the strange country. I don't know what we would do without the Salvation Army people. This will surprise you, Dandy, because Faither never told us before we left. Maybe he thought folks would laugh at him after all his drinking. In fact, George laughs behind his back now and I have to warn him. You see, when Faither went for that interview, these folk told him they could not take family men but they said that the Salvation Army would have officials on that same ship if he could afford to pay the fares; they could get him fixed up with a job on a fruit farm for a year. Then he could either get a free grant of land from the government and start up his own farm, or he could use the money he had saved from his wages to buy a small farm, twenty or thirty acres. It seems that folk with huge farms are selling bits of them off. The Salvation Army seem to know about every-thing and they see to the train bookings and things like that and see that the wrong people don't get hold of us when we leave the ship. One of their ladies reported that Mammie was sick and the ship's doctor came to see her. He gave Mammie something to calm her nerves. He told me not to worry, that Mammie would feel better when she got off the ship. He said we were unfortunate that the crossing was rougher than usual. I'm looking after Jack. He was a bit sick at first too. The twins have found a nice wee chum and her mother, Mrs Thomson, is quite happy to keep an eye on them while they play. The Thomsons are also being looked after by the Salvation Army and Mrs Thom-son said it would be nice if we ended up near one another. Mind you, it seems to be such a big

country from what folk tell me. When I think about
it I get frightened and wish you were nearer, Dandy
– you or Grannie.

Dandy found a lump in her throat when she got to
that part of the letter. She had let May down: May who
wrote like someone much older. All that responsibility
which she would have taken on her shoulders was now
dumped on May. It was terrible to be torn two ways,
but she had chosen her path and would have to make
the best of it.

The days at the mill dragged wearily on. The glorious
autumn colours meant nothing to those girls who still
talked of nothing but boys. Dandy had been met with
blank looks one morning when she remarked on the
changing season and said that she thought 1907 must
be giving one of the finest displays of autumn colours
ever. At times she felt like screaming. The older women
told dreary gossipy tales of neighbours; it seemed to
her in her rebellious state that they delighted in talking
of illnesses and hardship. She knew all about hardship
herself, but it wasn't something she wanted to talk
about. There were plenty worthwhile things to think
about – books and gardens, poetry. Her one mention
of books to Jenny had met with an astonished whistle.
'Don't tell me you read books when you don't have to?
I've never opened one since I left school. There are no
books in our house. We've more to think about.'

Aye! Bloody boys, thought Dandy, but she had managed to make some sort of diplomatic answer which
Jenny had taken as a compliment while Dandy
switched her thoughts to something much more to her
liking – her garden. Steadily she ran through all the
preparations she had made for winter. Nothing seemed
to have been missed. No, Uncle James would have
been pleased with her. Unfortunately it meant she had

nothing to look forward to for the next few months but letters from Canada.

The only thing that made the dreary sweeping possible for her was to recite poems in her head. Rachel's bookcase had yielded a rich store of those. As soon as she had finished her evening meal she would rush upstairs to check up on something that she had stumbled over in her long recitals over the ugly broom with its accretions of fluff, thread and sometimes worse, when the men had been spitting. 'Men are filthy creatures,' she told herself, remembering her father rolling drunkenly into bed in his dyeworks clothes. Then she would switch to Uncle James, fastidiously wiping his lips with his linen napkin, politely standing till his guests were seated – Uncle James in so many different little courtesies and then a flashing memory of Drew Keir relieving her of her heavy bag with the minimum of fuss. There was no need to dodge people like *that*, but she was damned if she would succumb to the charms of the likes of Andy Connell, who was Jenny's idea of a handsome hero.

The second letter had been written by her mother. Dandy snatched it eagerly from Aunt Margaret and found her hands trembling.

My Darling Dandy,

I want you to pass this letter on to your grannie and Aunt Margaret. Your father does not want to spend money on writing paper at the moment when we have so many things to buy. The Salvation Army people were waiting for us when we landed at Quebec. I was still feeling very queasy, but they guided us to our train and saw us settled. We were to go to Winnipeg first and wait in the hostel till your father got established in his job, then he would send for us. But, as it turned out, word came through that there were some disused houses available near where your father would be working and we were advised to go there since the weather was still good and see about patching ours up before the winter. So, we were soon on our way again to a little township near Vernon. That's in the Okanagan Valley district where they grow the finest apples. I must say my heart sank when I saw the cluster of houses – just huge log huts, really. The door wasn't locked and I could see why. There was nothing there to steal! There was a huge room with a stove in the middle and a sort of platform all round it with recesses for bunks here and there. There was one little room off with a sort of built-up platform for a double bed and another wee room with an old paraffin stove for cooking in it. The teeny doocot beyond that had the lavatory and the shower. The whole place was dusty – or sandy, I suppose you would say. The ground round about was very dry, you see. We were all so tired. The twins started to cry and that set Jack off. You know how that irritates your father! The two nearest houses were empty, but the fourth one – the furthest away – had curtains in the windows and we could hear hens in the backyard. We were just climbing down from the cart we had hired when a woman appeared round the corner of the house. She stared, then hurried towards us.

'Well, well,' she said. 'You comin' here? We're leavin' next week. Nobody stays long in these cabins. They all build, you see, once they get the land in order. Well, that place will be mucky. I'll give you brooms and Pa and the boys can sweep up. The rest of you come in and sit down in my place. We'll get the coffee pot on. When did you last eat?' I found it difficult to remember because we had travelled so long and yet I wasn't hungry, but it was great to smell the coffee. She took it for granted that the men should do the dirty work and I think they were too surprised to say anything. Then she asked me if we had noticed the big farm about half a mile down the road. I said the one where the dogs had been barking and she said that would be the one and did I see anyone. I said that there was a very fair-haired lady had come out from a barn to look at us. She said that that would be Marie and it would not be long till she arrived, she was sure. Well, Dandy, I soon found out what she meant. Marie Friedland – that's her name – arrived soon. She had guessed where we would be going. There she was, loaded with supplies: eggs, goat's milk, freshly baked bread, vegetables and fruit, a plucked chicken and a big lump of cheese. But, best of all, she had brought a paraffin stove that was in good working order and some pots and pans. What do you think of that? I'll tell you more about her later, but Faither is worried about the cost of paper and postage. Love to you all.

For the first time, Dandy missed her grannie. This was a letter to be shared with her somehow, even if it brought on – as it would have done – the usual complaints about the drunken dyer that Nettie had stupidly married when she could have had someone better, etc, etc. Grannie would have shared her worry about Mammie's plight in a way that her kind aunts could never understand. They had never been under the thumb of an insensitive domineering fellow like Will Baxter. Then suddenly she remembered the look that had passed between her parents that time they were laughing about how she got her name: that look which had disturbed her, giving her a glimpse of a completely different relationship which had somehow vanished. Deep down, it had made her afraid of ever landing in the same predicament.

'I've dared him to catch you, Dandy.'

'What?' Dandy had been dreaming. The weather was lovely. After enduring the dreary winter and fidgeting through the bright spring when she longed to work all day in her garden, Dandy was spending her lunch break with Jenny on a hot June day out of doors. The two girls had chosen a small stretch of grass near the mill dam where the sound of the waterfall, the Hammills, tumbling over the rocks made Dandy feel she was far from any thread mills. The spring planting which she had managed to fit in at the end of her long working day had turned out successfully and already the first roses were blooming against the south wall, candytuft made the borders a delight, the scent of pinks in a tiny crystal vase enhanced her little dressing table. Now she was kept busy removing weeds from among the seedling annuals.

'What?' she repeated. Then her thoughts focused and she sat up suddenly. 'What d'you mean?'

'I've dared Andy to catch you. It'll be fun to watch . . .' she tailed off, seeing Dandy's expression.

'I'll give you bloody fun,' said Dandy. Immediately she realized her mistake. All her pretence about going along with their ideas of fun would be shown up for false now.

'Language, language,' said Jenny, indignant in her turn. 'What's got into you? You laughed plenty when he caught Mattie Jenkins.'

'Aye, but I didn't dare him,' said Dandy, desperately trying to recover ground. 'Don't you see? You're making him big-headed. You should play it cool.'

'Is that what you're doing, just pretending you're

waiting for a rich old man while you play it cool?'

'Aye, something like that,' said Dandy.

'My, you're worth a watching. And we thought you were kind of stuck-up . . . different . . . Who would have guessed that you just play them like fishes? Wait till I tell the lassies.'

Dandy had plenty to think about as she walked home that night. Her seeming co-operation had worked for many months. It was stupid of her to let her guard slip. Now she would have to watch everyone – bloody Andy with his casual good looks as well as these stupid giggly girls. 'Am I an odd wee thing?' she asked herself again. That thought had occurred to her many times in these long months when it seemed impossible to fit in. 'I was the only one at school who could deal with the boys in the playground. Did the others maybe enjoy being tormented?' Yet when she had asked the aunts that same question they had made a joke of it. Aunt Alice *had* given her that wee lecture about inheriting things from Faither. Was she really telling her she was kind of odd?

Well, odd or not, she was keeping Uncle James's garden the way he would have liked it. That was a thought to treasure. Her step quickened.

At the back of her mind was always the thought of her mother's reaction to Grannie's death; to get that news so far from home, about a mother who had been her sole defence against Will at his worst. The letter when it came – delivered to the cottage this time – had been as bad as she had feared. It had been read so often that now she had only to take the crumpled paper in her hand and she could recite the contents.

The two letters which had come since then had been brief and colourless. But that one . . .

I just can't believe it. She was always so strong. I

don't remember her ever having anything worse than a cold. Your Aunt Jean says that she ate a grand dinner before she went up to bed. Of course, she would be excited with the travelling and leaving you, though Margaret tells me that you have a lovely home and the McLarens are good to you. Oh, pet, how I miss you here! We are more or less camping in a bare log house, but your Faither says that things will get better as we get on with the planting. It will be years before we have a crop of our own and even then we will be paying the company back for a long time, but Faither says it will be worth it. The house will have to wait. The boys are happy. They have chums, you see, and keep boasting about the muscles they built up in Paisley. There's a woman who lives alone on an older established farm near here and they have been earning the odd half-dollar picking apples for her. Maybe I told you about her before. Yes, I think I did. She brought us all the things when we first came in. Faither works long hours on the farm, learning the job. You'll be glad to know that he isn't drinking – nobody does round here. He is determined to get his own farm and build a nice house. The men get together in groups to help each other. It's the pioneer spirit, they say. Billy bought me this paper out of his earnings so that I could write to you. That's why I am blethering on, pet. May misses you terribly too. She cries at night, the twins tell me. She's a great wee help. The twins are getting quite independent. They have a lot of space and freedom here certainly, but space and freedom aren't everything, my love. I'd give a lot just to hear your grannie's key in the door and hear you singing in the scullery. The twins have taken to dancing and singing and some of the other mothers were saying that they thought they were natural comediennes. George said he didn't know whether to be flattered or flattened! The boys out here seem to grow up quickly. They copy their fathers as they work and learn a lot quite naturally. I think Mrs Friedland at the farm is good for George and Billy though, between ourselves, I think your Pa is a wee bit jealous. Oh, I said 'Pa'. That's what they all say here. I'd better stop. Give my best regards to Miss Alice and Miss Violet. Lots of love and kisses from all the family and,

Ma

p.s. It was good of you to go on taking Grannie's turn of washing the stairs till the house was given up. She would have been proud of you.

Dandy wondered what Grannie would have thought of her in her present occupation. She would have understood the independence which made her want to contribute to the household, yet she had always said that Dandy would learn nothing but good from these aunties because they were 'ladies'. Was she undoing that good by taking a job under pretence, a job where she was learning nothing at all – unless you counted dodging Andy's advances as something worth learning?

She had no one she could discuss this predicament with. Mammie was far away and must not be worried by anything. Probably she would never be able to discuss anything properly with her mother *ever* again. That was a sobering thought. Aunt Margaret? No. She always kept herself that wee bit remote. Still, it had been kind of her, letting Dandy pick something of Grannie's to keep. She had chosen the biscuit barrel and polished its silver bands faithfully every week. But Aunt Margaret's kindness was of a detached sort. Aunt Margaret would never let herself get too involved with

186

anyone, which was maybe a blessing – otherwise she wouldn't have been so pleased to let Dandy stay with her aunts. Aunt Margaret thought things out to her own advantage. She paid a woman to come and clean her house on the afternoons when she was at her bridge club. The woman looked after Betty's wee brother and gave Betty a titbit when she came home from school. The big fat lump was too silly to do things like that for herself. But was Dandy Baxter a big silly, working in the mill when she didn't have to: when her aunts could afford to keep her and when they could be teaching her things at home?

It hadn't seemed so silly in the winter time when there wasn't much to do in the garden anyway, but these lovely summer days were such a waste. Thinking of her favourite poems had helped to while away the tedious hours, but they had made her dreamy and now that Jenny, the giggly idiot, had issued her challenge to Andy Connell, dreaminess was dangerous. The noise of the machinery drowned the sound of footsteps, so she had to glance about her frequently.

She had managed to dodge him quite easily so far by the simple expedient of seeming to notice some dirt she had missed and veering out of his path to a safer area, but all this meant a stupid alertness which brought the futility of the job to the surface. The bell was going. Time for lunch. Thankfully she made for the broom cupboard and stacked the awkward brush in the approved fashion.

'Got you!' He was close behind her. As she whirled round he pinioned her arms and pulled her close. Dandy had not fought those playground battles for nothing. She wriggled like an eel and ducked out from under his grip. He lunged out to bring her back. Dandy seized the opportunity, grabbed his left thumb and gave it a fierce jerk backwards. Andy Connell, amazed, staggered and fell flat on his back right in the path of the foreman.

'Whit the hell's a' this?' he bellowed.

Dandy ignored him and addressed her victim. 'The next time you try your nonsense on me, you'll get worse. I'm warning you.'

'And I'm warning you they'll be nae next time, laddie. Just go to the office and get your books. You ken the rules – nae interfering wi' the lassies. Every one o' you is weel warned when you start here.'

Andy's face was chalk white as he slowly picked himself up. Dandy was appalled. In the playground, her rough justice had ended the trouble. Never in her wildest dreams had she imagined a situation like this. 'He never did anything . . . I mean he never got the chance to do anything,' she began falteringly.

'Naw.' A fleeting smile crossed his face. 'I got that impression. But rules are rules. On you go, Connell.'

Chapter 13

The machines had stopped. Everything was dead quiet. Then came a sob from the corner. It was Jenny. The woman nearest to Dandy said, 'I hope you're proud of yourself, you rotten wee bitch, getting a decent lad into trouble like that. You wait till Meg Elliot hears this. She's in the cop winding; led the big strike, she did, and she lives next to young Andy and his grannie. She'll sort you!'

Dandy knew all about THE BIG STRIKE. Some of the older women had discussed it ad nauseam during several lunch breaks. It seemed to be the only exciting thing that had happened in their lives at the mill. In all innocence, Dandy had asked when it took place and had met with astonished stares. 'During the Boer War, lassie. In 1900. Where were you that you didna hear o' it? They brought in this new patent, you see. It made the work heavier while the wages got smaller – no' that they were big to start wi', I can tell you. The lassies had to hump baskets o' yarn that were far too heavy. Of course, the foremen had their favourites. Aye, you ken whit I mean. Lassies they could take for a walk and get onything they wanted! Well, *they* didna have to hump the heavy things. Big Meg led the strike and that got things sorted out.'

Dandy recalled these words all too clearly as she turned and made her way to the changing room. She had nearly given her age away by not having heard of their famous strike. She would have to be careful. Word had already spread, she saw, by the stony faces that met her. She anchored a plait which had come loose in the struggle. All appetite had left her, but she went through the motions of looking out the packed lunch which Violet had prepared. She jumped as the door was thrown back on its hinges and a raucous voice bawled out, 'Where is she? Where's the bitch that lost Andy his job?'

Fingers were jabbed in Dandy's direction and there was a babble of voices as each one gave her version of the disaster. As the massive figure bore down on her, Dandy noted the muscular arms, the ruddy cheeks and the flashing green eyes. This was going to demand all her skill. Speed was on her side, she felt. She had coped with Andy. Surely . . . But she had reckoned without the mass indignation. 'Come on,' roared Meg. 'Get the claithes aff her back. Ah've brought the marking chalk.'

Dandy resisted desperately, landing a few painful punches before her arms were pinioned and Meg was ripping the buttons off her dress. 'That's it, lassies. Get her drawers. Get the tapes out o' them. That'll learn her – her and her stuck-up ideas. A fellow like Andy that's handed his pay to his grannie every Friday since he started. What that puir auld wife's going to dae, I don't know. He'll no' get a reference – a decent hard-working laddie like that!' Her indignation was arousing the others. Dandy saw the beautiful petticoat that Violet had refashioned from one of Rachel's being cut to ribbons by a young woman who had normally given her a friendly smile in passing. How could she ever explain? She had wished Andy no ill, just deplored his flirtatious ways.

'All this trouble just because o' a wee kiss. She didna ken when she was lucky. Naebody will want to kiss her when ah'm finished. There! My God, is she no' skinny? Here! Catch her! No, my lass, we'll write a pretty story on your bum – no' that there's much room.

But that flat chest would be just fine.' She was joined in her noisy laughter.

'Here! We'd better be quick or we'll get nae dinner,' warned an older woman.

'Aye! Aye thinking o' her stomach, Essie is,' said another. 'But you're right. What's that you've written Meg? Aye, she's a bitch all right. Whit about "Scum" or "Scab". She lost Andy his job, mind.'

'I'll no' forget that,' Meg assured her, 'and I'll see that this one never gets a chance to forget it either. There you are! I've written as much as I can get on. Watch her!

'Right, Dandy Bloody Baxter, you can go and show the foreman that lot and see what it does for you. We're off to our dinner and I hope you roast in hell for what you did to that wee lad.'

She was alone, free to let the angry tears course down her cheeks. The trouble was that she could understand their indignation in a way. A fellow who was good to his grannie like that ... well ... but she had never thought for a minute of doing him any real harm. It had seemed simple. As she studied her ravaged clothes she remembered Alice's warning about the things she might have inherited from her father. Quick to respond to a slight. Yes, she was. But what else could she have done to stop Andy? How did anyone stop someone like Andy? She studied her drawers. The woman who had pulled the tapes out of the casings had stuffed them in her pocket so there was no hope of getting them back in. Her chemise was ripped too, but it could be worn. She pulled it on, smudging the angry tears as she did so. She picked up the petticoat. It had been a beautiful thing, beautiful in itself as a piece of work – not just beautiful for her. How could anyone destroy anything like that? It was the sort of thing that her devils of brothers had done. Would she have done anything like

191

that if she had not had the McLarens as an example? Her dress had many buttons missing. It wouldn't stay shut at the back but, thankfully, she saw that the little shawl she had worn in the early morning was still stuck on its hook in the corner. They had forgotten that. She draped it round her then stood, automatically tidying her hair, uncertain what to do next. Then with a toss of her head she gathered her underwear into a bundle, held it under her shawl and hurried out.

The hot sun drew out the reek of the Espedair Burn, the drying mudbanks coloured with effluent from the dyeworks. Few people would go near it, especially in the middle of the day. Flies and bluebottles buzzed round her wet eyes and flushed cheeks. She was furious, indignant. But underneath that was a feeling somehow that she had changed sides in some way. The furious remarks of the women had been born of loyalty to a lad who would certainly have met with her grannie's approval – handing over his pay every week like that. Why did he have to be such a nuisance, though? They thought she was stuck-up when she refused his advances. Had she learned too much self-importance from her aunts? Was it because she was so much younger than the others that she saw a kiss as an assault, or was it somehow mixed up with the relationship between her mother and father – one that had probably started with happy kisses? These seemed harmless enough, but then they thought they could do that awful thing to you whether you wanted another bairn or not. 'He would roar the building down,' Mammie had said. It was an attack, that's what it was! Some women wouldn't put up with it. Aunt Margaret had her one of each and that was her finished with it. What made men want to attack like that? Yet they wouldn't all be the same. Uncle James would be gentle and loving with his Rachel. He would have loved their baby, but he'd never have insisted on ... that, not when she didn't want another bairn. No, not Uncle James! Would her aunts, unmarried and, in some eyes, pampered, understand these other women whose lives were so different? She rushed headlong through the weeds, desperate to be home.

She had expected the sisters to be shocked, but nothing had prepared her for the extent of their agitation. Violet, white as a sheet, staggered to the nearest chair in the kitchen. Alice, with tears coursing down her cheeks and her chin trembling, had advanced, put her arms round her quite helplessly, leaning more and more heavily till Dandy was practically holding her up. Then she felt her own courage evaporating. 'They've written all over me with marking chalk,' she sobbed, 'and the lovely petticoat ... Aunt Rachel's ... see!' She eased herself out from Alice's grip and held the pathetic tatters up before Violet's horrified eyes.

A strangled squeal was all the sempstress could manage. She swayed a little, grasping the table for support. Dandy watched, numb, while Alice, suddenly shocked into recovery, rushed forward to support her.

'Come now, Violet,' she admonished, 'we're not helping Dandy if we let ourselves go to pieces. Obviously the first thing required is a good bath. We'll have to open up the range, I think, but the water in the tank should be quite hot anyway – nothing to cool it in this weather. I'll see to the range while you make Dandy a nice cup of tea. Your parkin biscuits would be a comfort too, I think.'

Dandy choked a few times as she told her story, safely giving vent to her self-pity in the presence of her partisan listeners.

'But why did he pick on you to attack?' asked Violet.

'Well, you see ...' Dandy had to think a bit. The girls beside her had looked on Andy's presumption as a compliment: each stolen kiss a triumph. These aunts saw it as an attack. She saw it as an attack too, but her reaction was angled differently. She was thinking of her mother and what her father's kisses had done to her. Men who made advances, no matter how charmingly, were dangerous. Faither's kisses had led to that creaking in the bed. And that ... well, it had led to what Faither had called a pigsty: two overcrowded rooms and washing on the winterdykes permanently in front of the fire on wet days. There was so much that was beyond the reach of her aunts: impossible to explain, really, but she must try.

'The other girls like it. They giggle when they're telling each other that Andy caught them. I didn't know that there were such strict rules in the mill. I didn't know he was risking his job,' she finished bleakly.

'But think of it,' Alice responded briskly. 'Any fooling about near all that machinery could cause a disastrous accident. You say that the women's hair has always to be securely anchored. And, of course, it is time wasted in a big organization that is run for profit: an organization that gives gainful employment to many women who otherwise would find it difficult to get work at all.'

'Aye,' said Dandy, 'Grannie used to say that a woman who had a big family of girls in Paisley was considered lucky because they would all get jobs in the mill. She said it wasn't like that some other places where there were only engineering works.'

'Yes, your grannie was right. That is why the town has grown so quickly – all the weaving factories first of all, then the light engineering, the textile finishing and dyeing; and the thread mills are the biggest in the world. Oh yes, that's how the place has grown. Now, my dear, I think the water will be good and hot, but if that marking chalk has an oily base I think I should bring some olive oil and cotton rags up to the bathroom.

194

I don't think soap and water is going to remove it.'

Dandy blushed. Aunt Alice in the bathroom with her, seeing her with no clothes! But Aunt Alice appeared to think nothing of it. 'Call me when you're ready,' she was saying.

Dandy stood in her robe, hesitating. A shiver shook her in spite of the hot sun beating in the little window. Aunt Alice seemed to take it for granted. She hadn't seemed the least bit embarrassed when she said that about bringing the olive oil. 'Ladies' were funny. They worried about some things that she had never thought of, but they seemed to think you could take your clothes off in front of other people. Maybe it was because they had servants, nannies and things when they were children. They would be used to strangers putting on their clothes for them. Because of her brothers being around she had always had to be careful. Uncle James would have a bedroom all to himself even when he was wee so they wouldn't have to hide from him. She shivered again. It would have to be done. 'I'm ready,' she called, knowing that it wasn't true.

Aunt Alice tut-tutted over the various slogans as she plied the oil and rubbed vigorously. Dandy's shivering increased. 'I think you should have a nice hour or two in bed,' said Alice. 'You've had a shock, after all.' She opened the door and called downstairs, 'A hot-water bottle for Dandy, please, Violet.'

As she was tucked up in bed like a young child, Dandy felt the weak tears starting again. She was safe; she was in her own room; her aunts were on her side and as indignant as she could wish. But – and it was a big 'but' – she had cost Andy his job with her quick reaction; Andy whose plight was not unlike her own in previous years. Obviously he had never thought she would react differently from the other girls; thought she was in the same game of catch-as-catch-can. How was he feeling, having to go home and tell his grannie that he had been sacked: knowing that, without a reference, he was going to have an uphill struggle to find another job? How was his grannie feeling, having all her pride in her handsome grandson brought to nothing; losing her sure income? And it had been her fault in a way, though the aunts would never understand that. It was her fear of men like her father who used their charm to ensnare girls, trapping them into a life of constant pregnancies and poverty that had ruled her reactions to Andy. Her fellow workers hadn't known that, of course, when they labelled her 'stuck-up'.

She kicked the hot-water bottle further down the bed. She was feeling warm, wondering what the next step would be. What would the foreman say in the morning? How would the women react? Would she be constantly taunted or would they choose to ignore her? She tried to remember Alice's comforting words when she had announced her intention of working in the mill.

Her brain wasn't clicking, but she could remember the final phrase, 'And that will be the end of it.' Was this to be the end? Perhaps she had been stupid anyway. Her work in the garden was really a help to her aunts and they honestly seemed happy to keep her. Perhaps it was a strain on them knowing that she worked in such a place?

As Dandy, worn out, drifted into a troubled sleep, a war council was taking place in the sitting room. Alice had closed the door saying, 'She won't hear us from here.' Then she had plumped herself down in her favourite chair and said, 'I'm furious, Violet . . . spitting mad. I shall go to that mill tomorrow and see that those concerned are absolutely roasted. To do that to a girl like Dandy – a girl who has worked hard for her family, who took on that horrible job to repay us. Oh! It's unspeakable.'

Violet was quiet for a little while. 'I wonder, Alice. It's not quite so straightforward . . . Did you notice how often Dandy said, "I didn't think he would lose his job"? She was identifying with the lad to a certain extent. It would appear that he is popular with the older women because of his kindness to his grandmother. I feel she is as vexed about this as she is at being attacked by the other women – much though that has angered her, of course. I expect she treated them to some words that we don't know during the attack! She loved that petticoat! But I feel, dear, that if you get these women into trouble, that will only add to her feeling of guilt in a way. She has known what it is to be in similar circumstances to some of these people. We have made life different for her . . . Oh dear, I'm not good at expressing these things.'

Alice stirred. 'You're doing better than I did, Violet. I've been letting my anger blind me. This demands fin-esse. Of course, Dandy is bewildered. Part of it is due to the fact that she is pretending to be much older than she is and is expected to behave in a way that is strange to her and, I may say, holds no attraction for her. We let her go to work there against our better judgement. We were unwise in that, I think. She couldn't possibly foresee how out of place she would feel. She has begun to identify with us, but that doesn't work in the thread mill so her life is really a mass of pretences at the moment. The only reality is her garden. There she is sure of herself. No, we shall have to put our thinking caps on and we had better think quickly before that young lady comes rattling downstairs again.'

Two hours later, they had their scheme worked out, but there was no sign of Dandy. 'She doesn't usually sleep during the day,' said Violet.

'No, I think we had better check.' Alice was already out of her chair and making for the door.

Some of the bedclothes were trailing on the floor and Dandy was moaning restlessly, her long skinny arms jerking as they searched for relief. 'She's fevered, Violet,' said Alice, touching the hot forehead.

'I can see that. Should we fetch the doctor?'

'No, that could be awkward,' said Alice, straightening up.

'What do you mean?'

'The doctor is bound to ask her age. Then he might ask how long she had been in the thread mills. It's not likely, but we must be careful for she *did* tell a lie to get the job and we condoned it. Of course,' she added hastily, 'if I thought this was something we could not deal with ourselves, I should call the doctor. But I suspect that the fever is brought about by emotion and we should be able to cure her ourselves. Our scheme for the future should certainly help her. The immediate problem is to get the fever down. I think we carry on with the faithful old remedies, combined with love and care.'

Dandy submitted helplessly to their ministrations, shivering when they sponged down her burning skin and swallowing gratefully the hot lemon drinks which Violet supplied in a seemingly unending stream. Frequently she croaked her thanks: other times the slow tears would start flowing and she would sob, 'Aunt Rachel's lovely petticoat' or, more often, 'I didn't mean to lose him his job'. It was many hours before she settled into a deep and natural sleep and the sisters were able to retire, worn out, to their room.

The sun was high when Dandy surfaced. She saw with lazy pleasure the flowers on the curtains take on their natural colours. She was so lucky to have a room all to herself . . . she had waited so long for it . . . Then suddenly consciousness returned. She leapt from bed. She was late for work! She peered at the dressing table clock – five past eight. She was hours late! As if she hadn't enough to face in that place. What would they say? Would she, like Andy, be dismissed? None of them would be sorry to see *her* go. She dashed to the bathroom, letting her door swing noisily.

Aunt Alice was waiting by her bedroom when she returned. 'I'm late,' gasped Dandy.

'You are not going back, my dear – ever!'

'What?'

'We have other plans for you. Now, my dear, shall I bring you up some breakfast?'

'Bring me it up? Oh, no. That would be terrible. I'm not ill . . . but have they dismissed me too? Did they think I had encouraged him?'

'No, not at all,' said Alice. 'Let's get dressed, shall we, and go downstairs? It's another lovely day. We don't want to waste it. I'll tell you what we have worked out over breakfast. Wear something pretty but comfortable. We may be going out.'

The door was open on to the garden because, even at that early hour, the conservatory had gathered considerable heat. It was a good thing that Mr Forbes had thought of this useful addition to Uncle James's plans, Dandy told herself for the umpteenth time. Surely Uncle James would have revelled in it too. Maybe Mr Forbes thought that Uncle James could not afford the extra expense and did not want to embarrass him. That was probably it. What a contrast . . . sitting here in the beautiful sunshine . . . yesterday that nightmare!

'They'll dock money from my wages,' she said.

'You will never go back there again.' Alice's voice was firm, utterly reassuring. 'I have already written to that effect. Violet and I blame ourselves. We should never have let you go there at all. You were far too young and the work had no interest for you. We appreciate your motives, but we should have steered you clear for your own good.'

'I'll need to go back for my wages. They'll not send them here.'

'Forget all about that, Dandy. We know that you went to that horrid job to earn money for us but, believe me, Dandy, you owe us nothing whatever. Simply having you with us is a delight and the way you keep James's garden, well! We have all these books to sell, so we shall never starve. I mean it, Dandy. You hated the job even without yesterday's dreadful doings, didn't you?'

'Aye. The days dragged and I felt I wasn't learning anything, but it's going to be difficult. If I went back to school they would wonder where I'd been. I should be going to the big school by now and they'll want to know where I've come from . . .'

'You won't be going back to school, my dear. Violet and I have a plan. We thought it out yesterday afternoon while you were sleeping. Listen to this! Now, you know that we never went to school?'

Dandy nodded, wondering what this had to do with her.

'We spent many hours with our governesses and, I think, probably learned more that way than we would have done in a busy classroom. Of course, we have forgotten much of what we learned: that is inevitable, but, given the appropriate textbooks, we feel that we could teach you most of the things you would learn at any school. Fortunately, we tended to shine in different subjects and we have decided on a division of labour.'

Dandy was smiling broadly. 'That sounds a wonderful idea, Aunt Alice.'

'I'm not finished yet, my dear. There are other little advantages we see over a routine school. You are a keen student and we feel sure there will be little time wasted, so we think it would be sensible to adjust the hours of tuition to the weather to allow you the maximum time in the garden. That way, a wet day will seem a bonus to your studies rather than a loss to your gardening.'

Dandy gave a whoop of joy while the sisters smiled happily at each other.

'I propose, I mean *we* propose, to take you to Glasgow this morning. There is a big bookshop there which specializes in textbooks. We can have a delightful browse and study our requirements where there is little danger of bumping into anyone who knew you at school. Well, Miss Dandy?'

Dandy was clapping her hands too hard to waste time in speech. Then she quietened. 'I can't believe it, after that nightmare. But I can't help worrying about Andy. He was obviously surprised, I mean he thought I would be like the other girls, not an odd wee thing.' She paused for a moment. Was this the time to tell them her real name? Or could she tell them the truncated version she had thought up in bed that night she had learned the truth? Suddenly she sat up straight.

'Really I'm not Miss Dandy at all. I'm Miss Lily. I found that out when my father was looking out the birth certificates. I'm called after my grannie, you see – LILY JORDAN BAXTER. It seems that Grandpa Baxter used to ask how I was when I was a baby and my father would say, "Fine and dandy." Gradually it got shortened and he would say, "How's Dandy?" Our George picked it up and soon everybody used it.'

'So you're really *Lily*,' said Violet. 'And to think you used to envy me my flower name! I've always thought that you looked like a lily with that lovely yellow hair and your tall slender figure.'

'It *is* so appropriate,' said Alice, 'and yet, I don't know. "Dandy" has such happy associations for me.

Shall we keep "Lily" for Sundays? I'd hate to lose my little Dandy now.'

Dandy's heart was light as she skipped upstairs to dress. The thread mill and its problems were behind her: the hatred she had dreaded would not have to be faced. She was going to have two governesses! She giggled at the thought. *And* she was going to Glasgow. Other girls at school had visited Glasgow. She had always kept quiet. Though many of them would know that she had never had the chance, drawing attention to herself would bring pity or scorn, neither of which she wanted.

The arrival of the train brought back memories of Grannie's departure to Coventry. She had thought it lucky at the time that Aunt Alice was there with her. Now that she had got to know the aunts better she realized that Alice's presence was a carefully thought-out insurance policy in case Grannie changed her mind! Ladies could be quite fly, come to think of it. But they did it charmingly. It was worth learning.

She couldn't help smiling as they rattled along and Paisley disappeared from view, to be replaced by fields with cattle grazing. It took only a couple of minutes to be in the country by train. When she remarked on this, Violet told her to keep watching from the other side of the carriage and she would see Glasgow University. 'I think it's such an attractive building, my dear, but some architects say that it is a mixture of styles and they disapprove. It reminds me of the castles I used to like to read about when I was a little girl.'

None of the girls at school had mentioned the university. But, come to think of it, none of them ever talked about buildings at all, or gardens. Was she an "odd wee thing" as her Aunt Jean had said? She had always gazed in awe at the big red church in Paisley High Street, the one with all the steps up to it, the one where the boys sang so beautifully. The aunts had only taken her there once. They seemed to like to go to different churches every week. Now her eyes were fixed on the direction Aunt Violet had indicated. The countryside flying past confirmed that the train was going fast and yet it seemed ages before Aunt Violet said, 'There you are – see! On the hill: that's Gilmorehill. Sometimes I think it's a little like some of the French chateaux; then other times I am reminded of mad Ludwig's castles. We're lucky. The sun is full on it. Well, Miss Lily?'

Dandy chuckled without taking her eyes off the distant building. This name business was going to be fun! But Violet was waiting for an answer. 'It's magic, Aunt Violet. I don't know why nobody ever told me about it. Some of the girls at school used to go to Glasgow often.'

'Some people go about with their eyes shut, my dear. Perhaps no one has taught them to look, to study, to appreciate.'

'I'm so glad I've got you and Aunt Alice,' said Dandy. The window was open only a fraction, yet two seasoned lady travellers suddenly seemed to have smuts in their eyes.

Chapter 14

The huge bookshop was rather gloomy and forbidding at first sight. Dandy gazed uncertainly at the range of counters stretching into the near distance. Alice was reading a notice. 'That's what we want,' she said suddenly. 'Secondary One, this way.'

It was quite a walk to their counter. The piles of books were set in divisions with headings indicating the subject matter. Dandy watched as her aunts began to pick up a few. 'Are we allowed to do that?' she whispered.

'Of course, my dear. You can read them all if you like, but I am going to be looking for lunch before one o'clock, I warn you.'

Dandy started to pick her way round. 'They're very expensive,' she whispered.

'We don't intend to pay our governesses much and our gardener comes for nothing,' whispered Alice. 'And we don't need to whisper: we're not in church,' she said, still whispering in an exaggerated fashion. Dandy chuckled and started to enjoy herself. It wasn't long before both aunts had amassed a considerable pile. Dandy wondered how she was going to carry them home. She couldn't let the aunts do it.

'Well! I think I've got all I shall need. What about you, Violet?' asked Alice.

'Yes. If we find a gap, we can always come back at a later date for another look. My brain is beginning to go numb. It's easy to take too many and get confused, don't you think?'

Dandy's worry about the weight of the books had been unnecessary, she found, when they reached the cash desk and Alice was telling the assistant her address.

'They'll be out to you tomorrow, Madam,' the assistant was saying. Dandy wondered how she would have the patience to wait!

The sun and the heat hit them as they emerged. 'Now,' said Alice. 'Buchanan Street and lunch next, I think.'

Dandy grew more and more confused as her impressions of Glasgow mounted up. Central Station had been noisy in the extreme, but the streets outside had been every bit as bad. Tramcars were jammed all the way up Renfield Street, hawkers were shouting their wares in raucous voices. Whips cracked to control the nags, startled in their carts and fearing to move through the impossibly narrow spaces in the traffic. Both aunts had held her firmly by the hand all the way to the bookshop. But Buchanan Street was different ... dignified, yes, that was it. The shops were large and impressive, their windows elegantly dressed. As they mounted the wide marble staircase of their chosen store, Dandy looked about her in amazement. All that space! And she was allowed to walk in it. Of course, in the stylish clothes that Aunt Violet had made for her, people might think she was a young lady. The shoppers descending the stairs were all without exception elegantly dressed. But then, so were her aunts. She had been too busy registering the difference in her own lifestyle to notice that they too were able to make subtle changes. All the years they had lived beside her they had tended to be rather soberly dressed. They had looked like ladies, but you didn't actually notice their clothes much. 'If only May could have shared this,' thought Dandy, picturing her dainty sister in the sort of outfits Aunt Violet would have devised.

Entering the restaurant held no terrors now, but it was a thrill to get such a fine view of the other big stores. The stonework of the roofs was fascinating – so many interesting little statues that none of the shoppers down below would notice. She beamed at Alice and Violet as she lifted her menu.

The return journey in the packed train was stiflingly hot. All three breathed a sigh of relief as they threw themselves down in the cottage with all the doors open to the garden. Dandy felt she was in a happy dream and would be bound to wake up; surely all these wonderful things couldn't be happening to Dandy Baxter ... or was it Lily Baxter?

Even though the sun was still shining brightly on her beloved garden, Dandy was happy to clear away the evidence of their evening meal and settle down in the sitting room where Alice was already ruling large sheets of paper. 'This is our timetable,' she said; 'only a rough guide, obviously, because we intend to be flexible. But it is necessary to have a framework to make sure we cover as wide a range of subjects as possible.'

Dandy, an onlooker in the game, listened to one suggestion after another. Gradually she lost the thread of the various mild arguments that sprang up.

'We should take the more difficult things first in the morning, I think – while her brain is fresh, I mean.'

'But, Alice, you are assuming that the most difficult things are the ones you will be teaching.'

'Not at all. It's obvious how fond she is of poetry: how easily she memorizes it. That's your department. French will be much the same, I think. Now, Latin – that will be a different matter. You can't learn it parrot fashion. Remember what our Miss McEwan used to say, "There's no royal road to Latin." She was right, you know, Violet.'

'Yes, I grant you. We *did* have to work at it, but it

has such resonance. Dandy will appreciate that, I'm sure. Anyway, isn't it nice to start the day with something you enjoy?'

'Well . . . I see what you mean, Violet. Then, let's have a bit of a compromise, shall we?'

This is all for me, Dandy was thinking. She had everything a girl could ask for: the cottage with the beautiful room that was hers alone, the garden which was her responsibility and joy, two aunts who were 'ladies' now wrangling over who should teach her what and when. All for her! And what was happening to May . . . little uncomplaining May: May who had told her about the roster – 'Something like a hen.' She smiled at the memory.

'I think our pupil is finding our discussions amusing,' said Alice.

'No, it's not that,' said Dandy. 'I was just remembering May's description of the Keir family's roster.'

'Oh yes,' laughed Alice. 'Remember, Violet: "Something like a hen."' ' They were laughing when Dandy went off to make them a cup of tea. In the kitchen she stared at her distorted reflection in the copper kettle while her thoughts returned to May. How different her life. 'Oh, God, look after my wee sister,' she prayed. Then, as a picture of the whole family began to roll before her and stopped at the memory of the departing ship and her father's long arm waving the white handkerchief, she added, 'Look after them all, God.'

The two protagonists seemed to have declared a truce. The long sheets of paper were clipped together neatly, she noticed as she set out their cups. 'We have decided on a rough plan, Dandy,' Alice announced. 'Now, there is another little matter we wish to discuss. Since you moved in with us we have been visiting different churches every Sunday, seldom returning to the same one twice. Have you made up your mind which one you prefer?'

'Was it for me?' Dandy asked in amazement. 'I thought you just liked variety!'

'No, we aren't fibbertigibbets, your aunt and I. But we couldn't very well take you to the church we normally attended; questions would have been asked; your age would be bound to crop up – don't you see?'

'Oh, yes!' Dandy was at a loss. 'Well, shall we go to yours now?'

'We would like you to choose, my dear. After all, you are likely to be there much longer than we shall be.'

This was the first time they had mentioned their age. The thought had crossed Dandy's mind from time to time: these aunts were older than Uncle James; Grannie was dead. If they died, what would happen to her? She would hate to have to go to Aunt Margaret. But it wouldn't be long, really, till she was grown-up enough to look after herself – or at least to give Aunt Margaret the excuse to say that, she added realistically. It was lucky that Aunt Margaret was a socialite! But the aunts were watching her: waiting for a reply.

'I liked the big red one with all the steps at the front – the one where the choirboys sang,' she said.

'Yes. It is beautiful. I like that one too,' said Aunt Violet. 'Alice finds the steps a bit much, but we can go up the gentle slope to one of the side entrances, eh, Alice?'

'Of course. I liked the boys' singing too,' said Alice. 'So, that's decided. The singing does it!'

'They didn't sing like ordinary boys, did they?' said Dandy. 'I mean, my brothers didn't sound like that when they were singing – not that they sang very often, just daft football songs and that.'

'These boys are learning to use their head voices and

to float the voice. That is called "the cathedral sound". It *is* so lovely. Though it makes you think they are angelic, I know for a fact that these same little angels often have comic books under those snowy surplices and they manage to read them during the sermon. A lady whose nephew sang in that choir told me.'

'Wouldn't they be seen?' asked Dandy, intrigued.

'No. It seems that they can prop up the knee which is nearest to the congregation and the cassock and surplice hide the book. They have sweets in their pockets too. Very earthly little angels, you'll agree.'

'I'll watch out for them.'

'Oh, you mustn't do that. You'll miss the sermon, and Violet and I intend to examine you on it each Sunday when we get home.'

Dandy looked at them, startled, till Violet gave the show away by snorting.

In her bath that night, Dandy tried 'the cathedral sound'. It wasn't too difficult. With a little bit of practice she was sure she could do it. In their room, the sisters listened. 'Alice, I do think we shall have to buy a piano for that girl, don't you?'

'Yes, Violet, but not quite yet. One step at a time.'

Over breakfast Alice treated Dandy to another surprise. 'Violet and I were discussing botany last night. We hadn't really made provision for that in your curriculum. I know, my dear, that you studied the subject at school and did supremely well, but you had no opportunity for what they call "field work". Now that is the most enjoyable part of botany to my mind – finding something you have only read about in books. We had a governess who was an excellent teacher: used to take us up the Gleniffer Braes chiefly. Neither Violet nor I is fit for much climbing nowadays and the town is becoming so built-up that one has to go further afield.

Some of the unspoilt stretches of the west coast would provide some useful finds for us, so what do you think of trips there in the spring?'

Before Dandy could answer, there was a loud rapping at the door. 'Now who?' said Alice, but Dandy was already hurrying away.

'Is there a Dandy Baxter here?' asked a boy of about her own age. In his hand she saw a letter with the magic Canadian stamp.

'That's me,' she said, stretching out her hand.

'The postman's on holiday,' he said, handing over his precious burden. 'The other one couldn't make head or tail of it – the name wasn't on any door . . .'

'Aye! That's fine, thanks.' Dandy hastily closed the door and ran to the conservatory. 'It's a letter – not Mother's writing. Maybe George . . .' She was ripping it open as she spoke and glancing at the signature. 'It's Billy.'

It's such a long time since you got a letter and I know that Ma and May are worried but Pa will not let us spend money on paper. I told Aunt Marie though I didn't mean to, it just came out when she asked what I did with my apple money in the fall. That's what they call autumn you see. I told her that Faither took most of it but I had managed to buy Ma some writing paper. She's still got a wee bit left but he says that the stamps are that expensive and we must make every penny prisoner till we get our land and then we will need it for trees and tools and then we will have to build a house. We will have to help because that's what they do here. I'm fed up hearing him talk about saving. It's no fun. Mind you we do get some fun here. The boys know a good place to swim. We skinny dip. You know what that is Dandy? We take off all our clothes. Of course the girls don't get going to that place. I expect they go somewhere else 'cos everyone here can swim. And George goes fishing with some of the older boys and they get lovely fish for nothing. He gave some to Aunt Marie cos she gives us so many things and helps to show us how to do things for ourselves. The nice folk who gave us coffee when we arrived and saw the messy cabin gave us lots of things too when they moved to the real big house that their Pa and the other men had built. The bunk beds are quite comfy now with the special little mattresses that their mother had made. Folks make everything themselves here. They pluck the feathers from the hens to make quilts and things. Aunt Marie says it doesn't matter how much paper I use. She's got plenty and she'll stamp it and post it for me and you can write back to me at her house if you don't want Pa to know that you got this and she will write her address proply at the end so that you will know. It will be our little secret and she says that she is going to give me the stuff to make a pen for goats. I know how to do it for I helped her when she needed a new one and I like the goats and she says she will give me a couple of goats and Pa can't put them in the bank. She's funny but she says we'll just have to be clever and keep quiet. I've used an awful lot of paper. Tell Aunt Violet I showed Aunt Marie how to make Scotch pancakes and she let me take a big parcel of them home.

Love
Billy

Dandy was laughing at Marie Friedland's joke, but the tears were glittering on her lashes.

'I like the sound of his Aunt Marie,' said Alice. 'She sounds a sensible woman – and with a sense of humour too.'

'Fancy Billy remembering how to make pancakes,' said Violet. 'I must have made an impression on that young man. Remember how angry he was, Dandy, when you arrived and he lost his concentration.'

'Yes, and Aunt Alice told the one about the drop scones. That stopped him fighting, didn't it? It sounds as if this Mrs Friedland is good at that. She'll maybe be a help to Mother – or *Ma* as they say over there. I hope so!'

As Dandy went off to water her salad vegetables, the sisters sat quietly looking at each other. 'She still worries about them,' said Violet.

Alice's hope that they might fit in a surprise visit to the coast before the cool weather set in was not fulfilled. An unexpected storm removed slates from the cottage roof. The slaters were all busy and the Misses McLaren had to wait for attention. September was upon them; a tang in the air in the morning and the nights drawing in. 'Well, it's something to look forward to in the spring,' said Alice, and Dandy heartily agreed.

'Only we won't be able to smell the ozone,' said Violet.

Alice exploded into laughter. 'I'd forgotten that. You tell her, Violet. You were always better at imitating old Cranky.'

'Well, Dandy,' Violet started, 'it was like this. We had a governess that none of us liked very much – Miss Rankine. We christened her Cranky Ranky. She *was* serious about her work and I think our parents thought they were getting their money's worth, but she certainly wasn't much fun. She could be very scathing and one of her pet hates was people who sniffed the sea air and

212

said, "Smell the ozone." "What they are smelling," she used to say, "is rotting seaweed." '

'It isn't quite so poetic, though, is it?' said Dandy. '*Smell the rotting seaweed.*' She intoned the words with a grand gesture which had her aunts laughing again. 'I've often read about "the salt tang of the sea", but, surely, salt has no smell?'

'No, it hasn't,' said Alice, 'and yet there's something about the smell of the sea, even when there's no seaweed on the beach.'

'I'll sniff the Espedair Burn and smell the ozone,' Dandy said.

The Christmas and New Year festivities came as a welcome break to both sisters. Dandy was as keen to learn about cooking and baking as she was about nearly everything else. The kitchen with its glowing range, racks of shining pans, large scrubbed table and comfy armchairs by the fire was such a contrast to the tiny scullery she had had to struggle in when she was younger.

Violet was helping her make some new dresses as she had grown out of her previous winter outfits. One was a beauty in apple green velvet. Violet was going to teach her how to make a lacy collar for it. As she helped mix the fruit for the black bun, and practised how to ice the Christmas cake, Dandy was dreaming of that dress. The aunts had been urging her to join the Bible class at church. So far she had found it difficult to approach the young people of her own age. She knew that it worried Alice and Violet, but it was almost impossible to explain her feelings even to herself. Part of it was that disastrous affair of the thread mill. She still felt dreadful about Andy losing his job. It was her fault, though innocently done. Perhaps it went back further, though, to the time when she was always so caught up in household chores that she never had time to play with girls of her own age. They didn't have to cover up their father's drunkenness: the fact that he was sometimes so bad that he rolled into bed in his dirty working clothes. But she shouldn't be remembering those times, she chided herself. She should remember the ship stealing down the river and his long arm waving that handkerchief till he was out of sight. The white flag of surrender it could be – if you had enough imagination. Aunt Alice always tried to put things in the best possible light. She must learn to do the same. That green velvet dress! Aunt Violet said her yellow hair was perfect for it. The Bible class would be having a Christmas party. She could wear it. What was stopping her from joining? Nothing sensible. 'I think I'll join the Bible class on Sunday,' she said to Violet.

'Good. We'd better get your velvet dress finished before the party, then.'

The things you dreaded most often turned out to be nothing at all, Aunt Alice had said on one occasion and, come to think of it, what was there to worry about? If her new companions *should* turn out to be uncongenial she could sit and dream, thinking of the many new poems she was learning. There was nothing wrong with that. Even sweeping the mill floors had been tolerable while she was reciting poems in her head.

Aunt Alice was right. Everything was very informal and she was welcomed with smiles all round. Nor did she have to sit and dream of her poems because she soon found that the minister shared her enthusiasm and quoted one of her favourites in his address. 'He's always doing that,' Nan, the girl next to her, assured her. 'He sometimes asks if we know where the quote comes from. Usually I don't.'

'I'm glad I came,' said Dandy.

In the big church each Sunday where the congregation were well spread out she had the chance to observe many of them. One family intrigued her. The mother looked young and pretty, beautifully dressed in bright colours. She remarked on this to Nan. 'Oh, yes, she's beautiful, isn't she? That's Mrs Eadie ... you know, they have the big factory that makes mattresses; pots of money, but they say she's nice to work for – not stuck-up like some folk.'

It was useful to be in the Bible class. Often the titbits of information she received from her fellow members were of the sort that her aunts would be unlikely to pick up in their more circumspect circle. The minister and Dandy had been a surprise to each other. While she had been delighted to find how often he quoted poetry in his brief talks to them, he, in turn, was amazed to find how extensive her knowledge of each quotation was. It became almost a game: he would quote someone and then say, 'Dandy will tell you who said that.' As she became absorbed into the little group this would be the cue for someone to say, 'Bet she doesn't know.' Then there would be laughter and hand-clapping when she did.

She had never realized how lonely she was till she and her aunts were sitting waiting for the bells to welcome in 1909. The cottage was spotless. Every piece of silver and brass shone. Bowls of hyacinths had obligingly bloomed right on time – a luxury that had been unknown to Dandy. Sprays of her precious daphne scented some corners. The black bun and shortbread that she had helped to make were waiting on the beautifully decked trolley, but it was all so quiet! 'I wish some of the gang from the church were here,' she thought. Then her imagination set to work, wondering what they would say. Maybe someone would make up a daft poem and ask her who wrote that. Yes! That was the sort of thing that would happen.

215

'Look at that lovely smile, Alice! Our Dandy is happy.'

Dandy jumped guiltily, then rewarded Violet with a real smile, 'Of course I am.' She gave herself a silent pat on the back. She was learning to be a *real* lady, matching her behaviour to the occasion. The aunts were constantly putting themselves out on her behalf. She would do the same.

Soon the days were lengthening and it was time to prune some of her shrubs. The snowdrops finished and crocuses took over, followed by the daffodils. It was time to dig the vegetable beds and the cycle of planting began. She was hard at it one Saturday morning when she was surprised by a visit from Nan. 'Your aunt said I would find you here. I didn't know you were a gardener as well as everything else.'

Dandy was startled. 'What do you mean – *as well as everything else?*'

'Well, you seem to have read every book there ever was and you can make such nice clothes and then you can sing. I have to keep quiet in case I put everyone off. You're so lucky! But that's not what I came to ask. My mother wondered if you would like to come to tea tomorrow after the Bible class – just dumpling, nothing grand. It's my grannie's birthday and she thought you could keep me cheery and maybe sing something to Grannie – she was a singer when she was a lassie, though she's terrible now. You should hear her! But it would be nice for me if you would come.'

Dandy gazed in amazement. True, she had once been invited to Mr Forbes' house, but this was different. This was someone her own age inviting her. How would the aunts feel about it? They had encouraged her to join the Bible class: said she should have friends her own age. What would a *real* lady say to Nan?

216

'That sounds just lovely, Nan. I'll have to check with my aunts, but I'm sure it will be all right.'

The following evening saw her setting out in one of her new dresses. The neat little parcel she carried contained a box of Violet's delightful chocolate truffles for the old lady.

'We're losing her, Alice,' said Violet as they turned from the window. 'It's only natural and I should welcome it, I suppose.'

'Well, we *are* trying to fit her for life and, let's face it, we shan't be here forever. Her fine independence and application are all very well, but she has to learn to fit in. Her early years were spent either on the defensive or the attack. She must become more relaxed, and this sort of homely party – a cloutie dumpling, no less – is exactly what's needed.'

Dandy didn't know quite what to expect as she stood on the doorstep of Nan's flat. The varnish was well kept; the knocker shining and, she noted, the door on the other side of the landing was similarly maintained. Careful people, obviously. There was no sign of children: no marks of carelessly kicked balls on the landing walls. This building was more like Grannie's, she decided, than the cramped noisy quarters which she had been familiar with and which the Misses McLaren had endured with such stoicism.

Nan herself opened the door, but her mother immediately bustled to join her with a stream of welcoming words on her lips. 'Fat chance of feeling shy here,' Dandy thought, smiling her relief as she was introduced to Nan's father, Nan's brother and Nan's sister-in-law. The polite enquiries as to the health of the Misses McLaren were so obviously just part of the general stream of civilities that there was no need for her to suspect noseyness or feel diffident about answering. In her relaxed state she admired the enormous spiced dumpling with its jellied outer skin. 'I'll bet that's bigger than the one in *A Christmas Carol*,' she said. Several pairs of eyes looked puzzled. 'Our Dandy has read nearly every book there is,' Nan declared.

While Dandy disclaimed any such distinction, her heart felt warmed. 'Our Dandy!' That was what Nan – her own age – had said. She was accepted.

Chapter 15

Peace and continuity was what Aunt Alice had told
Aunt Margaret she was needing, and as the time flew
by Dandy rejoiced in the stability she was able to enjoy.
As week succeeded week, packed with interesting new
discoveries, and as the garden responded to her efforts
and people congratulated her on the results, she glowed
with satisfaction. No unpaid governesses ever had a
keener student – not merely a sponge to absorb everything they offered, but an inquiring mind which
made them examine the material they were expound-
ing.

Looking back later, Dandy thought that no year had
ever seemed to pass so quickly. The fact that she was
deliberately blotting out the memories of the thread
mills and facing up to the fact that worrying about her
mother and May was doing them no good, helped her
to bury herself in her studies. The botany lessons in the
summer were thrilling, based as they were on trips to
the west coast. Dandy never tired of gazing at the mountains floating in the sea.

Ruefully she noticed that her attitudes were changing.
As she grew in confidence, mixing happily with her
own age group, she began surreptitiously to mimic her
aunts. They were so old-fashioned! These ventures into
silent insurrection made her feel guilty. Constantly she
reminded herself of all these two had meant to her: the
haven she had found in their little flat when things were
desperate in her own home; the beautiful room in the
cottage which was hers alone; the garden where she

ruled supreme; the role they had assumed in acting as governesses when they might well have felt entitled to take life easy. Instead, they had thought up one ploy after another to make life interesting for her. On these trips to the coast each new site seemed to have something to offer in the way of flowers, and Violet was seldom stumped for an answer.

Soon it was autumn again and she was pruning and clearing up. Then with the cold weather she was cosily installed in Uncle James's book-lined sitting room. No wonder he became a recluse! The thought came to her more than once when the friendly crackle of the fire was the accompaniment to her exploration into new literary territory. Then she would think of her friends in the church, of the rounds of Christmas parties already being planned, the lovely clothes that Violet would insist on giving her.

The spring planting of 1910 gave her a feeling of *déjà vu*. It seemed no time since she had been engaged on the same job. Perhaps that meant that she was now a seasoned gardener. Perhaps that was how Uncle James's days had slipped by: the garden and books, from one joy to another. Some mild spring days allowed them to start on the trips to the coast again. This time Dandy knew which glens had the most spectacular carpets of primroses.

By August they had visited all the coast locations within travelling distance. The aunts announced one morning that her next treat was to be a trip to Langbank near the mouth of the Clyde to see a much-vaunted new liner go out on its maiden voyage. Aunt Violet had discussed her outfit as if they were going to meet the King and Queen. 'Well, you spend so much of your time grubbing about in old clothes in the garden. It adds to an occasion, I think, if you know you are looking your best. We must plan for changes in the weather, of course, but a fine warm day like this would let you wear that lovely big hat . . .'

Violet got her fine warm day and all three of them were glad of their shady hats as the minutes dragged by and the liner became long overdue. Nearby Dandy could see Mr and Mrs Eadie with two of their children, who were now becoming restless. Mrs Eadie, in a pale blue floating dress with parasol to match, looked a picture as usual. Dandy had watched slightly enviously when the father had given the boy a large package of sweets, whispering something in his ear before turning to offer the little girl a smaller pack. Mr Eadie saw Aunt Alice and, raising his hat, came towards them.

Their attention was suddenly drawn by the sound of the little girl coughing. Mr Eadie, turning, said angrily, 'John, I told you they were too big for Sarah.'

'But she wanted one of mine.' The boy spoke defiantly. The coughing developed into a whoop. With a startled look, John ran off, almost under the wheels of a passing coach. Mr Eadie ran to catch him while his wife struggled to close her parasol, then cast it aside impatiently to attend to Sarah, who was rapidly becoming blue in the face. Her efforts seemed to make no difference, the child grew worse and, just as Mr Eadie returned dragging his son, he was in time to catch his wife as she swooned. Dandy dashed quickly to Sarah, hoisted her towards a nearby boulder and squatted there with the child held firmly face down over her knee while she hooked the offending sweet out with her little finger. 'Stop crying. It's all over now, Sarah,' she said firmly, patting the child on the back. 'You'll mess up your pretty dress if you drop all that water over it.' Sarah, surprised at this abruptness, stopped crying and stared.

Violet was waving smelling salts under Mrs Eadie's nose while Alice chafed the blood back into her hands.

'I am deeply indebted, Miss McLaren,' began Mr Eadie. 'I do not know the young lady . . .'

'Our niece, Dandy.'

'How I wish we had you at home, Miss Dandy,' he said. 'We are in a pretty fix, I can tell you. Our eldest, Elizabeth, has a throat infection and has been fevered. Their governess, who has stayed at home with her, has a leg in plaster after tripping over a tree root. The nursery maid has gone home because of a crisis there and may not be back for all we know, and Nurse is busy with baby. We thought it would be a good idea to bring John and Sarah here today, but, really, they're too young . . .'

His wife joined in, 'An assistant governess would be a godsend to us. I can see that your niece is adept in dealing with children. I don't suppose you could spare her for a month or two?'

The aunts looked at Dandy. She seemed surprised but not unwilling. 'Well, Dandy, it's your decision,' said Alice.

'Would I get home to my garden sometimes?'

'Let's say Wednesday afternoons and Saturday night till Monday morning.'

Dandy shot a quick glance at her aunts, then, reassured, replied, 'Yes. I'd love to help you.'

That night, Dandy could hardly believe what she had done. As they sat in the conservatory with their coffee, she voiced her misgivings. 'I won't know my way around a huge house like that.'

'You'll be shown round the places that most concern you as soon as you arrive, my dear. Violet and I used to love showing new people where everything was.'

'Not just the house,' interpolated Violet. 'We liked to take them to our favourite parts of the garden – you'll enjoy that, Dandy. Oh, Alice, remember that French governess . . .' The two women burst out laughing while Dandy stared in amazement. A French governess – they had never mentioned *her* before.

Alice steadied herself. '*We* didn't have a French governess, my dear, nothing so grand! Friends who *did* have one were in a fix. They had been given the chance of a cruising holiday in the Western Isles by a wealthy family who had rather a grand yacht. This governess flatly refused to go. She had been extremely ill crossing the Channel and was dreading the return journey as it was. In fact, our friends were scared they might be saddled with her for ever! At least that's what they sometimes said. Anyway, they had no idea what to do with her for the three weeks they intended to be away. The decorators were coming in and Cook and most of the other servants were going on holiday. They asked our parents if we would like to borrow her for that time. Well, Violet and I took it upon ourselves to show her the garden not long after she arrived. The rose garden was all right. We even managed to answer some of her questions in our scanty French. Then we told her we were going to take her to the bit we called the little jungle. "It's guarded by a monkey puzzle," I said. Mademoiselle screamed and started to run back towards the house. "What's wrong?" we asked, pelting along beside her. "I hate monkeys," she sobbed.

'Oh, Dandy, what a time we had convincing her that we had *pas un singe*!'

The next morning was spent preparing for Dandy's departure. She had had a restless night, sometimes wrestling with monkeys who dropped on her from a huge monkey puzzle tree. She would wake up sweating. Then she would remember Uncle James, the only person she had ever heard give the tree its proper name.

'The Araucaria,' he had said. She would recite it softly over and over again till she fell asleep, but then the monkeys would be there once more. Sometimes they changed into the boys she had wrestled with in the school playground a long, long time ago. Sometimes they were her brother George and she would feel guilty when she beat him off. It was worse when they changed into Andy Connell and he was telling her that he had lost his job, 'And what will my grannie do now? I gave her my pay every week. It's all your fault.' Then big Meg was having a go at strangling her, saying, 'What's in a kiss? You'll be lucky if anybody wants to kiss you when I'm finished with you.' That was the worst dream of all and she woke with her nightdress wound round her like a tourniquet. All in all, the morning light was a relief and the flowers on the curtains a balm.

Violet was quite strict about which clothes she should pack. 'Aren't these too good?' Dandy asked.

'Not at all. They are not showy . . . very suitable.'

'But I'm only a servant, really, Aunt Violet.'

'You are assistant governess, not kitchen maid, Dandy. You are doing Mr and Mrs Eadie a favour in their present crisis. You will be polite and helpful as you always are to us, but I'm sure your employers will not expect you to be servile.' Dandy straightened up unconsciously while Violet turned to wink at Alice.

As they waited for the sound of the coach, Dandy issued her last-minute instructions as to which plants would need watering every night. 'And check my tumshie seedlings too,' she added. This had become a bit of a joke. The sisters, who had never heard the word 'tumshie' used before Dandy came to their garden, had immediately made it their own. 'Shall I boil up some crunchy tumshie?' Violet would ask.

The coachman dealt with her trunk while Dandy made her hasty farewells. 'I'll be back in a few days,' she reminded them.

'Of course,' said Alice, smiling.

They waved her off. As they made their way back towards the house, Violet turned to her sister. 'She's definitely growing away from us,' she said.

'That's healthy. We wouldn't be doing our job if she didn't,' replied Alice, wiping a tear.

The butterflies in Dandy's stomach were having a wild time long before the coach turned into the imposing drive and crunched over the red gravel. Her head turned from side to side as she tried to identify the trees and shrubs which lined their way. Then the drive widened and split: a space opened before them and she saw Braeval rearing up on the rise, its buff sandstone washed pink by the sunshine which turned every window into a shining beacon. 'And I'm to live here!' she told herself. 'Assistant governess! I wish May could see it.'

Her legs felt shaky as she stepped down and saw the heavy front door open. She was not to be treated like a servant, at least not like a kitchen maid. She was to enter by the front door. What was it Aunt Violet had said? *You will be doing Mr and Mrs Eadie a favour. You will be polite and helpful to them as you always are to us.* Come to think of it, her aunts had lived in a big house like this and they were just ordinary old ladies, only better educated. That was what made them behave differently from Grannie and people like that.

Mrs Eadie herself was at the door to welcome her and, at her side, a plump pleasant-looking woman – maybe ten years younger than her aunts – was smiling at her. Miss McGregor, the governess, she guessed before Mrs Eadie made the introduction. 'Your trunk

225

will be taken up to your room, Dandy. I have arranged for some tea to be brought to the morning room. I thought it would be a good idea if we three could have a little chat and work out a modus operandi.' Dandy, smiling her agreement, blessed Aunt Alice for insisting that she must learn some Latin. A year ago she had never heard of a modus operandi – it could have been an embroidery stitch!

Her duties seemed to be fairly general; in fact, it seemed that she was to be a pair of legs for Miss McGregor more than anything else. 'I *do* have to walk a little, of course,' said the governess, 'but I can't get up any speed and the children are naturally very active. If you could take them for walks now and again while I correct and prepare their work, it would be a great help. Sometimes it would be a help to have them separated for lessons too. I think John makes fun of his little sister's efforts at times – though not when I am present of course,' she added with a smile.

'I am sure that you will find Miss McGregor very understanding and helpful,' said her employer. 'Don't let the children bully you ... but I don't think you would, somehow.'

Dandy had to control her smile as she remembered how many boys had landed flat on their backs on the playground before they had half a chance to bully her. Obviously, such tactics would not be acceptable in this setting, but being bullied was not at the top of her list of worries.

'They are in the garden somewhere now,' said Mrs Eadie. 'Duncan, our head gardener, will see that they don't get up to any mischief. He is the boss down there and I leave him to it. They'll soon get their marching orders if there's any disobedience. Perhaps Miss McGregor and you would like to join them? If you feel tired, Morag, you can leave the children to take Miss

Baxter round the rest of the grounds,' she added in an aside.

There was obvious respect between those two women, Dandy noted. Well, it looked as if she had nothing to fear from a nasty governess: no Cranky Ranky here.

The children stared as she approached. 'Now,' said Miss McGregor, 'let's have a welcome for Miss Baxter. You've met her before, haven't you? What about shaking hands?'

John's face was flushed rather guiltily, but Sarah soon recovered and eagerly offered to take over the job as guide when Morag McGregor's steps lagged. 'I think it would be better if the two of you guided Miss Baxter. Then, if one forgets the name of a plant, the other may remember.'

'Top marks to Miss McGregor,' thought Dandy. 'Keep them within bounds.'

'If you meet Duncan – he's our head gardener, Miss Baxter – you will introduce him, children. Also, Jock – he's our odd-job man . . .'

'Jock's a joke,' said John. 'He's always doing this –' He and his sister pulled their hair up on top of their heads.

'That isn't funny, children,' said Morag McGregor. 'I've told you already. I will not have you making a fool of him. The poor boy is not quite right,' she added quietly to Dandy.

Now, Dandy assured herself as Morag departed, Mrs Eadie obviously thought that she could handle two active children. After all, they were just like George and Billy, even if their dress and speech were different. The same mischief was in them and you had to keep a thought ahead. 'Right! What do my guides think I should see first?' she asked.

The gardens were much more extensive than she had

imagined. When they *did* meet Jock, he gazed at her in open admiration, pulling his hair up in exactly the way the children had described. Because she was having difficulty keeping her own face straight, she decided to ignore their stifled giggles which went on quietly as they guided her to the west lawn. At the far end, the focal point of the view was a monkey puzzle tree. 'Just the stuff!' Dandy thought. 'Give them a laugh.' So, she retold the tale of her aunts and their French governess. 'And what a time they had convincing her that they had *pas un singe*.'

'What's that?' asked Sarah.

'"Not one monkey", silly,' said John scornfully.

'There's no need to speak like that to your sister, John. *You* didn't know what it meant when you were her age.' This was a stab in the dark. Dandy was relieved to find her guess correct as he mumbled, 'Well . . .'

'I think a brief apology would be in order, don't you, young man?'

'Sorry,' he muttered, his face crestfallen. Dandy suddenly conjured up Aunt Alice and how she could raise a smile to take away the sting. She threw her arms wide and declaimed, '*Absolument pas de singes*.'

John repeated her gesture, giggling, '*Absolument, Mademoiselle*.'

Sarah, not to be outdone, copied her brother. 'It means "absolutely",' he said kindly.

'First round to me,' thought Dandy. 'I wouldn't have believed that he would know it either: I was prepared to explain. Miss McGregor must set high standards. That's good. I'll probably be able to pick up some things too.'

'What would you like to see now?' asked Sarah when the tour of the grounds was completed.

'What about the schoolroom?'

228

John gave a groan, which he hastily stifled when Dandy caught his eye. 'It's upstairs,' he said. 'Would you not like to rest first . . . have a lemonade or something?' In truth, Dandy *was* feeling tired, but she knew quite well who it was that wanted a lemonade and, having gained the ascendancy, she was not going to let Master John dictate the programme.

'Not a bit of it,' she said. 'Lead the way.'

The schoolroom was spacious and sunny with a beautiful view over the walled rose garden. 'These children don't know they're born,' Dandy thought, remembering her early struggles to get an education. 'Fancy groaning about coming up to a marvellous place like this!' She looked at the varnished desks, the blackboard and the big table in the middle of the floor with a comfortable chair and footstool awaiting Miss McGregor. Well-filled bookshelves lined two walls.

'Would you like to see the music room?' asked John, eager to restore his reputation. Dandy was startled. She had never thought of a music room. 'Is it far away?' she asked.

'No. Just next door. It's handy for the schoolroom, you see, but a little further away from the nurseries so that the baby does not get disturbed.'

'I see,' said Dandy. 'Where is baby now?'

'Nurse has probably taken him for a walk in the woods. She says that the movement of the baby carriage soothes him and that trees give off oxygen and that's good for babies.'

'Rather good for us all, I should say,' smiled Dandy.

'Yes, we'd all be dead without it, wouldn't we?' He returned her smile.

'I'm winning,' thought Dandy, just as Miss McGregor appeared to announce, 'Minnie has taken your tea to the day nursery, children. I shall be taking Miss Baxter down to the drawing room and then I shall be up to see you. I expect good behaviour, remember!'

'Am I tidy enough?' asked Dandy as Morag McGregor led the way.

'Yes, of course. There's no wind to ruffle your hair today. What did you think of the gardens?'

'Lovely! Much bigger than I expected.'

'Yes. I think they've been laid out well. You keep getting surprises when you turn a corner, don't you?'

'We met Duncan. He seemed quite happy to answer my questions. Do you think he would let me help sometimes if I have a minute or two?' She hesitated before adding, 'Or would that not be the done thing?' Somehow she knew she could trust Morag McGregor not to sneer at her ignorance of procedure.

'I'm sure Duncan would be grateful. The seasonal workers are nearly all paid off by now. In the winter we have only Duncan, Alec, his assistant, and Jock. As you can see, Jock is brawn, not brain, but Duncan can manage him. I think Mr Eadie took the boy on out of sympathy. His mother worked in the kitchen here at one time, you see. She feels that he is safe here. Outside he had a rough time with other boys teasing him. Duncan always warns the seasonal workers quite strictly. Human nature can be a funny thing, Dandy. Perfectly pleasant young men can take a cruel pleasure in mimicking the likes of Jock. My father, who was a minister, used to say it was the devil's delight to torment the weak. But yes, at this time of year there is still quite a lot of dead-heading to be done and the weeds don't stop growing, so I'm sure Duncan would be glad of a hand there at least. You're keen on gardening?'

'Daft about it,' said Dandy succinctly.

*   *   *

230

Dandy's fears about not being able to find her way around soon proved groundless, as did her fear of not being up to the job. The authority she had established right at the start over John stood her in good stead. One worry she had not anticipated was Jock. He followed her around, grinning and dribbling. 'Never heed him lass,' said Duncan when he noticed her unease. 'He's a puir harmless creature.' Nonetheless, he always called the lad away to another task when he saw that his presence was troubling her. It was difficult for Dandy to explain this fear to herself. Jock was always smiling. She had never seen him look angry or heard an angry word. Why did her skin prickle when he got too near? And why did he loom up frequently in her dreams, his smile getting wider and wider with the horrible saliva trickling down and falling from his chin?

She tried to put those thoughts behind her in the schoolroom and particularly in the music room. Morag McGregor heard her singing something to the children one day and immediately decided that she must develop that lovely voice. The singing lessons were soon combined with piano lessons. Dandy threw herself into her music studies as she had embraced all the others – science excepted. It was nothing to her to rise early and creep along to the music room for an hour's practice before the others were up.

Morag McGregor was very understanding about her enthusiasm for the garden and would often tell her to go off while the children did their last written work of the day. Sometimes Elizabeth, the eldest child, would seek her out in the garden while the younger ones were playing. She was a thoughtful, serious child and Morag's easiest pupil. Her particular love was French, which she was always anxious to try out. Knowing that her shortcomings in the language could easily be detected, Dandy adopted the pose that she was very rusty and would welcome some practice with Elizabeth: then the child could tell her what she had forgotten. This policy was ideally suited to Elizabeth and Dandy continued her education without any loss of face. 'I'm thinking things out like Aunt Alice,' she told herself.

'Dear me, I *do* sound devious,' said Alice when Dandy aired this view the following weekend. 'Still, it *does* seem sensible, I must say. The only drawback we could see about your going to Braeval was that it would interrupt your studies. Instead, you are enjoying music lessons which were not possible here and your French is continuing too.'

'And I've learned a few more gardening tips from Duncan,' said Dandy. 'That's my own garden put to bed for the winter now. Only the daphne to look forward to. I always associate it with Uncle James.'

'I remember,' said Alice. 'You were so thrilled with it on your first visit. Doesn't that seem long ago! How different your life is now.'

'Thanks to you and Aunt Violet,' said Dandy. 'Oh, I must go and tell her a new trick I learned from the cook . . . when you're rolling puff pastry . . .'

She hurried off to the kitchen, leaving Alice fishing for her handkerchief.

Though gardening at the cottage was more or less finished till spring, much clearing up had still to be done at Braeval. Duncan and Alec were busy sawing logs, so Dandy took it upon herself to see that all the climbing plants were securely tied against the winter storms. There was only one snag and that was Jock. No matter which part of the garden she chose, he followed her there. Duncan had to concentrate on the job in hand, of course, so she could not rely on his intervention. It was too chilly for Elizabeth, who was subject to colds, and there seemed to be no escaping him. Dandy felt useless anger boil up in her. Why was she afraid? He had never said anything she could take objection to. Everyone agreed he was harmless and Duncan was working with him all the time. Surely he would know. She would have to ignore him and get on with the job.

She was busy with some tendrils of clematis, weaving them back into their trellis. From the corner of her eye she saw Jock approaching with the shambling walk which could seem comical to other people, but which her imagination turned sinister. 'Ignore him,' she said to herself. 'He's only a silly boy.'

'Miss Baxter . . .' his voice was wheedling. She turned. His trousers were undone. She gazed, horrified, as he quickened. 'It's big, isn't it? Feel it, Miss!' He was walking towards her. With a gasp Dandy was off, her dress catching on the bushes as she passed in a headlong rush. Within sight of the house she changed to a brisk walk. Morag McGregor met her as she made for her room. 'You're looking rosy. All that fresh air, all that energy – aren't you lucky!'

In her upset state, Dandy was tempted to blurt out her story. Morag was a sensible woman, calm and dependable. She would know what to do, Dandy was sure of it. But then Aunt Alice's training made her pause. 'Always think before you speak, Dandy,' she had said. 'It can save so much trouble and regret.' If she divulged this to Morag it was almost sure to reach her employers' ears. What would happen to Jock then? Probably the same thing that had happened to Andy. And she would be blamed by Jock's friends. Even if there were not a Big Meg to exact retribution, there was her own conscience, which still troubled her from time to time over the mill episode: a worry that could suddenly steal the joy from the present.

'It's really cold out there today. I was feeling quite

chilled so I hurried back,' she said. 'That rosiness is incipient frostbite, I can assure you.'

Morag McGregor went off laughing, little knowing that Duncan had just lost a valued assistant.

Chapter 16

Abstinence from gardening went against the grain with Dandy. Her walks with the children were almost a penance when she saw how many little jobs were in need of doing. It was a relief to hear that Duncan and Alec had finished with the logs. Little by little, she slipped back into her old ways. At first Jock seemed to be keeping his distance, then gradually he started following her about again. Dandy would warily change her position to be in sight of Duncan. Sometimes it meant leaving a task uncompleted – a thing she hated. Duncan, quiet and stolid though he might seem, didn't miss much. The lass who had always done her work in a way he fully approved now seemed to be getting flighty. He took to watching and saw that it was Jock who was upsetting her, making her fidgety and restless. She was daft to worry about the harmless bugger, he thought, but he would see that she wasn't troubled. After that, Jock was called away to some other task whenever he ventured too near Dandy. It happened so often that Dandy relaxed, sure that Duncan would see her safe.

It was a crisp cool day. Thinning out the shrubs necessitated the pruning saw – a nice warming job. She was enjoying herself. 'Miss – Miss – look!' The same wheedling voice, coming closer. 'Go away, Jock, I'm busy,' she said loudly without turning round.

'Jock!' Duncan's bellow echoed on the frosty air. 'Come here this instant!' Duncan in that mood was not to be ignored. With relief she heard Jock's receding footsteps; then found she was shaking. Slowly she picked up her tools and made for the house. In her own room she sat and stared in the wardrobe mirror without seeing herself. Why did men – some men – have to be like that? Her father when drunk . . . aggressive, merciless . . . She shuddered.

Next afternoon, she gave herself a talking to – Aunt Alice fashion. Running away would only punish herself. Why should daft Jock be allowed to keep her out of the garden? Duncan – comforting thought – was aware of her worries and would keep silly Jock, who didn't know what he was doing, at bay. Thus fortified, she sang as she snipped at the wood that had died back and rejoiced in the trim appearance of each plant when she finished.

Jock was there again, but she would ignore him. 'Miss – Miss – '

'I'm busy, Jock. I think Duncan wants you.'

'Oh, no, he can't.' He gurgled with laughter. 'I've locked him in the red shed, you see, and he can't stop me.'

'What?' Dandy took one desperate look then turned and ran. As she pounded along she tried to reassure herself. Surely he couldn't have . . . he was just saying it . . . he was daft. The shed was in sight and, yes, the key was in the door. She wrenched it open. Duncan, grey-faced and with blood dribbling down past his ear, tried to focus on her face. 'Duncan! What has he done to you?'

Duncan's voice seemed to come from far away, 'I've never known the daft bugger do anything like this before.'

Then there was a thud and the shed door slammed. The key ground in the lock. 'What's he at now?' asked Duncan.

Dandy stretched up to look through the tiny window. 'He's away to the old shed. I don't think he took the

236

key. Where's Alec?' She had to stoop to hear the reply: 'Stacking the dry logs in the cellar up at the house.'

'Then there's nobody near to let us out. Wait, I'll see what I can do.' With a silent apology to Violet for the destruction of her fine needlework, Dandy turned and ripped a strip off her petticoat. Then she tied it round his head, dabbing the blood as best she could. 'That will have to do till we get help. How long has Alec been away?'

'I don't . . . know.'

'Never mind, someone's bound to come soon,' said Dandy, with more courage than conviction. They were much too far away to be heard from the house. Miss McGregor was reading to the younger ones. Elizabeth was practising her piano. Nurse was out walking in the woods. She had taken Mel, the labrador, with her. Mrs Eadie had a committee going great guns in the drawing room. No one was likely to visit this part of the garden for some time. Alec was their only hope. Stacking those enormous heaps of dry logs would be bound to take time. It all depended when he had started. Obviously it was no use asking Duncan again. He looked ghastly. She began to be seriously worried. What if he was bleeding internally and should be receiving attention? She turned to the window again. Jock was coming near. 'Jock,' she started to call, then noticed what he held in his hand. 'Oh, God, no!'

'What is it, lass?' asked Duncan.

'He's got a can of paraffin.'

Duncan struggled to rise, then fell back in a heap. Dandy took off her shoe, smashed the window and started to scream just as Jock threw the paraffin over the hut. Some splashed through the window and on to her dress. With rising horror she saw him take a box of matches from his pocket. She screamed again, even more loudly, then, turning, snatched a flowerpot and threw it just as Jock struck the match. The flame leapt over his hand which immediately went up to his hair in the familiar gesture. The blue flame shot up like a torch. Jock, with a bellow, started running in the direction of the lily pond beating his bent head with his elbows. Dandy screamed repeatedly, all attempts at self-control abandoned. Footsteps came thudding. 'It's Alec,' she said, leaning in sudden helplessness against the wall of the hut. The key rasped in the lock and Alec stood, panting, in the doorway. 'Whit's wrang? Oh, mah Goad, Duncan! Whit happened, lass?'

'It was daft Jock . . . locked him in the hut. He was laughing when he told me. I wasn't sure, but I ran to see. Then he locked me in too. He came back with paraffin. He was striking the match – ' Suddenly she was interrupted by a loud bellow, Mel's furious barking and then high screams. 'That's nurse,' said Dandy. 'You watch Duncan, Alec – I'll go. He might be harming the baby!' She was off like the wind. Nurse's screams were joined by raised female voices and calls of, 'What's happened?'

Dandy arrived as Nurse, kneeling at the edge of the pond beside Jock's still body, tried to pull herself together. 'I'm sorry, losing control like that, ladies. When I first saw him, he was running towards the pond with his hair smouldering. He was bent with his arms half over his face. He tripped on the paving. I heard a terrible crack. I knew what it meant. Dreadful! His head had caught on the edge of the little statue. No hope.' Her lip was trembling.

'You've had a shock, nurse. Go to your room now. I'll see to baby myself.' Mrs Eadie moved to the baby carriage.

A babble of voices were offering help when Mr Eadie's voice rang out, 'What's all this?'

'Oh, you're home, thank God! My ladies were just

leaving, Charles, when we found there had been a dreadful accident. Poor Jock has cracked his skull. Nurse says there's no hope. She's very upset.'

'The children?'

'Morag came out, but when she saw what had happened insisted on taking them back indoors.'

'Sensible woman. Now, ladies, I am very grateful for your offers of help, but you can safely go home now. I'll take over here.' The hint had been given courteously but firmly, and the women drifted off, murmuring their concerns.

Mr Eadie turned to Dandy. 'Can you explain any of this, my dear, and why are you reeking of paraffin?'

'Well, he locked Duncan in the red hut . . .'

'Jock? Locked Duncan in the red hut? Why?'

'I think you'd better come and see him. I bandaged his head, but . . .'

'Take baby indoors, love, and join me in the study when you can. I'll need to get to the bottom of this before we send for the police.'

He hurried to the hut with Dandy. Alec had cushioned an upturned bucket with a sack and Duncan, still dazed, was sipping slowly from the bottle that was held to his lips.

'Don't try to speak, Duncan,' said Mr Eadie. 'Alec can tell me.'

'Well, sir, I had been up at the house putting the logs in the cellar and I was on the way back down when I heard the screams.'

'Was that the woman, the nurse – '

'No, it was Miss Baxter. She was locked in with him.'

'Jock locked you both in?' Dandy nodded. 'Look, Alec, do you think you could see Duncan back to his cottage and get him to bed. He's badly shaken. I'll send one of the servants down with some food and I think we'll get the doctor to have a look at him. Dandy, come

239

back with me to the study. I'd like to get this story straight before we bring in the police. It'll save time in the long run. You're shaking, my dear. Take my arm.'

Even in her distressed state, Dandy was amused to see the housemaid goggle as she passed on the master's arm. 'Some strong tea and biscuits in the study, Nancy, please,' he called over his shoulder. 'Three cups and saucers.' He led Dandy to a comfortable leather chair. 'Now, calm yourself, my dear. We'll wait till my wife comes so that you don't have to tell the story twice.'

They did not have long to wait before Mrs Eadie came bustling in. 'Nurse said she was ashamed of herself and would be all right now. She's preparing the things for baby's bath. That will soon calm her down. Now what have you been saying, my dear?'

'Miss Baxter has said nothing, my love. We waited for you.' He turned to Dandy. 'Now, what I've gathered is that Jock locked Duncan in the red hut; he then told you; you ran to the hut; Jock followed and locked you in too. Am I right?'

'Yes. And then he came back with a can of paraffin. I broke the window and screamed. Then I saw him with the matches. Just as he struck one, I threw the flowerpot. The flame lit up his hand and he stuck it in his hair – you know the way he does – and then he started running with his arms sort of over his head.'

'Phew! Have you ever seen him give any sign of trouble . . . ?'

Dandy hesitated. Was this to be a repeat of the Andy Connell affair? Mr Eadie was waiting for an answer. 'Well,' she said reluctantly, 'Duncan said he was harmless, so I just tried to ignore it.'

'Ignore what?' said the Eadies in one voice.

Dandy blushed and could find nothing to say. Mrs Eadie pressed her for details and, getting no answer, grew impatient. 'Please don't waste time. We must not delay in sending for the police. My committee ladies will have spread the word.'

'It was about a fortnight ago: he came to me when I was working. He was always following me around. I didn't like it but couldn't understand why. That time he opened his trousers and . . .' She stopped as Mrs Eadie gasped.

Mr Eadie gave his wife a stern look. 'Are you saying that he displayed his person?'

'Yes, that's it,' said Dandy.

Mrs Eadie's handkerchief was being twisted to shreds. 'To think such a thing could happen in our household! What will your aunts think of us: you are in our care.'

Mr Eadie laid his hand briefly on his wife's arm. 'Did Duncan know what brought today's attack on?'

'No. He said he'd never known the daft bugger do anything like this before.'

Mrs Eadie was shocked again, but a fleeting smile had passed over her husband's face. 'I think we must be careful what we say about all this,' he said. 'We do not want any unwelcome publicity for you, my dear.'

'No, we don't,' said Dandy fervently.

'Alec knows only that he locked Duncan, then you, in the hut: he then went to fetch paraffin and would have set the place on fire. The police are bound to make inquiries, but Duncan will tell them what he told you. That will avoid any embarrassing questions of a personal nature, I should think. It will be pronounced a brainstorm. I shudder to think what might have happened if you had not managed to hit him with the flowerpot. All that paraffin in the hut! Your case would have been hopeless. What happened to Jock was maybe a blessing. The poor idiot boy would have been locked up for the rest of his days.'

Dandy dreaded the police questioning. She had never

had any dealings with them at first hand but often had heard from her brothers of summary punishment dished out when they had been playing football in the wrong place. Yet here was Mr Eadie greeting them and making the introductions in his quiet authoritative manner. 'My wife, and this is Miss Baxter, our assistant governess, who has suffered rather an ordeal this afternoon. I think she has recovered enough to answer your questions. Our head gardener, who shared her plight, has been taken home to his cottage, but I'll take you down there when you have finished here.' He rang the bell for Nancy. 'Tell Nurse that the police are here and it would help if she could come. You could mind baby for her for a little while, couldn't you?'

Dandy found herself shaking violently. Attack had always brought out an answering violence in her, but here there was no opportunity to dispel that. It was as well that she was not being called upon to do anything that demanded control. Jock was dead. It was not a boyish prank that she could avenge swiftly. It was as well that Mr Eadie had no notion of her reactions. He simply thought she needed someone to speak for her and he was like Aunt Alice. He thought out everything before he spoke. All that was required of her was to keep quiet. That business about her ordeal had been a good touch. The sergeant and his young assistant had looked at her kindly. Any questioning would be gentle, she knew. She willed herself to hide her reactions. Nurse had been ashamed of her loss of control. She would be her normal efficient self when she told them of Jock's fatal fall. They would like that.

She was not wrong in her forecast, but, in spite of that, her legs were shaky as she mounted the stairs to dress for a dinner she had no wish to eat. It was Morag whose keen eye had noticed Dandy's trembling and who exerted herself to distract them all by talking of the children's varied reactions to a story she had read to all three. 'Elizabeth is fast growing away from them, now. You can see that she responds in quite a mature way. I think she will hold her own at school next year. In spite of being quiet and seemingly shy, she has an inner strength that will not allow her to be swamped in the wider world of boarding school.' Dandy, still trapped in the memories of that hut and only half listening, stared. Then blurted out, 'Is Elizabeth going away?'

'Yes, next autumn, to my old school,' said Mrs Eadie. 'We shall all miss her.'

'Then why . . . ?' Dandy started and then realized she was being rude.

'She will be very happy there,' said Mrs Eadie. 'I was, and I was shy like Elizabeth, believe it or not. It is the right age to be in a world of one's contemporaries. The opportunities for team games are there in plenty. They learn to be self-reliant, to compete and be gracious in defeat, and they are caught up in a team spirit which blots out petty selfishness.'

This was a lot for Dandy to swallow. It amazed her that Mrs Eadie could be thinking of anything so far removed from the awful drama of Jock's death. She glanced at Morag McGregor who had brought up the subject, but that lady's face was carefully impassive. It would be interesting to know what she really thought. Dandy, toying with her food, was relieved when the meal ended. Later, as they climbed the stairs together, and again as they parted on the landing, it was on the tip of her tongue to ask, but there was a subtle barrier which the governess could put up without seeming to do anything and Dandy knew that she would have to wait.

It was a bad night. When at last she fell into a fitful sleep, the dreams started. She was running towards the red hut and she couldn't get there in time. She heard Jock's bellow, Mel's bark and then Nurse's screams, and a blue flame shot up from the hut. Sometimes she managed to reach Duncan, but as she stretched out to help him up, there was a loud bang and the hut fell down on top of them. She woke from these fragments of dreams which repeated themselves time and time again, sweating and shivering. A crisp winter morning found her exhausted. Breakfast had no appeal, but she went through the motions. Miss McGregor waited till they were nearing the schoolroom. 'I see your appetite has not returned. Did you sleep?'

'Not very much,' admitted Dandy. 'When I *did* drop off, I always had nightmares about that hut.'

'I thought so. Well, I think you would not be much use in the schoolroom this morning. I suggest you wrap up warmly and go for a nice walk in the woods. The smell of the resin and the song of the birds will gradually soothe you, I'm sure. Perhaps the children will join you later – that is if they concentrate on the exercises I am setting them this morning.'

Her voice dropped. 'I'll use it as a bribe. You're a bit of a heroine to them now, you know. I chose to give them the outline of the story. It would have been useless to try to keep them in ignorance. One of the servants would be sure to slip up. Now!' her voice resumed its normal tone. 'Off you go for a brisk walk and you'll sleep well tonight.'

It was suddenly cool in the dark of the woods after the winter sunshine in the garden, but it wasn't long before she began to listen to the birds. Morag had been teaching the children the various calls. It was surprising how many different species there were, clear of the town and near the slopes of the Gleniffer Braes. And, really, when you thought of it, the sea was not far away. It was nothing to the waders to fly inland to some of the ponds fed from those hill streams. Everything here was so lovely. Jock had worked in these surroundings

244

for some time. What was it that made men so ...
obsessed with that part of their bodies, treating it like
a weapon? What was it Mr Eadie had said? – "Displaying his person." But Uncle James wasn't like that.
He adored his wife and would treat her with respect;
not like Faither who had treated Mother like a servant.
Mr Eadie was thoughtful and courteous to his wife too.
These were educated men, of course. Perhaps that was
what made the difference. Maybe educated people had
more to think about than displaying their persons. That
was a funny expression but it seemed to be the right
one. She would know in future. 'Oh, God! Don't let it
happen again!' Perhaps Morag McGregor could explain.
Like the aunts, she wasn't married, but she had lived
a long time with married people and she was very
observant: knew when to hold her tongue. You learned
a lot more when people were not put on their guard
by questions.

The clearing was warm, sheltered from the breeze.
She sat on a log and breathed deeply. She remembered
one of her mother's letters.

The air is wonderful here and there's a lot of it,
believe me. The boys are very happy. There are
lots of things to do – manly things, like sawing
logs and hammering in stakes and mending fences.
Because all the men do it, the boys copy them and
acquire skills at an early age. None of the men
round about here drinks. They are all determined
to succeed and seem to be able to work long hours
without getting tired. The Salvation Army officer
on the ship warned them that if they applied for a
job with liquor on their breath they would not be
taken. I thought he was exaggerating a wee bit, but
it's right! They *are* strict. Most of them don't even
smoke. Maybe that's why they seem so strong. I

don't know what I would have done without Marie
Friedland when we arrived. She has been a great
friend and she's taught the boys so much. She gives
casual employment to quite a lot of the young
people round about – says it suits her; she can trust
them all and it's good for them to realize that work
brings rewards. She's got a great way with her; lost
her husband before she was thirty but has kept
the farm going herself ever since then. Everybody
knows her and she'll fetch things from Vernon for
you when she goes in. Most of the women are too
busy to go there often. She has no children but is
always surrounded by them when we go there. She
keeps them working and makes it all fun.

That letter had cheered her; helped her to spurn the
guilty feeling that she should be out there in that strange
country helping Mammie – no, Ma – deal with Pa. 'Ma
and Pa.' She giggled at the amended names. They *did*
sound nice and friendly. Yes, Ma seemed to be settling
down fairly well and Billy at least thought that Canada
was a wonderful country. Did they think that she might
be coaxed to join them? Guilty or no, she was determined to stay where she was. But really, it sounded as
if Marie Friedland was helping a lot, showing them the
pattern of a useful productive life. And that was the
sort of life she, Dandy Baxter, could live here if there
was no daft Jock around to make things awkward.
    A mavis was singing proudly on a nearby tree. It was
infectious. Nobody could hear her in this remote place.
Soon Dandy was practising the scales and vocal exercises that Morag had set her. There was so much that
was lovely in the world. She would try to forget daft
Jock and Andy Connell: study the people who could
make life rich for themselves.

*   *   *

Over the next few months, Dandy found herself studying the couples she had met recently. Her visit to Nan's
house had been the first of many invitations to parties,
some simple and very homely and some quite extravagant affairs which meant hiring a hall and a dance band.
The home backgrounds of her contemporaries in church
seemed to be so varied. When the aunts proposed a
party for her, she demurred at first, knowing that it
would be bound to cause a lot of noise and bustle in
their quiet home. Hiring a hall was out of the question
because of the expense and, in any case, she had found
that the parties in other people's homes were much
more intriguing. It was often surprising to see how the
siblings varied from the member she knew.

Aunt Alice caught her unawares. 'Why do you not
want a party here, Dandy? As far as I can see, many
of your friends come from quite humble back-
grounds.'

'It's not that. The cottage is lovely, but they're apt to
get a bit noisy,' she said. 'Of course, that's often because
they have younger brothers and sisters who want to
join in the games . . . It would be a lot of work.'

'Well, we would expect you to help, naturally,' said
Alice matter-of-factly, 'but with Violet in charge of the
catering and me working out some quizzes and paper
games, I'm sure we could do something. It's a pity we
don't have a piano . . .'

'Agnes Wilson has a fiddle and two of the boys have
mouthies . . .'

'They have what?'

'Mouthies. Mouth organs. Harmonicas. Did you
never call them that?'

'No,' said Alice. 'We seem to have had a deprived
childhood, Violet.' She turned to Dandy again. 'You
see, Mama thought harmonicas were rather unhygienic.
James had a violin – a good one, I believe – but I think

he must have sold it when things were difficult. Well, your birthday isn't till September. What about having an Easter party?'

'Oh, yes,' said Violet. 'I could make an Easter bunny cake: make the icing pale green with narrow strips of angelica for grass, meringues for toadstools and little fluffy yellow bunnies – you can buy them – hiding in the grass. The beauty of it is that I could do it in advance. A rich cake improves. Plenty of sausage rolls, they're always popular ... Why are you two laughing?'

'Oh, Aunt Violet. How could I do you out of such a treat; working your fingers to the bone to make my party better than all the others. It sounds just wonderful.'

Though she was caught up in the preparations, spring was making Dandy restless in a way she had never felt before. Braeval was as comfortable as ever: her music lessons with Morag McGregor just as interesting. The trouble was that there was no one of her own age there. Her weekend meetings with her Sunday group were all too soon over and served to make her more restless still. Often she chided herself when she saw how the aunts were going out of their way to organize her party. They had not wasted any time. Aunt Alice had gone through old magazines and calendars, cutting out Scottish views.

'What are these for?' asked Dandy.

'This is the introductory game, "Know Your Scotland". I shall mount these on cardboard covered with some pretty wallpaper. There will be a clue with the rhyming word left out, under the picture. I'll fix them to the bookshelves all round the room and everyone will be given a paper and pencil when they arrive. They have to name the place.'

'I'm making home-made sweets and chocolates for

the prizes,' said Violet. 'I'll wrap them very smartly. Most young people like sweets.'

'It sounds marvellous,' said Dandy. 'What can I do?'

'First of all, find me a rhyme for Ballachulish. See – this view of the little ferry and a lone figure waiting to cross. He looks worried. Perhaps he's the doctor and anxious to get to a patient. It's a long way round the top of the loch, even though the scenery is so beautiful . . . see those reflections . . .'

'How would this do?' said Dandy, clearing her throat in an exaggerated manner.

'The wait at the ferry may make you quite mulish
But the scenery's grand at fair Ballachulish.'

'I wouldn't have believed it,' said Alice. 'I thought that one was impossible. You can jolly well do the rest of them. My efforts seem so tame:

'Just look at the water but don't fall in
The falls of Dochart are at Killin.

'That sort of thing. I don't suppose you could find something for Lochranza. This one is a feast for the eyes.'

'Lochranza . . . Lochranza,' said Dandy. 'How would this do?

'A vein of gold can be called a bonanza
But this little gem is known as Lochranza.'

'They'll never get that,' said Alice. 'I didn't know about a bonanza.'

'Nor did I,' said Violet.

'I heard Miss McGregor telling Elizabeth about it last week. I think she probably knows more than most governesses, for her father was a minister and very studious and she looked after him for years after her mother died.'

'Don't you think these children are very fortunate, Dandy?' asked Violet.

'Oh, yes, but they're sending Elizabeth away to boarding school. Mrs Eadie thinks it is good for her to be able to take part in team games and things like that, as *she* did.'

Alice shook her head. 'I find it difficult to understand why Mrs Eadie would think that way. She must have been happy herself, of course.'

'She's exceptionally pretty,' said Violet. 'The other girls probably fussed over her a bit . . .'

'Yes. That can be a doubtful blessing. Those of us who are on the homely side have to develop other qualities which are more lasting. That has been my experience. Girls who have things handed to them on a plate often end up self-centred and self-indulgent.'

'Do you think Mrs Eadie is self-indulgent?' asked Dandy.

'Oh, I wouldn't be so bold. I really don't know the lady well enough . . . though it struck me that day – at Langbank, remember? – she swooned away when her daughter needed her. Perhaps if she hadn't been used to people helping her out all the time she would have summoned the resources to do what was needed, as you did so promptly, my dear.'

'Well, these things happened all the time in our house, Aunt Alice.'

'Exactly! And you didn't faint once, did you?'

'No, and there wouldn't have been room to fall if I had!' she ended, chuckling.

It was a good start to the preparations for her party. Dandy soon realized that she had nothing to worry about. Her aunts were enjoying themselves thoroughly. Parties in their youth had been elaborate affairs with a theme, and the house decorated accordingly. 'Nobody else has had anything like this,' Dandy assured them frequently.

'Well, we are keeping to the spring theme,' said Violet. 'Everything must look fresh and new. I'll take special care with the salads. They can look so pretty if you picot edge the tomatoes . . .'

'She'll be crocheting the lettuce next,' Alice teased.

'It's bound to be a success,' Dandy told herself as she waited for the first of her guests to arrive. Alice had assured her that she was the young hostess and her aunts were just background. 'So you will welcome them all and keep an eye on the food and drinks to make sure that everyone is being served. You can wiggle your eyebrows at us and we'll see things right for you.'

The doorbell rang long and loud, making them jump. I'll bet that was Alec Campbell, thought Dandy. I hope he's not going to be too noisy. Alec indeed it was, closely followed by Nan and Jenny. Then there seemed to be an avalanche. The sitting room was soon packed. Agnes had brought her fiddle as promised and David and Willie patted their pockets reassuringly when she mentioned mouthies.

Her forecast about the success was soon proved right.

The decorations were enough to break the ice and the guessing game had them laughing hilariously as they tried to find rhymes. 'I'll bet Dandy made up those clues,' said Nan. 'I tell you, that girl reads too many books. It's a pity the minister isn't here. He can usually match her.'

'It's a good thing he isn't,' said Dandy. 'You'd have to behave yourself.'

'Hear that, folks? Dandy says we don't have to behave.'

During the ensuing roar, Dandy, glancing quickly at

her aunts, was relieved to see that they were laughing as heartily as the others. Everything was fine – fine and dandy!

Chapter 17

Inevitably there was a reaction. Preparations for the party had filled every spare moment when she was home. She had experienced the joy of being at the centre of a young, happy group and somehow nothing else could replace that – not the music lessons with Morag McGregor, the elegance of Braeval and its beautiful grounds, nor anything else. Her own little garden seemed so paltry when compared with what she had become accustomed to, but a flush of guilt and shame would creep over her when she realized how disloyal she was being to Uncle James. He had left a lovely place like Braeval and managed to create a little oasis for himself in the heart of the town. Remembering his definition of a lady, she felt that she was falling short.

She was jolted out of her introspection one afternoon when the three of them, Mrs Eadie, Morag McGregor and herself were having tea. 'I've something to tell you, ladies,' their employer began. 'This summer Mr Eadie's work will take him to London frequently, so we have decided to rent a house near the south coast. That will allow him to travel easily.'

Dandy blurted out, 'You won't need me any more, then, will you?'

'Well, my dear, we shall be sorry to part with you – as will the children, I'm sure. We have never forgotten what you did for Sarah that day at Langbank . . .'

'Oh, that was nothing,' said Dandy quickly. 'My aunts have been missing me rather and my garden certainly needs a bit of attention . . .'

Mrs Eadie brightened up immediately. 'Oh, well, that's all right. We didn't like ... I mean Mr Eadie ... I mean we would hate you to feel that we haven't appreciated your help. Duncan will miss you too. He told me you were a better gardener than a lot of the young fellows that had the cheek to come here for work in the summer. And, of course, he remembers how you saved his life that day ...'

'When do you leave?' asked Miss McGregor.

'The beginning of June – you'll be coming with us, of course.'

'Yes,' said Morag quietly.

'Then that's settled,' said Mrs Eadie brightly. 'If you'll excuse me, ladies, I have some telephone calls to make.'

Morag and Dandy walked slowly towards the woods where the children were playing. 'Are you not very keen on going to the south coast?' asked Dandy.

'No, I would prefer to be nearer home. You see, my cousin, my only close relative, has a weak heart. She lives in a little village in Perthshire. I always have the feeling that, were she to be taken seriously ill, I could reach her from here. From the south coast it would be a different story.'

'Could Mrs Eadie not get someone else for the summer? They won't be doing much in the way of school-work, will they?'

'No, they won't, but if I know Mrs Eadie she will soon become involved in social calls. That means someone reliable must be left in charge. I believe *she* would be quite happy to leave things to a stranger, but Mr Eadie wouldn't. He is a very caring father.'

Was she implying that Mrs Eadie wasn't a caring mother, Dandy wondered? She would have to tread warily or the governess would clam up on her, but perhaps now that she knew they were parting ...

'What's your opinion of boarding school, Miss McGregor?'

The governess paused and seemed to look round her for inspiration. 'It's quite warm,' she said. 'Shall we sit in the rose garden for a little while?' The minutes passed. The early roses were out on the wall. In another month, Dandy thought, the fragrance would be delightful. The tall walls would enclose and warm them, but nobody would be here to enjoy them: nobody but Duncan and his helpers, who weren't up to her own standard if Mrs Eadie were to be believed.

'I have no personal experience of boarding school, of course,' Morag began. 'I do not regret that. Many people who have been to boarding school will tell you they loved it – that's when they are being bright and sociable, but when you get to know them better you often find that they spent quite a lot of time disguising their tears. It's as if it were a sign of defeat to say that you were not happy at boarding school.'

'Surely Mrs Eadie must have been happy or she would not be sending Elizabeth there?'

'One would think not, but human nature is a complex thing, Dandy. Sometimes, people will not admit their real reasons even to themselves. Often, they are unaware of their motivation and can justify a course of action to themselves and other people quite convincingly.'

'I don't think I understand you,' said Dandy.

Morag took a deep breath. 'From what I have heard, Mrs Eadie's mother was a society beauty with a dazzling social life. Appearances meant a great deal to her. Let's suppose that she had little real maternal instinct; that her beautiful daughter was all right to show off now and again, but a drag when she expected to have her mother's company. So, she sent her to boarding school – for all the best reasons, naturally. Mrs Eadie sensed that rejection, but knew that it was all of a piece with the rest of her mother's life. She would use her beauty to charm the other girls at school into doing what she wanted. Queen it, in fact. This is all supposition, Dandy, but it is a possibility. The pattern she formed at boarding school then became the pattern for her adult life. It was how she could best bend people to her will. When she was at the peak of her beauty she met a fine man who obviously adored her and was in a position to give her the sort of home which suited her. This man was fond of children; had had a happy home life himself. Though she was not particularly fond of children herself, she played the part of a loving mother without actually doing much of the work involved. There have always been nannies, nursemaids and myself in due course. I have been the only governess. It could be that deep inside her there is still a little resentment towards her mother who did not value her company. This could make her react in a similar way to her own child. It would then suit her to repeat the arguments her mother used in favour of boarding school – a sort of self-justification.'

There was a long silence while Dandy digested this argument. Actually Miss McGregor had not answered her question. She would try it another way. 'Would you have liked to go to boarding school yourself?'

'Never! I loved my parents dearly. We were not ostentatious in our affections but they ran deep. The only disappointment which I shared with my mother was that no other children had arrived to keep me company. Boarding school would not have fulfilled that need for me. It had to be a deep and binding love in the security of the nest.'

'You think that it would be better if Mrs Eadie could make that sort of nest for Elizabeth instead of sending her away?'

'It would be my feeling, yes, but we must all do as we see right and Mrs Eadie is confident that she is right in this case. I don't have to say that all I have voiced is confidential, Dandy.'

'Of course. You have given me a lot to think about. I appreciate it.'

'I speak a little more freely than I might do, Dandy, if your circumstances were different. Your aunts have had no experience of boarding school themselves, so you may have a somewhat enchanted view of such a life. You will probably marry – you are a beautiful girl, Dandy – and it may be that you will have to consider such a subject when you have children of your own. I would urge you to think the matter over carefully when it arises. That is all. I have had the chance to observe such things in a way that your aunts may not have had.'

The subject *did* intrigue her. Morag seemed to think that she was likely to marry someone who could afford boarding schools. That was a laugh! What would she think if she knew the sort of home she had had before the aunts took pity on her? Mrs Eadie claimed to believe that boarding school had released her into a world of more opportunities, a world of team games and wider friendships. Morag was a deep thinker, watching and listening and quietly drawing her own conclusions. What had she concluded about her personal assistant? Did Morag, too, see her as an 'odd wee thing'? That was unlikely if she thought that Dandy would marry someone wealthy. She had never asked any personal questions, taking it for granted that Alice and Violet were really her aunts – or had she? She had never asked about her parents. Nor had the children, for that matter. Of course, if the Eadies thought they were dead they might warn the children not to ask questions. It was unlikely that Morag, who had given so much thought to her employer's motives, would not have set to work on the mind of her young assistant. Letters from Canada had always remained at the cottage to be devoured on her next visit home. Yet under that quiet scrutiny she could have given herself away; perhaps Morag had noticed that her speech patterns at times varied from those of her aunts. The more Dandy considered the problem, the more convinced she became that it was quite likely that Morag McGregor had worked out more about her than she had dreamt possible. But no questions would be asked! She could sit quietly like this, totally at peace with her surroundings.

A lot could be learned from Morag McGregor. What would she think of Dandy staying behind when the rest of the family went to Canada? Would Morag, who had longed for brothers and sisters, think her unfeeling that she let them go with few qualms and these only concerned with May? Her opinion would always be formed on the basis of evidence. Perhaps if she knew the whole story she would agree with Dandy that in staying with the aunts she had done the right thing: that her mother's lot was unlikely to change and she, Dandy, would simply be throwing away the possibility of a successful and full life here. Perhaps it would pay her to discuss the whole thing with someone impartial and understanding: someone who understood her love for May and her determination to do something for her as soon as she was able.

The following weekend Dandy broached the subject with Alice. 'They all think that you really are my aunts. Nobody has asked any questions. Did you mean it to be that way? Do you think they would not want me if they knew the truth?'

'We thought that we would leave it to you, my dear, to do what felt natural. As to our not being your real aunts, well, it would be difficult for us now to feel any other way. You have become such an important part of our lives. Do you feel that Mrs Eadie would wish to know?'

'Mrs Eadie? No, I don't think she would care much, but I wonder if Miss McGregor has her suspicions. She's a very thoughtful person.'

'Does it make you feel uneasy that you have not told her?'

'Well, it *does* seem a wee bit deceitful ... You see, she's told me quite a bit about her father – the way he looked at things and the books he encouraged her to read. They seem to have been happy together ...'

'In that case, I think you should tell her, especially since you will be parting soon. Unless she advises you to tell Mrs Eadie too, I should leave it at that. She has been with the family a long time and will know what is suitable. She is obviously interested in you or she would not trouble herself so much over your music lessons. A thoughtful, balanced person like that might be quite a comfort to talk to about your family. She is detached in her views in a way that would be impossible for us, having seen your early struggles. Also, in her father's parish there would be a wide variety of people from whom she could draw comparisons. Yes, she might be very helpful. Now: Violet and I have been planning a holiday for you but we didn't know when your work would finish at Braeval. After all, when they took you on, Mrs Eadie said it was to be for a few months, and you have been there more than a few. We must get ahead with the booking so that you can get a break as soon as possible.'

'But I couldn't go away ... I mean there's quite a bit to be done in my own garden.'

'Pouf! You need a holiday. We'll give you a hand in the garden and do our best, but what isn't done will have to wait. We plan to take you to a beautiful hotel

259

in Wigtownshire. There are lots of famous gardens near and we can make expeditions. No work, just pleasure, Dandy, for two whole weeks. What do you say to that? We think you deserve it.'

'Why are there so many famous gardens there?'

'Mild climate . . . the gulf stream . . . you'll see palm trees aplenty.'

'Really?'

'Yes and the hotel has such a beautiful setting. We'll have delicious meals, food without the effort of cooking . . . waited on hand and foot. What do you think? Can I book?'

Dandy looked at the eager face, threw her arms round Alice and said, 'It sounds wonderful.'

The news of her holiday was a ready opening for a talk with Morag McGregor when the children were playing hide and seek in the little wood. 'They're cooler under the trees,' said Morag. 'I think we can just let them get on with it unless any serious squabbles develop. And what is this news you are eager to tell me?'

Her reaction to the holiday was all that Dandy could have wished. 'It sounds exactly right for a garden lover like you. I've never been down in that part of the country. We spent a lot of time in the north. Are you familiar with it?'

Dandy drew a deep breath. 'I'm not familiar with any place but Paisley,' she began.

Morag remained looking straight ahead while Dandy's story unwound. It was only in the occasional tightening of the hands that the girl knew she was not so unmoved as she seemed. There was a long silence when she finished. Morag's hand stretched out and patted hers. 'Thank you, my dear,' she said, her voice husky. 'I guessed there were undertones, but I could never have imagined what you have told me now. I don't need to say that it will go no further. It is most wonderful that you have won through ... a credit to yourself and those kind aunts who recognized the gold among the grit. You are bound to have learned a lot from your earlier hardships – most of it good, I daresay. When we are young we are inclined to be very partisan. Your sympathy for your mother and the constant presence of your grandmother with her diatribes could have given you a very biased view of marriage. I have never been fortunate enough to win the love of a good man, and I suppose my music and my books have to a certain extent been a substitute for that, but I have seen that wonderful love working in the lives of my parents. I feel convinced that marriage is the highest, holiest and happiest alliance into which two people can be drawn. Your mother's frequent pregnancies may have given you a jaundiced view of physical love and with it a wariness of men in general. Even in the humblest of cottages I have observed that total love which makes the union of two people a glorious surrender in complete unselfishness.' She paused for a moment. 'Perhaps growing up in a manse makes me turn an answer into a sermon, my dear, but you are such a rewarding listener.'

The hotel sent its own coach to meet them at Stranraer. Dandy felt breathless with excitement as they bowled along the winding roads with constantly changing landscapes and seascapes. 'It's so different somehow,' she said. 'I mean, different from Langbank and Gourock and these places – no high mountains, just gentle hills and the far rocks, but the flowers are everywhere, right down to the beaches. It's wonderful!'

'Remember, Alice, our Aunt Edith used to say it was a mixture of Cornwall and somewhere in Wales that she was fond of. For myself, I'm quite happy to say it's

Galloway; stands on its own merits!' Violet turned to Dandy, 'What do you think?'

'Mmmmm,' said Dandy. Tears welled up in her eyes suddenly. Here she was – in a carriage, travelling through some of the loveliest countryside in the kingdom, exquisitely dressed, thanks to Aunt Violet; whereas May . . . what was May doing? That little sister who was too good to live, according to Grannie. The view of the blue waters of Luce Bay vanished in mist as she remembered May trying to bandage a doll, damaged by her rough brothers. And was it the brothers' fault that they were so undisciplined? By all accounts they were doing well in Canada. May had written from Marie Friedland's house:

Send your reply here, Dandy. We have to be careful that he does not know we are writing so often. He's that mean now you wouldn't believe it. But Aunt Marie makes it all a game. She found that I could crochet when she saw the twins in their party dresses. So she bought some yarn and got me to do her two blouses and she took me to Vernon and bought me lovely shoes. They are so comfy. I've never had any like them. Faither, of course, wanted to know where I had got them, but he couldn't say anything when I said she gave me them as a thank you for helping her with needlework. Faither should have married someone like Aunt Marie. She wouldn't let him up with any nonsense. You'll be glad to know that he is not drinking. There are no pubs out here and I think that even in Vernon folks have to go to a hotel if they want a drink. The apples they grow round here are eating ones – big and red – and someone said that they wouldn't be good for cider. I think it would be an awful waste anyway. Faither is determined to get thirty acres.

George says it is an obsession with him. Oh, George said to send his love. I said he should write, but you know him. Still, he's awfully good to Ma; slips her some money from his part-time jobs when he can. Billy would give the show away, so Aunt Marie gives him things to take home instead of money. You'll have heard about his goats. That was a really generous gift. We get loads of milk and Aunt Marie will sell any surplus kids for him. She takes things to market in Vernon, you see. I've given her the £1 note you sent in your last letter. She knows the banker and says that if he can't change it himself, she'll get him to send it to Winnipeg. It's awfully kind of you, Dandy. Faither is talking about re-engaging in the autumn for another year so that he can save enough money to buy his thirty acres and build us a house. He wants the land that lies at the back of Aunt Marie's farm. It would be nice if he got it because then we would be even nearer. We pass her farm on the way to school. That's how we know her so well.

Yes, her brothers were doing well. Perhaps if there had been enough space in their young lives, freedom to express themselves, they would have caused less trouble. While they had been struggling, living on top of one another, other people had been enjoying all this. Dandy could not help feeling she was in a divided world; pictures would rise up of the crowded poverty of her home; the washdays when she had to keep some order in that home while tending to the constant needs of the twins and Jack. According to May, the twins were more or less a law unto themselves these days. Perhaps it was easier to fit into a big family if you just ignored the others? No, that was daft. That wasn't what May had meant. They simply concentrated on the things that interested them, happy things like singing and dancing, and ignored Faither – or, as they called him, *Pa* – when he was grumpy.

'There it is!' said Violet. Well, Dandy?'

With a struggle Dandy tried to focus on the scene in front of her. 'It's a dream,' she said. 'I couldn't have believed it.' She was drinking in her first view of Rose-craig Hotel, nestling in flowers, and with the blue waters of Luce Bay behind it. As they descended from the coach, she gazed around her, bemused. Inside was so different too, with some sort of little conservatory off nearly every room. Whoever had built it had been a garden lover. 'It'll catch the sun at every angle,' she thought.

Though her aunts settled down quickly among the many elderly guests, Dandy kept roaming round, finding new treasures among the plants, indoors and out. Alice and Violet had not been wasting their time, how-ever. Over tea they told her of the advice they had been given by fellow guests and the girl at the desk. 'We asked which we should visit first,' said Alice, 'and they said Lindsay Gardens, which is the nearest one, is also the best. It seems we are in luck because the owner opens it only this one day a year for charity. The Captain likes to keep it to himself. The girl said that it would put us off the others. It is so special.'

'What's so special about it?'

'Well, there seems to be an endless list, but she said that she liked some little New Zealand palm trees par-ticularly and she likes the smell of the eucalyptus trees and there are countless lilies. He specializes in them. His grandfather started the garden, but his father really got it going when he came back from India with plants he brought from the Himalayas, Madeira and other places. The Captain devotes all his time to it.'

Alice's face was eager. This holiday meant a lot to

264

them. They were looking quite old, she noticed. Alice's hair was white in the bright sunlight and Violet's no longer had the dark streaks that had been there when she left for Braeval. Was it because she had been among so many young people that these signs had passed her by? If they died, what would happen to her? Would Aunt Margaret feel she had to take her in? Dandy gave herself a shake and thrust the horrible thought to the back of her mind. Morag seemed to think she would marry, and yet Morag knew about Jock. She didn't seem to think that an experience like that should put a girl off. Physical love, as Morag McGregor called it, should be a beautiful thing. Though a prim-looking governess, that lady was wide awake to other people's feelings. Dandy decided to forget Jock and Andy Connell. She would be like her twin sisters – enjoy the present.

Chapter 18

The drive leading to Lindsay Gardens was long. 'You see, it needs this shelter belt of trees,' the coachman told them. 'We never get frost here, but we *do* get high winds. The Captain's father brought a lot of plants from India and Madeira. They need the heat. Once you're inside, you'll find that the place has a climate of its own.'

Dandy felt the excitement rising in her. She had never dreamt that the gardens would cover such a large area. In fact, she had pictured them something like Braeval, only more exotic. When they got down she twirled round and round, studying the heights of the trees which hid most of the delights from her as yet. Aunt Alice paid the entrance fee and they were in! After only a few minutes' walk they turned sharp right and Dandy caught her breath at the sight of the rhododendrons: nothing like the lilac ones which grew wild in the woods by the Gleniffer Braes. These were huge and in every shade of colour imaginable. 'Look!' said Dandy, cupping one huge cluster in her hand. 'It's big enough to make a bouquet on its own.' She was in a fever of discovery as they moved from one bush to another, finding a thrill in each new variety and colour variation.

They passed through a stone archway into a clearing and there, in the centre, was a magnificent camellia, laden with exquisite white blooms.

'D'you know why it's called Camellia?' she asked her aunts.

'No,' said Alice, 'but I think you're going to tell us.'

'Uncle James said that it was called that after the man who found it in the Philippines, Joseph Kamel.'

'He was very fond of them – James, I mean,' said Violet. 'He would have liked one at the cottage but said that they have to be allowed to grow freely if you want to see them in their full glory. I've never seen a finer specimen than that one. It's so wonderful to have space like this to stand back and admire it.'

As they passed an admiring group, Dandy was all ears for their comments. 'It's a little past its best,' she heard someone say. 'It's a pity we couldn't have seen it a fortnight ago, though really, in a garden like this there are marvels right through the long growing season.' Dandy gave a deep sigh of longing. Fancy being able to see a place like this all year! And all that space. Everything was on such a grand scale. You walked and walked and it beckoned you on.

The next stone archway took them into the rose garden. It stretched, a riot of colour, into the distance. Over the top of the far-away wall, tall palm trees completed a perfect frame. They all paused to breathe the warm scents. 'They're intoxicating,' said Alice.

'Would you like to rest here for a little while?' Dandy asked, suddenly noticing that her aunts looked tired.

'That would be a lovely idea,' said Alice, while Violet nodded her assent.

They passed under a pergola to a rustic seat in a beautifully sheltered corner. 'Would you mind if I went on?' Dandy asked.

'Not a bit. We shall be happy here. It's so lovely I wouldn't mind just staying here till it's time for the coach. Off you go and explore! We shall enjoy it vicariously.'

Dandy skipped off. The map by the gate had said there was a lily garden. It was tempting to continue through the long rose garden to investigate the palm

267

trees, but Uncle James had felt that we did not do enough about lilies. She had read up lots about them. Perhaps she would see some of the rarer ones here. If she worked her way round the back of some of the main gardens, she might reach the lilies more quickly. She cut off at an angle through an opening in a tall rose hedge and found herself in a herbaceous garden. For a moment she stood confused, then cut off to the right, skirting the pelargoniums.

As she progressed, she saw that many of the beds here had younger plants – probably it was a sort of nursery area. The other visitors were sticking to the main paths, so she could hurry along. A tall gardener was coming through an archway. He turned suddenly, brushed by a tendril from a plant which was trailing in his way. Dandy watched as he put down his barrow and tried to fix it. Then she noticed that he had only one arm. She hurried forward. 'I'll do that!' He looked round, startled. Dandy did the job efficiently. 'That's better!' She looked at his barrow. 'I've never seen one with a crossbar before. Was it made specially for you?'

'Adapted,' he said, swallowing hard.

'You're lucky working here,' she said. 'I think it's wonderland. I've never seen anything like it. It's a pity he only opens it once a year, but it's lucky we landed here at the right time. I'm going to the lily garden. My Uncle James always said that we don't do enough about lilies in this country.'

'He was probably right. Of course, we're lucky here in that we seldom have frost.'

'So I understand,' said Dandy, sounding very like her Aunt Alice. 'You have the gulf stream to thank for that.'

The gardener seemed rather tongue-tied. He cleared his throat and said, 'Would you like me to show you the way to the lily garden?'

'Yes, please, if it won't get you into trouble . . . I mean

– if you're supposed to be doing something else.'

A young gardener approached to confer with her companion and touched his cap. Nice manners, thought Dandy, moving off a little. I must really look like a lady. Aunt Violet made a superb job of this dress. The conversation was finishing. She heard the young gardener say, 'Right, Sir, we just wanted to be sure.'

Suddenly it dawned on her. The man she had been speaking to was no ordinary gardener. Now she thought of it, his voice was very cultured. She had been so busy enthusing that she had put him almost in Uncle James's place in her mind. And of course Uncle James had been a very well-educated man. The tall man was moving to join her. In her new knowledge she found it difficult to behave naturally. He too seemed embarrassed. She walked beside him, wondering what to say. She could hardly say that she had changed her mind: that she did not wish to see the lilies now. They passed a grove of trees that looked like little feathery umbrellas. Her guide saw her studying them with interest. 'Tree ferns from New Zealand,' he said.

'I see,' said Dandy. No further words were exchanged till they walked through yet another stone archway. 'This is it,' he said.

Dandy's voice came out in a kind of whistle. The man smiled. 'Everyone feels like that, I think, when they first see them. I believe we have one of the finest collections in Britain – all the usual ones, of course, and five really rare ones. My father kept propagating them. He was scared they would die out and, I think, he was always hoping for a new variety. There was the occasional sport but he never achieved *Lilium macandrewensis*.'

'But the space! I know the whole garden is huge, but I had thought the lily garden would be just that – a big bed of lilies. You have lots of other flowers here. Somehow I was thinking of them as being white ... I know they come in other colours, but so many poems refer to the lily as white and pure.'

'Yes, they do. I've often thought of that. We have . . . twenty-eight beds, I think. Lilies by themselves could be rather wearing – too much exotica and too much height. It helps if they have a softening background – or some colour to relieve the green and white in certain cases. We keep one type in each bed and sometimes one colour in the bed. See – over there, a pink bed. These pink-spotted lilies seem to take a richer look when they are backed by pink hollyhocks and bee balm – at least, I think so. The soil here is fairly acid and some of the lilies need a little lime so their background plants have to be matched to that.'

Dandy laughed, shedding her embarrassment. 'I'll never recognize half of them,' she said, wonderingly.

'I wouldn't expect you to know our five rarest ones. *Lilium giganteum* can grow to ten feet tall: then there's *Lilium nepalensis*, *Lilium wallichianum*, *Lilium nanum* and *Lilium flavidum*. You won't find them in any other garden that I've heard of round about, but let's start here and see what you *do* know. This one?'

'That's easy. *Lilium candidum*, the madonna lily. It's much taller than I thought.'

'Mmm, five-foot stems and, see – nearly twenty flowers on each. It's one of the oldest lilies but difficult to beat. Dates from the fifteenth century in Crete. This is one that needs a little lime and I have to be careful that it doesn't dry out. What do you think of the fragrance?'

'It takes me into another world.'

Gradually Dandy became her own exuberant self. They were laughing together when she suddenly drew Violet's watch from her pocket and gasped. 'My aunts will be desperate for their lunch. I hope I have not kept you from yours.'

'Not at all,' he said politely. 'You are not hungry yourself?'

'I forget things like that when I am in the garden, I'm afraid.'

'You have the spirit of a true gardener.'

Dandy stared at him. 'Do you know, that's exactly what my Uncle James said to me the first time I visited him . . .'

The man stared at her, saying nothing. She kept still, not knowing how to break the silence. His colour rose a little but still he said nothing.

'I'd better get back to my aunts. They are in the rose garden. They like a little rest after lunch. I'd forgotten them altogether. I never get tired in the garden,' she was gabbling breathlessly.

'If you'd like to see more, come back tomorrow. See that little door in the wall with the sycamore hanging over it? If you branch to the right off the main drive, you'll reach it. I'll be here anyway and could show you . . . that is . . . if you care.'

'Ooh, wouldn't I just,' said Dandy. 'Now which way is the rose garden? I'm lost.'

'See those tall eucalyptus trees? Go straight past them and through the lilypond garden. Take the exit which is guarded by palms and you will find yourself in the rose garden.'

Her aunts rose gratefully when she appeared. 'I'm sorry,' she gasped. 'I forgot all about the time.'

'Don't worry, my dear,' said Violet. 'We both had a pleasant little snooze but we *were* beginning to wonder what could have happened to you. You look lovely in that dress, though I say it myself who shouldn't. It's the rosy cheeks that complete the picture.'

It wasn't just the swift walk to the rose garden that had brought that colour to her cheeks, Dandy knew. There had been something oddly disturbing about those last few minutes with the tall owner. He seemed shy. Why would anyone be shy with her ... especially a fellow enthusiast?

After lunch that day, her aunts managed to find out quite a bit about the owner of Lindsay Gardens. For once, Dandy was quite happy to listen to the chatter of the old ladies when they heard of their visit. It seemed he had been a dashing young man, an expert horseman and engaged to a very eligible young lady who was the toast of the county. That was until he went off to the Boer War and lost an arm. The society beauty could not face life with a disabled man and broke the engagement. The sight of all his father's fine horses which he could no longer ride filled Captain Hector McAndrew with bitterness. He became withdrawn and cantankerous. Life in the old house which had always been filled with laughter became grim. His parents were soon cut off from their old friends. His mother's health began to suffer. His sister in New Zealand begged them to join her for a holiday. She was shocked at the change in her mother and treated her like an invalid, which she in fact became. His father did his best, though he was not by nature a patient man. The inactivity irked him and he took to riding off on his own. He died in a fall when his horse stumbled in rough territory. Mrs McAndrew went downhill rapidly and died six months later.

There were those who blamed Hector for his parents' end. He sold off all the horses and concentrated on the garden which his grandfather had started, ignoring the outside world completely. It had taken all the pleading of the local doctor to get him to open the grounds once a year for a medical charity. The other women were amazed that he had spoken to Dandy. Normally he kept out of the way of the visitors. It was said that the garden became more impressive every year. The number of visitors certainly rose.

When they were alone, Dandy asked the aunts what they thought of her invitation for the next day. They urged her to accept, which was exactly what she had hoped for.

She dressed carefully next morning; she didn't know why. After all, she was going to a garden and even the best-kept garden could be dastardly for clothes. She wore her oldest things in the garden at home. Telling herself that it made Aunt Violet happy to see her show off her handiwork, she carefully coiled her yellow hair – that hair which Uncle James had admired, saying it made her look like a lily. Would Captain McAndrew think it made her look like a lily?

He was waiting by the door when she arrived, flushed and breathless after the brisk walk from the hotel. There was no reason for the speed: no reason to have her heart thumping the way it was.

'I didn't know,' he began. 'I mean, I thought your aunts might need you.'

'No. They've made friends with a lot of the old dearies –' She drew herself up. 'I mean, they've found suitable companionship . . .'

His quick smile startled her. 'I know what you mean. They're happy, so you can come and look at something else. What do you say to the wild garden? I've managed to naturalize some of the martagon lilies you saw yesterday – the deep pink ones. You didn't like their scent, remember, though that doesn't matter in this site. But your dress is so pretty . . . it would be a pity . . . of course we have made paths for the visitors, but I don't normally use them.'

'I'll take care,' said Dandy. 'I often envy you men your sensible clothes when I am working in my garden.'

Hector chuckled. A worker who had been spraying plants some distance away turned round looking startled. Dandy remembered the gossip: that he never spoke to anyone unless he had to; that he never smiled; only his old housekeeper seemed to think that he was the same Master Hector she had always loved, and talked bitterly of the 'selfish besom who wouldna take him when he maist needed her'.

She *was* a selfish besom too, thought Dandy. His smile makes such a difference; makes him look younger. But somehow it makes it more difficult to think of him like Uncle James.

Confusion about her feelings towards the proprietor of Lindsay Gardens made it difficult for Dandy to describe the wild garden to her aunts when she returned at lunchtime. 'It's so wonderful . . . so many different little corners, views – cameos, Captain McAndrew calls them. They are *his* creation. Most of the others were made by his father or grandfather. We didn't have time to see the half of it. Captain McAndrew said I should come back tomorrow and perhaps you would like to come to lunch – his housekeeper would welcome company. You could come early with me and rest in the shade if you wanted. I told him you like a game of bridge in the sunroom in the morning. He gave me the telephone number . . .' Her voice tailed off as she saw the stunned surprise on their faces. Alice gave Violet a quick look, then said, 'I think that would be a very interesting experience. Don't you agree, Violet? It will be lovely to have all that space all to ourselves – such luxury.'

Dandy went off to tidy up for lunch. 'Now,' said Alice leaning closer to Violet, 'I think we should not go till lunchtime tomorrow. If this visiting is going to become a habit, it would be better to have them think we hate to miss our bridge; that way they'll get more time together.'

Violet looked pensive. 'Alice, does this remind you of anything? What Dandy did for James, eh?'

'Violet, you've hit the nail on the head, but we'd better wait and see. Of course it's the garden that does it for her. She forgets to be anyone but her own bright self. Didn't she look pretty in that new dress!'

'But Alice, there's a difference between James becoming fond of our Dandy and this Captain McAndrew ... don't you think?'

'But surely he would know ... maybe not. She *does* look more than sixteen – nearly seventeen ...'

'That means he's nearly twice her age.'

'Yes. We'll have to be careful, Violet. Tomorrow should give us a chance to observe them together. The doting old housekeeper could be a help with information if we treat her the right way.'

Alice was soon proved correct in her surmise. Mrs McGuffie obviously held a privileged position in the depleted household. She had had little opportunity to share her mine of information for some time and revelled in the polite interest shown by the two ladies. 'Your niece is such a charming young woman,' she said. 'I don't think Master Hector has spoken to one since that besom – his fiancée, I mean ...'

'I can assure you,' said Alice, 'that our niece is so enthusiastic about gardens that it would make anyone forget to be shy.' Silently she noted that the woman had referred to Dandy as a young woman, not a girl; that her eyes had darted from Dandy to her master from time to time. It was obvious what she was thinking.

Later, Violet joined her in her speculations, though they assured each other that it was early days and nothing might come of it. 'They might forget each other when the holiday is over,' said Alice, without convincing herself or her sister. They watched, powerless, while the trips to the garden became a daily habit. Dandy never mentioned visiting any of the others. Captain McAndrew soon became 'Hector' and his name cropped up in every other sentence. A book on lilies which he lent her became her bible for a few days as she memorized the names. 'They look so difficult,' said Violet.

'Not really! If you think of them as poetry, Aunt Violet, it's quite easy – and, of course, the Latin names are easier than they would have been without my Latin lessons. I've told Hector he can quiz me on them tomorrow.'

Though 'tomorrow' turned out wet, Dandy was off as usual on foot, her only concession a tiny umbrella. Before she reached the gates of the main drive, she saw Hector coming towards her bearing one more than twice the size. His face lit up. 'I was afraid that your aunts would not allow you out in this and cursing myself for not being able to bring a trap to meet you,' he said. 'Put that silly thing down. This will cover us both if you come closer; hold on to my jacket.'

Dandy found herself blushing. She could find nothing to say. Holding on to his jacket made her very aware of his nearness. He seemed to be struck dumb too. The silence lengthened. 'I've brought back the book,' she said, holding up her bag.

'Oh yes! I think your lesson will have to be indoors.'

Dandy recovered some of her spirit. 'What do you mean – my lesson? I tell you that I have prepared my homework, Sir.'

'We'll see about that,' he laughed. 'You'll have to sample Mrs McGuffie's scones first, though. She was as anxious as I was that you might not turn up, but she thought that if she had her scones ready, it would be sure to bring you.'

'Scarcely logical, but it seems to have worked,' said Dandy.

Mrs McGuffie from her look-out post saw her beloved master laugh heartily as he held the umbrella carefully

276

over his companion. 'Bless the bonnie lass,' she said out loud as she hurried to the kitchen.

Both her young master and the bonnie lass did ample justice to her preparations and it was with a knowing smile that she closed the door carefully behind her. Hector blushed suddenly and Dandy found that she was in the same fix. Then he lifted the book and, laying it on a small table, placed two chairs beside it. 'Right!' he said briskly. 'Shall we begin?' He stretched his arm towards her. Dandy summoned her composure and took the seat he indicated. When he joined her, she felt the gentle touch of his knee against hers. The tell-tale colour was rising in her cheeks again. Furiously she fought for control. It's only a knee, silly! she reminded herself. He couldn't sit there without our knees touching. Pull yourself together, Dandy Baxter, or you'll look a right fool.

There was a broad ruler lying beside the book. He must have prepared for this, she noted. He turned a few pages then quickly grabbed the ruler and covered the name. 'What's this one?' The exam had started. Soon they were chuckling and their voices rising as Dandy guessed correctly time and time again. Mrs McGuffie, finding an errand that would take her past the drawing-room door, smiled with satisfaction.

'Well, you *have* done well,' he said at the end. You missed out on *Lilium nanum* and *Lilium flavidum*. These are both in the garden, but I can't blame you. Neither of them is very showy.'

The morning visit to the garden became a ritual. Sometimes her aunts joined them for lunch. Other days they had an outing arranged with their bridge partners. On these occasions, Hector and Dandy sometimes lunched in the big comfortable kitchen with Mrs McGuffie happily in attendance. All too soon, the end of the holiday was approaching and, though her own garden would be needing her attention, Dandy found herself filled with regret. Lying in bed at the hotel she was surprised to find that the thought of leaving Hector was almost as bad as leaving the garden. He's just like Uncle James, she told herself; then had to be honest. He was *not* like Uncle James. Was this how the mill girls felt about Andy? This thrill as he approached, his smile widening.

It was the last morning. She was as eager to get to the garden as usual but trembled at the thought that this would be her final visit. Hector, too, seemed excited at their meeting. 'That *Lilium giganteum* we have been waiting for seems almost about to break into flower. Perhaps by this afternoon . . .' They were walking close together all the way to the lily garden. Their halting conversation would stop and the silences lengthen while they stole glances at one another. Soon it was time to join the aunts in the house for lunch. For the first time, they had nothing to show for their morning, for neither had even stooped to pick a weed or snap off a dead head.

After lunch when the aunts had settled down in the shade, they wandered out into the garden again. It was warm and they walked slowly, the scent of the roses mingling with the sweet tang of eucalyptus. Hector cleared his throat. 'I've something for you in the summer house, Dandy.' She looked at him, startled. His face was flushed and he seemed keyed up.

The windows were open, but the smell of sun-warmed wood lingered. Dandy looked at the comfortable chairs and hammock with faded floral covers. Surely he didn't . . . ? No! He wasn't that sort or he wouldn't have invited her aunts. She found herself blushing with shame. He was blushing too as he lifted a book from the table. 'I wonder how you would feel if I inscribed this book as I would dearly like to.'

'What d'you mean?' asked Dandy.

'It's the book you enjoyed so much – my father's favourite – *Himalayan Journals* by Joseph Hooker; it includes your favourite lilies too. I'd like you to have it and I'd like to write, "To Dandy, Queen of the Lilies", because that's how I think of you, my dear.'

'It's uncanny,' said Dandy, 'how often you say the same things as Uncle James. He said I looked like a lily and that was before I knew that my real name is Lily.'

'It is? Then why . . . ?' As Dandy hesitated, he added, 'Let's sit down.' They were standing by the hammock and the most natural thing was to sit there. Dandy felt her colour rising. She mustn't show embarrassment. He was just being kind. Slowly she embarked on the edited version of how she got her name. The true version was out of the question.

'Well, well,' he said. 'You are a Lily, yet you're a Dandy too.'

'Aunt Alice suggested that we keep "Lily" for Sundays,' said Dandy.

'A good idea! I second that!'

Dandy's colour rose again. How many Sundays was Hector McAndrew likely to spend with her now she was going back to Paisley?

'You don't mind . . . if I write that?' he enquired tentatively. Dandy, beyond words, shook her head.

'There you are!' He was offering her the book.

With his one hand, she thought. Her own two were trembling as she took it from him. They were both blushing.

'I thought I might get thanked the pretty way,' Hector said hesitantly.

He wants to kiss me, Dandy thought. But this isn't like silly Andy Connell or daft Jock. This is different, very different, oh yes!

She leaned towards him, prepared to kiss his cheek but his mouth was on hers. A wonderful peace and joy crept over her. They separated gently and gazed at each other in wonder. Then his arm was round her and she was being drawn closer into a more lingering kiss. 'May I write to you?' he asked. 'Let you know when that *Lilium giganteum* finally decides to flower.'

It was a pretence and they both knew it. Dandy suddenly wondered what her aunts would make of it all. The thought lingered with her till they were about to leave Lindsay House and she caught the end of a conversation between Hector and Aunt Alice. 'It is most kind of you. Yes, your Mrs McGuffie has always made us feel most welcome. Of course it is still early summer; your plants are so ahead of ours that we tend to forget that, but, as you say, some of the more exotic ones are still not ready to flower. I think it will probably be quite suitable for us to return for a short trip. If you are writing to Dandy you can keep her informed.'

'Aunt Alice doesn't seem to mind,' thought Dandy. 'They probably think he's old and safe. I wonder if they know that he kissed me. What would they think if they knew that I liked it?'

It did not dawn on her that her love for Hector was giving her a bloom that the aunts had no difficulty in interpreting. As Alice said, 'I must confess, Violet, that I find myself very drawn to that young man. He shows every sign of being in love with Dandy and she is obviously in the same boat, but we do not want a repeat of his previous disappointment and we *do* have some responsibility for her, standing as we do *in loco parentis*. Luckily we do not have to worry about her intransigent father as we might were we living in England. She *could* marry at sixteen without his consent – not that I would encourage *that* idea. She is more mature than most girls of her age, but another year of study to give her a chance to grow up and know her own mind . . . What do you say, Violet?'

'Yes, Alice. We may find we have a ticklish task there. When Dandy gets the bit between her teeth . . .'

'Quite!'

Chapter 19

The garden she had been so proud of seemed to have shrunk in her absence. It looked pathetically limited. In the days that followed she had to chide herself constantly for disloyalty when she remembered her earlier life – a life that would be beyond Hector's comprehension.

The garden was not her only disappointment. There was no letter from Canada awaiting her return. There had been no letter for some time. That was worrying. She took to re-reading the carefully preserved bundle she kept in her room. Most of them were from May and written at Marie Friedland's house. Sometimes Billy's were more revealing. She turned to one of them.

I'm learning so much from Aunt Marie though I don't get much chance to visit her just now. Pa has gone daft since he managed to buy his thirty acres. He keeps us all working so hard during the school holidays. Ma has to come along too with wee Jack. Our George says Pa has no right to make Ma lift such heavy things; it's not good for a woman. It was Mr Keir told us that. I'm awfully glad he took us to that gym for the boys round here would have been able to beat us. They all do exercises all the time. George gets mad when Pa won't let him go fishing with his gang. Pa keeps saying that we've got to get the farm in order. Poor Ma had hoped to have a decent house by this time but Pa says that will come when our profits rise. I get sick looking at apples when it's harvest time. That's funny when you think how we used to wish we could buy them in Paisley. Aunt Marie says I'll make a good farmer. She thinks George is a good engineer but she says that with all the new farm machinery that's being invented every farmer will have to be a bit of an engineer anyway. I'll bet none of the boys at home would be able to do the things I can do on the farm. George laughs some times but I know when to take the goats to be mated and Aunt Marie sells the kids and we always have plenty milk. It's a shame George can't go fishing because Ma was always glad to get something for our dinner. Pa's that mean. Maybe I shouldna say that but it's true. May is that grateful for your old clothes. She says they're wonderful and sometimes she cuts things up and makes them for the twins. They seem to be happy with their wee chums and Pa never asks them to do much. I don't think he notices us. He's that daft about profits. Still he's not drinking.

That was one of the earlier letters. May's recent ones had had something guarded about them. It was difficult to put her finger on it. Something was missing. She scanned one. There was nothing about Faither in it – not a word; quite a lot about the twins and their performance in the school concert; Aunt Marie was good to Ma and May was often leaving Jack at her house on the way to school to give Ma a chance.

That was odd. Ma was supposed to have been benefiting from all that fresh air and the children's independence. Gentle little May would be reluctant to worry her. Billy was so caught up in his animals that he might not notice what was going on. George seemed to be worried about Ma. George wasn't the worrying type. George was the one who could answer her questions.

Dandy sat down there and then and started a letter to
Marie Friedland.

Dear Mrs Friedland,

I hear so much about you in the letters from my
family that I feel I know you already. I'd like to
thank you for all your kindness. I have found the
recent letters rather disturbing in that May seems
very guarded. She said that you were looking after
little Jack to give Ma a chance. I thought her health
had been good since she went to Canada. Billy said
that she had been lifting things that were too heavy
for her. I know that my mother would not want to
worry me and might be hiding something. George
never writes. He's the one who would tell me the
truth straight out. I'd be grateful if you could let
me know the true picture. It is very good of you
to let May use your sewing machine. I know what
a difference it makes to her to be able to alter the
things I send. She is the one I feel most protective
towards. The twins seem to be happily independent by all accounts and the boys seem to thrive
on the outdoor life. I am just back from a lovely
holiday and had expected to find a letter.

Hoping to hear from you,
Yours sincerely

She would have to wait patiently while the letter
made its way across the Atlantic and then was taken
by train all the way across that vast country till at last
it was delivered by a horseman to the outlying farms.
And if Marie was so busy helping other people it was
unreasonable to think that she could drop everything
to reply. Well! Worrying would not bring it any quicker.
Rain was forecast. She could plant a row of tumshies.
A little bit of digging and raking would stop her feeling
miserable. She would pretend that she was doing it

with Hector by her side. Soon she was singing lustily, so intent on the job that she did not see Aunt Margaret approaching.

'I thought I heard you, Dandy, so I just came round the side of the house. My! You're the one for gardening. Betty wouldn't dream of soiling her hands. Of course, we have help. Still, you seem to be enjoying it. There's no accounting for taste. I'm afraid, however, that you won't feel so cheery when you hear my news.'

Her voice had taken on a tone that Dandy always found extremely irritating. It was Aunt Margaret being 'sincere' and it didn't suit her one little bit. Dandy waited impassively. What was the silly woman about this time? She knew about their trip to Rosecraig; probably noseyness . . .

'I've had a very worrying letter from your mother . . .'

'What?' said Dandy, startled.

'Yes. Very worrying indeed. Of course it is natural that she should wish to confide in her sister. After all, I am her nearest relative – apart from Jean, I mean, and she's so far away . . .'

'I'm her eldest daughter. What did she say?' Dandy broke in abruptly.

'I'll read you a little bit, shall I? Perhaps we should go in to the house?'

'There's a seat over there,' said Dandy grimly. Margaret did not know how near she was to having her face slapped and the letter torn from her hand. Only Alice's training stopped Dandy from doing exactly that.

'Right!' said Dandy abruptly.

'Well, Dandy dear, you know that your mother was so relieved that your father was not drinking, even though she had to live in that awful house and did not get money for half the things she needed.'

'Yes, of course I know that. What else?'

'Well . . . unfortunately your father seems to have

285

resumed his old ways. He's been drinking . . . and, well, you're old enough to know . . . your poor mother is pregnant again . . .'

'God, no!' said Dandy loudly.

Alice came hurrying through the conservatory with Violet on her heels. 'Bad news?' she asked.

'Oh, Miss McLaren, yes, I'm afraid so. It's a pity to be telling such things when you are just back from holiday. Was it nice down there?'

Alice, hurrying to Dandy's side, ignored the question. 'What is it, my dear? What's happened?'

'Faither's been drinking. Ma's pregnant. I thought there was something funny about May's last letter and it's a while since I got it. She said that she was taking Jack to Mrs Friedland on the way to school every morning to give Ma a chance. Ma never mentioned any of this to me and I didn't know why she needed a chance. Oh God! She never gets a chance, does she?'

Dandy was trembling as Alice's arm went round her. 'I think we should go inside and have a cup of tea . . . could you, Violet?'

Violet responded quickly to the message from Alice's eyebrows – Margaret was there. Margaret was about the last person Dandy wanted to see at that moment; the sooner they gave her some tea and got rid of her the better. Soon she was wheeling in a trolley with her prime home baking and answering Margaret's questions about their holiday in a most satisfactory way. Alice never left Dandy's side.

'And are you off to bridge this afternoon?'

'Oh, yes,' said Margaret importantly. 'It upsets the arrangements if people do not show up.'

'It's good to have something to dress up for, I always think,' said Violet.

'Yes, of course, I shall be changing . . . Dear me! I'm afraid it is time I was leaving you. Thank you so much.

It is so good of you to give Dandy such a lovely holiday. Rosecraig sounds a lovely place. I must try to visit it some time . . .'

Alice rose and helped to speed the departing guest. Dandy sat, her fingernails dug in her palms. 'Is she away?' she asked as her aunts returned.

'Yes,' said Alice, exhaling loudly.

'She's a bitch,' said Dandy, then, mimicking Margaret, ' "I'm her nearest relative." What does she think *I* am?'

'I quite agree,' said Alice. 'It's a pity your mother chose to divulge her troubles to her . . . but she *is* her sister, of course.'

'Ma didn't want to worry me. I'm sure that's what it's all about. That's why May's letters have been a bit strange. I wrote to Marie Friedland because of that and asked her to tell me. If only George had written. He'll be that mad. Billy said a while ago that Faither was making mother lift heavy things and that was wrong. Mr Keir had taught them that. George will be feeling like murder. He's older now and getting protective about Ma. She's going to need him if that drunken bugger is up to his tricks again . . .' She paused. 'I'm sorry, I never thought this would happen. It was bad enough thinking that he was so mean, but it seemed for a purpose. He'll be wasting money on drink. Ma shouldna be having another bairn.'

'She certainly shouldn't,' agreed Alice. 'When did you write to Mrs Friedland?'

'Yesterday. She seems to be a busy woman, though. I'll have to wait a long time for an answer. Isn't it sickening? And to think I was enjoying myself so much and poor Ma having all this to face alone . . .'

'She's not alone, Dandy. May seems to be a wonderful help and those boys are turning out so well. The twins are happy so she doesn't have to worry about them. If, as you say, George is feeling protective towards your mother, he'll see that your father keeps within bounds.'

'He'd need to tie him up first,' said Dandy bitterly.

'Oh, my dear, I'm very sorry. You were looking so happy at Rosecraig and Violet and I were so relieved that life seemed to be giving you what you deserved . . .'

Tears started to roll down Dandy's face. 'Everything was so beautiful in Lindsay Gardens and Hector seemed to share everything with me. I forgot how different our lives had been.'

'But Hector's had his own horrors to overcome, my dear: his life completely overturned by disablement and his heart broken by the disloyalty of his fiancée. He must feel guilty too about the death of his parents. He'll know what other people say about it. He's very much alone in his sorrow – unless you count Mrs McGuffie, bless her!'

'Yes. I'm glad she's there for him,' said Dandy. 'I think Mrs Friedland is probably in the same sort of standing with Ma. She seems to go the right way about helping her – taking Jack, I mean. May said in one letter that Mrs Friedland had never had any children herself but she always seemed to like having them around and she knew how to entertain the wee ones; thought up simple little games for them and made cookies and things. Isn't it funny that she has none and Ma had too many of us?'

'I'm sure that your mother loves you all and wouldn't be without one of you, my dear. If only she had been blessed with a helpful, understanding husband, that would have made all the difference.'

'One of them – I think it was May – said that Mrs Friedland could have managed Pa. I wish to God she had got him. Ma would have been fine with a nice quiet fellow.'

Alice rose. 'Did you get your tumshies in before that aunt of yours called?'

'No. I was just at the raking. I suppose I'd better get on with it.' She rose stiffly and made for the garden. Alice wandered into the kitchen and joined Violet. They looked at each other. Nothing needed to be said.

There would be no letter for some time, but that did not stop Dandy from watching out for the postman. Again, the letter from Canada was written by May. She scanned it quickly. Everybody said the twins should go on the stage when they grew up – they had such talent. Billy knew so much about farming. Mrs Friedland obviously made a favourite of him yet she sympathized with George. He was threatening to go to Seattle when he was seventeen. Mrs Friedland said he would do just as well in Winnipeg or Vancouver. These were up and coming places.

Apart from a few details about her sewing, there was nothing else in the letter, which ended *Ma sends her love*.

'Well! That's not getting me any further forward,' said Dandy, attacking the weeds in the vegetable garden. 'It all depends on Mrs Friedland now.'

A few wet days might have added to her depression if Alice and Violet had allowed it. They insisted that it was time to get back to work if she was to be able to keep upsides with Hector in the botany stakes. 'You said you were so glad you had learned Latin,' Violet remarked.

Dandy, in a moment of bitterness, wondered how much good any of it was. At Rosecraig, and especially in Lindsay Gardens, she had felt that her education with the McLarens and Miss McGregor helped her to be almost upsides with Hector. Her family, by all accounts, had been doing well and the fear of disgrace was over. Hector had never asked about her parents.

He obviously thought her aunts had brought her up. The sort of home she had had would be completely beyond his imagination, she was sure. The poorest worker on his estate seemed to live in a decent cottage and most of these cottages had four little bedrooms upstairs. How could he possibly imagine a two-roomed flat with children sleeping at both ends of the bed? The gulf between them was hopeless. She should never have let him kiss her. It was cheating. Then she remembered that first kiss . . . the gentle touch, the wonderful feeling of peace it had engendered; and yet that peace led to a longing, a longing for something that Aunt Alice seemed to think she deserved. Or did they not understand? When they went along with Hector's suggestion of a return visit, had it no special significance for them? She knew that there was much more than a garden involved in her feelings for Lindsay House.

The first dry sunny morning meant that she could return to the garden and she was out early when the postman arrived. She looked at the postmark and made a quick dive for the house, scraping her shoes fiercely on the mat by the conservatory door, then removing them quickly. 'It's from Hector,' she called and ran upstairs to read it in the privacy of her room.

Alice raised her eyebrows to Violet. 'Things have gone further than I expected. I suppose we should have known that Dandy would never do anything at a normal pace.'

Dandy's heart was racing furiously and her hands trembling as she studied the gold letter-heading:

Lindsay House
   My dearest Dandy,
   This is to announce that *Lilium giganteum* (*Cardiocrinum giganteum*) has opened today. It is towering above *Lilium nepalensis* and *Lilium wallichianum*, but

I think they still hold their own in the beauty stakes. I'd like your expert opinion on that matter as soon as possible, my Queen of the Lilies.

Mrs McGuffie is looking forward to entertaining a house party and already the kitchen is filled with mouth-watering smells. Rosecraig Hotel will have to look to its laurels. I'd back my Mrs McGuffie any day. Miss Alice seemed to think there would be no difficulty in arranging for someone to look after your garden while you are away . . .

'So waste not time; but come; for all the vales
Await thee.'

'That's Tennyson! He loves poetry too. Wonderful! Wonderful!' She hugged the letter to her breast.

When she rejoined the aunts her sparkling eyes and flushed cheeks gave them their answer. 'Yes, of course,' said Alice. I spoke to Mrs Brown and she said her nephew was always glad of a little extra money. He knows the routine here now. We've nothing to worry about.'

If only that were true, thought Dandy. I've got my drunken father, my pregnant mother and my over-worked little sister . . . But, of course, worrying wouldn't help them. Some of Aunt Alice's old dresses might be useful to Ma now that none of her own would be fitting her properly. She would ask Aunt Alice at a suitable moment. Hector had begged her not to delay. She must start packing.

Their welcome was all that could have been desired. While the young couple dashed off to see the lily, Mrs McGuffie eagerly engaged the aunts in conversation, her remarks bordering on indiscretion as she relayed her young master's impatience to see Dandy again. They had already seen for themselves how young and almost nervous Hector seemed.

As they hurried towards the lily garden, he seized Dandy's hand. In his strong grip she again experienced that wonderful feeling of safety which had been hers at their first kiss. They stopped in front of the magnificent plant. 'It's eleven feet high. I measured it early this morning when I couldn't sleep. It's a good thing the flowers point downwards or you would never see half of them. There are nineteen on that stem.'

Dandy stood on tiptoe.

'I wish I had two arms and could lift you up.' Hector's voice came from behind her.

Dandy turned slowly. She knew that it was not just the beauty of the lily that brought the moisture to her eyes. She glanced up at him and was immediately in his embrace. When they drew apart she was laughing and shaken.

'I suppose I should be in the drawing room playing host,' Hector began. 'But, oh Dandy, how I've longed to see you again. There's been something missing in this garden since you went away. I keep longing to see that lovely yellow hair!' Dandy leaned against him as they walked hand-in-hand back to the house. Reluctantly they separated when they felt they were in sight, little knowing that they were too late. Not only the aunts but the housekeeper too had seen them.

The 'few days' they had promised themselves were extended without much discussion. The aunts took some sightseeing trips, but Dandy was far too busy in the garden. 'Really, Alice, it's all happening too quickly for me,' said Violet, and Alice was forced to agree that matters were now out of their hands.

Dandy was in heaven, revelling in each stolen kiss. All thoughts of her family were pushed resolutely to the back of her mind. Hector needed her help in the garden. He had suffered and she could comfort him. Hector loved her; said the garden wasn't the same with-

292

out her. She treasured that thought. One thing she *did* notice with a little disquiet was his ever more frequent references to his disability. 'You seem to manage most things,' she finally remonstrated.

'The fact remains that I am a maimed man. I expect you have heard my story by now. I'm not any less ugly . . . for any woman to look upon.' His last words were muttered.

'It's not so important as you think,' said Dandy.

'Isn't it?'

They wandered on. Dandy remarked on various changes and he made some sort of reply, but she could see that he was abstracted with no idea where he was going. Three times they landed back at the summer house. The third time Dandy paused. 'You're worried about something, Hector. What is it – your arm?'

'I'm tempted to take a risk, my darling, but I could regret it . . .'

'You know what the Marquis of Montrose wrote on the way to his execution, don't you?

> *'He either fears his fate too much,*
> *Or his deserts are small*
> *That puts it not unto the touch*
> *To win or lose it all.'*

'That settles it,' said Hector. 'Wait there till I call you.' He went into the summer house. In a few minutes she heard her name. When Dandy, puzzled, walked in, he was lying stripped to the waist, his face scarlet and grim. The hot blood rushed up in hers and her hand shot up to her mouth as she looked from the stump of the missing arm to the perfect one. Hector, watching her, sensed revulsion and, summing up the hopelessness of his cause, went white with despair. He half rose, then jerked up startled as Dandy reverted to the language of her childhood. 'The rotten bastards . . . the rotten bastards! If I could get hold of them!'

Hector's jaw dropped; then he roared with laughter. Dandy threw her arms round him, guiltily experiencing the feel of naked male flesh. He kissed her eagerly then thrust her away. 'Step outside, Dandy, while I get dressed. It wouldn't do for any of the staff to see me like this.'

His step was light when he rejoined her. 'I'll have to ask your aunts' permission to court you, my darling. I think it would be as well to keep quiet about my little experiment . . .'

'I had no intention of telling my revered aunts,' she laughed.

'You see I was terrified that you would feel disgust at the sight of me. I simply *had* to know. Though it was already too late for me. I could never stop loving you now, you little witch!'

It was really no surprise to the Misses McLaren to be invited to step into Hector's study. Their answer had been worked out on a pragmatic basis. They had foreseen his surprise too when he learned that Dandy was still a few weeks off her seventeenth birthday. 'I knew she was much younger than I, but I would have said twenty at least.'

'Most people think so,' said Alice. 'She has always been tall for her age and surprisingly mature. Her voracious reading helps in that respect, of course. You appreciate that she is too young for a formal engagement yet, but I'm sure that Violet agrees with me in trusting her to your care.'

Dandy was playing the piano when they entered the drawing room, but she ended with a crashing discord when she saw Hector's beaming face. With his arm round her waist he announced the verdict. Dandy was laughing and crying at the same time as she kissed her benefactors. 'This calls for champagne,' said Hector, 'and Mrs McGuffie must share it.'

Chapter 20

The short holiday had lasted nearly a fortnight when Alice and Violet finally tore Dandy away. It was only the thought of being a match for Hector that made her return to her studies. Once home, thoughts of her family returned to plague her. That bit about her mother having to carry heavy things was especially worrying. Grannie had always warned about that too, but of course Grannie worried about nearly everything. If only she could hear from Mrs Friedland! It was annoying that Aunt Margaret should get news that by rights should be hers. And yet, she could understand her mother's wish . . . not to worry her. There was little she could do at a distance – nothing, in fact. Still . . .

When the letter with the magic Canadian stamp arrived it was a fat one. She tore it open in the kitchen by the stove.

Dear Dandy,

I feel I may call you that because your name is seldom off May's lips. Your brothers too always speak so admiringly of 'our Dandy'. It is distressing to see what has happened to your Pa. He was certainly making a good job of the farm in spite of having had no training till he came here. I understand that he drank heavily in Scotland. We are lucky here that none of the local men have that weakness. Pioneers will never succeed unless they are made of stern stuff. Yes, your mother's pain is worrying. I have been trying some herbal remedies, but I feel that she has strained herself at one stage. That will probably disappear after the baby is born. It is the extra weight that is causing the trouble. George and Billy are champions and Jack is a little darling – so affectionate I could keep him. Billy has a natural gift for dealing with animals.

You said in your letter that George would tell you straight. Well, I have been bullying him and told him that not a cent will he earn from me till he writes that letter. He's here beside me now with a glass of lemonade to inspire him. I'll say goodbye and God bless you.

Marie Friedland

George's writing had not improved much, she noted, but at least she could interpret the little quirks.

Dear Dandy,

You know I'm not much of a writer but Aunt Marie seems to think I could let you know about Pa better than the others. Well, he was doing great on the farm, working hard but mean as hell about money. Poor Ma never gets any new clothes. It's damnable. Billy and I try to help but anything we can give seems to go on food or shoes. He had set his heart on a bigger farm than anyone else around and the bit of land he fancied was just at the back of Aunt Marie's here. Well, that was fine, but other men start on their houses as soon as the first planting is done. He keeps putting off, trying to get more trees and says the house can wait. Poor Ma has such a struggle in that dump. It's really only camping and she has to lift everything here and there because there is no real furniture. Other women have wardrobes and things. Poor Ma has to cope with a dump. Faither's hardly ever there. We put up with all that because he wasna drinking but he got a letter from an old pal and arranged to meet him in Vernon. He got all dressed up and said he would stay the night. He took a lot of money that was to go into the bank. He didn't come back the next day and Ma was up to high doh. I went to Aunt Marie on the third morning and she left me in charge of her place and took the trap into Vernon. She had a bother finding him and it was late at night before she brought him back. He looked like a tramp, Dandy – filthy and reeking of drink. He hadn't a cent on him. We think someone stole the money for he couldn't have got through all that drink. Aunt Marie brought him here and sent me home to tell Ma that he was all right. She sobered him up and gave him a good talking-to. Things were all right for a wee while. Then one day when we thought he was up at the farm we found he had gone into Vernon again. I feared the worst and I was right. When he got back he was drunk and I found later that he was keeping whisky in the hut at the farm. This letter will cost a fortune to post but Aunt Marie says not to mind. It's important to let you know everything. She's been such a help. We would never have got letters to you without her. Pa's that mean nowadays. Where was I? Aye! Next thing was that Ma started getting sick in the morning. I never thought much about it but I could see that May was real worried and then I found that there was a bun in the oven. It's ridiculous at her age and with all the bairns she's got. I felt I could have killed the old devil. I had to put up with a bit of tormenting at school at first but luckily my boxing is pretty good. That's thanks to Mr Keir. Remember he gave Faither a bashing! One of these days I'll do the same. Ma is feeling pretty rotten most of the time but Aunt Marie thinks she will be a bit better after the bairn is born. She says that Ma can come and stay at her house as soon as she likes but Ma feels it is her duty to keep the home together. Some home! Well, Dandy I think that lets you know what's happening here. You seem to be having a fine time with the McLarens. You certainly deserve it. Aunt Marie thinks I've probably told you enough. Don't worry about May. Billy and I will look after her.

Love,

George

Well, she knew the true story now, but it didn't really help much. Even if she were over there with them, what could she do? Certainly Ma wouldn't have had to lift such heavy things because she could have helped with that, but probably Faither would have insisted on her working on the fruit farm to make more money for him to drink. It was sickening. She wandered through to the sitting room where Violet was sewing and Alice was polishing silver.

'Oh, from Canada!' Alice exclaimed. 'We assumed it was from Hector.'

'No. I don't know what Hector would think of me if he knew the sort of background I come from.'

'I think he would separate you quite easily from your background and judge you as a person, my dear. You look troubled. Are things worse than you thought?'

'You'd better read it,' said Dandy, offering the letter.

'I haven't my spectacles, my dear. Please read it to us.'

Dandy's husky voice showed the strain she was under. This was one time when even Alice could find little to say in consolation.

The next letter *was* from Hector.

299

My darling Dandy,

I know it's your birthday next week. I've got a little something for you which I'd like to give you personally. Would it be at all possible for you to come back? I know it's rather soon to ask your dear aunts to repeat the journey. If not, dare I call on you in Paisley? I would put up at a hotel, of course. The weather has been fine and the garden is still in its summer glory but the darkness does come early. Sometimes I go into the summer house and imagine you are there. It is something about the lovely woody smell, I think, which brings you back. I was very aware of it while I awaited your reaction, that day. Oh, my dear, you have no idea what your loving courage does to me. To have hope of happiness when I thought all chance of it had fled. My darling, darling, Dandy. Do say 'yes' and let us meet again soon.

All my love,
Hector

Dandy found herself laughing helplessly with the tears running down her cheeks. Hector loved her. She had given him a hope of happiness. That should be heaven to her. But – and it was a big 'but' – what would he think of this tiny cottage, the pathetic little garden? Though they had never pretended that they lived in anything grander, she was sure that he would have a very different idea of their surroundings. He thought that the journey would be tiring for her aunts. Perhaps he was right, but it made it awkward for them to say, 'Oh, no, we would like to come to Lindsay House.' Didn't it? There was awkwardness every way she turned. She must not seem to disparage this cottage which the aunts had turned into a happy home for her. The garden which now seemed minuscule had been a

300

trust from Uncle James and he had given her so much – not least of his gifts had been the glimpse of what a decent man could be. She had measured Hector by that yardstick. Perhaps if she just put the problem in Aunt Alice's hands . . .

'I think he would quite like to come here,' said Alice. 'We have never pretended that the cottage was bigger than it is, have we? He knows what to expect. And perhaps he is thinking of appearances too. He is a very percipient young man.'

'Appearances?' asked Dandy.

'My dear. Hector is by way of being the laird in that district. You saw how his doings were discussed in the hotel. I think you can take it that a similar interest is shown in the farms and cottages round about. A pretty young stranger gets a recluse to welcome her day after day to his prized garden. Her aunts seem to welcome the intimacy that develops. Are they out to "get him"?'

'They'd never think that about you and Aunt Violet, surely?' Dandy was aghast.

'My dear Dandy, it is possible that someone will and the rumour will spread. People will look and see what they wish to see. That is human nature, I'm afraid. Hector, as I said, is aware of this. By coming to see you here instead he will avoid that. Only Mrs McGuffie will know and she is loyalty itself and very much on your side.'

'My garden will seem so wee . . . I've got nothing rare . . . I mean, Uncle James did wonders, but . . .'

'Dandy, your garden has *you* – the Queen of the Lilies, as Hector put it in that lovely inscription. He wants to see you and nothing else. He has enough thoughtfulness to consider your reputation – and ours, I suspect.'

'You think I should tell him to come, then? What hotel is best?'

It was Violet who answered, 'This one.'

'You see?' said Alice. 'Mrs McGuffie is not the only one who could match Rosecraig Hotel. I think we can be proud of our chef and, as you see, Dandy, she is just dying to try.'

'Shall I write and invite him or is that wrong? Will it have to come from you and Aunt Violet?'

'I think we dare be informal now. Just tell him that we would be delighted to have him here.'

'The spare room isn't very big.'

'Your Hector probably went to boarding school and slept in a dormitory or cubicle. Do you think that being under the same roof as his Dandy would not be worth a little inconvenience? If you say "yes" I shall think that you do not know Hector as well as I do, my dear.'

Dandy sat at her little writing table for some time before putting pen to paper. There were so many 'ifs' and 'buts', but Aunt Alice was never wrong and she seemed to think that Hector would be quite happy to take pot luck, and of course she was right about the cooking. Aunt Violet would have everything planned to the last detail and there would be nothing to be ashamed of in that department and, really, if Hector was too grand to fit into the cottage he would not be a true gentleman like Uncle James. Surely Hector could match his behaviour to the occasion! He valued her loving courage – what a lovely compliment.

My darling Hector, she began.

When the letter was sealed and posted she returned to the garden with vigour. Small it might be, but she would see that it reached as near perfection as was humanly possible.

When she entered the house by the back door, the smell of lunch was vying with that of shortbread. Violet had started in her methodical way with the things that would keep well in tins. Dandy had a fleeting worry that these devoted efforts might be in vain, but banished it instantly. Mrs McGuffie had gone ahead with *her* baking, feeling that it would bring Dandy through the rain to Hector's side. Who was she to have a lesser faith!

She did not have long to wait for an answer.

O my darling Dandy,

I am delighted to accept your aunts' kind invitation. To be under the same roof as you . . . I can't wait. You seem worried that I shall find the cottage small. I'm not a giant, am I? I can assure you that I spent many holidays camping with my father when I was young. Fitting into a tent is surely much more difficult than anything you can offer! Oh, my darling. That's all I can say. To know that you are there only a few steps away from me at night is bound to fill my dreams with rapture.

It will be especially enjoyable because I always feel here that, even though we are isolated in the garden, my comings and goings are noted. I suppose it is inevitable. My engagement was announced in *The Times*, you see, and the cancellation too. Though all that is a long time ago, folk memory can serve a life sentence on the subject of its interest. Mrs McGuffie will just tell them that Master Hector has gone to Glasgow for some shopping. Perhaps you will be able to get her out of her habit of calling me that. I've tried everything from shaking an imaginary rattle to speaking in a schoolboy falsetto!

I'll get the morning train from Stranraer on Thursday. I'm afraid the hours will drag till I feel those lovely arms round me.

Give my warmest thanks and compliments to your aunts,

Your devoted

Hector

After that it was full speed ahead in the cottage. Violet issued her orders and four willing hands obeyed. There was a discussion about meeting Hector at the station. 'Really,' said Alice, 'you should not be there unchaperoned. But if there were no danger of bumping into someone like your Aunt Margaret – oh, dear, I *am* uncharitable about Mrs McMillan – and you would be getting a cab from the station. Well, I really feel that there is no need for us to climb those stairs. What do you think, Violet?'

Violet, meeting her sister's intense stare, replied that she thought they could risk staying at home. Dandy felt her colour rise. She would be on that platform alone, waiting for her beloved Hector. She would watch the carriage doors open; see his tall figure coming towards her. Would he kiss her? No, probably not in public. Would he think it odd that she was unchaperoned? Aunt Alice had weighed things up and decided that it was probably safe. Aunt Alice had given her a good reason for their not coming with her – those station stairs. Was that Aunt Alice being devious? It was difficult to tell. She must be looking her best. Which dress? It would depend on the weather. Wasn't she lucky to have such a choice, thanks to Aunt Violet!

She set off for the station feeling that her feet hardly touched the ground.

She was too early, of course. There were a few people there. She studied them obliquely. No, nobody she knew. She would have to be careful not to draw attention to herself. The minutes dragged. What would he say? He seemed so happy to come, even to the wee cottage, but what would happen when she had to tell him about her family? The aunts had not said anything about telling him. She had dreaded being told that the time had come and he must know. Would that be when they were going to get engaged? He had accepted an invitation to the cottage very happily, but she tried to imagine his feelings when she told him how his Queen of the Lilies had spent her childhood – in conditions worse than the poorest of his employees. It was asking a lot of someone brought up like Hector with a grandfather who had started a place like Lindsay Gardens. All her grandfather had bequeathed her was her nickname. And when could she ever tell him *that* story? She was still blushing over that memory when the distant rumble became a vibration and the noisy engine steamed in with a squealing of brakes; then there was a slamming of doors and all was confusion. A quick glance showed Dandy that he was one of the first on the platform. Then he saw her and lengthened his stride. She stifled the instinct to run towards him and throw her arms around him. Aunt Alice had not issued any advice or warnings, but her training told Dandy to be careful. There *was* a danger that someone in the crowd might know her.

His smile was wide and a little unsteady – like her own, she guessed. He placed his luggage on the platform and stretched out his hand. It was the strength of his grip that told her of his desire for a more intimate greeting. When would he kiss her, she wondered – when they reached the cottage? In the cab she was all too aware of his nearness. He was talking about the garden – all innocent stuff that the cabbie could listen to if he chose – but while his voice went on matter-of-factly his arm was creeping round her waist. She gave a long sigh. She was safe. Hector was here and it didn't matter how small the cottage was.

His greeting for the aunts was rather a shy one, she noted. Of course he was not on his own territory any longer. Her memory took her back to some of the conversations in the hotel: he never went anywhere nowadays; sometimes the doctor and his wife were at

Lindsay House in the evening; the minister included him in his round of visits; an occasional shopping trip to Stranraer or Glasgow – that was about it.

But Alice was speaking to her. 'Will you show Hector up to his room, dear? Then we can have a little drink in the conservatory before lunch, I think.'

Dandy's legs were trembling as she led Hector up the narrow staircase. The thought that he would find the spare room pokey was still at the back of her mind, but the first thing was his kiss. It was sure to come now. He had been shy, rather formal, downstairs and had addressed all his remarks to her aunts. Of course, that was right, but . . .

'Here you are. I put some flowers in – small ones.'

'I shall treasure them, my love.' His suitcase was down and she was being drawn towards him. Then came the gentle kiss she had longed for; but it did not end . . . just got deeper and deeper till she felt she had no breath left. They finally drew apart, laughing and gasping. Hector's arm went round her again. 'You've no idea how I've longed and longed for that. I don't know how I am going to wait till you grow up, my darling.'

'I feel grown-up when I am with you,' said Dandy. 'In fact, I feel grown-up most of the time. I think I grew up early.'

'Possibly because you were being brought up by rather elderly aunts,' he said.

This was dangerous territory. Dandy racked her brains but could think of nothing. 'They will be wondering what is keeping us,' she ventured.

'I'll be very surprised if they don't know,' said Hector. 'I don't think they'll mind waiting . . .'

This was indeed true as far as it applied to Alice, but Violet was beginning to worry about her carefully prepared lunch some minutes before she heard their hasty steps on the stairs and saw their flushed smiling faces. Hector, sizing up the situation, refused the offer of sherry in favour of making straight for the dining room. In a dream, Dandy endorsed Hector's opinions as he praised Violet's cooking and in a dream she sat beside him in the conservatory after the meal was over, instead of hurrying to the kitchen to make the coffee. Each minute was golden and had to be cherished. It was Hector who finally urged her to take him on a tour of her garden. 'Tour!' she said. 'A few minutes will complete it.'

'Not the way I intend to inspect it,' said Hector. 'You will have to look to your laurels, Miss Baxter.'

'There aren't any,' said Dandy. 'I hate the things.'

'Well, that's another thing we have in common,' laughed Hector as he followed her out.

Alice joined Violet in the kitchen. 'I think we've lost our coffee maker, my dear.'

'Yes, and our dishwasher, Alice, but I don't mind in the least. I felt decidedly *de trop* in there.'

'Well, he *did* appreciate your cooking . . .'

'I doubt if he was in a fit state to disapprove of anything with his Queen of the Lilies sitting there beside him, and did you see how dreamy Dandy was. I doubt if she could tell you *what* I made!'

'Well, isn't that just how it should be? Remember James and Rachel?'

'Yes . . . but she *is* so young, Alice, and what is going to happen when she tells him about her family? She'll have to tell him sometime. I have the feeling that she is dreading it.'

'Of course she is. I don't know whether I should urge her to tell him now or not. It is a dreadful responsibility. The fact that she is dreading it will be bound to make her awkward in the telling. It isn't that I don't trust Hector . . . to have the character to cope, I mean, though it is bound to be a bit of a shock . . . It's wonderful to see her so happy. I hate to mar a moment of it for her.'

'What I'm scared of, Alice, is that it might be taken out of our hands. I thought of it that day when Mrs McMillan arrived with that letter. She *is* Dandy's aunt! I mean, if she found out she could make things awkward. Hector is only supposed to be here for a few days, but supposing she sees them together or someone asks her who the handsome man is who's been seen with her niece. Wouldn't she just love to poke her nose in . . .'

'Exactly! I was very aware of that when Hector asked permission to court Dandy. I had no right, and Mrs McMillan could take exception to my giving it. But Dandy comes first and I beg to think that we can further her happiness in a way that Aunt Bloody Margaret is incapable of doing!'

'Alice! You said . . .' The well-bred Misses McLaren were in each other's arms and helpless with laughter.

Chapter 21

Dandy, who had dreamed her way through the meal, was still lost in a dream of happiness as she led him out into the garden. Holding hands could be dangerous when they were overlooked from every angle, yet Hector's nearness was so real to her that she felt her hand tingle as if in his strong grasp. 'That's clever,' he said when they passed through the first archway to find another cunningly contrived vista. 'I thought I had been rather smart with my cameos but I could never have managed it in such little space. Top marks to your Uncle James.'

'Just wait; you haven't seen the best one,' was all Dandy could say. She longed to feel Hector's arm creep round her, his lips on hers; longed for the space and privacy of Lindsay Gardens. Everywhere they went in town they were liable to be noticed. Perhaps she could offer to take him for a walk up the Gleniffer Braes. There would be plenty of quiet spots there, but there was always the danger of meeting people on the way. It was a well-known venue for courting couples. She might meet some of her friends from church . . . or someone who knew Aunt Margaret.

They turned a corner and came to the tiny lawn surrounded by shrubs. 'Oh,' said Hector, stopping in his tracks. 'Magic in miniature.'

'The first time I saw it I thought it looked the sort of place where the fairies might dance – not that I believed in fairies, of course!'

'No?' said Hector, raising an eyebrow. 'After what

has happened to me – meeting you . . . I mean . . . Well, if I don't exactly believe in fairies . . . I believe in magic. You said this garden was overlooked from all angles . . . Come here, between the birch tree and the escallonia. Yes – I thought so! We are completely screened, my darling.'

Dandy's arms wound round his neck as she lifted her face to his. All her pent-up longing was in that kiss, her young pliant body pressing eagerly against his. Suddenly Hector tore himself from her grasp. 'I'm sorry, Dandy. I shouldn't. It's not fair . . . you're so young . . . I should have known better. We shall have to control ourselves. You're so young. Your aunts trust me to look after you.'

Dandy gazed at his crimson face, her lip trembling. 'What did I do wrong? Why do you keep saying I'm so young?' Then awareness rushed through her – her father, daft Jock – Hector too? Of course, that was the explanation! That was what was behind her own dreams. That was the desire that drove her to long for Hector's kisses. And she was too young. It would probably be years before her aunts would let her marry Hector – that is, if he wanted to marry her. Of course he did! That was why he longed to have her with him. That was why he felt bereft in Lindsay Gardens without her.

She found herself shaking uncontrollably. 'Steady, my love!' Hector's hand was on her shoulder. 'I think we should make our way back now, don't you?' Dandy nodded dumbly.

If Alice noticed the two flushed faces she gave no sign. 'I've been thinking, Dandy. Isn't your Aunt Margaret at bridge this afternoon? This would be a good time for us to show Hector some of the sights of Paisley.'

Hector turned inquiringly to Dandy. 'I take it that this Aunt Margaret is one to be avoided?'

'She's nosey,' said Dandy. 'A socialite.'

'Sounds dreadful,' said Hector. 'Sightseeing it is!'

'I'll fetch my hat,' said Dandy.

They set off with Alice on Hector's arm and Violet following with Dandy. It had been decided that they would start with the abbey and work their way westward. 'Twelfth-century,' said Dandy, who had done her homework. 'Founded by Walter Fitzalan, the first high steward of Scotland who was brought here from Brittany by King David I, "The Sair Sanct".'

Their footsteps echoed on the stone slabs as Dandy took on the role of guide. Before very long Alice and Violet were glad to sit down while Hector and Dandy walked round the tombs. They were crouching down to read the inscription on one when Hector surprised her with a quick kiss. Dandy looked round hurriedly, but was relieved to see that only the figures on the tombs could have seen. After that it became a little game with Hector to ask her who was in a particular tomb – always in the dimmest spot possible.

It was a relief to emerge into the sunlight and admire the solid town hall on the banks of the river. 'Now,' said Dandy, 'I want you to see the church we attend and where the boys sing like angels, though they're far from that once you get to know them.'

'What boy is?' said Hector, laughing. Violet looked at Alice, sure that she too was remembering the gossip in the hotel; that the Captain was a recluse who never smiled. By the time they reached the church and Dandy had fetched the key from the church officer, who knew her well, Alice and Violet were glad to sit down in a pew and let Dandy lead Hector off. 'There's something here I'm sure you've never seen before,' she was saying as the door beside the pulpit closed behind them.

'I would have thought that there were many things

here that he'll never have seen before,' said Alice. 'That big marble pond, for example.'

'Don't you remember what intrigued her most the first time she was shown over the building, Alice? It was the changing room where the panelling opens and the big rubber saucers appear. Remember how she giggled? She said it was like a conjurer's trick. I'll be surprised if that is not what Hector is being shown right now.'

'Would she know how to work the mechanism?'

'That's probably what she was discussing with the church officer: remember he was stretching and going through the motions of pulling something.'

'And what is this wonder I have never seen before?' Hector was asking in the echoing corridor.

'Just wait!' She threw open a door. 'Now, you stand there and watch this.'

Quickly she approached one of the panelled walls, muttering, 'It's here somewhere.' Then she stretched up and released a tiny bolt, stooped and released another and she was walking backwards pulling an enormous frame which enclosed a large rubber saucer.

'What in the name . . . ?' Hector started.

'The people who have been baptized come here. There will be curtains round these rails of course: they drop their wet robes in the big saucers. Clever isn't it? There are four of them in this room and four in the men's changing room.'

'I wouldn't have believed it. But then, I wouldn't have believed I would be here with you . . . If anyone had told me . . .' His arm was round her and she had no wish to end the ecstasy of the kiss that followed.

It was some time before guide and pupil appeared and Violet was proved right. 'Who would have dreamt it,' he was saying . . . 'in a church! You're right. It *is* like a conjurer's trick, my love. Now, I'd like to study the carving on the pulpit. It's quite something! Though I'm not so keen on the angels on the ceiling.'

'Neither am I,' said Dandy. 'In fact, I think it's the only thing I don't like.'

'Again we are of one accord,' said Hector, grasping her hand as they moved forward. Alice answered Violet's smile with a rueful lift of the eyebrows.

Dandy's eager voice faded in the distance. 'She'll be taking him down the winding stairs to the lecture hall,' said Violet.

'I think we might as well settle down for a little snooze,' said Alice.

They woke with the sound of 'Oh for the wings of a dove' coming from the choir stalls. Dandy stood proudly singing for the man she loved. There was dead silence when she finished; then Hector's footsteps approached from the back of the church.

'Could you hear me?' she asked.

'Every syllable. I didn't know ... your voice is wonderful ...'

'I wasn't singing loud. That's the cathedral sound. You float the voice ...'

'I've never heard anything more touching,' said Hector, his heart in his eyes. There was a long pause.

'I hate to bring you down to earth,' said Alice, 'but if we wish to avoid your Aunt Margaret we had better be on our way soon.'

'Why don't you sing in the church choir yourself?' he asked when they were safely back in the conservatory.

'Well, when I was working I couldn't get away for the choir practice ...'

'You were working?'

'I was helping out as assistant governess to a family in church. They moved down to the south of England in the spring and I was no longer needed.'

'I'll bet you were the youngest governess they had ever seen!'

'Probably, but the senior governess was excellent. I enjoyed my time there. She taught music too, you see. The children did what I told them, so that was no problem.'

'I seem to have a lot to learn about you, Dandy.'

Dandy tensed up and glanced at Alice, who sailed smoothly in. 'I daresay you will both have a great deal to tell. I cannot see time ever hanging on your hands – or boredom setting in for that matter. I've been thinking, Dandy, isn't it likely that Mrs McMillan may come with a birthday gift for you?'

Dandy was about to reply that Aunt Margaret had never given them presents – there were too many of them, then she stopped herself in time. 'She might. You never know. Still, we can't keep Hector prisoner here because of Aunt Bl . . . Aunt Margaret.'

Alice rose hastily. 'You carry on with your sherry. I'll see if Violet would welcome any help.'

'She knew what I nearly said,' thought Dandy. 'She's away through to tell Aunt Violet.' The sound of subdued laughter from the kitchen confirmed her suspicion. She glanced at Hector. Had he picked up her slip of the tongue? But Hector was gazing at her with a look that melted her bones.

'My little songbird!' he said. 'This engagement is going to be murder. It's wrong to wish time away, I know, but I can't wait for your growing up.'

'Me too!' said Dandy with a fervent sigh.

'As for being kept a prisoner. I can't imagine a nicer fate than being a prisoner with you – and your kind aunts,' he added as an afterthought. Dandy reflected that that was just how she felt herself. The tiny garden, the conservatory, the sitting room – they all had a magic for her when Hector was near. Was this what had persuaded her mother to marry 'a drunken dyer'? Obviously, Hector was a different proposition from her father, but would the same pull have been exerted...? It was impossible to tell. She was lucky; she had met Hector, and he felt the same magic; the aunts supported her cause with him. But there was one snag. She was going to have to tell him about the family some time. The prospect had not seemed too daunting when reports from Canada had told of her father's sobriety, but now! Aunt Alice never broached the subject. That in itself was odd. Did she, too, see it as a great barrier that might put Hector off? The chasm between his upbringing and hers seemed in her gloomier moments too vast ever to be bridged. And yet, Aunt Alice had allowed the courtship to go ahead ... indeed had smoothed its path. She *must* think there was a way through.

'You're very thoughtful, my litle birthday girl.'

'It's not my birthday till tomorrow. Are you really quite content to stay around the cottage, or would you like to go somewhere ... There is some lovely country-side on the outskirts of the town.'

'All I want is to be with you. When we're outside I have to be so circumspect. Your aunts are very understanding. I think we can relax very well here, don't you?'

'That's the way I feel, but I wondered...'

'Come here!'

When Dandy reluctantly drew out of his embrace, she wondered out loud if she should be helping Violet in the kitchen.

'No, under no circumstances,' he assured her. 'I have my orders. Let me whisper. There's a birthday cake being prepared and you are not to know anything about it. There!'

'Sir, you are a traitor, betraying a secret like that,'

said Dandy, winding her arms round his neck. Then she remembered, blushed and drew apart.

'D'you see?' said Hector. 'It is as well that I live not too near. This engagement isn't going to be easy for either of us – at least a year, and there's no saying what might happen in that year.'

'What do you mean?'

'The situation in Europe. I don't like it.'

'What situation? I don't understand.'

'No, I suppose if you were busy teaching children you would not be following those things. We all thought we were fine after the *Entente Cordiale* – oh dear, you would only be . . . let me see . . . nine or ten years old when that was drawn up, so I don't expect you heard it discussed. That was an agreement between Britain, France and Belgium, Dandy – mutual support, you know. But now the armaments race is on. Germany is re-arming like mad and there's this trouble between Russia and the Austria–Hungary alliance. There's no saying where it will all end. Oh dear, I shouldn't be worrying you. Perhaps they'll all see sense . . .'

'You think there might be a war . . . for us, I mean?'

'We could very well get caught up in it through our alliances.'

'But you wouldn't have to fight – your arm . . .'

'No. I'm pretty useless.' His voice was grim.

'Would Canada be in a war too?'

'Good God! Why Canada?'

'I don't know. I just wondered.' Dandy bit her lip in vexation. This business of keeping quiet about her family was not easy; yet the prospect of telling Hector was one she simply couldn't face. Perhaps later . . . She thought of May's recent letter:

We are taking care of Ma and Aunt Marie is marvel-lous. I think I told you she has some herbal medicines that are supposed to help make things easier when the time comes. I wonder how wee Jack will take to a baby in the house. He is such a manly little fellow now, you would laugh, Dandy. Aunt Marie gets him to 'help' her carry things. She calls out 'strong man wanted' and he comes rushing. Of course the things are never really heavy! She says that every boy should be taught right from the beginning to use his manly strength to help others. I can never remember what I told you in my last letter. Aunt Marie has taught George to ride. She says you never know when a doctor would be needed during the night and that would be the quickest way to fetch him. I wonder if she is thinking of Ma. Billy is learning now too. He loves animals and is very patient at the feeding and all the horrid cleaning out that they need. I think I'd rather crochet – not that there's much time for that because Ma needs to rest and I cook as much as I can at night time. If only we had a decent house. So much time and effort is wasted humping things from here to there and back again. She's doing a little bit of knitting, though, and I think we'll have enough clothes for the wee one. It'll be funny having a baby in the house again – and no Dandy and no Grannie. She used to annoy us a bit with all her moaning, but sometimes I feel that Ma just longs to have her here to support her. It is lovely to hear of all the nice places you are visiting, Dandy. I tell the girls at school about you. The clothes that Miss McLaren sent have been a godsend to Ma. I made the odd little alteration, shortened them a wee bit, but they're fine. That's us! Write when you can. We read all your letters over and over again. I'd love to meet that nice captain who lost his arm in a war. Ma and the twins send their love.

How would Hector ever understand her family set-up? And yet, as time went on, it was going to be more and more difficult to tell him. He was bound to ask sooner or later what had happened to her parents. Aunt Alice must think it would be a stumbling block or she would have made her tell him before now. Aunt Alice understood Hector so well.

'Isn't that your aunt calling?' asked Hector.

'I didn't . . . yes, you're right.' Dandy opened the door to the hall. Alice was hurrying down the stairs with her hat on. 'Your Aunt Margaret is coming. Take Hector out the back way while I am at the door. Slip down by the burn. I'll pretend I was going out. Violet will hold the fort. She'll hang out a towel on the line when the coast is clear. That's the bell!'

Hector and Dandy were stifling giggles as they tip-toed round the side of the house. 'Bravo to your Aunt Alice,' he said. 'Putting on her hat like that! Will she actually go out?'

'She may, if she thinks she can take Aunt Margaret with her. Violet is busy baking so she can't go, but she's pretty good in her own quiet way at getting our Margaret to think of something more interesting to do.'

'Well, it's a long time since I played this sort of hide and seek,' said Hector, 'and never with such an adorable companion. I could think of lovelier perfumes than your Espedair Burn however.'

'It's an advantage on this occasion. That's why few adults ever venture near,' said Dandy.

Hector's laughter was hastily stifled. 'Oh glory! We don't want your Aunt Margaret to find us after all Alice's machinations. But if it were not for your delectable company, my love, I think I would rather meet twenty Aunt Margarets than endure this stink much longer.'

'Let's have a peep. Aunt Alice may have managed to

take her with her . . . yes! There's the towel on the line. That didn't take long. Good old Aunties!'

'I really feel that the army could use a few strategists like that,' said Hector, stepping out smartly.

Violet was waiting for them. 'Mrs McMillan brought you a birthday present, Dandy, and there's a card . . .' She stopped herself abruptly. 'You mustn't open them till the morning. I've put them in your room. Well, what do you think of our fragrant burn, Hector?'

'Let's just say I have no wish to renew its acquaintance in spite of my charming guide.'

Dandy, joining in the laughter, wondered what it was that had made Violet check herself. 'And there's a card,' she had said. Nothing unusual about that unless . . . She excused herself and slipped upstairs to her room, leaving Hector happily scraping up the crumbs from a baking tray.

The envelope was addressed to her, care of Aunt Margaret. Hastily she tore it open. The card was of the home-made variety; a log hut with pine trees, animals . . . were they goats? With shaking hands she unfolded the letter which was tucked inside.

My dear little daughter,

   I am sending this early to your Aunt Margaret to make sure you get it on your birthday. I'm sorry that I have nothing nice for a present but Marie says that that doesn't matter, all you want is our news and our love. I expect she is right. Miss Violet seems to be making you lovely clothes.

   How your life has changed, my little love! It is wonderful to think of you having a holiday in a hotel. I've never had that in my life! And this poor captain with the one arm seems to be so kind, inviting you to visit his garden like that. Margaret was sort of surprised that nobody had mentioned him to her. Of course, she's always interested in people who have big houses – a social climber, your grannie always said. She said she was taking you a little birthday present this year because we were so far away. I expect she will be hoping to hear more about the big house and the hotel and all that sort of thing. Still, it's kind of her. I'm finding things more difficult this time – probably it's my age, and of course this house is a bit of a jumble. I wish your Pa was not so determined to wait till he had everything else before he starts on the house. The other fellows would help, you know. They all help one another here. Most of them have been something different in the old country – plumbers, engineers, painters and things. So what one doesn't know, somebody else does. Marie is so good. She says not to worry how long this letter is but she tells me that I shouldn't let Will dictate to me the way he does. I suppose I was just too young when I married and then I'd never been used to a man like that. My father was so quiet. Grannie did all the bossing. I wondered if Marie's husband had been very quiet. She says not a bit of it, but they were a team and respected each other's abilities. It sounds a nice sort of set-up. Well, Dandy, we will be thinking of you on your birthday. The twins made your card at school and we've all signed it.

All my love,
Ma

Dandy's eyes were misty as she looked at the variety of signatures. Even little Jack had made an attempt – probably with someone guiding him. May's was the neatest, of course. George and Billy sprawled a bit, but it was firm writing. The twins had tried to do something fancy with theirs ... all little twiddles ... but it was

her father's that was surprising. He had signed himself
'Will'. She couldn't really remember what his writing
had been like before. She had never paid any attention.
The picture came to her again of her father's long arm
waving the white handkerchief as the ship moved out
of sight. Was Aunt Alice right that his daughter's low
opinion of him had hurt? She dashed her hand across
her eyes. Hector would be wondering what was keeping
her, and Hector's time was short. She must treasure it.
This card would have to be kept hidden. Aunt Margaret
had probably put a card in her little parcel, so Hector
would think that was the one Violet had been talking about. That was his voice calling her. Of course,
dinner had been nearly ready when Aunt Margaret
arrived. She hurriedly tidied her hair and ran downstairs.

'Dinner awaits you, my lady,' said Hector, offering
his arm with elaborate courtesy. 'If I may venture a
criticism, you are not supposed to giggle in the dining
room.' He paused, then added, 'Even when you know
that Aunt Margaret will be too busy partying all day
tomorrow to pay you a birthday visit.'

'Who said?'

'The lady herself, according to a reliable source.' He
winked at Violet.

'Oooh! We'll be able to enjoy the whole day. Even if
other folk see us and report to her, it'll be too late! Oh,
Hector I wish you could stay longer.'

'We all do,' said Alice briskly. 'But Hector is being
sensible and is protecting you from gossip, remember.'

Dandy *did* remember. He was protecting the aunts
too. A prolonged stay with them could give rise to
criticism.

'Oh, I wish I was older,' she said, then blushed furiously for having given herself away.

'The rest of us wish we were younger,' said Hector

laughing, 'and remember, "Time may be relied upon to remedy that."'

'He's always got an apt quote,' thought Dandy gratefully. 'Life with Hector will never be dull.'

Alice and Violet declared themselves tired and proposed retiring to bed early. 'Don't keep the birthday girl up late,' warned Alice as she left them.

'I think I'd better not,' whispered Hector when the door closed. 'In fact, I think we should sit in separate chairs. Oh, Dandy, has anyone ever told you that you're dynamite?'

'No. I've been called many a thing,' she giggled then quietened. 'Did you not feel ... I mean ... have you never felt that way before?'

He flushed, looking at her steadily. 'I thought I was in love. We seemed so obviously suitable; met at all the same things; horses, of course, were very important to both of us. Everyone expected us to team up. She was thrilled to see me in uniform ...

'I was very bitter, Dandy, when ... No doubt you have already heard about that. Now I realize that I took my disappointment out on other people. I'm certainly not proud of that. There seemed no gleam of hope for me. The garden was a funk hole where I could hide and recreate some of the beauty that had gone from my life. That's silly. I'm not expressing myself well ...'

'I understand,' said Dandy, simply.

Hector stared at her. 'That is the funny thing. You're so young, so innocent in many ways, and yet you seem to have a deeper understanding of me than anyone else has ever had. You can sweep away the clouds that hang over me at times. Oh God! I hope I can make you happy, my little love. I simply cannot imagine life without you now ...'

'I feel exactly the same,' said Dandy rising. There was no hiding her longing as they clung together. At last

Hector pushed her gently away. 'I think we should wend our way bedwards, don't you?'

I wish we could, thought Dandy. Together.

It was a long time before she fell asleep. Hector was only a few steps away along the corridor. She knew now what Hector wanted to do . . . why he broke off suddenly from those embraces, leaving her aching with frustration. Did other girls feel this pain? Her hands slipped down over her tight breasts, her flat, tense stomach to massage the aching flesh. Was she an odd wee thing? Nobody had ever told her anything about being in love. Till that time Faither handed her the birth certificate she had never thought of her parents ever having known anything like this. Was it this sort of longing that had made her mother marry a drunken dyer, just to let him . . . ? But she mustn't think of that. Hector was different. Hector was . . . Hector. She longed to be pulled closer and closer till he was right inside her. What would it be like?

Chapter 22

Her birthday morning dawned bright and sunny. Closer inspection from the window showed a few clouds to the south west. Might rain later, she thought, but who cares! Aunt Margaret won't be here. We can go out or stay in. Quickly she made her choice from the lovely dresses in her wardrobe. This was their last full day together. Why waste it in 'ifs' and 'buts'?

She was brushing her hair when she heard Hector's door open and his swift step on the stair. He was down before her. Faint sounds from the kitchen indicated that Violet was already at her post. He said in his letter he had a little something for me. I wonder what it is, she mused. Opening the bedroom door, she paused for a moment. My seventeenth birthday! I wish it was my eighteenth.

He was standing just inside the sitting-room door, waiting for her. Dandy watched the quick colour flood his face and his eyes light up. 'My birthday girl,' he whispered, drawing her to him. Then he broke away abruptly. 'I've got something for you,' he said, producing a tiny parcel from his pocket. 'I hope you like it. It comes with all my love.'

'I'm sure I shall,' said Dandy, fumbling with the wrappings. The tiny box bore the jeweller's name embossed in gold. With shaking hands she drew out the shining fob watch on its gold chain. 'Oh,' she breathed, gazing at the tiny spray of flowers that decorated the gold-rimmed face. 'Oh, Hector, it's exquisite.' Her eyes were brimming with tears. 'I've never had anything so beautiful in all my life.'

'Neither have I,' said Hector huskily, encircling her with his arm. Dandy leaned against him. 'Nothing will ever be lovelier than this,' she thought. 'This moment, this birthday, this happiness that's so wonderful that it hurts.'

His arm was still round her when they drifted into the dining room. No one ate very much. Dandy was too busy opening her birthday gifts and the others too busy watching her delight.

'I'll have to add a tiny fob pocket to your dresses,' Violet said, 'so that the watch can be tucked away when you wish. Swinging free, it could be damaged when you are up to some of your tricks.'

'My tricks?' said Dandy in wide-eyed amazement. Hector, laughing heartily, had noted how frequently her hand crept towards his gift and was well satisfied.

'It looks like being another fine day,' said Alice. 'We've no Mrs McMillan to think about; what about engaging a cab to take us up the Gleniffer Braes? Violet and I could sit in a sheltered spot while Hector and you roam free. On a working day like this, the place should be almost deserted. What do you think?'

Dandy looked at Hector. 'Roaming free with my birthday girl sounds like heaven to me,' he said, then blushed furiously.

'Then that's settled,' said Alice briskly. 'It's some time now since we saw that view – eh, Violet?'

'What? Oh, yes, whatever you say – certainly, a good idea.'

'We'll need our shady hats, Violet.'

'Oh yes . . . well pinned! There's usually a breeze.'

'Sounds perfect,' said Hector.

'Well, when?' asked Alice.

Hector, his arm round Dandy, suggested, 'Any time.'

325

'Shall I prepare a picnic?' asked Violet. 'Then we can take our time.'

'We'll have to book the cab for the return journey.'

'I know, Alice. What about three o'clock? We would have a leisurely lunch *al fresco*, then back home in time for tea in the garden or the conservatory and nothing to do but enjoy ourselves till dinner.'

'Aren't we going to enjoy dinner, then?' Hector asked cheekily.

And that's the man they said never smiled, thought Alice. Our little Dandy is a wonder girl. If only there weren't that barrier about her family. We'll have to get round to it some time, but they're in heaven today. I can't bear to spoil things.

In her large shady hat, Dandy sat upright but it was not long before her hand was imprisoned in Hector's. He was making no effort to conceal his feelings. Usually the aunts were so particular about observing the proprieties. Hector seemed to be exempt in certain respects. Was it because he was older that they trusted her to him? If they knew how she longed to . . . longed to be closer and closer in his embrace; longed to be old enough to marry him; longed for things she would never dare put into words, to them or anyone else, would they still be so trusting?

Hector was announcing his appreciation of the view as the road wound higher and higher. 'Just wait,' said Dandy. 'It's wonderful at the top – though it's difficult to say what *is* the top. You see a little mound and you run to it; then there's another that seems higher . . .'

'Sounds very promising,' said Hector, twinkling at her.

He means he'll enjoy chasing me, thought Dandy. He's not thinking of the scenery at all. All he wants is to have me to himself. But then he'll push me away because . . . Oh dear, I never understood those things before. I thought I knew everything, but I didn't know about *feelings*. Maybe I should be ashamed of them. But they're so wonderful. Did Uncle James and Rachel feel like this? I'll bet they did! That's why he wanted to keep the cottage all to himself. It was there that Rachel gave herself to him just as I long to give myself to Hector. A quick flush rose in her face and she glanced round to see if anyone had guessed her thoughts, but Alice was pointing out landmarks to Hector and Violet was smiling dreamily. Probably planning the dinner that Hector was so cheeky about, thought Dandy with a smile.

The sun was hot on their faces, but Alice and Violet soon found a spot shaded by some birch trees. Hector spread their rug for them and placed the picnic basket under a bush.

'Now! Which way?' he asked Dandy.

'Well, as you see, we have miles along the top. Let's try this way first. We should be able to see the sea if there's no haze.'

'When is lunch?' asked Hector. Dandy bit her lip. He was certainly getting bolder – letting the aunts know that he intended keeping her away for some time. But Alice and Violet didn't seem put out. They were consulting and deciding that they might as well make it the same as usual – one o'clock. Hector stretched his hand to her and they were off . . . alone in this wide world . . . free. There had been children's voices from the other direction, which had helped her choose this particular route. 'The only people we are likely to meet are other lovers,' she thought. 'And *they* won't be interested in us!'

'This is wonderful,' said Hector as they strode along. 'But I'm not sure if it is wise.'

'What d'you mean?'

He turned and looked at her so intensely that she

327

found herself blushing. 'I thought you said you understood . . . I thought you felt the same.'

'I do, but what should I have done? Refused the
chance? It seemed so wonderful . . .'

'It is – I've just said so! Oh, my darling, it's heaven
and hell all wrapped up together. I'd kill anyone who
laid a finger on you and yet I long and long . . .'

'I know,' said Dandy.

'I'm older. It's up to me to look after you. I was
wondering: the aunts seem to accept our . . . what shall
I say . . . liaison as a *fait accompli*. I have been thinking.
It might make things easier for us both if I could pin
them down to dates: when we could get engaged, when
we could get married. If we knew how long this suffering was to last, we might find the strength to cope.
Look! That little hollow with the whins half-way round
and the trees behind. Shall we sit down?'

'No rug for us,' said Dandy. 'I'll have to be careful
where I put my dress.'

'Seems quite clean turf to me. See, I'll not sit too close.
Then we can talk without distractions. Well, what do
you think about dates?'

'I hadn't really thought about it . . . only that I wish
– oh, how I wish – that I was much nearer your age
and we didn't have to wait.'

'Well, to take a positive step, how would it do if I
suggested that we be allowed to get engaged this Christmas and married the day after your birthday next year.
You'll be eighteen. That sounds much older than seventeen somehow.'

'Oh, yes. I'll certainly be old enough then. I'm sure
I'm older than most people of my age –' She stopped
abruptly. Again she had nearly taken herself into difficult territory. Brought up by her aunts, he would think.

'It would be as well to broach the subject as soon as
we go back for our picnic. Then we shall know how we

stand.' He had edged closer as he spoke. 'Isn't that sun wonderful! Out of the breeze here ... I feel sleepy. I didn't sleep much last night, thinking of you and your birthday; hoping that you would like your present...'

'It's just ... oh, I can't find the right word.'

She was silenced by his lips on hers. Quickly she unpinned the obtrusive hat and cast it behind her. The scent of the broom was sharp and sweet; she could hear lark and peewit; everything round her was lovely and she was alone with Hector. But he was disengaging her gently. 'Let's have a little snooze. We've plenty of time before lunch.'

The sun was warm, the breeze was scented with wild flowers and Hector was only a few feet away from her. She drifted into sleep. She was floating ... floating ... floating but wanted to land on a hillock. Somehow she couldn't; something was pressing against her breast and something hard was against her back. She wriggled and tried to open her eyes but the sun was red; then she heard Hector curse. She was freed suddenly and he was up in an instant and running towards the trees. What? Was there someone there watching them? Then it dawned on her ... that weight ... that pressure ... daft Jock. But how could she think of daft Jock in relation to Hector? She shook herself vigorously.

Hector's face was pale. 'I didn't hurt you, did I?' Dandy shook her head.

'I was fast asleep, I assure you, or it would never have happened. Oh, Dandy, I don't think you understand ... brought up by your aunts!'

'Hector, we can talk about anything, surely. We're going to be married, for heaven's sake. I was dreaming that I was floating and wanted to land on one of these hillocks but I couldn't. Something was pressing on my breast and there was something hard against my back.'

'My hand was on your breast and well, you can

329

maybe guess what was pressing against your back –
why I had to run to the trees. Oh God! What would
your aunts think of me? They put you in my care and
I can't even trust myself to fall asleep without . . . Well,
this shows, if anything does, that we had better not see
too much of each other – alone, that is – till we can tie
the knot. I wonder that you aren't afraid of me . . .
Dandy?'

'Never!'

'Well, I reckon we shall have to fill our lives with
something else; keep busy. The time will pass. Look
how fast my visit has gone. It seems like minutes since
I came and yet I'll be saying goodbye to you tomorrow
morning.'

'Surely you could stay another day or two?'

'Don't, Dandy. We have to avoid gossip – and not
only for your sake; there are your aunts to consider. In
a rather secluded area like mine, gossip flourishes. It
can be kindly meant – usually is – but there's always
the odd troublemaker. I want to present you proudly
as my bride with nothing for anyone to whisper against
you.'

Dandy shivered suddenly. What if he knew about
her family, her upbringing? How proud would he feel
then? She would have to tell him some day, but surely
not today . . . this lovely day when they had the freedom
to acknowledge their love. But what if someone else
told him first? Who could? There was only Aunt
Margaret and she was busy all day today. Hector was
getting a cab to the station in the morning, so there was
little danger there. The bitch would have to be on the
station and that was unlikely. She imagined the disastrous job Aunt Margaret could make of telling Hector
and found herself shivering again.

'You *are* upset, my love.' Hector was holding her
hand tightly. 'Take a few deep breaths, tidy your hair

a little then put on your lovely hat. There now! Let's step out briskly and surprise your aunts by arriving in plenty of time.'

'D'you think they'll have any idea, Hector?'

'Let's say, "a limited idea". They're both well read, but when it gets down to the practicalities . . . well, no! And as for that, I had no intention of introducing you to them before we were married. I despise myself for my lack of control.'

'Don't say that, Hector, or you'll make me feel guilty too.'

'It's not your fault that you are beautiful as the lilies and as attractive as honeysuckle to this bee. That's better. A smile! Keep it up. We've been for a long brisk walk, remember.'

'Don't they look healthy?' said Violet. 'Hector talking so earnestly and look how pretty Dandy is – such a graceful walk and that happy, shy smile.'

'*Shy* is not a word I would normally apply to our Dandy,' said Alice.

'But Hector is different, don't you think?'

Alice lowered her voice to a mutter. 'I wonder if we are allowing them too much freedom. James was never allowed to roam the hills with Rachel, I'm sure. It's a dreadful responsibility, but she's so eager, so much in love and deserves it if any girl ever did.'

'I'll fetch the basket,' said Violet, rising. 'Feeling hungry?' she called as they approached.

'Of course,' said Hector. 'All that fresh air and this lively girl by my side.'

'If you two could take this wine bottle to the well over there and take turns of holding it under the cool flow, we'll get the foodstuffs spread out.'

'Your wish is my command. Come along now; step out smartly,' he said to Dandy.

'Oooh!' Hector drew his breath in sharply. 'I see what they mean by cool flow. It's amazing how it can stay like that on a hot day like this.'

'It's always cold. Quite a tradition for young people to walk up here on Sundays and take a drink. By the time you've walked up you feel you deserve it. Did you think the aunts noticed anything? They know me so well . . .'

'Violet, certainly not. Alice? Well, she's very good at disguising her feelings. I sensed a slight preoccupation there, but it could have been the result of a little sleep. I don't suppose they stayed awake long on a day like this. Here – your turn with the bottle.'

'Dare we walk again after lunch?'

'We *did* say we would . . . yes, I think we walk again, but keep walking. If we linger beside them talking after lunch, we need walk only a short time before the cab comes to pick us up. Your hands are blue. Here, I think the wine's ready. Let's enjoy the picnic, love. It means so much to Violet. No sense in letting our problems upset them. We'll write often to each other when I get back. That should be safe enough, eh?'

'Yes. Are you going to ask about when . . . the engagement . . .'

'Yes, tonight.'

'Tonight' kept ringing in Dandy's ears all the way back to the cottage. She stared unseeing from her seat in the conservatory.

Luckily at dinner Hector was able to keep up the flow of conversation with stories of his father's sojourn in India, his stop off at Madeira on the way home and the many plants he had brought from there. 'Some were unsuccessful, of course, even under glass, but it was surprising how many thrived and that was before our shelter belt was as thick as it is today. I've often toyed with the idea of building a few really large greenhouses to try some rare fruits and flowers.'

'Where would you put them?' asked Dandy.

'Just beyond the wild garden ... the little paddock that I let out to one of my tenants from time to time. We used to have horses there, of course.'

'Won't he be put out? The tenant, I mean.'

'He'll make other arrangements. It's *my* land, after all.'

Dandy found herself blushing. The gulf between their social standing was so wide. Hector had grown up the son of a landowner and had known all his life that he in turn would be one. How could she ever describe those two rooms which had been the ambit of her young life?

'The work in the garden is lessening at this time of year, of course, though by October we have started most of the felling and logging. A scheme like this would be just the thing to keep me occupied into November when the weather is rather dull. I'll send you sketches of my ideas, Dandy, as I work them out. Perhaps you could all come for a short stay at the beginning of November to see how things are going? Mrs McGuffie is most keen that you should come for Christmas and New Year, of course. She remembers what it was to have the whole house decorated and full of guests; assures me that she will have no difficulty in hiring extra help in Rosecraig.'

Dandy volunteered to make the coffee – glad to get away to the privacy of the kitchen where she stood with her hands on her burning cheeks for a few moments. He was going to ask permission to become engaged at Christmas. But he didn't know ... Was it fair? 'It's *my* land, after all' thumped repeatedly in her head. He was bound to find out one day. There would be letters and, of course, she had no wish to deny the others – only her father. But Aunt Alice seemed to think that her father too deserved some sympathy from his daughter. A picture of the long arm waving the white handkerchief floated before her again. Why, why, why had she been given this glimpse of heaven with Hector if she had to turn her back on it? She remembered his look of concern – 'I was fast asleep, I assure you, or it would never have happened.' That was Hector who longed for her with every fibre of his being, just as she longed for him. But they were waiting for their coffee. She had better get on with it. Would he have started his speech to the aunts? No, he would probably wait till they were settled comfortably with their feet up as usual. He seemed very quick to notice a pattern of living like that and to fit in. 'A lady adapts her behaviour to the occasion,' Uncle James had said. The same would seem to apply to a gentleman. But what an adaptation Hector would have to make to the idea of her upbringing! That was asking a lot. She concentrated on the tray she was carrying and laid down Hector's cup without daring to look at him.

She felt her breath draw in sharply as soon as he stretched forward to place his cup and saucer on the table. 'We have something to ask you, Dandy and I,' he began. The spoon danced in her saucer as the colour flooded her face. 'I don't think it will have escaped your notice that we are desperately in love. The disparity in our ages is a barrier we both regret but might not seem so bad if we could have a time fixed . . . for our hopes . . . Oh dear, I'm making a mess of this. What we would like – I'll put it baldly – is to become engaged this Christmas and to marry the day after Dandy's eighteenth birthday.'

There was dead silence. Violet gazed at Hector as if mesmerized, while Alice fixed her intent stare on the object of his desire. 'I know what that means,' thought Dandy. 'She thinks that he will have to know. If I tell

334

him it may spoil everything. I can't bear the thought of seeing him change.'

There was fear in the look that she returned. Alice registered it before speaking. 'Thank you for being so frank, Hector. What you suggest is quite a momentous matter. I don't think we could give a snap answer. Perhaps Violet and I could have some time . . . let's say that if we pay your proposed visit at the beginning of November, we could give you our decision then?' Dandy released her breath slowly. Alice might have brought the subject up there and then, but she had given her time . . . not yet . . . not yet . . .

Alice and Violet retired early, saying that they had been rather long in the sun that day.

'I think we shall be retiring early too,' said Hector. 'What did you think of Alice's verdict?' he asked when they were alone.

'Quite fair, I think.'

'Mmmm, I suppose you're right. She gave it quite a cool reception, I thought. Maybe she thinks that *someone* had better stay cool since we can't. Still, she's accepted the idea of a visit in November. We'll be writing, of course, and I'll get down to designing those glasshouses. You'll be singing in the church choir, I hope. What else will you do – plan your trousseau?'

'Aunt Violet will be sure to want to do that. I tend to do the machining and leave the twiddly bits to her.'

He laughed. 'I'll think of you slaving over a hot sewing machine. Hasn't the time passed so quickly? How the minutes fly when I'm with you! I think we'd better get upstairs soon. Come here, let's have a proper kiss here and then we can have a modest one on the landing in case they are listening.'

'Of course we could give them a shock . . . do them good,' said Dandy.

'You monkey!' said Hector as her arms wound round

his neck. 'You little Delilah, I do believe you enjoy piling on the agony for me.'

'Of course I do. Why should I be the only one to suffer?'

He laughed, quite unaware of the depth of her suffering.

Dandy herself was only too aware of it as she tossed restlessly through the night, recalling Hector's remarks. 'I want to present you as my bride with no one to whisper anything against you,' kept running through her head, while, 'It's *my* land,' beat thunderously in the background. Telling him the truth could put an end to all her dreams – and Hector's dreams as well. He was building his hopes of happiness on her, Dandy Baxter, the daughter of a drunken dyer. What would it do to him when he found out the truth? Would he feel betrayed yet again? It was bound to be worse a second time.

Morning found her pale and subdued. Hector too looked as if sleep had eluded him. The aunts were obviously preparing to come to the station with them, so there would be no opportunity for further talk.

'I ordered the cab in plenty of time,' said Alice. 'I don't think we shall come upstairs with you at the station, but I wondered if you would like to do any shopping in town afterwards, Dandy, or shall I retain the cab for our return journey?'

'Er . . . yes . . . retain it,' said Dandy. She was trying to read beyond Alice's words. They would certainly come upstairs at the station if they saw anyone liable to be interested in Hector – Aunt Margaret, for example. Retaining the cab was not really for their benefit – they would normally have walked slowly home. They were thinking she might be upset. She glanced at Hector. He was looking rather grim. *He* wasn't finding it easy either, but he had no dark secret to hide – a secret that could make their parting permanent. Yes, she might be glad of that cab.

The aunts said their goodbyes in the cab and Dandy slowly mounted the stairs, almost afraid to look at Hector. I love him so much, she thought. If I have to tell him in November, this may be the last time we part as lovers. He's finding it difficult even though he doesn't know it may be the last time. He *must* love me. Of course he does! I'll have to pull myself together . . . leave him with a happy smile. There were few people on the platform before them but she knew that the train would be busy on a Saturday morning and found herself scanning each new arrival. 'Don't look so worried, my little darling,' said Hector. 'I'll write to you as soon as I get back and I'll start on these designs. If we keep busy, November will be on us before we know it! Look how quickly those precious days have passed. I'm pretty sure that Alice will give her permission. She just needs time to get used to the idea. If you were *my* ward, I can tell you I'd be very suspicious of any fellow who came along and wanted to marry you.'

Dandy's smile was not far from tears. She wasn't Alice's ward. Life would be a lot simpler if she were. It wasn't suspicion of Hector that kept Alice from giving her permission. It was her sense of justice. He would have to be told. There was no way round that. Hector was talking again . . . about the garden . . . about Christmas and the party he proposed to give to the tenants if Alice gave her permission to the engagement. The train was due soon. No one she knew had appeared. Oh, God! Keep them all away, she prayed. Let me have this last wee while with Hector.

He turned to her as the train approached. 'D'you think there is anyone here who would report us?'

'No.' Her arms went round his neck and she clung unashamedly as he put his heart into their farewell kiss.

In a mist of tears she watched him enter the carriage, heard the door slam and the train shunt noisily on its way.

Alice took one look at the dismal figure approaching and alerted the cabman; then Dandy was inside and could cry as freely as she liked. They left her alone – then, and in the conservatory where she threw herself down in despair as soon as they got in. A few minutes later, Alice appeared. 'Drink this!' she ordered.

'What is it?' asked Dandy. 'Smells horrid.'

'Coffee with brandy. Do you good; drink it up.'

Violet drifted in with a tray and watched while Dandy sipped obediently.

'Now,' said Alice, 'I know you are upset at not being allowed to become engaged, but I want to tell you why I delayed granting permission . . .'

'I know,' said Dandy. 'I've got to tell him first. That's why, isn't it?'

Alice sighed heavily. 'Yes, that's why.'

Dandy dabbed at the tears which had begun to flow again. Violet crossed to lay a comforting hand on her shoulder while Alice went on. 'I know it's hard for you, but it has to be faced. Hector is a fine man and must be treated fairly. There has to be absolute trust between you or any thought of future happiness is hopeless.'

'It's pretty hopeless anyway. Did you hear how he said, "It's *my* land, after all"? We're miles apart. He's a landowner and I'm the daughter of a drunken dyer who was only good for fathering children he could not afford . . .'

'Stop that!' said Alice. 'Listen: let's suppose *you* had been brought up in comfortable circumstances, like Hector – like Violet and me, come to that. Suppose you had met Hector, a fine, handsome man who was educated and keen on music and poetry; suppose you

338

had fallen madly in love with him and he with you. Now, suppose he were to tell you that his upbringing had been far different from yours; that he had had to struggle to get an education; that he had worked assiduously at the things that so many better-off people took for granted? How would you feel about your handsome Hector then? Would you despise him? Would you not be more likely to admire him, to appreciate the understanding that his struggle had brought him? Think it over, my dear, during those weeks which separate you. Carry on with the studies which are bringing you closer and closer to his standards of literacy and which you find so rewarding in themselves. And, Dandy, you are at church every Sunday . . . doesn't faith come into this? Doesn't it seem possible that God meant you for each other? Well, I've said my piece! I'll leave you to mull it over. When the time comes, in November – I mean, if you still feel unable to tell Hector yourself – I am perfectly prepared to do it for you. However, I think it would come more acceptably from the lips of his own Queen of the Lilies, don't you?'

'Maybe,' said Dandy.

Chapter 23

Though Dandy had her reservations about how Hector would take the news, Alice's programme sounded quite sensible. She could certainly do with a deeper knowledge of languages if there were the prospect of travelling with Hector after they were married – if ever they got married. And of course there were his letters to enjoy. While he remained in ignorance, she could still write freely to him. He had tested her out in the names of lilies; now she took to testing him in poetry quotations. This interesting game became the excuse for many letters which she sought eagerly.

'One from Canada today,' the postman announced one morning.

'It's from Mother,' said Dandy as she joined the aunts at breakfast. She scanned it quickly before reading it aloud.

My dear Dandy,

As you can see I have moved to Marie's farm. Recently I've had quite a lot of pain and she thought it was time I should rest in some comfort. Jack just loves it here anyway. George has come with me. He seems to rub his father up the wrong way. Marie says that would happen anyway with a big growing lad asserting his manhood. She's full of ideas like that. You wouldn't believe how George has changed. He doesn't look like a boy any longer – so big and broad and his voice so gruff. Billy is tall now too, but somehow he's still boyish. The animals are all he cares about. May is such a help, never needs to be told what's needed. The twins, well, they're just in a wee world of their own most of the time. It's a good thing they get on so well together. Marie says it is good to have George here. She started him off horse-riding nearly two years ago and now he is really clever at it. She says you never know when that might be needed. Last winter she started him skiing and she says as soon as the first fall of snow comes this year, she will take him out. I wonder if she is thinking of having to fetch the doctor when the bairn arrives. The snow here is like nothing we ever saw in Paisley. Folks get snowed up and can be prisoners for days on end. But the neighbours all look after one another when they can. Some have snow ploughs and can get the horses to open up a path to the door for you. Marie knows everybody for miles around. You can't walk down the street in Vernon, even, without folk greeting her right, left and centre. There's a native Indian who wanders around and always calls on Marie. He says that the snow will come early this winter. Seemingly he watches the animals and birds and knows how they are preparing. She says she's never known him to be wrong and that's why she is anxious for George to improve his skiing. I wish I could give you a good report of your father, but I'm afraid the drink has got hold of him again. I wish I had the strength of will that Marie has. She would sort him, as Grannie used to say. How I miss your grannie and you, my dear wee Dandy – though by all accounts you're a fine young lady now. It's lovely to think of you so happy with the McLarens. Give them my best wishes.

Love from Ma

Dandy's voice was husky when she got to the end. Violet looked at Alice, who cleared her throat before venturing, 'Isn't it good that that fine Mrs Friedland has taken charge of affairs. It takes a load off your mind, Dandy.'

'Yes. It would be bloody hell without her,' said Dandy abstractedly, 'Faither drinking when she needs all the help she can get.'

'You never know,' said Violet. 'That same Mrs Friedland might manage to do something with your father. He is bound to be visiting when your mother is there.'

'Aye, I'm glad George is separated from him, though. I can imagine how he is feeling – Mammie like that and the devil drinking.'

'It could be, Dandy,' said Alice, 'that your father is as worried about your mother as you are. It is simply that drink is the only way he can suppress his anxieties.'

'Aye,' said Dandy bitterly. The dishes clattered as she started to clear the table.

October brought some fine weather mid-day after sharp mornings. Alice saw to it that Dandy was kept at her studies when she wasn't clearing up in the garden.

'It's the best we can do for her,' she confided to Violet. 'I know how much she's dreading having to tell Hector. I think the world of that fellow, but her family *is* rather a difficult pill to swallow. Just think how we would have felt about James associating with that sort before we lost our money. You have to try to see it through his eyes.'

'I think his eyes are streaked with the juice . . . what's that in *Midsummer Night's Dream*?'

'Oh Violet, you *are* a laugh! That had something to do with hateful fantasies, if I remember rightly, but I hope you're right and Hector's are streaked with something nice!'

* * *

342

'Well, at least the garden has been put to bed for the winter. I don't think I've neglected anything,' said Dandy as the cab jolted on the way to the station. To herself she added: Tonight I'll be sleeping just a few yards away from Hector – maybe the last night he'll be in love with me if Aunt Alice makes me tell him tomorrow. I'll not have long with him tonight – just a quick look at the garden in the afternoon before darkness falls.

All the way in the train she was dreaming. Sometimes a smile would curve her lips as she pictured their life together; then her thoughts would return to the confession which lay ahead of her. These changes of expression were not lost on the sisters, who could not fail to share her perturbation. They sensed its deepening on the last lap of the journey when the cab wound its way round the shore road and Luce Bay was spread before them. He'll be longing to see me just now, thought Dandy. I wonder how he'll feel by tomorrow night!

Their welcome to Lindsay House was all that they could wish. Hector kissed Alice and Violet on the cheek and then, in spite of Mrs McGuffie's hovering presence, drew Dandy to him in a deep embrace.

'Yes, tea would be lovely,' Alice was saying. 'We had a picnic lunch on the train.'

It was misty and the light was going by the time they had finished, but Hector insisted on taking Dandy on a tour of the garden. Once out of sight of the house, he said, 'There's really nothing to see. The rain has knocked the last petals off most of the things that were still blooming last week. Let's go to the summer house. I always feel that you are really mine in the garden.'

His nearness made her forget her worries for the moment. Eagerly she responded to his kiss, being pulled closer and closer into his embrace. 'Oh, Dandy, when you are mine I shall feel like a king!'

'O God, let him still feel that way once he knows,' she prayed time and time again through dinner and the pleasant evening by the drawing-room fire that followed. It was nearly dawn before she fell into an exhausted sleep.

Alice, coming into her room before breakfast, felt a pang of pity when she saw the pale young face. 'You *must* tell him today, my dear. It has been put off too long.'

'What shall I do if he is angry ... berates me ...? Shall we have to go home?'

'I don't think it will come to that at all, Dandy. He may be hurt, and justifiably so, that you have not seen fit to confide in him sooner, yet somehow I feel that his love is too deep ... I feel guilty that I have allowed this seeming deception to go on, but we have been tilted into a situation, an unusual situation that could not have been foreseen. Because you are so young, perhaps we were not so alert as we should have been.'

'You mustn't blame yourself, Aunt Alice, ever!' She paused. 'Don't you think I could have today, one last perfect day, before I tell him? I hardly saw him yesterday!'

A brief smile touched Alice's mouth. 'You mean *we* hardly saw you once you saw Hector ... Oh, my dear ... one last perfect day, then, but he simply *must* be told tomorrow and no surrender!'

'Right! We're going to do some pruning this morning if the rain stays away.'

'I expect Violet and I will remain indoors. It is still dampish. I wouldn't be surprised if we end up in Mrs McGuffie's kitchen. Violet and she like to discuss recipes and she always seems desperate for company. It's funny how things change. When we were young

344

our elders hardly ever went near the kitchen. We were allowed in only when Cook was feeling indulgent.'

'When I was here last Hector and I sometimes took lunch in the kitchen to save her trouble when we had been working in the garden. One of the maids used to peek through the crack in the scullery door. I never let on I saw her. I would never have dreamt of watching that crack if I hadn't done the same thing myself.'

In the garden the air was damp but mild. Hector was near and Dandy sang as she worked. Then the song was interrupted as his arm came round her. 'Happy, my love?'

'Of course. I like pruning, getting rid of the dead wood, seeing things take shape. It's satisfying somehow.'

'And is this?' She was drawn closer to him and his lips were on hers.

'I've to tell him tomorrow,' thought Dandy. 'Maybe he'll never feel like doing this again.' She clung desperately, feeling no shame as she urged her body against his. Again it was Hector who broke off. 'My God! Do I never learn? It's just not seeing you for all these weeks, my love, and dreaming of you at nights. Roll on next September and an end to this agony.'

The rain started in the afternoon. Alice and Violet decided to have a little siesta. Hector led Dandy to the library, where she gasped with envy. 'Oh, you lucky devil! Hundreds and hundreds of them – have you read them all?'

'No, and I don't think you will either, even when you're mine and the lady of Lindsay House. Some are pretty dry, I think, and dated in style. Really, I don't know why I keep them. It's just a case of ... they've always been there, I suppose.'

Dandy had stopped listening. 'The lady of Lindsay

House,' he had said. Would he think her fit to fill that role once he knew more about the Baxter family? She shivered suddenly.

'You're cold, Dandy. Let's go back to the drawing room. There's a lovely fire there. We can sit on the kissing sofa; that should be safe enough!'

'What's a kissing sofa? Oh, is that the sort of twisty one? I didn't know and I didn't like to ask.'

'Yes, it's the "sort of twisty one" as you put it. We can kiss, but we are facing different directions and separated by the curve of the sofa. I think the fellow who designed it must have suffered too. We should be safe there till your aunts join us for tea. I feel quite hungry. It's your delightful company, my dear.'

Dandy, on the contrary, realized that half the perfect day which Alice had allowed her was already gone. There would be no further postponement. Paradise might fade from her grasp. How could she ever face life without Hector? Again she shivered.

True to Hector's forecast, the aunts appeared in time for tea. Then Mrs McGuffie herself, followed by the kitchen maid. 'What a marvellous spread,' said Violet with the true appreciation of "one who knows". The firelight caught the gleam of the silver; everything was arranged so beautifully and Hector was near her and gazing at her fondly every time she met his eye. Suddenly there was the sound of a carriage drawing up. 'Wonder who that can be?' said Hector. 'The minister has paid his parochial visit . . . Can't think . . . I'd better go and see . . .'

The drawing-room door had been left open. Dandy heard Hector's deep tones and then, to her horror, Aunt Margaret's affected drawl. 'Yes, of course, her mother's sister. Dandy is the eldest . . .' Her niece stood up slowly as Hector ushered in the person she least wanted to see at that moment.

'Your Aunt, I believe, Dandy. She has some news for you.'

'What a journey I've had,' said Margaret, who looked as if she might have been crying. 'You said you were going to Rosecraig for a few days,' she turned on Alice.

'This *is* the parish of Rosecraig, Mrs McMillan,' said Alice.

'Well, I thought you meant the hotel and then I found it was closed and when I asked somebody about it they told me you were here . . . and I had meant to stay the night.'

'Thank you, Mrs McGuffie,' said Hector, as that lady bustled in with fresh tea and an extra cup and saucer. 'Miss McLaren will pour, thank you.'

'He doesn't want her to know anything,' thought Dandy. 'And he's not offering to put Margaret up for the night. She's heaving with disappointment. Oh God, I hope she doesn't burst into tears. What will she do? And what's she here for, anyway?'

It was Violet who ministered to Margaret while Alice stared, tight-lipped. 'Mrs McMillan, you have come a long way. What is it you wish to tell Dandy?'

'Oh, Miss Alice . . . Oh Dandy . . . it's sad news, I'm afraid . . .' she choked suddenly. 'Your mother, Dandy, it was too much for her at her age and the baby too, I'm afraid.'

Dandy stood like a statue and stared. Alice shook herself angrily. 'Mrs McMillan, what precisely are you saying?'

'My poor sister, Dandy's mother, is dead!' There was silence in the room. Dandy's mouth opened but no sound came. It was Hector who finally broke the silence, staring at Dandy. 'I thought you were an orphan!'

'Is that what she told you?' Margaret spluttered through her tears. 'Disowning my sister! I'll have you know that she married beneath her. There was nothing

347

wrong with my sister. We were well brought-up, just as my children are. No, she *would* marry that no-use . . .'

'Mrs McMillan,' Alice cut in brusquely, 'could you please tell us what happened? Have you a letter?'

'Yes! Out of the blue. How do you think I felt? It's from that woman with the funny name . . .'

'Mrs Friedland?'

'Yes, that's it.'

'Perhaps you could let Dandy read it.'

Margaret McMillan started rummaging in her bag. 'I thought I should break the news personally, you know . . .' As she handed the letter to Dandy, she turned to Hector. 'It wasn't easy for me to get away today. I had an important bridge match this afternoon, but I thought I probably wouldn't be able to think what I was doing anyway, and I *am* Dandy's closest relative in this country . . .'

Hector, watching Dandy intently, said not a word. He noted how her hand shook as she unfolded the sheets, but she remained standing as she read.

Dear Mrs McMillan,

I have very sad news to impart to Mrs Baxter's eldest daughter and, in view of her youth, I thought it might be better if you broke it to her. Nettie died in childbirth two days ago. The baby was dead too, I'm afraid. She had been having a lot of pain and I feared that things were not going to be easy. You probably know that she had been staying with me for some time. Things got very bad two nights ago and I had to send George on horseback all the way to Vernon to fetch the doctor in the middle of the night. That boy's a hero. You can all be very proud of him. I did what I could for Nettie to ease her pain while we waited, but it was no use. The doctor said she had twisted something badly and that had damaged the baby too.

348

Naturally the family are shattered. I managed to get Will to the funeral, sober and decently clad, but I'm afraid he will seek solace in the bottle as usual. May is a little angel and keeps things going in that dreadful house in quite a remarkable fashion. The children are turning out well in spite of, or maybe because of, their father's weakness. In justice, I must say that he has worked hard since he came here, but he has become fanatical in his wish to have a bigger farm than the others. Nettie was too soft with him. I told her so often, but it made no difference. All the reports tell me that Dandy is a wonder girl. I hope she will be able to cope with what must be a dreadful blow. Tell her that I am keeping an eye on her brothers and sisters, and give her my love.

Marie Friedland

Without a word, Dandy handed the letter to Alice, who drew her chair nearer to Violet's as they read. Dandy, still dry-eyed, stretched out her hand to the nearest chair and slowly sank into it.

'I'm going to be too late for the evening train,' said Margaret hopefully.

'No,' said Hector, rising. 'I'll get one of my tenants to send his son with the trap . . .'

'Won't that be cold?'

'No, he has an awning and we shall see that there are rugs and a hot-water bottle there for you.'

Margaret pouted but could offer no other objection. Hector went off to make the necessary arrangements. Dandy stared sightlessly ahead of her while even Alice could not bring herself to say anything. When Mrs McGuffie came in to clear the dishes, Alice rallied, however, and made the necessary polite remarks.

'The Captain's been on the phone,' she informed

them. 'Jo Scott will drive the lady to Stranraer. His father is coming to speak to the laird on business, so you're asked to excuse him for an hour or two. Dinner will be at the usual time. He tells me that there has been a family bereavement and none of you will be feeling very hungry or wish to talk ... Maybe a little bit of sole ... ?'

'I think that would fill the bill very nicely, Mrs McGuffie; how thoughtful of you!' said Alice.

Margaret sniffed, whether in disappointment at not being part of the dinner party or in tune with the bereavement statement, it was difficult to say. Thereafter, Violet made heroic efforts to keep the conversation going.

It was a relief to them all when the trap drove off with their visitor, but even then Dandy found it impossible to speak for the bleak thoughts which hammered in her head. Her mother was dead but somehow the thought would not register. She should be weeping, but she had the rest of her life to weep. It was all so unreal. What *was* real was the look that Hector had given her. She had dreaded telling him, but that was for her own sake. Her mother was dead. Was God punishing her? She had been so busy enjoying herself while all that trouble was going on in Canada. If she had been there, things would never have been so bad ... or would they? It was Grannie, really, who had controlled Faither in the old days. She herself had never been anything but an irritant to him. Marie Friedland seemed the only hope, but there was a limit ... and anyway it was too late now to save Mammie. The childhood name came to her lips naturally. They would go home tomorrow. Obviously Hector could not stand the sight of her after this. Alice and Violet were talking of Marie Friedland; of George and his adventurous ride. The talk seemed to come from far away ... she was drifting ... 'Let her sleep, Violet,' Alice was saying. 'It's emotional exhaustion, I think. She didn't sleep much last night. Hector won't join us till the young man returns from the station – and perhaps not even them. No, that is unjust. He will be polite and considerate even if he is burning with anger inside. It is his training. I could have avoided this if I had made her tell him earlier, but I knew that the more he saw of Dandy the more he would find to love. I suppose I was hoping that that would outweigh all other considerations. Now I think it is maybe the thought that he was kept in the dark which is the most difficult to swallow. He certainly kept his head. Did you hear how he dealt with Mrs McGuffie and stopped her bothering us?'

Dandy was dozing when Alice roused her gently. 'I think you should tidy up a little. It's nearly dinner time. Don't worry about looking sad; Mrs McGuffie will expect that. But *do* remember to live up to your reputation of being a fine young lady.'

I owe it to the aunts, Dandy thought as she started to brush her hair. Then the thought came: This may be the last time Hector sees me if he bothers to turn up in the drawing room. In the morning it will just be a bustle to say goodbye. How do I want him to remember me? I must memorize his face too, if I get the chance . . . his eyes . . . they look grey sometimes; other times they're green. I'll wear my prettiest dress. It won't mean a thing to me afterwards. There's nobody else I care about! That's maybe not fair to Violet. She goes to such trouble. I don't feel like dressing up one little bit, but it may stop me from making a fool of myself if I try . . . play the part. Come to think of it, being a lady often means playing a part. You can't do whatever you feel like. You put on a show for other folk. I'll be glad when it's all over and I can think about Mammie . . . I wonder if he *will* say anything to me . . .

Mrs McGuffie had been told the ladies would not feel like talking, but her nature would certainly not allow her to serve these treasured guests in silence. She spoke in a comforting way. 'The Captain and Mr Scott just had trays in the office. They're still at it, but it won't be long till young Jo is back and I expect we'll get Master Hector ... I mean, the Captain, to ourselves again.'

'I'll never have Master-Hector-I-mean-the-Captain to myself again,' thought Dandy. 'It could have been so lovely.' She blinked away a tear and automatically sat up straighter. She would play the part that Alice had set her.

The meal was over and they had adjourned to the drawing room before the sound of the trap was heard. Soon Mrs McGuffie appeared with the coffee tray. 'The Captain is just saying goodbye to the Scotts now. I expect he'll not be long.' Dandy's hand shook when she tried to lift the tiny cup.

When he *did* appear she found it impossible to raise her eyes. Aunt Alice as usual made valiant efforts to keep things normal on the surface. Hector assured her that Jo had seen Mrs McMillan off safely. 'We don't have to worry about gossip there,' he added. 'Jo Scott has no interest in two-legged creatures. He's daft about horses and they are the only creatures he bothers to talk to.'

So he *had* been worried about gossip, Dandy noted. He was going to hush things up. Would he feel as bitter about her as he had about the first one who had let him down? That time his grief had landed him in talk he had not bargained for; he would take care to be more skilful this time. Her head throbbed. 'If you'll excuse me,' she said suddenly.

Hector moved quickly to the door and opened it for her. He stepped into the corridor, then, speaking in a

low voice, 'I thought I knew you through and through
. . . you seemed so honest . . .' She gazed hungrily at
him. His eyes had brown flecks among the green; there
were two deep furrows down his cheek that weren't
usually there. His mouth was a taut line as he returned
her stare. Without a word, she turned and ran to the
safety of her bedroom.

Hector's face was grim and his voice tight as he
addressed his guests. 'If you'll excuse me, ladies, I have
more work to do in my office.'

'No!' said Alice brusquely. 'I want you to sit down
and listen to me. I feel I am to blame for a lot of this.
Please sit down, Hector. Your work can wait, I am sure.
This is important.' Violet gasped, but Alice ignored her
while she steadily willed Hector to do as he was told.

'Now, I shall begin at the beginning and tell you
everything that is needful,' she said when he had
settled.

'Violet and I were brought up in a house not unlike
this one on the borders of Renfrewshire and Ayrshire.
We had an exceptionally happy childhood with loving
parents, ponies, holidays . . . all the things that children
of wealthy parents could wish for. We were in our twen-
ties when all that ended in a clap of thunder, so it
seemed to us. An adviser whom my parents and others
in our family business had trusted absolutely turned
out to have feet of clay. Money which was supposed to
be safely invested had been purloined to be placed in
madcap schemes to retrieve his gambling losses. My
mother's health had not been good for some time. The
blow was too much for her. She took another heart
attack – this time a severe one, and died.' Hector made
a murmur of sympathy, but Alice drove on relentlessly.
'Two days after her funeral our father, who had hitherto
enjoyed perfect health, died of a stroke.' She paused.
'You can guess how distraught we were. Our brother

James was engaged to a lovely girl, Rachel, the daughter of one of the directors of our firm. Their marriage had been planned. He was now penniless like the rest of us. Rachel, bless her, refused to give him up. James managed to obtain employment, a very modest post as a clerk in Paisley, and took his lovely young bride to the little cottage you have seen.

'Friends were kind. Of course, many of them had had their fingers burned in the collapse of our firm. Violet and I had offers of accommodation from some who were not affected. We refused – rightly, I think. I suppose we could have offered ourselves as governesses, but that would have meant splitting up and, after losing our parents, our lovely home and our money, I think we clung together more closely than we might have done. We decided to follow James to Paisley. We had very little to support us, just jewellery and things we had manage to dispose of, so we had to rent a flat in a very poor area. The flat above us was occupied by Dandy's family. Brace yourself, Hector, while I describe the sort of life that plucky child led . . .'

Chapter 24

'But why was I not told all this earlier? She seemed so direct . . .' Hector drew his hand across his eyes. 'I mean, there she was, vowing to make up to me for what I had missed! That's ironic. What *I* had missed! Why couldn't she tell *me*, of all people?'

'Because you offered her a glimpse of absolute heaven, Hector, and till we took her under our wings she had never experienced life without trials, deprivations and disappointments. Even with us, there was the disastrous affair at the mill. That was all because the dear child was trying to repay us. And I – God forgive me! – was too afraid to make her tell you . . . just in case.'

'You thought I might shun her? Surely . . . ?'

'I was fairly certain you would overcome any such prejudices but the dear child herself was so fearful; perhaps that's why I let it go on so long. She had promised me she would tell you tomorrow. This was to have been her last perfect day. She begged me to grant it.' Alice ended with a gulp.

'I had better check up on her,' Violet whispered. 'She's lost her mother and she thinks . . .'

'She thinks I would desert her,' murmured Hector. 'The truth is quite the opposite. Had I known this, I would have been more anxious than ever to be her protector. If only she were a little older and I could have her in my care . . . She would never have to worry again. All that courage would be re—'

The drawing-room door was flung open suddenly and Violet stood white-faced in front of them. 'She's gone!' she croaked. 'Her dress is on the bed and her watch on the table. She isn't in the bathroom. I tried . . .'

Hector strode to the door and held it closed. 'Go to your rooms, ladies. Do not undress . . . in case. I shall tell Mrs McGuffie that you have retired early and I am having a little walk in the garden – may have left a book in the summer house – something like that. I'll tell her I'm taking the key so she can retire.'

'Where could she go at this time of night? It's dark,' said Violet.

'She wouldn't have any hope of transport. I'm pretty sure she's in the garden. Pray God I'm right.'

'She might be saying goodbye to it,' said Alice hesitantly.

'We'll hope that's what she's thinking of,' said Hector grimly. 'I'll take my warm cape . . . just in case . . . She could have tripped . . . I know every inch . . .'

They heard his voice in the hall below as they made their reluctant way to their rooms. 'He has great presence of mind,' whispered Violet.

'I wish I'd had as much,' said Alice when they had plumped down together on her bed. 'Seeing his reactions tonight makes me realize that he is a more capable guardian for her than either of us. Did you see how he dealt with Aunt Bloody Margaret? Polite but no nonsense. Got her off to her train in time. We'd have been stuck with her and Dandy ready to boil over. D'you know, I'm beginning to think it will be a big relief when they *do* get married. Her family can never bother her again . . . Well, I'm being a little ridiculous. It's only her father who presents a problem now.'

*   *   *

Hector cursed as he tripped over a trailing strand of greenery. He had been faced with a choice – a lantern or a walking stick – and had chosen the lantern. If Dandy *had* stumbled and needed help, he would have to see her. On the other hand, lighting a lantern with one hand was a task he had not yet completely conquered. It might have been more sensible to get some help with that from one of the gardening boys, but most of them would be down in the village enjoying themselves at this time of night, if they weren't already in bed. And his instinct told him that the fewer people who knew of this, the better. Or was it instinct? Could it be that he had been in the habit of shutting people out of his life and this applied even when Dandy might be in danger? He hurried on. The air was damp. Violet had not taken time to check if Dandy had taken anything warm with her. Her pretty dress was on the bed. Had she changed into another ... his impetuous little love? Where would she make for on her last perfect day? Of course! The summer house ... where he gave her the book, and that first wondering kiss that had led to so many ... Oh God, let her be there!

The door was pulled to. He wrenched it awkwardly, the lantern swinging in his hand. 'Dandy?' There was no reply. 'Dandy?' he repeated anxiously. Then his eyes adjusted to the darkness and he moved forward and stumbled. The sobs she had been stifling broke through. 'Dandy, oh Dandy, are you hurt? Damn this lantern! I can't manage it properly with one hand.' He dropped the matches, fumbled for them and then dropped them a second time.

Dandy sniffed loudly. 'I'll do it.' Her hand shook violently as she held the lighted match; then Hector was steadying her and adjusting the flame before placing the lantern on the floor beside the door. The hammock rocked as he threw himself down beside her and gathered her to him. 'You're shivering. What have you on?'

'My mantle. I didn't want to dirty my dress in the dark.'

'Here, take my cape – I brought it in case . . . let me tuck it round you.' He kissed her, fierce in his relief. 'There! I should really be spanking you for keeping me in the dark all that time.'

'I was afraid . . .'

'Afraid of me? Surely . . .'

'What do you know about me?'

'Everything. Alice told me the lot. Oh dear, you're still shivering. This won't do and your aunts will be nearly demented. I think we'd better get back. Talking will have to wait. Do you want to keep the lantern lit? I thought that the fewer people who knew about this the better, but if you should stumble . . .'

'No, I won't. I know this garden as well as if it were my own.'

'It *is* yours, Dandy, in every way that matters, just as I am. Remember that. Trust me! Your teeth are chattering. I'm afraid you've got a chill . . .'

His words were repeated by Alice when she thankfully led Dandy into her bedroom. 'Violet has crept downstairs to make you a hot drink. Hector says he doesn't think Mrs McGuffie will hear. The room she sleeps in is what used to be the gun room and is separated by another door from the kitchen premises. Anyway, she takes a little tot of whisky last thing and sleeps like a baby, so he says.'

She's just blethering away to give me a chance to pull myself together, thought Dandy. If only I could stop this shivering . . . my face is hot but my hands are icy . . .

'Here, let me help you,' Alice said. 'The sooner you

have a hot bath the better – just a quick one. Don't lock the door in case you feel faint. I'll be around. Hector says I have to call him when you are safely tucked up.'

Violet's tray was already by the bedside when Dandy returned. 'I wouldn't bother plaiting your hair tonight, Dandy,' she said. 'Look – I'll tie it back with a ribbon for you.'

'I'm being spoiled,' said Dandy through chattering teeth.

'It's about time,' said Alice, 'that someone spoiled you, and I know a young man who is dying to do just that. Shall I tell Hector he may come now?'

He approached the bed shyly. 'She's still shivering,' said Alice. 'I think that Violet and I should take turns to sit up . . .'

'Yes,' said Violet. 'It's very like the last time . . .'

'I wouldn't dream of it, ladies. I shall sit up. If Dandy needs you, I shall call. It's only a few steps along the corridor.'

'But you'll be tired . . .'

'No, Alice. I'm an old campaigner. I shan't be tired, I assure you.'

Violet opened her mouth then closed it again as she met Alice's eye. They said their goodnights and departed.

'Only you and me,' said Hector softly. Dandy sketched a shaky smile.

'Have you finished with that drink? Here, let me take it. Now, snuggle down and I'll tuck you in. Traipsing around in the dark in November, indeed! Careful – we mustn't catch your lovely hair. That's it. I'll spread it over the pillow. How lovely and silky! I'm looking forward to the day after your eighteenth birthday, young lady, so you must take care of yourself. No more adventuring without me. There now, you're still

359

shivering. I think you have a bit of a fever. If I stroke your brow, does that help?'

'Mmmm,' said Dandy.

'Go to sleep, my love. I'm here. That's it. Gently. Go ... to ... sleep ...'

It was all right; Hector was watching her; he would never abandon her; she was safe, wandering in the garden. The flower scents were mixed ... lilac ... roses ... honeysuckle ... chrysanthemums – that was funny: all together! But there was a smell of burning in the summer house and daft Jock was laughing. Hector would be burned. She struggled but was caught up in the fire. The heat was awful. She would have to get her clothes off ... She was laughing – or was it daft Jock again?

'Hush, my darling. No, don't struggle. Let me dab some cold water on your brow ... steady ... steady.'

'Fire!' croaked Dandy.

'Yes, you're on fire, I know. A nasty fever. Doctor in the morning, I'm afraid.'

'For I'm to be Queen of the May,' murmured Dandy.

'What's that?'

'Queen ... call me early ...' She tossed and turned, her voice rising. 'Call me early ... no, it's too late. Aunt Margaret's here ... Aunt Bloody Margaret. She'll tell him. He won't understand ... my last perfect day ... Oh, Hector, Hector –'

'Hush, hush, I'm here, my love. Let me bathe your forehead ... No, don't struggle ... gently ... gently ...'

'I've got to ... it's got to be a secret. It's my own lovely room – "Dandy's room" they call it. Faither would grudge me it ... he couldn't do anything about it ... he couldn't. That's Jock laughing in the summer house ... Hector ... my book!'

The door opened and Alice came in softly. 'I heard her laughing. Is she delirious?'

'Afraid so – I think I should phone the doctor.'

'Won't that be awkward for you, Hector? I mean, she will probably talk about her worries . . . perhaps about her mother's death, and if people thought she was an orphan . . .'

'What the hell – I beg your pardon – I mean, what does that matter if she needs attention? Listen to her! She's delirious all right. Doc Anderson has known me for years. He'll be Dandy's doctor too in the not too distant future, I hope. There's no harm in putting him in the picture.'

'It seems a shame to call him out at this hour of the night, but she *does* seem to be getting much worse.'

'Definitely. I'll ring him from my office in case the tinkling of the bell wakes anyone. Then I'll stay downstairs ready to open the door when I hear his trap. You'll be all right here?'

'Oh yes. Violet is still awake. Here she is! Off you go, Hector. We'll carry on here.'

Dandy's voice was rising again. 'I should have been there. It's too much for May. It's my job, I'm the eldest. Oh Mammie . . . She's on the big ship . . . but Grannie needs me too. I've to wash the stairs . . . I mustn't miss my turn. She won't like that. No, Grannie, I haven't forgotten. But Grannie doesn't like flowers . . .' She quietened down for a moment or two while Violet stroked her forehead with cool fingers. Then she was groaning again. 'Aunt Margaret doesn't want to take my rosebuds. Still Aunt Alice will sort her!' She gave a hoarse cackle. 'Hector can sort her too. Thought she was staying the night . . . ha! ha! ha!'

'Try a little sip of this, dear,' Alice was urging. 'Violet, could you help to hold her up a little? I don't want her to choke.' This time their ministrations seemed to have an effect and Dandy's breathing gradually steadied. The sisters looked at each other in relief.

'She may sleep for the rest of the night,' whispered Violet.

'I wouldn't count on it. Remember last time?' came the whispered answer.

It was not long before the silence was broken by the clip-clop of hooves. They heard the mutter of voices and the snort of the horse. 'He'll be giving it a nosebag to keep it quiet,' whispered Violet.

'Quiet,' murmured Dandy. 'Quiet . . . Hector mustn't know.' She stirred restlessly. 'Aunt Bloody Margaret will tell him. He's a landowner . . . lots of land . . . Faither! . . . A drunken dyer, aye . . . in a pigsty . . . poor Mammie! 'She shot up suddenly, screaming, 'Mammie's dead . . . she never had a chance . . . never. I wouldn't go to bloody Canada . . . wouldn't go . . .'

Alice was busy dabbing her forehead while Violet tried to hold her still when Hector opened the door for the doctor.

'Now what have we here?' he asked, advancing to the bed.

'A feverish chill,' said Alice promptly. 'We've had to deal with this before, Doctor. It was frightening at the time, but she was bright as a button in a couple of days.'

Dr Anderson laid his left hand on Dandy's forehead while he felt for her pulse with the right. 'Let's take her temperature, shall we?' he suggested after a moment. 'I wouldn't trust her not to bite it so, if one of you ladies could hold her arm . . . yes, I'll get it tucked in her armpit . . . keep it tucked in . . . Now, young lady, calm down! I suspect you've been out in the cold with too little on. Young ladies have a habit of doing that.'

'I didn't get my dress dirty . . . no!' muttered Dandy. 'Jock was laughing in the summer house.'

The doctor raised inquiring eyebrows. Alice

answered, 'She witnessed a near disaster when a gardener's lad – not quite right in the head – tried to set fire to a hut. She saved the head gardener's life by her quick-wittedness on that occasion. She seems to be linking it with the summer house here and thinks something dreadful will happen to Hector.'

'Mmmm, worries often seem to get transferred in these cases.' He studied the thermometer. 'I thought so: 104 degrees. I've brought some powders. Give her one now, in a little milk – hold her nose, if necessary – and another in three hours' time. I'll be back before morning surgery. Keep sponging her down and give her lots of cool drinks; anything that gives her a little peace. It may be that there's more than a simple chill to account for this, some worry . . .'

Yes,' said Hector. 'I'll explain on the way down.'

As the door closed, Violet raised her eyebrows at Alice. 'I don't know,' she replied. 'But I'm sure it will be an edited version.'

They had not long to wait. Hector assured them that they could return to bed: he was quite able to look after Dandy. He held the door open for them, then stepped into the corridor, murmuring, 'I told the doctor that her mother had died in Canada; Dandy was feeling guilty about refusing to go there with the rest of the family, but she was so fond of you two and you of her. I think that will seem quite a reasonable explanation.'

Returning to the bedside, he stroked Dandy's hair. She murmured incoherently before falling asleep. He had dozed off for a short time himself when he heard her stirring. 'Fire, fire, it's so hot!' She tossed and turned, then jerked up in bed, knocking the sponge out of Hector's hand and tearing frantically at the buttons of her nightdress. 'I'm so hot!'

The loose cambric floated lightly round her as she managed to wriggle her arms free. Hector gazed

363

enchanted, then started gently sponging and alternately dabbing with the soft towel. 'Is that better, love?'

'Mmmm . . . better,' she said. Hector hesitated, then with a groan leaned forward and buried his face in her breasts for a moment before kissing them gently time and time again. He pulled himself away reluctantly, but Dandy, with a gasp, snatched at his hand and held it to her breast, then she was guiding it down to her stomach and further . . .

'No!' said Hector, wrenching himself free. Dandy, arms thrashing, started to cry. 'Hush, darling,' he whispered. 'Let me put your arms in.' He kissed her gently on the cheek while he tried to get her to slip her arm into the nightgown. Perspiration was dripping from his forehead as he considered Alice and Violet's likely reaction to the scene. 'Oh, Dandy, if only I had two arms,' he groaned.

'Bloody bastards took one,' she said, quite distinctly.

'Hush, darling. You don't want to wake Alice and Violet.'

'Shhhhh,' she said, fingers to her lips. 'Kiss me, Hector. No, not on the face.' Her firm young breasts were being offered to him.

'If you'll promise to put your nightgown back on.'

She pouted for a moment, then nodded. Again his lips caressed the silky warm skin; Dandy was wriggling provocatively against him. 'Let's go to the summer house, Hector. No one will see us there.'

'You promised me, Dandy. Now let's get your nightgown properly fixed and then we'll have a little sleep.'

'Will you put your head on the pillow beside me?'

'All right, if you promise to sleep.'

'Mmmmm.'

Alice, entering the room a few hours later made a hasty exit before rattling the doorknob and speaking over her shoulder to Violet. This time Hector was in the chair by the bed, smoothing his ruffled hair.

'Did she sleep?'

'Yes. One restless spell, but then she seemed to calm down. I fell asleep myself.'

'Good,' said Alice. 'Would you like to go down to breakfast now? I heard stirrings below. The doctor said he would call before surgery.'

'Oh yes. If you can take over now . . . thank you . . . I *would* like to freshen up.'

'Yes and pick those yellow hairs off your shoulder,' muttered Alice softly when the door had closed behind him.

Doctor Anderson smiled with satisfaction. 'Temperature's well down, but it often is by morning in these cases. She could be propped up for a while during the day but we'll have to keep her carefully wrapped. There's always the danger of pneumonia. Right, young lady. Stay there and do what these kind nurses tell you. They'll be tired after sitting up all night.'

'Hector looked after me,' croaked Dandy.

The doctor laughed. 'I just can't see that young man in the role of nurse.' He was still laughing when he made his way downstairs with Alice.

'Hector did indeed sit up with her, doctor,' she said. 'He insisted.'

'Well, that's a stumper! I heard rumours, of course, that he was smitten by your fair niece. Couldn't be more pleased! He's cut himself off from life long enough. Good stuff there, you know.'

'Yes, I appreciate that.'

'You say you've had to deal with this sort of fever before, Miss McLaren. Was it purely a chill then, or was there an emotional strain?'

'Definitely an emotional strain. She is a girl of strong

feelings and strong character. She and Hector will be good for each other, I'm sure. It is a great pity she is so young.'

'Young? What is she – twenty?'

'Seventeen. Hector would like to marry her the day after her eighteenth birthday.'

The doctor started laughing. 'I'll bet the young ass doesn't realize that the girl has to choose the date, smart and all as he is. She looks older. Why do they have to wait? Hector's not penniless. My mother married at seventeen, produced five healthy sons, kept active all her days.'

'You think I am being cautious. I know she could marry without anyone's consent at sixteen, but somehow I was afraid . . . she's so impetuous – but fiercely loyal too. Hector and his garden are her idea of heaven.'

'Well, why make them wait?'

'There's her mother's death too – in Canada.'

'Mmmm, well, I suppose that would make a big affair out of the question, but if I know Hector he would probably prefer a simple ceremony here in the house. Young Sandy – Sandy Crawford, our minister – would be happy to oblige, I'm sure. Let's hope we've caught this thing in the early stages. You say the last bout took a couple of days?'

'Perhaps we were being over-anxious, but it seemed longer. Her family had gone to Canada and we were taking our responsibilities very seriously, you see.'

'I'd let Hector take over if I were you. It's time he was married, taken out of himself. From things I've heard, that young lady is just the one to do it. Mrs McGuffie, for one, is warm in her approval and she would not be easy to please where her Master Hector is concerned.'

'No indeed!' agreed Alice. No sooner had she handed

the doctor over to Hector than she hurried to consult with Violet. A lift of her eyebrows summoned that lady into the corridor. 'The doctor thinks a lot of the fever is caused by emotional strain. He thinks we should let them get married sooner. Honestly, Violet, I am beginning to feel my age. Seeing how Hector copes makes me realize that I am making heavy weather of things.'

'Well, maybe . . . but we must get her well first before we think of anything else, and don't you think the cottage will seem awful without her now?'

'Yes! We're a couple of dull old dogs – or should I say bitches?'

'Dandy would,' said Violet.

'What are you laughing at?' asked Dandy as they entered.

'Just so pleased to see you less fevered, isn't that so, Violet?'

'Yes. That's right. We've to see that you stay wrapped up.'

'Where's Hector, Aunt Alice?'

'I'm not sure. Don't you think that young man deserves a little rest after sitting up all night?'

'Mmmm, I want him beside me. I wish I was eighteen.'

'Yes. We've heard that song before. Now just settle down, Dandy. Shall I ask Mrs McGuffie to make you a little toast?'

'No toast.'

'A hot drink, then?'

'A hot drink and Hector.' She started to weep. The sisters looked at each other in despair. Then there was a knock at the door. 'Hector?' croaked Dandy.

His smile was quickly replaced by a frown when he saw her tears. Ignoring the sisters, he hurried to the bedside and put his arm round Dandy's shoulders. 'Here, here, this won't do. You have to get rid of that chill and be well and strong soon. Now, let Aunt Violet give you your powder and then your drink, and then you can try for a little sleep. If you're very good, I may have some thrilling news for you when you wake up.'

'What is it?' Her voice was muffled.

Hector leaned over and kissed her brow. 'I'm not telling you till you've had a little sleep.'

'Will you sleep beside me?'

Hector flushed. 'I have a few things to do, but I'll be in that chair when you wake, believe me. There now! Aunt Violet is ready to look after you . . .' He made his way to the door, sending a message to Alice as he went. She followed him out.

'Let's go into my office. There is something the doctor said that I'd like to discuss.'

And I've a good idea what that is, Young Lochinvar, thought Alice as she padded along beside him.

He ushered Alice to a seat, but prowled around restlessly himself for a few minutes before settling down and starting in a staccato voice: 'The doctor has known me for years; he says he doesn't see why we have to wait till Dandy is eighteen.' He blushed as he continued, 'He says that physically she is well developed and he can't see anything to worry about there. You told me once that she has always seemed older than her age and now that I know her history, that is not to be wondered at. I would guard her with my life – you know that – and we are so desperately in love . . . Don't you think you could relent a little . . . ?'

'Dear me, Hector, you *do* make me sound a hard-hearted Hannah! Relent indeed! Violet and I love that child as if she were our own. It is only because of that that we have been chary of her impulsive ways.'

'And my history, no doubt?'

'Well, to be honest, that has weighed too. We did not wish you to be let down twice if her feelings should change. I certainly can't see that happening now. You are the beat of her heart: that's obvious. In that respect I feel you are an extremely fortunate young man. There are some things too precious for money to buy.'

'I was thinking of it from another angle. I am not proud of the way I reacted to my disappointment: the way I took it out on others who were entirely blameless. Hearing Dandy's story doubled my guilt in that department. Well, I've said it before. We would dearly love to belong to each other. I swear I would try to make up to her for her lost childhood. Well, what do you think?'

Alice looked at the whitened knuckles, the flushed brow and the intense eyes. 'When you put it that way, Hector . . . Of course I should like to consult Violet . . .' They both knew that Violet would fall in with any plan that Alice favoured.

Hector relaxed in a broad smile. 'Could we think of Easter?'

'Why not June? The roses will be in their full glory. Where were you thinking of – for the ceremony, I mean?'

'We've never discussed that. I've no left arm to lead her back down the aisle on . . . and yet it seems a shame to do my beautiful Dandy out of a grand wedding in that lovely church . . .'

'So soon after her mother's death? No, I don't think that would be suitable. Dandy is so happy here that a quiet ceremony – perhaps in the rose garden, if the day is fine . . .'

Hector beamed. 'That's exactly what I would have chosen.' He kissed her impulsively. 'Please hurry and consult Violet; then I'll be able to give Dandy the news.'

'Hector, that fever may flare up again. I don't know that she is in the best state to understand. She has such a volatile temperament – needs care.'

'Well, there are three of us to see that she gets it – and that's not counting Mrs McGuffie,' he added with a grin.

Chapter 25

'Hector?'

'Mmm yes?' He was burying his chin in her hair.

'There's something I want to ask you.'

'Let's go into the summer house then. It's probably full of spiders, but it's better than trailing your skirts through all these wet plants, I'm sure.'

'Well, I wanted to have you to myself . . . to say good-bye properly.'

'Mmmm, your aunts weren't fooled for a moment. They know there's nothing worth looking at this week. Now, here we are; it's none too warm but at least it's dry.'

'And it still has that woody summerhouse smell . . .'

'I had never really paid any attention to that till you did. Now, what is it that you wanted to ask?'

'Well . . . I don't know quite how to put it . . . when I was ill – I mean at the beginning when I was very fevered, I had some terrible dreams. Sometimes I woke up and you were there.'

'Not surprising. I sat up with you the first three nights. After that, Alice insisted that they take turns. You see, you kept asking for me during the day too – utterly shameless, that's what you are.'

'Shameless?' She looked at him searchingly. 'What do you mean?'

'Propositioning me in the most blatant manner. In fact, I'm thinking of telling Alice that they have not brought you up properly.'

'Stop tormenting me!'

'I've got you worried now, haven't I?'

'Hector, please!'

'All right. What's this all about?'

'I had terrible dreams ... I keep remembering one of them. I hope it was a dream ...'

'Yes?'

'I was in a fire and too hot and I had to get my clothes off and then you were sponging me and ...'

'And you were beautiful,' Hector whispered. 'Beautiful as Aphrodite. Oh Dandy, my little Queen of the Lilies ...'

'So it wasn't a dream?' said Dandy, blushing furiously.

'On the contrary, it was a dream of delight which I hope to repeat in ... about seven months from now, my fair charmer. I hope you will be as eager then as you were when in a fever. Now, if I could only find out what triggers off your attacks ...'

'Hector McAndrew, you're a ...'

'Bounder? Rake? Libertine? Or what about, "The man who is going to love and treasure me for the rest of my days and never refuse my offers of beautiful breasts to kiss"?'

'It's a good thing I'm going home,' Dandy muttered into his chest.

'I quite agree. Not for long, of course. In three weeks' time you will be back for the Christmas celebrations. Three months after that you will be enjoying an Easter safari to darkest Wigtownshire. In between I may have the odd shopping trip which necessitates a visit to Paisley to see you slaving over a hot sewing machine. And then *June*, flaming June when we ... when we ... Oh Dandy! It's a good thing you're going home. Now, quick march! The carriage will be here any minute.'

Dandy managed to smile bravely as she waved goodbye to the tall figure on Stranraer Station. 'Well done,' said Alice. 'We look like having the compartment to ourselves. Good! Now, Violet has been telling me some of her ideas for new outfits. They sound lovely to me. There's nothing like keeping busy to make the time pass quickly. Hector is taking a bold step in reviving the Christmas celebrations at Lindsay House. I gather that they have always been based on the carols and the children's party. Next year he hopes to revive the New Year junketing. It would not be very suitable for you so soon after your mother's death. One thing that has disappointed Violet is the thought of the quiet ceremony in June. She had visions of your wedding dress – her *pièce de résistance*.'

'But Hector thought of that,' said Dandy. 'He's got a plan. Though we'll be married quietly at Lindsay House, he would like to see me in a proper dress. He says that a friend who was in the army with him has a sister who is married to a famous portrait painter in London. He thinks he could get him to paint me afterwards.'

'That would mean going to London,' said Violet.

'No, Hector thinks that the painter would be quite glad to come to Lindsay House and stay there while he is doing it. His wife could come too, if she wanted. He says he has neglected all his old friends and now he wants to show me off . . .' she trailed away, embarrassed.

'Good. I've got some lovely ideas. I can picture you looking like one of those beautiful lilies . . .' Violet was off in a dream and soon Dandy was smiling gently to herself. It was only a few weeks to Christmas, then it wouldn't be long till Easter, and then – if she had all that sewing to do and her own garden to leave in perfect condition – well, June might well be upon them before they had time to fret. The only dark spot in the picture was the thought of Canada – particularly little May.

Hector had offered to send the money for her to come home – indeed, for any of the family Dandy wished to have with her. But she knew how May would worry about leaving them – even Faither. In fact, May seemed to have taken on her mother's mantle of plodding, ungrudging service. At least the boys were more aware of things nowadays and weren't the worry they had been in Paisley. If only Aunt Marie could keep Will Baxter off the bottle!

The cold November mists went unheeded as Violet led Dandy on extravagant shopping sprees. 'You can never have too many pretty blouses – particularly when you will have someone to launder them for you. Alice and I used to have some lovely things. It's like re-living those days, isn't it Alice?'

'Maybe,' said Alice. 'The difference is that Dandy always looked outstanding even when her clothes were anything but grand. I think nature always needed rather a lot of help where we were concerned.'

'I always thought you were lovely – so ladylike,' said Dandy simply. 'Won't you love coming to visit us at Lindsay House? It will be a bit like your old home to you.'

'It will be most pleasant,' they agreed, nobly omitting to voice their feelings about the cottage minus the Queen of the Lilies.

As the two women had anticipated, Dandy threw herself into the preparations with a will. Hector was entranced by her appearance at his Christmas party. 'I was dreading what you might call "going into society" again,' he told her afterwards, 'but having my beautiful Dandy to show off made me forget to be shy. You looked so happy all the time.'

'I wish I didn't have to go home,' said Dandy.

'I know, dearest, but I can understand your aunts' decision to leave tomorrow. They are making sure that your reputation will never be damaged. Violet seems to be enjoying herself, at least – designing your trousseau.'

'I'm not sure Aunt Alice is so happy about being left to do most of the cooking, though. In a way, it is good to see Violet the dominant one for a change.'

'I can imagine! Now there is something important we have to decide. I had always planned to take you to Italy for our honeymoon – Lake Garda, to be precise. There are so many beautiful gardens round about and the setting is out of this world. A poet I haven't introduced you to yet, Catullus, was born in Sirmione, which is on that lake. He may burn your ears at times . . .'

'What d'you mean?'

'I'll tell you when you are an old married lady. No, it's no use flourishing your engagement ring at me. Let me continue. There is one snag: Lake Garda will be very, very hot in June.'

'I don't know why we have to go away at all. I can't imagine anything lovelier than being here with you. We could always go away later, maybe the autumn or the next spring.'

'You were worried last time when I told you that I fear the war clouds are gathering. Germany is supporting Austria and Hungary. We have our alliance with France and Belgium. If we put off our visit to Italy, we may be prevented from going for a long time. Wars always leave devastation and bitterness in their wake. Goodness, I've just remembered! Last time – you asked about Canada. Now I understand. That is something else you may have to face if the worst comes to the worst – there would be no possibility of your going to Canada or of your family visiting you till it is over. Of course, it might be that your eldest brother would be in it too.'

'Oh, no!'

'I'm a fool, worrying you like this. But I *do* feel I'd like to take you to Italy. Now, the wedding is to be a

375

quiet affair because you are still officially in mourning. Suppose we risk leaving the Italian visit till October. Then we can have a party for the estate workers when we get back – a celebration.'

'There's something you seem to have forgotten, Hector. Suppose I get pregnant right away . . .'

'I've no intention of landing you in that state at such an early age. I'll take care of you.'

Dandy flushed then shivered. 'Come on,' he said. 'This summer house was never meant for winter weather. One of the items on my spring programme will be to see that it is spruced up and painted before our wedding, since it means so much to you.'

'Well, it was here that you gave me the book . . .'

'And you let me kiss you, and after June there will be no end to the kissing . . . Oh, for pity's sake let's get back to safety, you little temptress!'

Dandy recalled these words often on the journey home, which was lengthened by atrocious weather conditions. It was a great relief to see smoke rising from the cottage chimneys when their cab drew near. 'Mrs Brown hasn't neglected us, I see,' said Alice. 'It will be lovely to have tea by the fire.'

'And the range is going merrily, I see by the smoke,' said Violet. 'If she remembered the shopping too, a good hot supper is on the cards.'

Dandy was ashamed to think how little the cottage meant to her now that Lindsay House was soon to be her home. The big log fire in the drawing room with Hector sitting near, talking eagerly. That was home! But those feelings would have to be hidden . . .

'There's one for you from Canada,' said Alice, who had picked up the pile of mail from the hall table. Dandy looked at the untidy writing and her dreamy mood was shattered immediately. 'Looks like Billy,' she said, tearing it open.

'Aye,' she scanned it quickly. 'Oh God, what now? Are we never to get any peace. Poor wee May!'

'Bad news?' asked Alice.

'Is there ever anything else?' Dandy's tone was bitter. 'Here!' She handed the letter to Alice while Violet quietly set the tea things before them. Dandy sipped abstractedly while Alice read the untidy script.

Dear Dandy,

Things have been happening here and Aunt Marie says I am probably the best one to tell you for George is not speaking to anyone and May is too upset and never likes upsetting anyone else but really she has had a rotten time. The weather has been awful cold here and Pa has been drinking so much since Ma died. He forgets to give May money for food and she has had a terrible time. Even the vegetables are frozen in the ground and it's only the things we saved in sacks that we have to eat. Aunt Marie doesn't know just how bad it is. She would give us food but May says that it is not fair and we've not to tell her how bad things are. Well, a few nights ago May had made a sort of soup. It hadn't much in it but potatoes and turnips and a wee bit barley. Pa was drunk and when she put it in front of him he said he didn't want that dish-water and threw it at her. May got scalded all over her hand. She cried sore and you know May she doesn't usually cry much. The twins were crying too in sympathy and George suddenly got up with a roar and he shouted at Pa, 'I've had enough from you, you drunken old bugger.' He pulled Pa out of his seat. George is awful big and strong now you know and he started punching and punching Pa. At first Pa was roaring and cursing but he couldn't beat George. May was crying on George

377

to stop but he wouldn't. He went on punching Pa and he told me to see to May's wrist – put a paste of baking soda on it and he told the twins to stop greetin' and to get on with doing something instead of leaving everything to May. Then he stopped punching Pa. He sat with his head in his hands for a while and then he put his macinaw on – that's a warm jacket with pockets over your belly – and he warned the twins they were to help May and he came over to me and said that he was going to Aunt Marie's. He couldn't stay in the house with that devil any more. See that May gets something to eat, he said and then he gave her a sort of wee cuddle and went out in the snow. Aunt Marie came over later. She had stuff to cool May's scalds and lots of bandages and she bandaged Pa too and said she would talk to him later when he was fit and she was keeping George at her house meantime and she asked me how I was getting on and she praised the twins for helping, said they would have to learn to look after things themselves if they hoped to have a career on the stage. Self-sufficiency is very important, she said. There's not much Aunt Marie does not know. Well, I was at Aunt Marie's today and she says that she is trying to get an opening for George in a place in Vancouver. A friend of hers knows somebody in an engineering works there. She says I am the farmer of the family but she thinks if we could get Pa to give up drink he could be a good fruit farmer too. I hope every-thing is fine with you. May doesn't know I am writing this but I'm sure she would send her love. Give my love to Aunt Violet and Aunt Alice and tell them I can still make pancakes.

Billy

Alice looked steadily at Dandy. 'There's one compensation, my dear. I sense a lot of family loyalty there. Your siblings are sticking up for one another very nicely.'

'D'you think,' Dandy began uncertainly, 'that things might have been different if I had gone with them?'

'They wouldn't have been better – might have been worse. You couldn't have kept your mouth shut and yet you could not have controlled your father. Things would definitely have been worse. George has managed it with sheer physical strength, which you don't have, and George's remedy is unlikely to be of lasting use, but it may open the door for Mrs Whatshername to work on him. She seems to be forceful and subtle at the same time – an unusual combination. Yes. My money is on that lady. I'm sorry your homecoming has been spoiled, my dear, after such a wonderful time with Hector. Hang on to the lovely things in your life. Help where you can and trust where you cannot. That's my advice.' Dandy's face gradually cleared and she managed a grin.

Violet extended her sewing instruction from dressmaking to household goods. 'You may be lucky enough to have people to make curtains and things like that for you,' she said, 'but if you know something about it yourself, you can tell a good piece of work and know a sensible price for it. Some of the valuable old curtains in Lindsay House could do with a little careful repairing ... a matter of darning in loose threads invisibly, strengthening weak parts – that sort of thing. Knowledge will never let you down, but lack of it might. There is nothing clever about throwing money away.'

'They're preparing me to be the lady of the house; they want Hector to be proud of me. That's what these lectures are all about,' she thought. 'But I know that all Hector wants is his Queen of the Lilies, his Aphrodite

... he longs to kiss my breasts: the curtains can fall down for all he cares.' She smiled kindly at Aunt Violet and gave every impression of paying attention.

Dandy found it difficult to sit still. The train seemed to her to be crawling. Every time they were held up at a signal she sighed with irritation. Alice and Violet smiled indulgently. 'Hector will be just as restless,' said Violet. 'Longing to see his little bride, I'm sure. The weather seems set fair. That's a wonderful idea – getting married in the rose garden, I mean.'

'I think the drawing room with its magnificent view would be lovely too,' said Alice. 'We don't really have to worry about the weather.'

'If Hector's there, I don't care,' said Dandy.

'Well, without Hector it would be an odd wedding,' said Alice.

'I hope Aunt Margaret doesn't make it odder.'

'She won't,' Violet assured her. 'She'll love dressing up, Dandy.'

'I think it was wise of Hector to include her,' said Alice. 'To be able to say that she is your mother's sister, well, it introduces a note of normality. There could have been less acceptable people, if you think of it. At least she knows which fork to use.'

Chapter 26

Alice and Violet had said their fond goodbyes and
borne Aunt Margaret off to the hotel with them. 'She
wasn't too bad, now, was she?' said Hector.

'Aunt Margaret? I didn't notice her much. Your minister seemed rather shy and yet Dr Anderson says he
is very sporty and the children of the parish cluster
round him whenever he appears.'

'Our minister was struck dumb by the vision of loveli-
ness drifting before him. The bridegroom was not in a
much better state, I can tell you. Did you hear how I
croaked my responses?'

'I think I whispered mine. All of a sudden it seemed
such a big thing and I thought that my mother had taken
those same vows and had hoped for the happiness we
hope for ... and then I got a waft of the roses and I
peeked up at you and your jaw was set in that determined way and I knew you were a man of your word
and I was safe with you for ever ...'

'I'm looking forward to seeing you in your gorgeous
dress again. We were lucky that the famous fellow was
available next month.'

'Aye, but I'm glad we have a few weeks to ourselves
first, Hector.'

'True! Now, we have this whole garden to ourselves.
Mrs McGuffie knows I have taken a key. She is sensible
enough to know that we don't want to see her again
tonight. The rest of the staff are celebrating in the village
hostelry – drinks at my expense. Since you whispered
your desire to start our marriage in the summer house,

I was prudent enough to secrete some more cushions there today – and a rug, in case the night should become chilly, though I don't expect you to suffer from cold . . .'

Hector was leading her towards the summer house. She shivered suddenly. 'He can't wait,' she thought in panic. 'It's so deliberate . . . I don't feel the way I sometimes do. I couldn't . . . not feeling like this! Men seem to be so . . . they think of one thing . . . even daft Jock . . .'

They were inside and he was locking the door. 'One of the things I made sure of when I had the place smartened up,' he said. 'A good lock.' Dandy had a sudden memory of the hut and daft Jock. She shivered again violently.

'What's wrong?' Hector asked, his arm firmly round her. She went on shuddering, her teeth chattering. 'What's wrong?' he repeated, but she shook her head. 'My darling, you have nothing to be afraid of.' Still she shivered helplessly. 'Look, you were all right when we were walking in the garden. Let's go out again. It will be light for ages. Then we'll go in. I'll sleep in the dressing room tonight – leave you alone, if that's what worrying you. My darling, I can't have you like this. Did you think I would ever force myself on you?'

She allowed herself to be led out again and gradually the soothing perfumes of the eucalyptus, roses and honeysuckle worked their magic. Hector turned his steps towards the house, but at an intersection of the path she pulled gently on his arm and nodded towards the summer house. He looked at her keenly. 'Are you sure?' She nodded.

'Let's sit down,' he said, patting the space beside him on the hammock. 'You seemed quite calm at the actual wedding. Did I say something to frighten you, my darling?'

'I remembered the hut and daft Jock ... and my mother and father. I used to hear things ...'

'Oh dear. I had seen our love as a beautiful poem, my little Queen of the Lilies. I thought you did too.'

'I did, I did! I don't know why it happened.'

'Stage fright, maybe. Now don't think of anything else. I shan't touch you. Stay here beside me and let's be happy together at the end of such a wonderful day. Could you hum some of the songs you sang in the drawing room the other night? Liz Anderson told me what a pleasure it was to accompany a singer of your calibre. Go on, Bridegroom's treat!'

Not the treat you were expecting, reflected Dandy. She leaned closer as she started humming. The dress she had chosen for her walk in the garden was a simple one on flowing lines with large buttons down the front. Gradually, singing softly, she eased the buttons open; then she was slipping the dress off her shoulders. Next she started unhooking her bodice. Hector tugged at his cravat. 'You'll have to help me,' he said. 'Bob Anderson got me into this. It's a different fastening from the thing I usually wear.' Deftly she stripped him to the waist before discarding her bodice. He buried his face in her breasts and the rush of desire she had experienced in her fever returned to swamp her.

In a dream, Hector, naked himself, watched her remove the rest of her clothing. 'Aphrodite,' he whispered as she stood before him. 'There isn't all that much room,' she murmured, looking at the hammock. 'Shall I ... shall I lie down?'

'No. I'm scared to touch you. No, I shall lie down and you ... you can do what you like with me. Only, listen! If I tell you to separate, don't waste any time. You understand? We don't want to land you with a pregnancy. You *do* understand?'

'Yes,' she said, lowering her pliant young body on to him.

'Your skin is like silk,' he whispered.

She gave a long sigh. His body was exploring hers, setting up tremors all over her. Eagerly she pressed down then lay still. Hector's lips were devouring her while he explored deeper and deeper. His breathing was more agitated. She was being torn apart. It was painful but a wonderful pain. Suddenly, his lips tore away. 'Leave me,' he gasped. Then more frantic, 'Leave me!' But Dandy, floating in a world she did not understand, moaned helplessly and lay still. It was a long time before they could bring themselves to dress and return silently through the midnight garden to their room. 'Oh, God, I hope I haven't landed you, Dandy,' said Hector, perching on the edge of the bed. 'I thought you understood.'

'I thought I did too, but I didn't know that anything would happen to *me* – just to you. I was helpless. It wouldn't be a disaster, would it? We can afford a baby.'

'I know, but it's your age that worries me. When I told Alice I would look after you, that was one of the aspects I was thinking of. And I must confess, I selfishly hoped to keep you to myself for a little while.'

'I'll always be yours, Hector.'

'Bless you! Of course you will. Let's hope that we've been lucky this time. I'll certainly take more care in future. Now, would you like me to sleep in the dressing room, or dare I join you here? It seems that I can't guarantee my good behaviour as far as you are concerned.'

Dandy chuckled. 'I think I might be lonely in a bed this size . . .'

A few weeks later, Dandy was able to tell him that they had indeed been lucky. 'Thank goodness for that,' he said. 'Maybe the fact that you are so young had something to do with it – I mean ... not quite ready ... and yet, oh, my darling, you are such a joy to love. Marriage seems to be making you even more beautiful, if that were possible.'

Her aunts, on their visit to celebrate Dandy's birthday, confirmed his opinion. 'Isn't she blooming?' asked Violet.

'Yes. I'd say that being Mrs McAndrew certainly agrees with you,' said Alice.

'I still can't quite get used to that, but I've already been asked to lend my name to some worthy causes. It was a good thing Hector warned me.'

'I have to inform you that my wife writes excellent speeches – concise but with a lyricism which is all her own. I am extremely proud of her.'

'And how did you get on with the artist?' asked Violet. 'We thought the portrait would be here.'

'No. He did the essential parts here but felt he needed a lot more time to do justice to the dress, so he has taken it away with him to finish when he has completed a portrait of some dignitary he has to paint in his new robes of office.'

'I think we made him too comfortable,' said Hector. 'He seemed to spend rather a lot of time strolling in the garden, planning his setting, as he put it.'

'I suppose this would be a pleasant contrast to the bustle of London,' said Alice, 'but I must confess I am anxious to see the finished production.'

The week's visit the women had planned was extended by another week and then another. Then Alice said firmly that it was time they were home, looking after things, getting in coal for the winter, and so on. Dandy, in her dream world of happiness, was unaware of the effort it took for the two of them to face the cottage without her.

'They must have enjoyed it,' said Dandy that night.

'No wonder,' said Hector. 'Seeing you so well and happy was bound to be a relief.'

'A relief? Surely they expected me to be happy!'

'Things do not always live up to our expectations. Well, we gave them a nice time; they're happy and I'm happy to have you all to myself, my eighteen-year-old wife.'

'Yes. I'm eighteen now. Hector, I'm fed up with this "taking care" business. Couldn't we just enjoy ourselves now?'

'You really mean ... you wouldn't mind? Oh, it's tempting, but you're still only eighteen ...'

'I would be nearly nineteen if anything *did* happen.'

'Oh, you little siren! You mean I may take my wicked way with you?'

'I wonder what that is like,' said Dandy with a giggle.

'I'm sorry I wasn't back in time,' said Hector. 'The lawyer was so long-winded and his clerk couldn't find the deeds; then the rain was plumping down on the way back and one of the horses skidded on some mud. The driver was cursing. Well, what did he say?'

'He said I was to congratulate you on a bull's eye. The next generation should appear in late June.'

'Oh!'

'Is that all you can say, Captain-about-to-become-a-father-McAndrew?'

'Well, we didn't get much time to enjoy ourselves, did we?'

'I thought you might be just a little proud and thrilled ...'

'Oh, that wasn't what I meant. I mean, it's all right for me. It's you I'm thinking of – so young ... to go through that ...'

'Dr Anderson says I'm the fittest young woman he has ever met and that he's sure my love of gardening has something to do with it – all that fresh air and bending and stretching and so on.'

'Well, you'll have to give up that now, won't you . . . I mean, take plenty of rest.'

'Oh, Hector, you're priceless. It's only a teeny, weeny wee thing at the moment; doesn't make the slightest difference to my going about.'

'No? But I'll be banished to the dressing room . . .'

'Not a chance, Sir! Dr Anderson says that we can carry on as before, avoiding the days I would be out of commission anyway, as he put it.'

'Did you ask him, you bold little hussy?'

'Didn't need to. He didn't seem the least bit embarrassed. Well, I didn't exactly expect a whoop of joy, but I *did* think there would have been a kiss going . . .'

'A kiss! You don't know the half of it.'

The Christmas preparations had a deeper meaning for them that year. 'Just think,' said Dandy, 'next year we will be hanging up a special little stocking.'

'Yes, and people will send masses of fluffy bunnies – the same people who would shoot any rabbit that dared cock its ears on their land. That's something that has always struck me as so incongruous.'

'Never thought of it. Toys were few and far between in my life. I'm going to enjoy playing with the bairn's things.'

'It's a bit early, but what are we going to call this bairn of ours?'

'Well, it depends on whether it's a boy or a girl.'

'It has a good chance of being one or t'other, Mrs McAndrew.'

'Indeed, Captain! And which would you prefer?'

Hector hugged her fiercely. 'All I want is my darling Dandy, safe and well.'

'So, if I made it a Shetland pony you wouldn't mind? Now, seriously . . . ?'

'Honestly, Dandy, I'll be delighted with either. The important thing is that you should be safe and well. When do we start telling people?'

'I'd like to hug the news to myself for a little while but, in all fairness, I *should* tell the aunts. They'll see themselves as grandmothers, I daresay.'

'Well, it won't be long till they're here. Let's keep the news as a sort of extra Christmas present.'

'What about Mrs McGuffie?'

'Soon after we tell your aunts, I think, would be in order. Then after Christmas we'll have nothing to do but think about names till the spring planting calls us forth.'

'And do some planting in the new greenhouses.'

'Yes. Somehow they don't seem so important now that we have this to think about.'

A letter from Canada gave Dandy fresh thoughts on the subject. Before the wedding, Hector had read Dandy's collection of letters from Canada. From his reading, he had formed a good opinion of Marie Friedland. 'She sounds the sort of person one could rely on. I think that after the wedding I should send her a sum of money, suggesting that she treat the family – a sort of substitute celebration. She'll know how best to spend it – on clothes or whatever. She seems to be able to deal with your father in a way that your little sister never could.' The result had been a regular correspondence and cheering news of George's progress in Vancouver and Will Baxter's abstinence. This letter from May was certainly satisfactory.

Dear Dandy,
    You will be pleased to know that things are going

388

so much better here. Aunt Marie has managed to keep Pa off the drink. He is working hard again on the farm. We have lots of meals at her house. Wee Jack stays there all the time now, you see. He has come to think of her as his mother. One of my school friends said that Aunt Marie has asked her father to try to help Pa to kick the drink habit and she thinks that some of the other men are helping too. We have parties now. The crop was very heavy and I think Pa made quite a lot of money in the fall. Anyway we eat much better now and your lovely clothes are making me the best-dressed girl in school. I'm getting quite good at sewing. What I'd really like to be is a nurse. Aunt Marie says I could start my training in Vernon. But of course I could not leave the family till the twins are grown-up. I'll tell you a secret. I think Pa is sweet on Aunt Marie. At first I thought I was imagining it, but I've watched the way his eyes follow her when she's doing things. She can make him laugh too. That's good, isn't it? Billy works hard on Pa's farm but always finds time for his animals. Wee Jack follows Aunt Marie around and helps feed the hens and collect the eggs. He talks to them while he's working. It's funny! Your husband sound wonderful. He has been so kind remembering us. I would have loved to see you in your wedding dress. Give my love to Aunt Alice and Aunt Violet.

Lots of love from your wee sister,
May

When they had talked of a name for a boy, Dandy had suggested 'James' because of its associations for her. Hector had been called after his father, so that would

389

automatically be included. 'What about your own father?' Hector had asked. 'Definitely not,' was Dandy's reply and he had not pursued the subject. Now, thinking about May's letter, she wondered if she was right. Aunt Alice's opinions about what had made her father the way he was – a late child of an over-indulgent mother – returned to her. With her own child stirring inside her she found her thoughts softening. Marie Friedland seemed to think there was something worth saving there. *And* there was the memory of that long arm waving a white handkerchief till the ship was out of sight. Was that her father's way of showing that he cared for his first-born; his first-born who had shown that she despised him? Had she allowed herself to be too influenced by her grandmother? Hector had regretted the way he had treated his family and had been man enough to admit it. Maybe James Hector William would help to heal the wounds. That is, if he didn't turn out to be Janet Rosemary Alice Violet. She laughed at her fancies. Mothers-to-be were notorious for the daft things they thought up!

In the June heat, Dandy was glad to sit in the shade. It amused her to see how often Hector's work seemed to bring him in her direction. He likes to pretend he's not fussing, she thought fondly. What is his excuse this time?

'A letter from Canada,' he announced, sitting down beside her. 'Marie Friedland.'

'Oh, good! It seems no time since the last one. Goodness, hear this, Hector:

By the time you get this I shall be Marie Baxter. I hope the shock isn't an unpleasant one for you. Your father has made a tremendous effort to get off the booze and is really making a success of his life now. Before I agreed to marry him I made him swear on the Bible that he would never touch another drop. There are some people who can never drink in moderation and your father is one of them. Luckily most of the men around here are TT anyway so that should help him. Little Jack is like my own baby to me now, and I think he will be happy with the new arrangement. Some of the men are going to help Will to build on a couple more bedrooms here, but we will manage quite well in the meantime. Billy will share with Jack and the girls will be in one big room. I'm hoping that George will come for the wedding. It will be awkward for him, but I've been keeping in touch and he knows his Pa is a changed man. The wedding will mean a fresh start to their relationship, I hope. I knew there would be no question of your getting to the wedding with your confinement so near, so there seemed nothing to wait for once we had made up our minds. I'll look after your loved ones, never fear. Give my regards to your wonderful husband.

  With love,
  Marie Friedland

'Well!' said Dandy.

'An excellent arrangement, don't you think?'

'I suppose so, but it takes a bit of swallowing. It's not that long since Mamm . . . Mother died. They seem almost to have forgotten her. All these years when she worked so hard . . .'

'I shouldn't think for a moment they've forgotten – look how they remember you and praise you to Mrs Marie Whatsit . . . It should take a load off your mind. You can stop worrying about the lot of them, I reckon. Marie seems happy to cope.'

'Aye, you're right. I *have* felt guilty at times – letting my mother go to fend for them all on her own. And then, hearing that May was doing *my* job.'

'Your job is to keep well and be happy with your loving husband. You'll soon have your own little family to look after, though I'll see to it that you have plenty of help where it's needed. You're going to have time to play with their toys. I want to make up to you for what you lost in your childhood, my darling.'

'You do, darling – many times over. Hector, I'm not sure but I've had some funny little twinges while I was sitting here today . . .'

'I'll phone Dr Anderson.'

'Don't be daft. It's nothing like that yet. I've seen my mother hanging on to the furniture before she would send for the midwife. It wouldn't happen as quickly as all that. I'll get plenty of warning.'

'I'll have a word with him just in case.'

'It's Saturday. He'll be at our famous cricket team – miles away.'

'I'll phone and have a word with Liz. She'll tell him when he gets in.' Dandy shook her head and smiled as he hurried away.

Yes, there it was again. A funny sort of twinge that came without any warning. It was difficult to tell exactly where it was. She stroked her swollen stomach. At times it seemed there and yet it shot through her back too. Perhaps a little walk round the garden would help . . .

Hector's voice sounded urgent. 'Dandy! Where are you?'

'Here, among the lilies.'

'You had me worried. Are you all right?'

'Yes. I felt a little cramped. What did Liz say?'

'She says a first baby usually takes a long time so I've not to panic. It might be nothing at all, but she'll get Bob to see you this evening. She's managed to unearth that song she had mislaid and she'll bring it along.'

'See, it can't be anything serious or she wouldn't be talking about bringing songs.'

'No, I suppose not, but somehow I can't think about singing. You've got ten days till it's due, but Liz says that a first can be early *or* late.'

Dandy realized that she didn't feel like singing either. She was restless. It would be a comfort to hear what the doctor had to say.

Dr Anderson was thoughtful. 'Mmmmm, something *does* seem to be starting, but it could be a false start; you often get that with a first one. Nurse Samson has no other bookings at the moment. I think I'll give her a ring: tell her to get her bag packed. She would be able to keep an eye on things.'

'I could get someone to fetch her in a trap,' said Hector.

'Aye, but tomorrow would probably do. No, wait a minute: Sunday tomorrow. Folks would probably be taking their traps to the kirk. I'll see – if she's ready and willing to come tonight, that might be wiser. Meantime, Dandy, just you carry on singing. This could be a false alarm and you could be waiting for another fortnight.'

'A fortnight!' said Hector, horrified.

'Look at him,' said the doctor, chuckling. 'You'd think *he* was having the bairn.'

Nurse Samson was indeed ready and willing to leave right away. Hector busied himself arranging her transport while the doctor went out to fetch some drugs he wished to leave. Dandy gave up any pretence of singing. 'You're restless, Dandy?' enquired Liz.

'Aye, I feel I'd like to get on with something active, cutting the grass, pruning the roses ... something active. . .'

'My mother told me that she always started a minor

393

springclean the day before her bairn arrived. I can't say it ever took *me* that way – I got too fat and lazy. My loving husband used to declare I was like a big white slug!'

'He didn't!' said Dandy, shocked.

'Aye, men go daft when they're worried about you. I think he was trying to minimize the situation or something like that. I'm told the doctors are the worst and I can quite believe it. In a way, you're sort of out of their control and they don't like that. Here they are.'

'Mrs McGuffie is seeing to the nurse's room, though I expect it is perfect. She told us it was ready weeks ago, didn't she, Dandy?'

'What? Oh yes.'

'I'll sleep in the dressing room, shall I?'

'Aye, I'm restless. Are you going home, doctor? It's early yet.'

'Well, I think it would be a good idea if the pair of you had an early night and, in case you get up to your tricks tomorrow, Dandy, I intend doing the same. Come on, Liz. Quick march.'

Dandy remembered Liz's conspiratorial wink as she tossed restlessly in the big bed. There had been a few of the twinges. Maybe it was her imagination, but they *did* seem to be getting stronger. Nurse had said she was to tap on her door if she felt that anything was happening, but there was no sound from her room and it seemed a shame to disturb her. There had been a few creaks from Hector's dressing room in spite of the whisky that the doctor had advised him to drink. Liz's wink had been linked to that, she was sure. The whisky was meant to keep Hector out of the way. She missed him and yet she was hot and restless: definitely needed the bed to herself. Hector had said that he had been born in this room, though he couldn't be sure that it was the same bed. 'I suppose in a way I'm making history,' she told herself, then winced as another pain hit her. It was closely followed by another, severe enough to make her gasp. The floorboards creaked and Hector was beside her. 'Pain again?' he asked. Dandy, her lips tightly compressed, nodded. 'I'm going to wake the nurse.'

In a few minutes Nurse Samson appeared, fully dressed. 'I had two twinges quite close together,' said Dandy, 'but it's all right again.'

'If you'll leave us, Captain, I'll examine your wife,' the nurse said brusquely. While her capable fingers probed, she was asking questions. 'I think I'll give you the sedative the doctor left. I'd like you to get some sleep if possible before the real business starts.'

'Will you need to bring the doctor back?'

'Not yet awhile. A first baby is never all that quick, but he *did* tell me that you are exceptionally fit and that may mean that your muscles will help things along. Aye, don't you worry. I'll know when to send for him. Drink this. I'll just sit in the big chair till you fall asleep.'

'My husband . . .'

'Aye, husbands! I'll tell him to sleep while he can.'

She doesn't think much of the breed, was Dandy's thought as she drifted into a welcome sleep. The pain that woke her a couple of hours later left her confused, but Nurse Samson was alert on the instant. There was a clatter from the dressing room and soon Hector was knocking on the door. 'Wait!' said Nurse imperiously. 'Mhm. Things have started now. Let's tidy you up a bit. It'll be a while yet, but I think I'll let that impatient husband of yours phone the doctor. He'll give us no peace otherwise. Mind you, the doctor won't thank me for keeping him twiddling his thumbs here. Should I? ... Aye, we'll risk it. Captain!'

Chapter 27

Looking back later, Hector and Dandy always laughed at Nurse Samson's discomfiture when her prophecy of 'a while yet' proved to be inaccurate. From the hall, the two men could hear Dandy's cries of pain. Hector in a frenzy had run up the stairs with the doctor struggling behind him. 'Non-combatants stay out,' the doctor warned him. 'Down to the kitchen, man, and see that the water is kept hot.'

One look at Dandy had made him speak gruffly to the nurse as he scrubbed his hands in the basin made ready. 'The bairn's nearly here. Why didn't you fetch me sooner?'

'She's been so quick, doctor.'

'Aye, I warned you. Hyperactive type with efficient muscles.' He hurried to the bed. 'Right! Mrs McAndrew, hold it there. Wait! Now – push harder! The head's down. NOW . . . ONE BIG ONE! *There* we are! Good girl. Well done, you've got a fine boy! Nothing wrong with his lungs either. Hear that? He's been listening to his mother. Wait till I get this tied. Right, here you are, Nurse. Now, Dandy, Nurse will clean up the baby while I'm attending to you. Then she can freshen you up and it won't be long till we can let that fellow who's prowling about on the landing see the pair of you.'

'He's been so worried, Doctor . . . thought I was too young, you see.'

'You were made for it, lass. Count yourself lucky.'

Dandy did indeed count herself lucky and, thanks to

Alice's training, had the tact to restore Nurse Samson's self-respect by careful questioning about previous cases and quoting to her Liz Anderson's remark about a first baby always being slow.

With the arrival of his son, the barriers that Hector had erected against society seemed to vanish. Brimming over with happiness himself, he happily concurred with all Dandy's wishes. 'They'll think it's odd that you don't want a professional nurse, but that's up to you. If you prefer to manage with a young nursery maid, that's fine – especially since Mrs McGuffie has recommended her.' They were amazed to see how easily Dandy handled the baby. This gave Dandy many a wicked chuckle when she and Hector were alone together. 'One baby seems a toy to me. Ever since I was old enough to hold one, there was a tribe of them needing attention. But oh, how different this is ... our own wee son and in this lovely home, and he'll grow up surrounded by those beautiful gardens ...'

'And break the windows of our expensive glasshouses playing football, I have no doubt,' Hector teased.

The hot summer days were filled with joy for her. Alice and Violet, incoherent with delight at her choice of name, were thrilled with little James. They brought news of Morag McGregor who had visited them in Paisley. Alice confided, 'She's very lonely now. She went up north to look after her cousin. Then, when she died, there was little to interest her there. She has no real home, you see. That's the worst of being a governess, even in a good place; when you get too old, you're lost. Violet and I were thinking it might not be a bad idea to ask her to come to us. The cottage would be too small now ... for you visiting, I mean ...'

'Aye, we'd probably put up at a hotel. She could have my room at the cottage and then you could bring her with you when you come to see James. I could have some music lessons when she's here.'

'The same old Dandy,' said Violet, laughing. 'The eternal student.'

A sudden storm a few days after the aunts reluctantly left for Paisley kept Hector, Dandy and their workers busy clearing up. 'Different wind direction,' said Hector, when Dandy remarked that the shelter belt for once seemed to have been insufficient. Not only the new glasshouses had suffered but the beautiful old stables. 'I'll need to get those slates fixed immediately,' said Hector. 'It never pays to let a roof go. That way leads to disaster.'

'Hector, I've just had a thought: those old stables . . .'

'Yes?'

'They're never used.'

Hector's face tightened momentarily. 'You know why. Perhaps some day James . . .'

'I've got an idea. Remember I told you about Alice and Violet's plan to invite Morag to the cottage.'

'Mmm . . . seems sensible. Three old ladies are safer than two.'

'Those beautiful stone stables, all on one level, the big sunny courtyard in the middle . . . Couldn't they be adapted to one-storey houses for the aunts and Miss McGregor? I wouldn't have to worry about not being able to look after them . . . they would see the children growing up . . .'

'Children? How many? I thought you'd had enough of big families.'

Dandy chuckled. 'I *did* visit a big family once – Mr Forbes, the builder – and I thought, "That's the sort of home I'd like to have when I grow up." You see, they all had space and seemed to have fun together instead of getting on one another's nerves.'

'Well, judging by the speed with which you produced

young James, I think I'd better engage a domiciled doctor for future occasions. Mmmm, the stables. There *are* drains, water supply, etc. But no gas . . . The internal walls are not too thick. Archways between to make biggish rooms. Those little conservatories such as they have at Rosecraig Hotel would allow easy access to and from their bedrooms. Yes, it's a possibility. Like you, I've been wondering what would happen when Alice and Violet get beyond making the rather tedious journey here. I'll have a word with the builder in Stranraer before we sound them out. I'm pretty sure the aunts would be only too happy, but there may be snags we wot not of. Hold your fire for a little while.'

The more Dandy thought of the scheme, the more suitable it seemed. The builder when he visited could see no difficulties but advised engaging an architect to check the plans that Hector had drawn up. Dandy listened eagerly to their discussions. 'You've never had any trouble with drainage, Captain?'

'No. Of course, in autumn there has to be constant sweeping of leaves or we would have trouble.'

'That's local . . . of no consequence. I meant drains being operative . . .'

'Everything was kept spick-and-span. Our horses were as well cared for as their riders.'

'The buildings have been like this, unused, for . . . did you say fifteen years?'

'Roughly.'

'In this climate, I think that should not matter; little salt in the air thanks to all your planting . . . I can't see any difficulty, Captain.'

Dandy held her fire till the aunts paid their birthday visit in September, this time accompanied by Morag McGregor. She was relieved to see that Hector, who had welcomed Morag with reserved politeness, was soon talking comfortably to her and congratulating her on her music teaching. 'I get the benefit of a tame little songbird – did I say tame? Perhaps I should think of another adjective.'

He waited till the laughter had died down. 'Now my not-so-tame little songbird has an idea which she would like to place before you. Speech! Speech!' he sat back applauding.

'Well,' she began tentatively, 'you've seen the stables . . .'

'Miss McGregor hasn't.'

'Stop interrupting, Hector!'

'Merely stating a fact.'

'Behave yourself, Hector,' said Alice, 'or she'll be disappearing to feed young James and we won't hear her idea at all.'

'That's the stuff, Aunt Alice. Now, these handsome stables have lain empty for years. They were built in prosperous times and it seems a shame that no use should be made of them. Hector and I were thinking that they could be turned into two comfortable houses for you three ladies. There's a nice big sunny courtyard and we would have little conservatories like the ones in the hotel – Miss McGregor won't have seen them – but it would make it easy for you to step outside from any of the rooms. The builder and the architect think that the idea is feasible. What do you think?'

Violet was the first to recover speech. 'It sounds wonderful to me. We were just saying how tiring the journey is . . . I don't mean . . .'

'That's exactly what I said,' said Hector, coming to her rescue. 'Of course, Miss McGregor must find this a little overwhelming. Ah-ha, that sounds like Peggy coming to summon my little songbird.' He opened the door. 'I was right. James wants his mother. I would suggest, ladies, that if you are feeling refreshed, you might care to take a little stroll in the garden. There are plenty of seats, Miss McGregor, and Alice and Violet could show you the stables at your leisure. It would give you a chance to discuss the scheme.'

Morag McGregor gave a warm smile of appreciation. She approves of my tactful husband, thought Dandy, hurrying off to the nursery.

It gratified her to find that all three women were thrilled at the idea. The talk at the dinner table was all of selling their houses and choosing which furniture they would bring with them. 'We could store most of it in the billiard room till the new places are ready,' said Hector. 'I got rid of the tables a long time ago. The builder says it will be a few months before he can start – some hold-up with materials for his present job. But there's plenty of room here. The important thing is to be sold up and have that worry off your mind. You've all a good chance of being here in time for Christmas. This year I intend to reinstate the New Year celebrations.'

Buoyed up with the exciting prospect of their move, they took their departure for home quite cheerfully. 'Went off well, didn't it?' said Dandy.

'Yes, but I'm not sorry to have my little wife to myself. We'll have to hope that the builders get a move on when they *do* start. It could be quite a strain never having the drawing room to ourselves in the evening.'

'I was looking forward to having Morag to play my accompaniments. I've a long way to go before my playing is up to her standard, but I know what you mean . . . Alice and Violet are pretty tactful. They'll play patience.'

'You said on your first visit that they were fond of bridge. Bob and Liz are too. We might be able to arrange something there.'

'And we're always alone in the bedroom . . .'

'Ah, the bedroom. I vote we have an early night

tonight, after you've sung for your supper, my gorgeous songbird.'

Though they had seized on the idea of being with Dandy, both Alice and Violet found themselves distressed when it came to leaving the cottage which reminded them so much of James. 'It seems disloyal somehow,' said Alice.

'Indeed, that's how I feel . . . and yet, wouldn't James have jumped at the chance of Lindsay Gardens!'

'He certainly would, Violet. I'm so glad that the Rattrays are garden lovers. I would have hated to sell it to anyone who didn't care. Wasn't it funny to hear Mr Rattray say that he had always longed to see inside this garden?'

'Yes, and that they were always hoping the house would come on the market – so near the shops, just the right size and with a garden small enough to manage themselves. You know, Alice, when I was remaking Rachel's clothes for Dandy, I used to feel that she would approve. After all, Dandy made such a difference to his life.'

They were quiet for a moment, then Alice said slowly, 'It's difficult to put some things into words, but, when you think of it, we linked Dandy to James and now in a funny way I feel that she is linking us to him in her lovely garden . . . sort of binding us together. Oh, I can't really explain it.'

'I feel it too,' said Violet quietly.

Christmas did indeed see the three women installed in Lindsay House. As yet the stables were untouched. The site that the builders were engaged on had flooded, delaying the work there. Dandy knew that her aunts' feelings were very divided – joy at being with her at Lindsay House and a feeling that they were taking

403

advantage of Hector's hospitality. As Alice explained, 'It is one thing being in the stables houses and paying a rent but we all – Morag particularly – feel that we are imposing upon Hector's hospitality here and it is difficult to know what to do about it.'

The idea of the McLarens paying a rent was a new one to Dandy, but she closed her lips on any remark till she had consulted Hector.

'Yes, I *shall* take a rent from them. Let them keep their independence. Don't worry. It will be modest – in line with my other tenants. They will have sold their cottages, and that money, invested, will amply cover their expenses for the rest of their days. We must never let them feel that they are accepting charity. Naturally we will keep our eyes peeled for any sign of need ... All the vegetables and fruit from the garden here will be at their disposal, and when Bob bestows the odd salmon on me from a successful fishing trip we shall invite them to dinner. We will find other excuses to invite them. Mrs McGuffie has been told to take on any extra help she needs. I can trust her absolutely. She's happy as a sandboy having all these ladies to praise her cooking.'

Dandy was surprised to see how easily Morag fitted into the local scene. As a daughter of the manse she naturally gravitated there and was made welcome by the minister and his wife. When it was revealed that she was keen on chess she was recruited to play with Jim Napier, a retired headmaster in the village who was starved of suitable opponents. Soon he was added to the group in the drawing room at Lindsay House in the dull February evenings. Often Dandy found Hector consulting Jim on his opinions of world affairs. Morag was able to take her part in these discussions in a way that Dandy envied. She realized that Alice and Violet had been unable to teach her about a world from which

404

their early training had sheltered them. Morag's father had taken the scholar's view that knowledge was to be sought and appreciated: nothing was barred.

It was the first week of March. The daffodils were out and the builders had at last begun. Dandy walking with the baby carriage in the garden breathed deeply and tried to forget the troublesome talk of the night before.

'We're going to be drawn into it eventually,' Hector had stated. 'There's no stopping Germany. Ever since they took Alsace Lorraine there's been resentment in France.'

'Wherever you turn,' Morag had said, 'there seems to be some sort of uprising, rooted in old resentments.'

'We daren't ignore the German armaments race,' interjected Jim Napier. 'They are supporting the Austria–Hungary Alliance right now. The Habsburg Empire is finished and they know it. What worries me is that the whole thing is going to spread: sooner or later they will turn on France and we will be drawn in through the *Entente Cordiale*.'

'And this won't be the sort of little party I got engaged in,' said Hector. 'This won't be a skirmish with the Boers but a global war. I've heard rumours of some of the weapons the Germans are working on and I hope they are just rumours . . .'

'It's a good thing your son is weaned,' said Bob Anderson. 'You are frightening one little mother here.'

Hector was taken aback to see Dandy staring at him with big frightened eyes. 'We'll be all right here,' he assured her. 'This is a backwater.'

She tried to console herself with this thought in the days that followed while she avidly scanned the news-papers she had tended to ignore before. The sound of picks clanging on stone and the rumble and crash of

405

falling rubble punctuated her worried thoughts. Hector looked tense, she noticed. In fact, the only time he seemed totally at ease was when he was playing with his adored son. When the weather permitted they took their afternoon tea in the garden. Dandy would spread a rug for James to crawl on. In no time Hector would be down beside him and they would be chuckling together.

'Aren't they alike!' Violet remarked one day.

'James is much fairer,' said Alice.

'I was fair too when I was at this stage. There is a painting up in the attic . . . I was a little older than James because I am standing, holding a fluffy ball.'

'Why haven't I seen that?' demanded Dandy.

'Because I never let anyone see it,' said Hector

'Why?'

'I expect he is wearing skirts and petticoats, as was the fashion,' said Alice.

Hector roared with laughter. 'Got it in one, Alice. All those frills . . . Oh, God! Excuse me . . . ladies present . . .' he was relieved to see that all the ladies present were laughing heartily. 'I'll show you it when we are old and grey,' he said. Then, looking at Dandy, 'I think I'd better lock the doors to the attic or a certain lady will have it out tomorrow. But isn't it good that he resembles me, wife of my bosom? Keeps it all so respectable!'

'He's certainly got over his shyness in company,' thought Dandy as she joined in the laughter.

Soon they found that they had a new worry. In digging deep for the foundations, the workmen found an underground stream. Hector was dumbfounded. 'I've never heard a word about this. It isn't in any plans I've seen and the architect didn't find it.'

Further investigation showed that it was nearest the surface at that point but was flowing quite steeply downhill. 'And of course there are so many trees down there,' the surveyor said, 'that the roots would absorb the seepage where the stream slowed in its tracks.' It was decided that it would have to be culverted before any more work could proceed.

James's first birthday came and went and still the bungalows were not completed. 'I think Hector would have thought twice about his kind offer,' said Alice, 'had he known how long it was going to take.'

'We've plenty of room,' said Dandy, 'and it has made things so much easier for Hector to enter into a wider social life. He used to hate people seeing him unable to cut his food properly. Now he never thinks twice about asking for help.'

'He's certainly an excellent host at a party,' said Alice. 'It takes us back to a life we had almost forgotten. The builders seem to be making less noise now and the water pipes are in for our kitchens, laundries and bathrooms. Hector was saying that the large part of the stables which has not been converted might be a useful place to dry clothes on a wet day. Isn't it wonderful to have so much space!'

'It's something I always longed for,' said Dandy simply.

'Oh, my dear, how happy we are that you have been so rewarded – Hector, little James, this house and the magnificent gardens . . .'

'If only it weren't for all the talk of war,' said Dandy. 'Hector has no doubt it is coming. D'you know, Aunt Alice, he thinks he will be back in the army.'

'What? Never!'

'He says that he could brush up his French: he used to be quite good at it. He reckons they'll be short of officers who can liaise . . .'

'But his arm – I'm sure, Dandy, they would never take him. I can't imagine! He would know that surely?'

407

'He says they won't be able to be too fussy this time. All able-bodied men will be needed for combat. The old rules will no longer apply.'

'I can't believe it,' said Alice.

Aunt Alice was seldom wrong. Dandy hugged that thought to herself as the hot days of July gave way to August.

'It's happened!'

'What?' said Dandy. 'Oh, no!'

'That was Bob Anderson on the phone. We are at war! I knew it. I knew it. I knew it. Some folk thought I was scaremongering. Oh, my darling!' He crushed Dandy hungrily to him. 'Why are men so mad . . . when they could create gardens . . . they spend time trying to avenge old defeats. Oh Dandy, it's such a mucky business. I'm glad you will be out of it here . . . and James.'

'And his little brother or sister . . .'

'What?'

'You are not very observant, Captain McAndrew. I have not been "out of commission", as our dear Bob would put it, for quite a few weeks.'

'So, when would that . . .'

'In the spring when all life is new.'

'I reckon there will be countless corpses by the spring.'

'Hector!'

'Oh I'm sorry, my love, but it's a hell of a time to be bringing a child into the world. There, don't cry. I'm a stupid ass. Don't cry. It's just that I've seen this coming. I should have looked after you better, but you'll be all right here, you'll see! The aunts and Morag will look after you, and Bob will be too old to go – needed here anyway. We'll lose a lot of our younger workers, I should think; may not get the stable houses completed if the builder loses his men ... I'm sorry, I've upset you. I think you should lie down.'

In the vast bed, Dandy sobbed as she had not done for years. It had been too good to be true – all the love and beauty that surrounded her, Hector doting on his little son. One whiff of war and he had no interest in another child. She remembered his words: 'It's a hell of a time to be bringing a child into the world.' Surely when all seemed to be destruction in so many parts of the world, that was the time you wanted something pure, something creative, something to give you hope for the future.

It was Morag who slipped into her room some time later and sat quietly by the bed. Dandy's breathing gradually steadied. 'You know?' she said.

'I met Hector. He said he had bungled things: is calling himself all sorts of names.' She paused, then spoke consideringly, 'He is a man of action – a powerful, creative man who has seen the mad posturings of the various leaders and known that they could lead only to disaster. The loss of his arm has made him more aware than ever of those things than he would otherwise have been, Dandy. He does everything thoroughly – even the unwise things like cutting himself off from human intercourse. That is now at an end, thanks to you and your love which has so enriched his life. If he were a different type of character he could sit back and say that he had done his bit, suffered and been maimed; life owed him some reward; let others carry the burden. He is not like that. He will fret at the bit till he has made the effort to share in this dreadful enterprise. If it's any consolation to you, I do not think for one moment that he will be accepted for any sort of active service. To be brutal, he needs assistance in quite simple things and could be a liability in a fighting situation.'

'It's not just that, Morag. He said it was a hell of a

409

time to be bringing a child into the world. I thought that when he was so happy with James . . .'

'I can understand that reaction. He wants everything that is best for his children – a steady home with two parents. At the moment he thinks he will not be here to support you. I feel he is wrong in that supposition but have refrained from telling him so. He will certainly need consolation if he is judged to be of no use in the struggle. The coming child will then be invaluable in focusing his thoughts on a happier future. I said that Hector is a strong person. You are a strong person too, Dandy. He will have need of your strength. There may be times when your womanly instincts will be right and he will be reluctant to admit it. Stand up for what you feel to be sound, my dear, but always make your home a happy place. It is a gift you have, a strength and a tool you may use to handle your husband.' She laughed shortly. 'Here am I, an old maid, telling you how to handle your husband – but years in a parish with a wide variety of people and a frank father have taught me much that is denied to most unmarried women.'

Dandy, sitting alone, thought over her words. She would have to be wily; that was the truth of it. Her apparent weakness in pregnancy would have to be used; confronted by it, Hector would be at a loss, but she would have to be careful not to diminish him. The last thing she wanted was a weakened Hector. Life was not going to be easy for some time.

She watched her husband carefully, noting how he fretted restlessly for a few days, spending hours in discussion with Jim Napier. Then he announced that he was going up to Glasgow to see an old officer friend. 'He was due to retire, but this turn-up will have altered his plans, I'm sure.'

'Couldn't you phone him?' said Dandy.

'No. There will be things to discuss.'

410

Dandy did not go to the station, but, remembering Morag's words, embraced him warmly before he left. Home was to be remembered always as a place of love and comfort.

It was a long day – not helped by a phone call from their builder. Three of his younger men had not turned up for work and he had learned that they had already volunteered. 'That might not be the end of it,' he announced gloomily. 'There's other two that fancy themselves in uniform and won't see sense.' As possessor herself of a husband who 'wouldn't see sense', Dandy had sympathy for the distraught employer. The postponement of the housebuilding seemed a comparatively small part of her worries at that moment.

To her initial relief and surprise, Hector returned that evening. She had expected a phone call to say he was staying in Glasgow ... and perhaps worse ... that he had re-enlisted. One look at his taut face told her that he had been thwarted. 'Tell Mrs McGuffie I don't need any dinner. I'll have some sandwiches in the office. There are things I have been neglecting.'

It was Dandy who carried in the tray. 'Well?' she said.

'My God! Well, anything but! It appears that I am no bloody use to anyone. They might hide me in a back room somewhere. I suppose he was doing his best, old Tompkin. "They *are* taking some experienced people back for the new recruitment centres, but you understand ... your arm ... hardly much of an encouragement, I mean. For anything else ... likely to be France ... everybody has to be 100 per cent fit. Understand?" He was embarrassed as hell; said he *might* manage to wangle me in a back office somewhere but frankly he didn't think I would fit in. "Go back and grow food for the nation, young Hector. Our merchant ships are going to have one hell of a time. You've done your stint with

411

the army. I always thought you'd get something . . . a gong . . . surprised, really. No, go home and think yourself lucky. This is going to be a bloody business.'' He really thought I'd be happy at home while others are in his bloody business.'

'I'm sorry for *your* sake, Hector, but very relieved for my own. It isn't going to be easy to relax with another child on the way, our workers disappearing ''like snow off a dyke'', as my grannie used to say, and the three women to keep happy. They're wonderfully kind but they *are* old. I'm worried about Canada: will our letters get through, things like that. How shall I be able to help them?'

'I don't think they'll need all that much help, Dandy, now that the outfit is being run by Marie Whatsit.'

'Marie Baxter.'

'Yes.' He smiled briefly. 'Your brother George is not much younger than yourself. He might be in it.'

'Oh no!' said Dandy.

'A good chance to visit us, perhaps. There has to be *something* good in this mess.'

It was the first thing he had said that could be termed encouraging. Dandy stored it. There must be a way of snatching that 'something good'. She would cudgel her brains.

She was not alone in this occupation. Hector had disappeared before breakfast the following morning – off to one of the farms as Mrs McGuffie informed them. They all knew without being told that he was finding it difficult to face everyone. They were in the garden at afternoon tea when he finally joined them. James immediately demanded his attention and, while Hector was seeming to concentrate on his son, Alice spoke up. 'We three old ladies have an idea, Hector. What about opening the gardens to the public every Sunday afternoon in aid of the Red Cross? We three could take turns

412

at collecting the ticket money. People will crave beauty if all the news is of ugly destruction.'

'I was urged by a senior army officer to go home and grow food for the nation. I'm afraid the gardens will not be the haven of beauty that you find them now. I shall be ploughing it up gradually.'

'Oh, no you won't! You bloody well won't.' Dandy stood like Boadicea, her face a stern mask. James, grasping her skirt, started to cry.

'It's got to be done. We have to make sacrifices.'

'Over my dead body,' said his Queen of the Lilies. Neither of them noticed that the three ladies who had sparked off the row had taken themselves off.

'You don't understand,' he said, scooping the whimpering child in his arm.

'I understand only too well, Captain Bloody McAndrew. You didn't get your own way up there today so you are cutting off your nose to spite your face, destroying years and years of work – generations of work, come to think of it: work that was meant to create beauty for the future, for people like James.'

'Tompkin said that the nation will need food.'

'Tompkin couldn't think of another bloody thing to say to you, but *I* can and I say that it's your duty to keep this place that your father and grandfather worked in and to improve it for James and his children and all the other people who will enjoy it. The aunts had a good idea. Money for the Red Cross and a respite from wickedness and ugliness – that's what this place should be. And if all the young men are joining up, where in heaven's name do you expect to get workers to plant and weed and gather? Your tenant farmers will be at their wits' ends as it is! There's a lot of space in the glasshouses that we haven't got round to filling yet. We could grow tomatoes there. In this climate they would be early. The Glasgow market would grab them if no merchant ships are getting in to the Clyde.' She paused, her face red and her chest heaving. Hector looked stonily at her, then put his son in her arms and turned on his heel.

He did not appear at dinner. Mrs McGuffie announced that the Captain had to visit some of his tenants and asked the ladies to proceed without him. She had made the meal a light one since it had been such a hot day. All agreed that she was wise. Morag gave her hostess a steady look, but nothing was said.

Dandy was bathed and in bed when he finally appeared. 'I'll sleep in the spare room, if you like, but I had to come and apologize. You were right about my being cut up; nevertheless, it was no way to take the news of the child – our child. Please forgive me.'

It was costing him a lot, she could see. What was it Morag had said? But why bother about what other folk said? Dandy stretched out her arms. Her nightgown, unbuttoned, gave tantalizing glimpses of her still firm breasts. 'Oh, Dandy!' he said, lost. The reaction to their disagreement made Dandy merciless in her demands that night and Hector was fiercely glad to vent some of his frustration in meeting them. There was little sleep for either of them and morning found them exhausted. Hector, hauling himself out of bed, stooped to kiss a bleary-eyed Dandy. She moaned slightly in reply and he gave a short laugh as he left for his bath.

She was still there when he came back. 'Not having any breakfast this morning, Mrs McAndrew?'

'Hector, I think I've been silly.' She gave a little groan.

'What d'you mean?'

'I shouldn't have . . . last night . . . it was the wrong date. I'm bleeding and I've got pains.'

'Oh, my God!' He rushed off to the phone. Soon he was back. 'He's coming. What can I do?'

'Fetch some towels from the bathroom cabinet.'

'What now?' he asked returning.

'Spread them. I'd better not move but I think it's too late. I've got pains now and I'm bleeding like a pig.'

'I should be shot.'

'Don't be daft. I needed you.'

'Shall I summon Alice?'

'No! just us – and Bob. I think I hear him.' It was as if the relief of knowing that help was at hand released her from all constraints. Dandy was writhing and groaning loudly by the time Bob Anderson entered the room. It didn't take him long to sum up the situation.

'Can you stay upright, Hector, or should we fetch Mrs McGuffie?'

'I'll do what you say, Bob.'

'Right. Do him good to see the results, eh, Dandy?' She groaned in reply.

'Aye, I'm afraid you're going to lose this one, lass. Try to relax between the pains. It'll soon be over.'

Chapter 28

It was an episode that neither of them could ever forget and it signalled the start of a new relationship. Dandy, trying to puzzle it out, came to the conclusion that their marriage had grown up. She lay in bed, enjoying being pampered since it helped Hector to direct his emotions. The scheme of opening the gardens on Sundays had been given official approval from the Red Cross. Tickets had been ordered and Morag had drafted notices.

On her first day out of bed, she was walking hand in hand with Hector in the garden. 'I've got an idea,' he said. 'It's a little more ambitious than the Sunday-viewing lark, but I felt I would like to discuss it with you before saying anything to our Three Graces.' Dandy chuckled as she always did when he used the new name he had coined for his guests. 'It's like this. There are lots of casualties already and anyone who knows anything can be sure that they are going to multiply soon. Hospitals in the south of England will be overloaded before long and they'll gradually bring the poor devils further north. It's not only hospitals they will need but convalescent homes for the buggers who land like me, minus a limb. I thought it might be feasible to offer the stables to the War Office for the duration. Water is already in at several points. Small wards are more homey for this sort of treatment. There is plenty of space to store wheelchairs and other equipment. What do you think? Would the women be upset at the notion?'

'I think it's a marvellous idea, Hector. Why didn't I think of it?'

'Did you think you had the monopoly of imagination in the McAndrew household, my Queen of the Lilies?'

'Well . . .' said Dandy and paused, teasing. 'The place isn't finished yet. The builder can't get enough workers . . .'

'The War Office would soon see to the completion if they accepted. They could get everything done by the army. It really wouldn't need a great deal. So many things necessary in an ordinary house would be unwanted in a hospital. Space for their own fitments is what they want. What about the Three Graces?'

'They'd be delighted. They could write letters, do errands, darn socks or, perhaps more important, be a listening ear.'

Hector found it a relief to have something positive to do. His offer brought an RAMC officer to view the site, closely followed by an officer of the engineers. James, held aloft in his father's arm, chuckled when he saw them salute each other. His little starfish hand went up in imitation. 'Oh, ho, my little soldier lad,' said Hector. 'Let's put you down while I talk to the officers.'

'Seems ideal for us,' said the RAMC officer after a brief inspection. 'It all depends on this lot –' Turning to the other officer – 'How long do you think it would take you?'

'Well, if Captain McAndrew could tell us of some space nearby where the men could be quartered and our materials stored, I reckon it could be done in under three weeks.'

'How many men?' asked Hector.

'Two dozen.'

'Tents?'

'Yes.'

'They could go in the paddock here and the materials could be stored in my empty glasshouses.'

'Sohjass' soon became James's favourite word. Dandy encouraged Hector to take his son to view the work in progress, knowing that it gave him a vicarious satisfaction to see the war being prosecuted in his backyard, as it were. James's salute was assiduously practised till it approximated to the real thing.

James was beside himself with excitement. The wounded soldiers were to arrive that afternoon.

'I had been thinking of going down myself to meet them,' said Hector, 'but now I think it would be a good idea if you came along with James. The sight of my Queen of the Lilies and this little bundle of mischief would be as refreshing as water in the desert to men who have been in the trenches.'

'Won't they want peace to settle in?'

'Oh, yes. I was simply meaning that you should be visible to wave to them. I'll have a brief word with the MO, check that they have everything they need and then leave them.'

This ploy meant a lot to Hector, Dandy thought as they made their way to the stables. She breathed deeply. 'All these wonderful scents are bound to make them feel better.'

'Well, some of them may be in a bad way, don't forget. It'll take more than a beautiful garden to get them over what they've been through.'

They took up their places by the edge of the drive leading to the stables. 'Sohjass?' said James hopefully.

'Soon,' said Hector.

After the tenth similar exchange, 'They're late,' said Dandy. Maybe we should have stayed up at the house.'

'No. The ambulances will drive right round here. We'll have to learn to be patient. Wars don't work to a timetable.'

'Hector, d'you know what I'm thinking? If this thing goes on and on, one of these fellows some day could be my brother. I wish I'd managed to see them all before the war started.'

'Well, I *did* warn you it was boiling up. Listen! Here they come. Now, James, I'm going to put you down. You will stand up straight like a soldier. Yes, like that!'

'Oh, darling, you're expecting a lot. He's only a baby.'

'This is important. See, James? A big ambulance! Coming to see James . . . Now – salute!'

Two wan faces peering from the window of the wagonette broke into grins. The Lady of Lindsay House swallowed a lump in her throat before giving them the benefit of her radiant smile. She swung her son into her arms and turned to make for the house. 'Dada,' he called, stretching back.

'Dada is going to see that the soldiers are comfortable, then he's coming for tea. I think Mrs McGuffie is making something special for James. Honey cakes! What do you think of that?'

For answer two chubby hands patted her cheeks and, chuckling, he buried his face in the soft skin of her neck.

Glossary

blethering	chattering
close	common entry (to flats)
cludgie	dry lavatory
cranky	irritable
doocot	dovecot (i.e. a small place)
factor's man	official from factor's office (repair man)
faur frae	far from
flit	move house
fly	devious
gey	very, extremely
girning	moaning, complaining
greetin'	weeping
hirple	hobble
peevers	hopscotch
Sair Sanct	Extremely Holy
sleekit	sly
stramash	disturbance, riot
sumph	oaf
swither	to be faced with a difficult choice
tawse	leather strap used to punish schoolchildren
thrapple	throat
wean	weaned child
winterdykes	clothes horse
yin	one